THE LETTERS SHE LEFT BEHIND

A NOVEL
BY CL WALTERS

Mixed Plate
Press
Hawaii

Also by CL Walters

Swimming Sideways

The Ugly Truth

The Bones of Who We Are

The Stories Stars Tell

In the Echo of this Ghost Town

When the Echo Answers

The Messy Truth About Love

The Ring Academy: The Trials of Imogene Sol

Books by Maci Aurora

In the Shadow of a Wish

In the Shadow of a Hoax

In the Shadow of a Dream

In the Shadow of the Truth

In the Shadow of an Obsession

The Secrets of Roan Island

The Accidental Sereph

THE LETTERS SHE LEFT BEHIND

A NOVEL
BY CL WALTERS

Mixed Plate
Press
Hawaii

The following story is fictional. Any characters, places, events are from the author's imagination. Any similarities are coincidental and unintentional.

Mixed Plate Press, Honolulu, Hawai'i

Cover Art: Sara Oliver Designs

ISBN: 978-1-7342568-0-2 (pbk)
ASIN: B07QVFRYJ2 (ebook)

To Vince, My Kāne,
I love you.

Dear Reader,

First, thank you so much for making a choice to read this story. An expression of gratitude seems small knowing how many choices are available, and you selected this one. Thank you for taking a chance and allowing a bit of my heart into your life. It is my sincere hope that this story is worth the time you spend reading it; the characters find their way into your heart as they have mine; and you enjoy *The Letters She Left Behind* so it lasts beyond the close of the final page.

I wrote this story many years ago. I remember when the idea coalesced. I'd been writing in my own journal, and I had a fleeting image of a husband picking up his wife's journals. What he found were a lifetime of letters that started with his name: *Dear Adam...* After many drafts, revisions, and rejections, I put the manuscript away and moved on. In the meantime, I raised my children, taught multitudes of students, and wrote several more novels. Fifteen years later, I decided to go back and reread this story as an exercise. When I finished reading, I remembered why I fell in love with these characters. Now, with many revisions and updates, I present *The Letters She Left Behind* to you.

It's important to note that Hawai'i—the island of O'ahu—is a very important aspect in this story. My home. I love where I live and have always wanted to share it beyond the pretty picture or the tourist *lu'au*. Sprinkled throughout the text are small bits of culture as I understood them though I haven't been able to capture the true cultural beauty with my non-Hawaiian eyes. From *'ōlelo Hawai'i* (Hawaiian language) vocabulary, to locations, to a protagonist of

Hawaiian descent, there is a dusting of the beauty of this culture. Please note those choices weren't made to appropriate culture; the decision was made as a testament to the love affair I have with this home, this land, this place, and my Hawaiian husband. Knowing that, I fictionalized most things except for a few: *Zippy's* (which is a local restaurant and a local favorite), the Stadium where Trey plays his football games, Aloha Tower, Chinatown, and finally, the H3 where Emma and Adam go for a drive. Kaimana Beach is the name of an actual beach that exists east of Waikiki, but in the imagining of this story, the Kaimana Beach referenced is a fictional place near the real Sandies. Everything else is reimagined, though the essence of my home lingers.

I can't wait to hear what you think about the book. There are lots of ways to do this: Post a review to Goodreads, Amazon, and other social media platforms. Another way is to connect with me on Instagram (@cl.walters), TikTok (@clwaltersofficial), and Facebook (CL Walters). You can keep up with my books and writing on my website (www.clwalters.net) where I often post new short stories and fun excerpts as well as announce news. You can sign up for my author newsletter there too. I look forward to hearing from you.

Sincerely,

C-

PROLOGUE
(HONOLULU, 1979)

T he crowd inside the fraternity was packed so tight the slightest shift in one body was felt across the room in another. Hawai'i State's football team had pulled off their first victory in two seasons with local boy Adam Kāne at the helm, so the crowd was a live wire. Adam, said starting quarterback, was feeling proud, rather cocky, and invincible. He was also very drunk.

The beer he was drinking with his friends went down with the ease of cold water, thanks to the earlier tequila shots. He was loose and courageous, more so than when he was sober. Long on the road of total inebriation, his adrenaline after the victory and his male urge to find a willing female sex partner were the only things keeping him from falling on his face.

He'd been scanning female faces all night. There were several who met his criteria, but his eyes continued to return to one *wahine* who'd caught his attention early and held it. After an hour of watching her, and the misguided thinking he was irresistible, the hunter in him took over.

Keeping her in his sights, he started across the crowded room. She was pretty: soft wavy, dark brown hair, gorgeous shape, heart-shaped lips. She wasn't a local girl, but it didn't bother him she was a *haole wahine*. What stuck with him, however, were her vibrant green eyes, the color of the football field in the fall as the sun rises and dew paints each blade of grass. It was *hoailona*—a sign. What made it more exciting was she repeatedly glanced at him as he made his way toward her.

Tension welled up in the pit of his stomach the closer he got. He wasn't one to instigate conversation with a woman to whom he was attracted. While he wasn't shy, he was reserved and waited for moments to present themselves. His football self was far more aggressive, but it was necessary on the field. When it came to football players and women, there were enough football players who ran the stereotype. He didn't want to be one. Usually.

Now, as he worked his way through the sea of partygoers, it felt necessary to pursue what he wanted, but maybe, it was the alcohol. Tonight, he was filled with enough self-importance, arrogance, and alcohol to charge his courage until he was standing behind her, close enough that her backside fit nicely against his groin; closer than he should have been or would have been had he been sober. He leaned forward and said, "Dance with me." She smelled so good: gardenia. Home.

She stepped away from him, "I already have a date, so…" and she turned. The last of her words died on her lips when her eyes met his. A smile worked its way across her face along with a becoming blush that stained her cheeks.

He smiled back. "I'm Adam," he told her and offered his hand.

They were standing so close, there was barely a breath between them.

"AJ," she answered, taking his hand in hers.

The transfer of heat between them sent electricity up Adam's arm. Their sexual chemistry was a strong, heady elixir that swirled through him, even though all they'd shared was a simple touch.

"Is that short for something else?" His heartbeat thudded in his groin.

"Yes," but she didn't elaborate.

"Where's your date?" Adam glanced around.

"Around."

"Not very smart of him. Or her." He cocked an eyebrow.

She blushed and said, "Him. Probably not," then lifted the cup of beer to her lips and drank.

When she moved to wipe the foam from her lip, Adam stopped her by grabbing her hand, then laced his fingers with hers. His other hand rode the curve at the small of her back and drew her closer. Then he leaned down and waited a moment, measuring her interest. She looked at his lips, so he leaned forward and kissed the foam from her lip. The feel of her quick intake of breath caressed his lips. He noticed the frantic beating of her pulse against the olive skin of her neck matching his heart's rhythm.

Adam pulled back, just enough to look at her face. Her heavy lashes fluttered up and her green eyes, hazy with something primal, assessed him. Not worried about the fact he knew nothing more than her name and his desire to make a sex partner of her provided she was willing, he kissed her again. Heat exploded in his bloodstream as her soft lips molded and shifted under his. The warmth of their tongues entwined and was enough to send his inebriated brain into an oblivion of sexual need.

Adam ended the kiss, glanced around, and still holding her hand, drew her through the crowd.

Privacy. They needed privacy.

"My date," he heard her say over the music.

He stopped and looked at her. "Would you rather be with him?" He waited, giving her a chance to choose.

She looked at him, her eyes grazing his face, mapping him as though she might find out what she needed to know there. Then she shook her head. "No."

It was all he needed.

3

He led her into a hallway, far less crowded, but still occupied by curious eyes and continued deeper into the labyrinth of the fraternity. When he reached a secluded nook, he turned, took her face in his hands, and kissed her again. It was fire. She matched his rhythm with her tongue, and her hands clutched his back, her touch burning his skin like flames. He gently pushed her into the shadows against the wall.

Once there, he fitted his body against hers and charted her with his tongue. He outlined each of her curves with his hands, then pulled her tighter against him attempting to ease the need he felt. Her moan filled his mouth and added fuel to his lust.

"I lied," she finally said into his mouth.

"About?" He wasn't overly interested in her morality at the moment and kissed her again aware of little more than the urgency throbbing inside his pants.

AJ turned her face away forcing his mouth to find her jaw. Then her neck. "My date. I don't really have one. I've been using it excuse so I wouldn't get picked up on." She gasped as he ran his mouth and tongue over her exposed shoulder.

"I'm not sure it was very effective." Adam placed strategic kisses against her collar bone, then drew his tongue across the exposed mound of her breast hidden under her strapless shirt.

She moaned, pressing her body closer to his. "It was until you came along." She ran her hands through his hair bringing his lips to meet her own.

Adam picked her up, then used the wall for support. She wrapped her legs around his waist, the skirt riding up to her hips. Heat radiated between them. He pressed his erection against her exposed core, and he moaned.

Another drunk snickered as he passed. "Get it," the guy slurred. "Touchdown." He disappeared down the hall.

Releasing her legs, AJ pushed against his chest and tried to right herself.

He stepped back as she found her feet, but kept hold. She was too good a catch to let go.

"I'm sorry." She tugged at her skirt. "I'm drunk, and this is feeling entirely too good."

"I'm not sorry," Adam answered with a smile. "I just saw an amazing looking woman across the room, and I reacted."

"I'm sure the liquor helped," she teased.

"That it did—for bravery," he answered with a smile. "You have the most beautiful eyes."

She reached up to touch the dimple in his cheek. "You can have any girl you want."

"I want you," he answered, and turned his face to kiss her fingertip and rolling his tongue against her hot flesh.

Her green eyes ignited with a passionate fire, her gaze dropping to his mouth. "Kiss me," she demanded. She grabbed his face with her hands, pulled him back to her, and kissed him with urgency as she fumbled with the doorknob behind her. It was locked. "Damn," she mumbled, then grabbed his hand and took her turn leading Adam through the hallway trying doors as she went.

On the third try, a door opened to an empty room.

They ducked in, hands clutching, arms encircling, legs tripping. Adam kicked the door closed and reached to lock it. His mouth explored hers and his hands pushed her sleeveless blouse to her waist while her hands worked the buttons of his pants. After drunkenly trying to disrobe each other, they switched to taking their own clothes off while devouring each other with their mouths.

When they were naked, bared, he took a step back and ran his hands over her breasts. She shivered, her skin glowing in the moonlight. "You are beautiful," he said, and then kissed her again. Her lips were full and swollen. "You want this?"

Her breathing matched his. "Yes. Please."

Adam dove back in for another intense kiss. He was drunk, really drunk, but he couldn't remember feeling like this—ever. His hand clutched her perfect ass. Bending his knees, he ran his hands along her thighs and lifted her. She wrapped her legs around him. "I want you," he whispered, the hunger raw and aching in him.

He tried to carry her to the floor, but alcohol made his muscles disconnected from his tired, aching body. He stumbled; she slipped from his grasp, and they ended up on the floor in a heap, Adam over her. She giggled. He smiled—too drunk to care —and stopped for a moment to look at her. The goddess *Hina* did beautiful things against AJ's skin. His hands roved over her body to smooth the moonlight and the velvet created by the light. She sighed, her eyes closed, and her body arched under his touch.

He was ready to jump from the top of the mountain he'd climbed, but he thought about her, cognizant he wasn't alone in this. He leaned down and kissed her mouth again, then worked his tongue down her neck, over her breasts, down her belly until he was tasting her at her most intimate place. It was hot in all ways: her, her sounds, the quivering of her body as she came. Then he kissed a trail back up, slipped on a condom retrieved from his stuff, and positioned himself to join his body with hers. He pushed into her.

She cried out.

He stopped. "You okay?"

"Yes. More." She drew herself up to kiss him, using the strength of his back for support.

They moved together. Her sounds pushing him toward the edge faster than he wanted, but the numbing effects of the alcohol blessed him with added staying power. So, he lasted until she cried out, and he jumped from the edge himself.

Adam collapsed against her, physically and sexually spent. The alcohol coursed through him. He was tired. "That was good, AJ," he murmured, his eyes heavy with exhaustion.

"I can't believe I did that."

Adam slid off her onto his side and nuzzled her shoulder, his arm draped across her. Fatigue rushed toward him, like a black tunnel surrounding him. He tried to keep his eyes open, but it was becoming difficult. "You smell good," he murmured.

She placed her hands over her face and was quiet for a few

moments before saying, "I've got to go."

"Stay here," he said but even his own voice sounded far away. "We can do it again in a few minutes." His body weight shifted as she sat up, but he didn't try to get up with her. His legs were jelly from the game. From the sex.

"We're both drunk," she said.

"A good excuse, don't you think." He rolled to his back and smiled in the dark with his eyes closed. "Come back. Lay with me."

"Look, Adam, right? I've never done this before. I'm not... I'm going to go." He heard her moving around, looking for her clothes.

With his eyes still closed, he drifted toward sleep. He wasn't particularly aware of her words, only the satiation of his pleasure. He wanted her to stay, but doing it again, although nice, was beginning to sound impossible. His eyelids felt cemented.

"AJ," he muttered.

"Yes?"

"Maybe I can call you?" He heard the denim of her skirt slide over her skin. "Will I see you again?" he asked as he drifted in and out of hearing patches of sound. He didn't hear her answer but felt the whisper of fabric on his body as she covered him with a sheet. The last sound he remembered before falling into the oblivion of sleep was the latch on the door clicking shut.

CHAPTER ONE
(Honolulu, 2006)

A silhouette darkened the student essay Alex was reading. She looked up from the typed page at a figure whose face was obscured by the sun. The outline of the shadowy form was male: tall, built, and sinewy. The muscles of his frame outlined by the sunlight. She shaded her eyes with one hand and held the essay she'd been grading against her lap to keep the soft breeze from blowing the pages away. She squinted at the figure. "Can I help you?"

"I've been looking for you."

Alex's breath caught at the familiar voice, deep and resonant. She'd have recognized it anywhere. "I find that hard to believe." She looked down and hoped she sounded detached. It wasn't how she felt. Her heart raced now that she knew it was Adam, just like it always had. But instead of anger, this time the bridge between them had been burned by death.

Adam Kāne crouched down in front of her, and she met his gaze. Still the perfect picture of a man. His chestnut-hued skin, the handsome Hawaiian features, large chocolate eyes, and a strong nose framed his face. His lips were the perfect shape, kissable, masculine, appealing, but what undid her—always—was the dimple when he smiled. He wasn't smiling now. The strength of his arms and legs were obvious in his cotton pull over shirt and his blue jeans, both taut in his present position. He still looked the athlete, even at forty-seven.

Alex suppressed the urge to reach out and run her hand along the dark skin of his forearm to feel the velvet of his skin but resisted. *So inappropriate*, she thought and shook her head.

"You shouldn't be surprised," he said.

"Why not? After the last time we spoke?" She made a noise of dismay that caught in her nose.

He was quiet, then asked, "May I?" He nodded to the space on the bench next to her.

Alex lowered her foot to the ground and scooted a fraction. She looked away from Adam as he sat. The outside of his thigh pressed against hers, and the heat of his body burned through the layer of skirt into her skin.

The significance of this particular bench was not lost to her, though she was sure he hadn't made the connection. It was where they had officially met so long ago. He had been the all-American quarterback then. The only Hawaiian quarterback to lead Hawaiʻi State University to two major bowls.

He leaned forward, the shirt stretched across his back, his elbows rested on his knees. He still wore his wedding ring and twisted it around his finger with his thumb. He cleared his throat but didn't talk.

Alex looked away and waited for him to speak. She knew he would when he'd worked out what it was he wanted to tell her. So, she waited, staring out at the trees beyond the walkway in front of her. Students milled about in a rainbow of colors, but she didn't focus on any of them more curious as to what Adam was there to say. The last time she'd seen him, he'd berated her at Megan's funeral. That had been almost a year ago, time she'd spent running from her grief alone.

Last year, she'd been so consumed by the haze of working, numb to anything other than the refuge of being busy, she hadn't had time to focus on her own pain. Then, after what Adam said, she hadn't had them—her family—either. While she usually enjoyed her summer off and spent the months traveling, the summer had provided little more than free time to spend grieving the loss of her best friend and life as it had once been. The last four weeks back at work provided the relief from the loneliness and the opportunity to bury herself in the monotony of her existing world at school. It was difficult to believe that November would mark one year since Megan's passing.

"I owe you an apology," he said, breaking the silence between them.

Alex looked at the green pen she was rolling back and forth between her fingers. Her eyebrows arched a moment in disbelief.

"I said some terrible things to you, Alex. Things I'm ashamed to have said."

"But things you believed nonetheless." Alex turned her head to look at him.

He scrutinized his hands, calloused from manual labor of his youth. They still looked like quarterback hands, strong and wide with long tapered fingers.

"Do you still believe what you said that day?"

Adam hesitated.

She noticed the planes and ridges of his back and wanted to run her hand along the muscle to feel his strength. She was stupid longing for something she would never have.

He turned his left hand over and looked at it. The gold of his wedding band gleamed in the afternoon sun peeking through the trees. "It was wrong of me to say them."

Alex shoved the essay and pen inside her satchel. "I guess there's nothing left to say then." She stood to go.

He grabbed her wrist.

She turned to look at him. His touch was gentle, and her skin burned beneath it. Though she was fuming, his brown eyes kept her from yanking her hand away. His gaze held a look of regret, of anguish. She had never seen that look in their depths before. Even in the heat of their best battles, she had never seen anything other than control and at times amusement. Her heart quickened, and her resolve faltered.

"Please stay," he said. He pulled her with a steady pressure back toward him.

She might have jumped in his lap with enough coaxing. Instead, she wrenched her hand free and returned to the spot she'd vacated, but she didn't get comfortable, keeping to the edge of the bench.

"I did believe my words at the time. Wait, let me finish," he said when she moved to stand again. He grabbed her hand, holding it with his strong one, but all Alex could feel was the gentle stroking of his thumb against her palm. The motion, the contact with his skin against her own ignited a longing she'd repressed. A million bolts of lightning electrocuted her lower back.

"A year can change a person and his perspective."

Alex couldn't fault him for that truth. She had spent the last year wondering if his vitriol had been right.

"My anger that day was wrong, and I'm sorry for the things I said. They have no significance anymore."

She pulled her hand free and turned on him. "You self-centered, self-righteous son-of-a-bitch." The venom of her words hit their mark when he leaned back. "No significance? Let me call you a bastard and then accuse you of trying to break up my marriage because you didn't want your best friend to be happy. And while I'm at it, let me rip away the only family you've known for the last thirty years."

Alex noticed his jaw flex. She had struck a nerve. It had always been this way between them. "Is this why you were looking for me, Adam? To rub it in. To throw that day in my face and make me feel worse?"

He looked away. "No." The tight sound of his voice hinted of his strained patience.

"Then what is it? I have things to do."

"I found something."

Panic seized her. She could think of only one thing that would have him come looking for her after the way he'd shared his true feelings the last time they were together. Did he know? Alex remained silent afraid to give away her fear, but she held his eyes with her own when he reconnected with her gaze.

She could easily feign disinterest. She'd been doing it for years.

"Look, Alex. I know things have always been–" he paused looking for a word– "strained between us, but I need your help."

"You? The great Adam Kāne. Hawai'i Businessman of the year five times running." Sarcasm laced each word. "How could you need the help of a lowly college professor?"

"It's for Megan."

As she anticipated his response, she'd been brainstorming possible retorts to whatever he might say, but Adam's words stopped her short. Megan was all she needed to hear to calm her. The tears pooled in her eyes and blinked them away. She wouldn't cry in front of him. She wouldn't cry in front of anyone. She still could not believe that her best friend, her sister, was gone.

Alex had met Megan when she and her mom had moved to California. She had walked into her Kindergarten classroom afraid and alone. California had seemed a new country to her five-year-old mentality. She'd entered a classroom to cold stares from the other kids who didn't really know any different how to behave toward strangers. The only kindred spirit, a little blond girl who'd come over to show Alex her new shoes. A kinship had been born. She and Megan had been inseparable from that moment on, even attending college together on the very campus where she now taught.

Alex fiddled with the black leather satchel in her lap. She waited for Adam to continue, her anger simmering.

"She left me journals and letters. Journals she'd been writing since she had Emma."

Alex felt the panic again. "I know." She'd known they existed, but the secrets they contained were a mystery. She wondered if Megan had included the one secret that would prove Adam right.

"You knew about them?" His eyes narrowed in anger.

"I assumed you did too. You *were* married to her."

Adam stood and ran his hand through his short black hair to the back of his neck. The other hand rested on his hip. He took a deep breath. "You're right. I'm sorry."

She nodded, accepting his apology, but surprised by it as well. This was new territory for them.

"I did, but I didn't think about them until I rediscovered them in her office a few months after she died. I couldn't bring myself to read them until a few days ago. They're like reopening old wounds—reliving memories of our relationship."

The panic hit Alex again and nausea gripped her. She blinked to right the world that seemed to be spinning. She measured her words, "What does that have to do with me?" She watched him move his feet. He'd put his hands in his front pockets which pulled at the front of his jeans.

Her stomach twisted.

"I don't think anything. That's not exactly why I'm here. I found something that doesn't make sense to me. I thought maybe you'd know what it is. You knew her so well."

"What is it?"

"She underlined words. At first, I thought they were just underlined for emphasis, but the more I've read, the stranger the words. Some are nonsensical. We both know Megan was too deliberate to do something that didn't make sense."

She thought about her own letter. "Even toward the end?" Alex asked, remembering Megan in her last days fighting cancer. It made her feel heavy with sadness. Megan's coherence had been thin.

"They began—the notations—with the first entries. I don't think so." He crossed his arms over his chest. He looked vulnerable, like a boy, but trying not to be. "I'd hoped you might take a look at the entries—you might know what Megan was doing."

Chills ran a course along her skin. She wondered if it was a good time to tell him about her letter. "Do you have them with you now?" Maybe it was a coincidence. She was overreacting. She was good at that too.

Adam shook his head. "Can you come to the house?" He looked down at the ground and shifted his weight from one foot to the other. A memory of him surfaced in Alex's mind:

She'd left the library to go to her next class. Adam had been waiting for her, his mannerisms of today reminiscent of that day so long ago. He'd looked nervous and a bit unsure of himself—a rarity for him. Though he was humble, he'd never lacked self-confidence.

Alex hesitated, though she wasn't sure why. She had nothing to worry about with Adam. He hated her. This olive branch was for Megan and his grief. "When?"

"What about now?"

"I can't. I have a class in thirty minutes," She glanced down at her watch. "What about later?"

Adam nodded. "Thank you."

After agreeing on a time and offering an awkward farewell, Alex watched him walk away, his stride assured and confident. He put a hand in his pocket and pulled something from his jeans. Then he disappeared around Jensen Hall, a brick building across the mall of trees.

Alex went to her office to spend a few moments trying to calm her racing heartbeat. She leaned against the closed door and shut her eyes. Images of Adam reeled through her mind's eye like a slideshow.

His smile—that dimple.

His adoration of Megan.

Holding his children.

And even deeper and further, his hands on her. She shook her head of the errant thought, pushed away from the door, and set the satchel on her desk while collecting what she would need for her next class.

She couldn't let him do this to her—not again. She couldn't allow Adam to break her resolve to move forward, to move ahead with her life.

Like you've been doing any moving forward, she heard her inner voice say.

I have, she snapped at the voice in her head.

When you stop lying to yourself, then you might begin moving forward, the voice answered.

A sudden sense of loss so glaring hit Alex, and she was blinded by the ache of it as tears filled her eyes. She sank into her desk chair. Her inner voice was right. She hadn't finished her grieving process. About Megan. But also, about Adam. Alex didn't know if she could move forward until she faced Adam with the truth. But that, she knew, she could never do.

CHAPTER TWO

Most nights Adam would finish a second scotch—or a third and fourth—in front of the TV and then take himself to bed to lose his loneliness in sleep. Over the course of the last year, days and nights ran together with no beginning and no end. Just moments mixed up without Megan.

But tonight, Alex was going to be at the house putting a doorstop in his routine existence. For some reason, knowing it made his heart palpitate against his chest in an awkward rhythm, reminding him he was human.

The last time he'd seen Alex, before today, he'd been so raw. It had been after the funeral, and she'd been a rock. So, when he'd turned at the sound of her voice to find her standing inside the doorway of the office with the same pain he felt etched on her face, he'd had a desire to grieve in her arms. The fleeting wish had been followed by such ravishing guilt for even thinking it. His wife just in the ground even if it had been over a year watching her die. He'd lashed out at Alex, made his terrible accusation, even though there was a time in their history he'd been sure that was exactly what she'd done.

Now, he moved through the kitchen toward the living room and stood at the top of the two steps that descended into the space. That's where the box was now. Full and waiting.

He'd carried it down a few nights ago having remembered it was in the office all that time. The last ten months taunting him with its existence. Megan's office was a room he avoided because it reminded him the most she was gone. And something in him acquiesced to its call, a loosening in his chest that reminded him he was still alive. So, after nearly a year, he'd finally opened the door to her office, collected the box, and brought it down into the heart of the house he'd once shared with her.

He recalled stumbling into the office a few days after Megan's funeral. He'd gone there to be closer to her because his grief felt like his body was being crushed, every bit of air in his lungs pressed out. The space was exactly as she had left it before she died. He imagined the smell of her perfume lingered. It didn't. She'd spent so little time in her office the last year before she passed. Instead, they'd spent it in the awful in-between prison of the wait.

Chemotherapy.

Radiation.

Waiting.

Hoping.

Praying.

Waiting.

Dying.

Everything in there, however, was Megan. The L-shaped desk pressed against the wall was neat, a place for everything and everything in its place. Each picture frame, each craft made by the kids, every paperclip in order. The large chair was pushed under the desk, and her closed laptop sat in the center. Waiting. For her to return. Just like him, but she wasn't ever going to come home.

He knew that now, but then, amidst her things, in the room that felt like maybe she would just walk through the door and get right to work, Adam had sunk to the floor and broke. All of him—his essence—peeled away from his soul and melted, as though he'd never return to the land of life, where his kids needed him, where his business was circling, waiting for him to come in for landing. When he'd found his breath again, opened his eyes to the ceiling, nothing had collapsed. It all looked so normal despite how wrong his life felt.

He'd gotten to his knees and that was when he'd noticed the box marked with Megan's perfectly capitalized penmanship sitting on the floor next to the file cabinet—out of place and out of character for Megan. Where he was unorganized and cluttered, Megan complimented his nature by keeping him in order. She'd kept everything neat, just like her office. He remembered teasing her she was meant to be an architect with handwriting like the structural scrawl on blueprints he worked with every day. The block letters matched her personality.

Adam had known he was supposed to find that box.

With care, he'd removed the lid. Inside had been several bound books in a nondescript burgundy color with gilded edging. He'd looked at each of them removing them one-by-one, recognizing them as the same books Megan had written in each day before she left her office for the evening. He'd always assumed they contained ideas for her work. There were twenty books in all.

When he'd opened one and saw her neat handwriting decorating the page, he scanned it. Midway down the page he saw a heading that read, *Dear Adam*, and it was dated four years earlier. Adam had flipped through the journal and eyed the dates. Megan had written him each day. Some entries were pages; others were single lines. Each entry started with *Dear Adam*. He'd dropped the book back into the box as though he'd been burned and left the room.

He hadn't been back in there until a couple of days ago, finally ready to face her words. It hadn't been that he didn't want to read her words. God, he had. Every fiber of him wanted to immerse himself in her world, but her words weren't enough. He'd wanted her. He'd wanted her arms around him, her voice in his ears. He wanted to bury his nose in the space between her shoulder and her neck. He wanted to kiss her and hear her laugh. Adam remembered he'd felt the wall around his carefully preserved emotions crack as his heart imploded. He hadn't been sure he could ever read them.

He poured himself a scotch, instead.

As time passed, and the pain grew less acute and more like the dull ache of an abscessed heart, Adam finally returned to her journals. At first, the idea of reliving the relationship they'd shared through her eyes was frightening. But when he started reading, he'd had difficulty putting the books down to reconnect with the real world—a world without her.

Now, he drew a book from the box, part of his routine, the first journal. It had what he needed to show Alex. He opened it and smiled as the memory of giving Megan the first journal caressed the edge of his consciousness. It had been the day after Emma was born. "Write your story, Meg," he'd said, then kissed her. They'd only been married a year and barely old enough to start a family.

He returned to the kitchen, mixed himself another scotch, settled in an overstuffed chair in the far end of the family room, and opened the book to read.

> Dear Adam. . . I never thought this. I never thought about how full I would feel when the baby was placed in my arms. I love you so much Adam, and when Emma arrived, that love exploded into a supernova of emotion. I didn't know I could feel this way. To see her and to recognize you in her face. To know that we made her through our love. To understand that we created this tiny creature dependent on us for her life is awesome and frightening...

> Dear Adam. . . Remember the day we met?

Adam smiled at the recollection. Though the edges of the memory were faded like an old photo because of the years, he could still see her, a new freshman at Hawai'i State University. He been a sophomore football player testing the waters of what it meant to be a man.

She was walking the mall pathway that was lined by parallel trees. There were grassy knolls on which to sit, benches to stop for a break, and all along the outer edge of the trees were concrete buildings. Adam caught sight of her and couldn't look away. He was sitting with his football buddies talking about a party they'd all been to the prior weekend. He'd been so drunk, he could barely remember what he'd done, but there were flashes of a gorgeous girl though no details remained. It made him feel embarrassed he'd gotten so wasted, so he avoided the banter with the guys and spied a hot ha'ole wahine walking toward them, a piece of paper in hand.

Taken in by her ingénue appearance, he appreciated her angelic smile. Her rich golden hair slicked straight and sliding midway down her back. Her hazel eyes, adorned with the natural color of her light skin, turned at the corners when she smiled. And that smile nearly knocked him clear off the back of the bench where he sat so that he'd had to steady himself by grabbing hold of it. She wore those sexy hip-hugging pants and tight top that showed off the skin of her abdomen and her curves.

Oblivious to feeling timid around a group full of overgrown jocks, she approached the bench where they gathered. "Excuse me?"

"You lost?" A fellow teammate asked, his tone mocking.

"Actually, yes," she replied and arched an eyebrow in challenge. "Can any of you point me toward Anderson Hall?" His friend backed off, and Adam was impressed by this female who didn't seem intimidated by a bunch of overgrown jocks.

Another of his friends, Michael, the one notorious for thinking about his next lay, spoke up. "Sure. I'll take you." He climbed from the bench and stood beside her. "Anyone want to come?"

"I have to hit the library anyway," Adam lied trying to seem cool. "I'll walk with you." He gave his remaining friends a quick jock version of a handshake, then followed Mike and the beautiful blonde. As they walked, he noticed the brunette. Michael attempted to charm the blonde, strolling ahead of Adam and another woman.

Unsure of what to say, he walked in silence. From the corner of his eye, he checked the brunette out. She was also a knock-out. Her dark hair, streaked with red highlights, was wavy around her face and dropped below her shoulders. Her green eyes, framed with dark lashes, were downcast as they walked, looking up every so often to check their progress on the path. Her body, rounded in all the right places, filled out her clothing. She was so pretty, Adam couldn't even string together a coherent sentence. Looking at her, though, a tug of something familiar nagged him. He tried to reach for it but wasn't sure how to grasp onto the hazy feeling.

When they reached the library, Adam hesitated to go, but for the sake of appearances had to follow through. He slapped his hand against Mike's, which turned into a handshake. "See you at practice," he said. "Ladies." He nodded to each.

"I'm sorry, I didn't catch your name," the blonde said before he walked away.

"Adam."

"I'm Megan," she said and offered her hand. She flashed him that heart-stopping smile, then introduced him to Alex, but he'd barely paid attention. He couldn't concentrate but for the feeling that his hand was on fire from her touch.

Adam stared at the page in front of him. He watched the words come back into focus, pulling him from his memory. He picked up his drink, took a sip, and returned to Megan's words.

If I remember correctly, you had a thing for <u>Alex</u> at first.

21

Adam smiled rereading it and replaced the sifter on the coaster.

I'd been so jealous you'd chosen to walk with Alex instead of me. I was the one who noticed you right away. It had been my idea to coerce you into helping me find my class. I knew where It was, but it seemed the best way to get your attention.

You'd been sitting on the back of the bench surrounded by other <u>football</u> cronies. And you barely noticed me when I came to ask directions. I'd told Alex prior to approaching the group I could get you to talk to me. She'd said you didn't seem like that type of guy. I was so irritated that she'd been right. She told me later, after I'd pestered her to know what you talked about on the walk to the library where we'd parted ways, that you hadn't said a word. She'd been right. You'd been too nice to try to get into either of our pants with slick words you didn't mean.

After that day, before our first date, I looked for glimpses of you everywhere on campus, but the only place I could find you was at the practice field, so I took to dragging Alex with me to football practice every day so I could watch you. Oh, the sight of you dropping back and throwing the ball as though it was an extension of yourself, so smooth and perfect. It was such a turn on. I laugh remembering how I couldn't stop talking about you. Poor Alex, she just listened and supported my infatuation.

He set the book in his lap, picked up his scotch, took another sip, and closed his eyes. *More interested in Alex? What could she have been thinking?* He set the book on the table, stood, and walked into the kitchen.

When had a monster started growing out of the sink, he wondered? He glanced around, walked the main floor of the house, realizing everything was in disarray. *Megan is scolding me from heaven,* he decided with a smile and recognized his ability to smile when he thought about her had only begun to happen.

He glanced at his watch. Alex was probably on her way over. "Shit," he muttered. There was no way he wanted Alex to be witness to his weakness.

He went from room to room and picked up stray items, threw away junk mail and old food containers. As the rooms began to hint of their original selves, he felt a shift in his attitude. The constant pressure that weighed on him over the last year eased.

Adam went to the kitchen and tackled the messy sink. The hot water steamed the window that afforded a view of the stream behind the house. Though the blue-gray night obscured the view and instead offered a strange reflection of him in the misty, glass pane. He washed the dishes, scrubbing the food, rinsing, and placing them in the dishwasher and thought of Megan standing in that same spot with a daughter on each side. He and Trey clearing the dinner dishes away from the table, teasing the girls until they were all laughing, the dishes still undone.

Adam wondered if he had envisioned the complete happiness they would share together as a family when he first knew Megan was the woman with whom he wanted to share his life. He knew for certain he'd never envisioned the heartache.

The night he'd realized that he wanted Megan to be his wife he'd taken her to a tiny little Italian restaurant on the edge of the HSU campus. It had been a cliché little Italian place with the red checked tablecloths and the half-burned candlesticks in recycled cans with sand to hold the taper. They'd passed the time getting to know one another, sharing their goals and laughing about stories each had of their life. It was as though they had been created to share the other's space. In the candlelit moment of their camaraderie, it dawned on Adam why he'd been so nervous about asking her out, about making a good impression. Subconsciously, he'd already known this was the woman he wanted to marry. He just couldn't have predicted where that would lead them.

Adam finished the dishes, wiping the counter around the sink with a cloth. He looked around the kitchen and family room at his handiwork and appreciated the sense of accomplishment. He wrote out a note to call a cleaning service the next day, and was attaching it to the refrigerator with a magnet when the doorbell rang.

He opened the large, wood door. "Since when did you start ringing the bell?" The sound of his voice was harsh to his own ears, and he chastised himself. He didn't want to be that way with Alex. He didn't want to restart in anger. There was just so much history, so much bitterness and resentment that had built walls between them.

"I didn't think you'd find it very appropriate for me to just walk in." Alex's smile was subdued and didn't reach her pretty green eyes.

He had the distinct feeling she wanted to be somewhere else other than his doorstep and supposed he didn't blame her after what he'd done at the funeral.

He moved away from the doorway to allow her entry. "Sorry. That was a stupid comment considering."

"Right."

"Can I offer you a drink?" he asked as she passed him. He noticed her light gardenia scent and frowned.

"I'm not sure," she walked into the kitchen.

Adam followed her and scolded himself for looking at her shapely backside in her black pants. He shook his head. *Get it together, Kāne.*

She stopped, turned at the bar, and looked at him as he walked into the kitchen. An internal battle waged across her face, then she nodded as though giving herself permission. "Thank you. I'll have what you are having."

"Scotch?" Adam stood in the center of the kitchen and waited for her reply. He was unsure of how to proceed with her and felt ridiculous because of it. He could deal with multimillion-dollar projects, negotiate with owners and corporations, wheel and deal with architects, suppliers and subcontractors. But being alone with Alex felt like walking on ice, treading a very slippery slope. They had never coexisted in peace, their battles epic. He hadn't wanted to seek her advice, to reopen old wounds, but he didn't know where else to turn.

"A scotch would be perfect. Neat. I'm sorry I couldn't get away sooner. I just…well, the life of a teacher is never convenient." She stood at the end of the counter looking as though she was as unsure as he felt.

Adam finished pouring her a scotch. "Would you like to go into the living room?"

"This is fine." She chose a barstool facing the kitchen.

Adam placed the drink in front of her and remained on the opposite side of the counter from her.

She was reticent. Adam wondered where her thoughts were as her gaze drifted with the waves in the glass of amber liquid she swirled. Then she broke the silence and said, "I really miss her."

He turned away from her and walked to the kitchen sink, creating more distance between them. What could he say? He turned back to her, then, and leaned against the counter. He crossed his legs at the ankles and his arms over his chest.

"I–" she started but stopped.

"What is it?" Adam paused. He watched her stare at the glass in her hand and continue to swirl the liquid around into a whirlpool. A piece of her mahogany hair, styled so that it shone and waved against her tanned skin, fell forward as she looked down. She pulled the lock off of her face and tucked it behind her ear. She looked up to pin him with her emerald gaze.

The look connected with his spine and threaded it with a new

25

strand. Something confusing. He'd always viewed Alex like the snake in the Garden of Eden, whispering in the ear of Megan, tempting her away from him. At least that was his justification for accusing her of trying to break up his marriage. Now, as she looked at him, and he at her, heat spread through his body chasing away excuses for all the reasons he'd blamed her. It was a heat he didn't want to acknowledge, a heat built from memories, and those memories weren't her fault.

"Maybe you were right," Alex stated and stood.

"Right about what?" He walked into the sitting room to retrieve his drink, needing to do something with his body, move, spend the energy moving through him. His thoughts were not sane.

"I shouldn't have come."

He turned and looked at her. Her nervousness perplexed him. "Alex," he said with more control than he thought he possessed at that moment. "I asked you to come, remember. I'm the one who needs your help."

She sat again, but Adam had the distinct impression she would bolt toward the door with any sudden movement. He treaded with light steps and careful words. "Would you like to see the journals?"

"I should have mentioned this earlier. But I didn't."

Adam waited.

She stared at her drink, then lifted it to her lips and sipped.

His gaze fixated on her lips, and his stomach fluttered thinking about them. And kisses. Moonlight. More.

He looked away.

She set the glass back on the counter. "Megan left me a letter. She wrote it before she died. You mentioned that there was something strange about her journal entries."

"Wait. What?" The disorienting effect of her admission on his mind had to be written on his face. "Why didn't you say anything about the letter?"

She stopped swirling the glass with her hands, and her brows arched over her eyes, incredulous at his last question. He thought maybe they looked like mirror images, both of them stubborn and defensive. "Because it was my letter," she said, and then her brows dropped, coming together with ire. "And why should I? Because, like you, I didn't think anything of it. I'm sure there all kinds of reasons I didn't have to tell you Megan wrote me a letter."

"So like you, Alex."

"What's that supposed to mean?" She stood. She shook her head and reached for her bag. "I knew this was a bad idea."

"Can't you put yourself in my shoes for one second?" he asked. He hadn't wanted to fight with her, but here they were right back to where the path they tread always led them.

"So like you, Adam," she parroted back at him.

He stared at her.

She stared right back.

The warmth that spread through him, the sudden urge he had to take her in his arms, wasn't welcome. He didn't like the vision he had of kissing her until she didn't have any fight left in her. And he certainly didn't like that he felt that way when he shouldn't. He was a widower. He blinked the images from his mind, focused on the infuriating, obstinate woman in front of him.

He just missed his wife. *That* was all.

Alex took a deep breath the tension draining from her back and shoulders. She sank back onto the stool. "She did the same thing in her letter." Her anger was gone.

"Did what?"

"She underlined words there too."

CHAPTER THREE

Alex pulled a worn envelope from her purse and glanced at Adam who was motionless across the room. He leaned against the back of the couch, his glass of scotch held in one hand, loose, like it might drop to the floor. His other hand gripped the sofa's spine. His eyes watched the envelope, as if she'd pulled the embodiment of Megan from her bag. If it wasn't for the grief, it might have been worth a smile, but Alex understood his pain. She understood the desire to find Megan in the concrete objects of the world around them.

"Would you like to read it?" She held it out, the weight of the words far more than the paper that held them.

"It's yours." He looked down at his drink, brought it to his lips, and took a sip.

She set it on the white marble countertop in front of her and cupped her hands around her own glass of scotch.

A strained silence ensued; one that epitomized the canyon between them. On one side stood Adam, who'd made it clear he blamed her for everything that went wrong in his marriage. He carried a love for his wife in the very essence of his identity. On the other side was where she stood, and she'd made it clear Megan and her family—by extension, him—was everything to her, the very essence of her own identity. She loved Megan like a sister, and Adam... well, Adam was complicated.

Being there was bittersweet.

She'd spent most of her adult life sitting on this barstool and laughing with her best friend. She could picture Megan, blonde hair drawn into a ponytail, chasing one of the kids—probably Bekah, who'd done something naughty again—through the room. Alex smiled despite herself, wishing things were different, that Megan was still here. She pictured Emma, the oldest, on one barstool doing homework and Megan on another working on a new article, with Alex in between grading essays. But being alone with Adam had been infrequent. Perhaps only after the kids had been born, and he and Megan had needed help.

She sighed wishing things were different.

"Adam, I—" she started.

"Look, Alex—" Adam said at the same time.

They both stopped when they heard the other's voice.

"Let me," he said and crossed the room, stopping on the opposite side of the counter.

She looked up at him and her frustration effervesced like steam. Despite the animosity that existed between them, they'd fought silent wars of passivity and disconnection for the most part. Only on occasion had they openly engaged in verbal warfare. And when battles of open warfare were instigated, they'd been waged by Adam. She'd been willing to keep the peace because, to her detriment, she couldn't stay mad at him. It would have been easier if she could.

He looked at his glass and then up at her. His eyes were room-temperature whiskey. "I don't want it to be like this between us. Megan was important to both of us. I don't want...you know, being able to be in the same room to be only because of her." He set down his drink and ran a hand over his face. "Honestly, when I came to find you today, I was still bitter. But when I saw you, and you threw the same words I'd hurled at you after Megan's funeral, I understood I wasn't angry at you at all. I was pissed at myself. Then and now. I just took it out on you."

Alex looked at him, delved into the fathoms of his brown eyes and glimpsed regret. They'd softened, the edges worn down by time and grief, and a narrow plane of something she didn't recognize in their depths.

"I'm sorry for what I said that day. Hell, for the last twenty-something years between us."

The hope stirred by his words was almost too much. It made her uncomfortable wanting the words so much but being afraid of them. "Me too."

He smiled, a real one that transformed his handsome face and reminded her of a night so long ago, his guard down due to alcohol and the bravery to go after what he wanted. He'd smiled like that then.

Alex's heart split in two and raced in opposite directions.

"Peace treaty? A real one?" He stepped around the end of the counter, and she followed him with her head.

She nodded. "A peace treaty," and swiveled around in the stool as he walked into the family room. His back to her, she took a moment to appreciate him—his wide back, the sinew of his muscles, the taper of his waist, musculature of his legs. *Still surfing*, she thought. He picked up a book from the table and returned with it, sitting on the barstool next to hers. After setting the book on the counter, he pushed it toward her across the countertop.

Alex caught the scent of his clean, citrusy cologne and leaned toward him to take the journal. Her hand brushed his as he transferred the journal to her. She drew back, the heat of his touch leaving an imprint on her skin and suppressed the familiar feeling she was used to tamping down.

"The first post-it," he said.

Alex flipped the book open to the entry Adam had marked. She read it and noticed the underlined words. "I see what you mean." She turned to the next entry, then another. "What were you trying to tell us?" Alex muttered and continued through the entry—a letter to Adam about when they'd met.

If I remember correctly, you had a thing for <u>Alex</u> at first.

Alex's stomach clenched, constricting with anxiety, but she tried not to overreact. She checked the date and breathed a little easier. It was written long before she'd ever told Megan her secret. "Megan was deliberate about everything." Alex turned the page.

"My thoughts too."

"We can assume she underlined these words with purpose."

If Megan was trying to communicate something to Adam through her journal, why would she do the same thing in a letter to her? Could Megan have been trying to bring them back together? Alex was confident Megan knew she and Adam would have fallen away from one another after her death if for no other reason than Adam's stubborn pride. Without her as the bridge between them, how would they cross to one side or the other? An ache encircled Alex's heart thinking about her friend.

"Have you made a list of the words, yet?"

Adam shook his head. "No. I've been preoccupied with reading the entries. I noticed, though, she stopped underlining the further I get into the books." He reached across and flipped it open to an entry in the back of the book free of markings. "See. There are none in later journals."

"Let's list the words."

Adam retrieved paper and a pen from a desk in the kitchen. "You write. I'll read them out."

They traded.

Twenty minutes later, heads together and bent over the same paper, Adam and Alex looked over the list of underlined words compiled from the few journals and Alex's letter. They weren't any clearer about them.

"Let's read them aloud. Would you read them to me?" she asked, pushing the paper to him. 'Maybe if we hear the words?"

"Sure." Adam held up the list, leaned back, to recite the words and phrases. "First one, 'dependent on us for her life'."

Alex closed her eyes and listened to the words as he read them. The first one she pictured Emma, Trey, and Bekah, Adam and Megan's children.

"Alex."

Alex couldn't imagine why Megan had underlined her name. But she imagined Megan smiling at her, pictured her as her roommate challenging her to do something brave.

"Football."

Alex pictured Adam, sleek and sinewy, dropping back into the pocket for a pass. The image made her body ache. So, she pictured Trey, now a sophomore at HSU—a quarterback like his dad.

"Hide."

That one seemed strange. Hiding like her? In work? Her feelings?

"Campus."

Alex worked on a campus. She and Megan had met Adam on a campus. Both of which included HSU. Trey played football for HSU.

"Assumptions. Rose-colored lenses."

What could she possibly mean—to look at the message ideally—to look at this pragmatically?

"School in Hawai'i."

Which? There were over thirty high schools alone. Ten colleges and community colleges. Countless other schools to consider. It was like a needle in a haystack. Except, Alex thought, she'd thought of HSU more than once.

"Ignorance."

Alex opened her eyes and stole a glance at Adam as he continued to read the list. He'd put it back on the counter and leaned over it, his arms folded in front of him. His eyes were focused, a thick fringe of long, dark lashes, and a strong, masculine profile. *Was he still ignorant to her secret*, she wondered? She took a sip of her drink to purge the direction of her thoughts.

"Been blind."

She glanced at him again. His dark hair, interlaced with silver was cut short, but long enough to look soft and touchable. His brown complexion was vibrant, healthy. His features bold, like rocks in an ocean tide. That all-familiar tug pulled at Alex's innards and she denied it.

Adam continued reading pausing between separate words. "Malicious. Anger of. Family. Ignorance of. Families."

"Wait." She tapped the paper. "Read those again," Alex said, "But try and combine them."

"Malicious. Anger of family. Ignorance of families." He glanced at her. "They kind of do."

"But whose family?" Alex wondered.

Adam continued. "Go with my instincts."

Whose? Alex wondered? Megan's instincts? Someone else's?

"Don't let."

Alex ran her finger a long a gray vein of the marble and thought of most of her adult life spent in denial. She'd never allow herself to want.

"Do that to our kids."

"Adam!"

He stopped, looking up from the list.

"Read the last two together." She leaned toward him and pressed closer to read the list with him.

"Don't let do that to our kids."

Alex turned her face to see him better. They were so close their noses almost bumped. She sat back. "She thought your children were in danger. What would motivate her to be cryptic? You. The kids. Your safety."

She stood up, paced the floor between a couch and the barstools where Adam still sat. "Megan must have found out something she thought put you and the kids in danger."

"That seems… far-fetched. Why not just tell me?"

"I don't know." Alex said and bit the nail of her thumb of one hand, the other pressed against her belly. "Try read the underlined words from the letter."

"Adam. Emma. Trey. Bekah. Take care of them. Scared."

She moved back to the barstool excited and laid a hand on Adam's shoulder. "I remember thinking when I first read them, she was scared because she was leaving you all behind. That she was scared to die. But what if she was scared about something else?"

"How would they be in danger? Who could possibly want to hurt the kids?" He shook his head. "It seems… ridiculous." Adam glanced at her hand, looked back at the list, but didn't shrug away from her touch.

Self-conscious, she removed her hand, flexing it by her side. "Maybe, but Megan wasn't illogical about things she did. That's what we have to figure out. We need to figure out what the rest of these words mean and how they relate."

"They are all looking the same to me."

"Let me snap a pic of them, and I will try to make some sense of them too." Alex took out her phone.

"What about these numbers?"

Alex glanced at his finger pointing to a six-digit number on her letter. She paused. "I'm not sure. I thought you might know." She put her phone away.

Adam sighed and shook his head. He stood and walked back into the kitchen carrying his glass to the sink. "Would you like another drink?"

Watching him move, the slope of his shoulders, and the way his shirt stretched across his back, an unbidden flutter vivibrated against her nerves. She recalled that night so long ago—the one she was supposed to have forgotten. Emotions—guilt, relief, grief, want—

overwhelmed her. She stood.

"No. Thank you." She gathered her things. "I should go. It's late and I have an eight o'clock class tomorrow morning." She took the letter and her purse and walked past the kitchen into the hallway.

Adam followed her.

Tears threatened, the burn of them tormenting her earlier peace. She didn't want to cry. Not in front of Adam. And she knew her tears were for the wrong reason now. The overwhelm wasn't for Megan—it was about her.

"Slow down. There isn't a fire," Adam joked and caught up with her in the foyer. "This has been rather enjoyable." He turned her around to face him by her elbow. "I liked…wait. What's wrong?"

Alex kept her eyes fixed on the dark tiled floor. She didn't want him to see her crying. She never wanted that. "I just miss her," Alex said and looked up at Adam. That was the truth. Then she couldn't help herself and heaped more coal into the fire, "As much as I wished for her life, I want her back." Tears spilled leaving a trail on her cheeks.

Adam pull her into his embrace, and she collapsed against him. Though he'd hugged her briefly after Megan's passing, this was different. Then, it had been consolation for news, two people clinging to one another in the high tide of grief, both drowning. This felt like comfort, as though he'd become a sheltering island in the storm while it crashed around them. She should step away, but she didn't.

"I miss her too," he said his lips moving against her hair.

"She asked me to watch over you and the kids before she died. I failed her."

"Alex." His voice was soothing, his hands comforting as they caressed her back.

"Don't," she said. "I have." She tried to compose herself, and she took a step away from him the feel of his compassion more welcome than he understood. But he didn't let her go, his hands still on her shoulders. She looked up at him. "I have stayed away when

35

Megan asked me to help you and the kids through your grief."

He reached for a tissue on the table in the hall and held it out to her.

She accepted it, then stared at it as she rubbed the soft paper between her fingers.

"How could you have, Alex? I was so awful and hostile at the funeral. I guaranteed you'd stay away. It took me ten months to apologize. Why would you—should you—have done any differently?"

"I should have. Megan would have," Alex answered. "She would have known you were hurting." A fresh wave of tears hit her.

"Please don't cry, Alex. You were hurting too."

Adam took her face in his hands and nudged her to look at him. He wiped a tear away with his thumb.

She searched his eyes, while they darted around her face. Alex saw that look again from earlier, the one she couldn't name, soften his features.

You don't remember do you, Adam? she wondered. But she knew the answer to that question. He didn't.

He leaned in and kissed the place on her cheek where he'd wiped away the tear with his thumb.

Warmth spread from the graze of his lips on her cheek into her body like a wildfire. She stepped away when reason stepped in to remind her who she was. Who he was. She noticed he'd also stepped way, his expression stunned.

"I'm sorry, Alex. I shouldn't have done that." His hands were up.

"Maybe you were right, what you said that day." She took another step away from him toward the front door. "I've spent countless hours analyzing your words, poking holes in your argument," she said, and looked up. "Even as angry and hurt as I was that you said them."

She paused with her hand on the door and turned back to face him. "Thank you for the drink." She reached into her purse and withdrew the worn envelope. "Here's Megan's letter," Her tone impersonal, business-like. With equal efficiency when he didn't take it, she set the missive on the table in the entryway. "I've got to go."

"At least let me walk you out?"

She shook her head. "This is far enough. I'm okay, Adam. I've always been okay." She turned. "If I think of anything, I'll let you know." Then she willed herself to walk away.

Adam watched Alex get swallowed by the night.

He took a couple of steps after her but stopped on the front porch of his house unsure why he was trailing her. She started her car and drive out of the driveway. A bizarre sensation tugged at him, a sense of urgency perplexed by her words: *Maybe you were right.* It was as though the sea were rolling under his surf board, but he couldn't find his balance. Unfamiliar territory with her, and he wasn't sure what to make of the new emotions colliding within him.

Adam shut the front door, picked up the letter Alex had left, and went back into the kitchen where the light felt inviting and safe. He glanced at the spot she'd occupied while there, and the emptiness of the house suddenly felt cavernous and lonely.

He sat back down at the bar and opened the letter Megan had written to Alex:

Alex, my friend, my sister:

I don't know where to begin, really, how to tell you my heart, but it needs to be done. So, I should start with the blaring truth of the matter. The cancer has returned and my doctor fears I have less than a year. I could ramble on about how angry I am, and I'm sure I will have already done that with you by the time I give you this letter. I've already beaten this disease once, and I was willing to come out victorious again—but it isn't meant to be this time—this time I'm meant to put my responsibilities in order, my ducks in a row, so to speak. Who could I trust more than you, Alex, and Adam to help me?

Alex, you have been the best of friends. You have been there for me, guided me when I ventured off the path, and counseled me with the truth, even when it wasn't what I wanted to hear. What kind of friend you have been to help me see light when sometimes I was enshrouded in darkness? Know that I respect you and respect the choice you made so many years ago when you shared what you did. There was nothing to forgive, and I hope that you know that.

Adam stopped and reread the last paragraph contemplating the meaning behind Megan's words. But he couldn't puzzle it out, couldn't connect the dots. It made him curious. What had she meant? What could Alex have thought that Megan needed to forgive her for?

Alex, I don't know how my family will take the cancer and my inevitable passing. I'm frightened to think that they won't be able to move on. Though that sounds vain and presumptuous, I know that if I were to lose Adam, or one of the children, I could imagine myself getting stuck in vicious cycle of denial, anger, self-doubt, and hopelessness. Promise me that you will <u>take care of them</u>.

I know you and <u>Adam</u> haven't always seen eye-to-eye. I can appreciate how patient you have been with him. Please continue to be. He is notorious for being hard-headed, but he isn't hard-hearted. He is a loving, kind, and generous man, and though I know you are well aware of that, I know how easy it is to lose patience with his stubborn streak. He is prone to fighting tooth and nail against that which he perceives as a threat, even if he misunderstands. He will go to battle for those he loves, and Alex, despite your differences, I know that deep down Adam loves you too, just as I do. I don't presume he will never move on after I'm gone, Alex, but please make sure that he knows I don't want him to waste his years. That I want him to find love again.

Please watch out for <u>Emma</u>, <u>Trey</u> and <u>Bekah</u>. They all love you, their Aunt Alex, and on days that their terrible mom wouldn't let them get away with being awful humans, would have gladly called Aunt Alex mom. I am so blessed to have them, and I'm very proud at how they have grown into beautiful souls with so much promise of being wonderful adults.

Emma is just married, and I know that within time will think about starting her own family with Grant. Oh, my heart aches to think that I won't hold my own grandchildren, but Alex, you can. You will be able to be there for Emma when she experiences the ups and downs of motherhood. Please tell her when she feels as though she's ready to go insane because she's lost herself in them that it won't last. That one day her selfless giving to her children will mold them and she will return stronger and more vibrant than when she began the journey of motherhood. Tell her how much I loved her. How she made me strive to be a better mother, because my inadequacy was always so transparent.

Trey makes my heart feel full. Though I love each of my children, I love them in their own unique ways. Where Emma makes me proud, she humbles me for I see me in her and can remember all the choices I made that I would change. Whereas Bekah fills me with joy, she reminds me of mortality, for I'm frightened of them leaving me behind. Trey makes me rest in today and acknowledge that today is more important than yesterday or tomorrow. It is written in James, chapter four verse 14, "Why you do not even know what will happen tomorrow. What is your life? You are a mist that appears for a little while and then vanishes." Please tell Trey when the time is right how very much, I loved him. How he changed me to enjoy each day of my life and to keep living purposefully.

Oh, my Bekah, my baby, my joy. I will miss her in ways that are indescribable. I'm saddened that I might not see her graduate from high school next year. That I won't see her graduate from college or watch her continued to develop into the strong, independent woman that she is becoming. Alex, I ask that you help Bekah realize how strong she is as a woman. That she shouldn't defer her dreams to anyone or anything. That she can be exactly who she wants to be—she can have it all if she wants it. That she can be just like her Aunt Alex. I know of no better person to guide Bekah than you, my friend, the epitome of a woman of strength, who knew her mind and followed it. Please tell her how much I will miss watching her grow into the woman I know is there, waiting to bloom.

Alex, I will miss your fellowship. Though we aren't related by blood, I don't think that blood would have made you more of a sister to me than you are. I'm so blessed that I have you as a friend. I'm so blessed that I shouldn't feel <u>scared</u>, because I know that you will take care of my family. And I thank you for your loyalty and devotion. There aren't many people who would exemplify such dedication. I love you, Alex, for all that you have been in my life and for all that you will continue to be even after I'm gone.

Grief welled up in his chest and flowed into the deep recesses of his heart. He fought to control the emotion that threatened to spill over, and his throat constricted as he held back. He imagined Megan writing those words. Her feeling like she needed to take care of her family and turning to the one person that she knew would. Guilt hammered at him for having pushed Alex away, begrudging her presence in his wife's life, being angry she was always there.

Emotion stung his eyes and spilled down his cheeks. He dropped his face into his hands and leaned against the counter, allowing the tears their time and space. The loss of Megan was still deep and alive, but there was a new rawness scraped over his heart. While he missed his wife, he accepted she wasn't coming back. He'd spent the last ten months grieving. Hell, he'd spent the last year and a half grieving as Megan wasted away in front of him. He'd been left behind to exist as a shadow.

Today though, like seeing the house for what it had become and picking up the clutter, his tears felt cleansing. He was renewed knowing his wife had loved him so deeply; she'd sought the aid of her best friend to keep watch over them like a guardian angel. He felt, for the first time in a year, hope that he might be able to find peace in existing without her.

Adam wiped his face and folded Alex's letter, putting it back in the envelope. He imagined her and her face as they'd gone over the words. Her eyes closed and a myriad of expressions traipsing across her face like a parade.

He picked up her glass and remembered her tears, her words: *Maybe you were right.*

He frowned.

The moment he'd offered comfort, his lips against her skin, he recognized where his thoughts had gone, and an image of a woman lit by moonlight on a drunken night over thirty years ago. He reached for it, but it was hazy. He remembered being drunk and hadn't thought much about that night. Alex had made him think of it. Her words: *I've got to go.* The way she'd said them. Something painted his periphery, but Alex had walked out. He'd dismissed the distant feeling watching her leave.

Adam carried Alex's glass to the sink and set it inside. He looked up at his reflection in the darkness of the window. Before today, he'd been able to disconnect from Alex in his anger. The peace didn't offer distance. And, like the warmth of their peace treaty, Alex was a newly sprouted seed in his heart.

CHAPTER FOUR

The shrill ring of the telephone pierced Adam's sleep like a scream startling him awake. He grabbed for it on the nightstand next to the bed knocking over a frame in the process. "Hello?" His voice sounded as though it needed to catch up with his body. He swung his legs around and sat up, his back to the empty space of the bed behind him.

"You still sleeping, Dad?" It was Trey.

"Were you hoping I was?" he asked his son.

"Maybe, but I figured you'd be awake already. You're usually up so freakin' early to surf."

Adam buried his face in his hands, the phone held with his shoulder, and rubbed the sleep from his eyes. He hadn't been much of an early bird since losing Megan. Then, with his hand holding the phone again, he got up and walked to the bathroom.

"Being your alarm clock wasn't the reason I have blessed you with this call though," Trey continued.

"Okay." Adam flipped the light on in the bathroom.

"I found out from coach last night that I'm sharing time with

Miles in tomorrow's game."

"What?" Adam stalled in the middle of the room. "And you're only calling me now? That's great news!" He smiled.

"I didn't call last night because I was embroiled in a major video game tournament."

"Video games? Is that what my money pays for?" At the sink, Adam leaned forward and looked at his face. He needed a shave.

"Didn't you catch the vocab, Dad? Embroiled? Besides, the semester just started, and major book time doesn't start until midterms."

"I don't remember that about college." Adam rolled his eyes.

"Things have changed since your day, old man."

Adam could hear his son's amusement on the other end of the line and imagined Trey's smile. "Well, I will look forward to your grades. Maybe I can save money and get some cheap labor in the process." With the phone between his shoulder and his cheek, Adam pasted his toothbrush.

"No worries, Dad. I got it all under control. Football scholarship stipulates tutor support anyway—so I'm in the clear."

"Did you just use the word 'stipulate'? You must be picking something up from your computer thesaurus feature on your laptop." Adam chuckled. "So, Jonesy is still starting, though?" Adam asked referring to the other quarterback on the team.

"Yeah. Coach said I'm going in for the second offensive series."

"Congratulations, bud. That's great. Shows Coach's confidence in you. You'll have to work twice as hard to keep that position, though." Adam said, thinking about his own experience. "There's always someone better waiting in the wings."

"That's me. I got this, Dad."

"I know you do, but just in case... you've always got a job with me at the company if the college and football thing doesn't work out."

"No thank you!" Trey made a disgusted noise, and Adam smiled imagining his son squeezing his eyes shut and scrunching up his nose. "I'm going to milk this college thing as long as I can."

Adam laughed and then completed the pregame tradition: "Touchdown?"

"Touchdown," Trey answered. "Gotta go. I've got to work out before class. Oh, and by the way—get up!" Trey ended the call.

Adam's chest filled with joy thinking about his son as he hung up the phone. He set it on the bathroom counter and brushed his teeth. He stood up and stretched, thought about how he used to cherish the early morning and decided he needed to start surfing again—it had been too long—since Megan passed. Being in the ocean was healing, but it was also spiritual for him. He hadn't been able to face it, but looking in the mirror, he decided he was ready. He was tired of running over the land and needed the water again.

The bathroom mirror framed with large, round lights reflected his weary face and his brown eyes were lined with fatigue. Too much scotch, he decided, and realized it was time to make a change there too. His black hair, laced with traces of silver, was a bit overgrown. The black and silver stubble on his chin had grown from a shadow into the beginning of a beard overnight.

As he scraped the razor across his skin, his mind wandered, thinking of the work he had to do at the office. The cleaning service. Then he thought about Alex and stalled. He shook his head. He didn't want to think about Alex and turned his thoughts instead to Trey's phone call as he resumed scraping the razor over his brown skin. Adam's reflection was an older version of his son, though Trey's edges where a bit more angular, taking after his mother. And he'd been blessed with her hazel eyes—all their children had her magical eyes.

He rinsed his face and ran a hand over his skin to check for missed spots.

His children were his world now. Though they had their own lives; he didn't get to spend as much time with them. Emma was married and had her own life to think about. Trey—a sophomore— and Bekah—a freshman—were both in college now living with roommates. He could be thankful they'd remained in Hawai'i to go to school instead of on the continent.

After splashing on some after shave, Adam went to his closet to dress. He was really looking forward to Trey's football game. Seeing his son in that uniform as the quarterback for the Hurricane's would feel like coming full circle in a way. Though he wasn't one of those dads who lived vicariously through his son—he'd been there after all—he was just so proud.

Adam glanced at his watch. He still had a few minutes before he needed to leave for work. So, he made a cup of coffee, a bite to eat, and settled at the counter to read some of Megan's journal.

Dear Adam... Remember the first time we went out? I think about it now and laugh; Alex and Michael were so funny arguing with each other about the feminist movement.

He remembered going out that first night, but he hadn't remembered that particular bit about the night. Mike had asked Megan out and coerced Adam to joining him for the double date Megan had insisted on.

Adam closed his eyes walking down memory lane.

Mike told him on the way to the dorms: "Dibs on the blonde, 'kay? What was her name? Margaret? Mary?"

"Megan," Adam replied. It was bro-code not to poach a friend's conquest, even if it irritated him Mike couldn't remember her name. Adam hoped Megan was smart enough to see through the other man's bullshit.

"She's bringing along that hot brunette."

Adam remembered her from the walk to the library. She had been pretty if quiet.

He and Mike met Megan and Alex outside their dormitory and walked to a diner at the edge of campus. It was a cool night. Trade winds moved through the leaves, and the sky was clear, the stars sparkling like crystals refracting light.

"What's your major?" he finally asked Alex, breaking the silence as they followed behind a chattering Mike and Megan.

"Women's Studies."

"You're a feminist?" Adam asked. He hadn't meant it to be rude. He was down with the movement, but she bristled at his question.

"You got a problem with that?" She looked at him then, her ire making her bold. The shadows played with her features as they walked, and Adam had that sensation again that he knew her.

"Not at all. I'm down. What does one do with a Women's Studies degree?" he asked.

"Haven't decided yet. I either want to specialize in women's literature and eventually teach at the college level, or I'm thinking about doubling in international relations and joining the Peace Corps to work with women in third-world countries."

They continued walking behind Mike and Megan, who were deep in conversation.

"That's impressive." He glanced at her and recalled again just how pretty she was. Her hair rippled with loose waves down her back. She was wearing a green dress. He was about to ask if they'd met before, but she asked him a question.

"And your major?"

"Business."

"Why business?"

"I want to own my own construction company."

"Intent on being the corporate man, huh." She smiled.

"I suppose so." He returned her smile and held the door open for her when they reached the restaurant.

"Thank you," she said with a gleam in her pretty green eyes.

Had she been interested then, and Adam hadn't seen it? He remembered feeling like she hadn't been. But then, he'd been so enchanted by Megan, he hadn't really been paying attention.

Adam sat next to Alex when they got to the booth, which afforded him a nice view of Megan on the other side of the table. Megan gave him one of those beguiling smiles, and he was as affected by that as the realization he was on the verge of poaching.

He slipped off his jacket and brushed Alex's bare arm with his own, then wondered if he'd imagined she'd jumped. Heat crawled through him in response to the contact. He ignored it.

The rest of the evening was fun. While it was obvious that Mike was laying it on thick, Megan seemed into it. Conversely, Alex was a worthy opponent of Mike's in the word play department. She was quick and witty though very serious about her opinions. Adam liked it, especially the banter between her and Mike that left the foursome laughing more than eating.

By the end of the night, as they walked Megan and Alex back to their dorm, Adam was glad he'd joined the date. Until they reached the entrance and Mike walked Megan into a shadowy alcove of the walkway for some privacy.

"Thank you, Adam." Alex turned to face him.

"You're welcome. I had a good time, Alex, even though you think I'm a corporate monger bent on greed and destruction of the little guy." He tried to focus on his date, not what may or may not be happening in the shadowy alcove where Mike had disappeared with Megan.

She laughed at his joke. "Or gal."

He smiled and searched her pretty face. Her green eyes sparkled. He fell a bit deeper into them and was aware of the sensation again that he knew her.

She opened her mouth to say something, closed it, and then finally said, "You don't remember, do you?"

"Remember what?" He tilted his head. "I do feel like I know you from somewhere but can't put my finger on it."

Disappointment seeped into her green eyes when they locked on his brown ones.

And as though on cue, Megan bounded up the stairs toward them splitting the moment into a before and after. "Thank you, Adam. I had a great time. Be sure to give us a call soon, okay." She flashed him a smile, then she grabbed Alex's hand and waved at Mike who'd stayed at the bottom of the stairs.

"See you later," Alex said as Megan pulled her toward to door.

"Right." He moved away from the door as the two women disappeared into their dorm, then walked back down the steps. The confusion about Alex's question melted away as he fell into step with Mike, his curiosity about how far his friend had gotten with Megan at the forefront of his thoughts. "So?"

"Nothing."

Adam sighed. It was one of relief, but Mike must have interpreted it as a sympathetic sigh. "She wasn't into me, man. Didn't you catch on?"

"What are you talking about?"

"I wouldn't have gotten anywhere with her. She was more into you than me." Mike slapped him on the back.

"What are you talking about?"

Mike ignored his question. "So how far did you get with Alex?"

Adam, still immersed in his friend's revelation about Megan's interest in him, replied, "No chance."

"I guess we go home horny." Mike laughed.

Mike's crass joke sifted past him as though it was passing through a sieve. Adam was immersed in his own thoughts about Mike's comment that Megan was possibly into him.

That was how he remembered their first night out. He closed the journal, filled a travel mug with some coffee and left the house. As he navigated traffic, he thought about Alex's question that night so long ago: *You don't remember, do you?* He thought about her leaving last night. Her tears over Megan but the sense something additional fueled them.

He parked his car in the lower parking garage and took the

elevator to the main office of Kāne Builders discarding the thoughts of Alex and incongruent memories. The historical three-story building sat on the edge of Chinatown overlooking the Honolulu Harbor. It wasn't the industrial hub of most of the company's contracting operations, the warehouse a few miles away, but it was the face of his company. It was where Adam spent most of his time reading contracts, meeting sub-contractors and architects, troubleshooting changes to plans, and dealing with the accounting side of being a contractor, estimating, and all of the day-to-day operations.

He walked into his office, set down his satchel and went to the window that overlooked Honolulu Harbor. A large cruise ship, white with blue detailing, was making its way toward Aloha Tower, the clock face of the landmark looming high above the crystal blue water in the port. He turned away and sat at his large desk to shut out the world without Megan and enter a world where only work existed.

"Your essay on the Alvermoon book is due two weeks from today," Alex stated as she passed out the white handout that listed the expectations she had for the essay.

"Dr. James? Would you explain how Alvermoon's assessment of media is connected to women's studies?" An older student at the front of the plain room asked.

Alex moved back to the front of the room. She set down the left-over handouts she'd been passing out and pulled a print ad out of her pile of teaching materials. "Anyone tell me what this is?" she asked.

"A magazine ad," came the obvious answer from somewhere in the back row. It wasn't an overgrown class of a hundred plus, which was usual for entry level liberal arts courses. However, it was one of her larger sections as a lower-division women's studies course.

"Correct," she said. "What is it advertising?" She held the ad in front of the older woman who'd requested an explanation.

"Soap," the student answered.

"Right." Alex walked up an isle between the desks so those in the back could see the ad clearly. "And yet, is the soap pictured anywhere on the ad?"

"No," a male voice answered.

"What is?" she asked the young man.

"A close up of a woman's body. She's naked."

"Good. It's from the bottom of her breasts to the top of her pubic bone." Alex walked back to the front of the room. "No face, no identity," she stated. "A woman as an object." She paused. "Remember, people, media offers us a snapshot of cultural value. In looking at this ad, we could conclude the value of women in this culture is as merely objects to sell. Understand why we're reading Alvermoon?" She glanced about the room assessing her students' faces and nodded. "Have a great weekend."

After answering some individual questions after class, Alex collected her things and walked down the concrete corridor. She exited the building to return to her office a short distance across campus.

The sun was hot—typical for the waning hurricane season of late September. She was thankful she'd donned a light, linen tank top dyed a soft yellow, and the coordinating linen skirt. The azure sky was peppered with high cotton clouds vying for a clear space, moving swiftly in the trade winds. The leafy green trees provided a canopy of shade along the walkway and made the walk to her office bearable.

Alex passed students moving toward their classes. Some meandered with friends chatting animatedly. She smiled remembering the impetuousness of youth. She'd been there. A blush crept up her face at the memory she'd never been able to escape. She pushed it back, shaking her head to shake it loose, and lose it among the many others. Afterall these years, she knew she wouldn't.

"Aunty Alex?"

Alex turned to see Trey, Megan and Adam's son, a few feet away. He was sitting on a bench outside of her building, the same bench where she and Megan had met Adam. It had been the football player hangout then, too, which gave her a sense of déjà vu.

"Trey!" Joy welled up at the sight of him. He looked so much like his father.

He stood and walked toward her. He was tall, well over six feet now, his Hawaiian heritage obvious in the light-brown hue of his skin. Though his hair, a chestnut brown, had natural streaks of gold from days spent in the sun. His hazel eyes were just like Megan's. She'd missed him. She missed them all.

She slipped the shoulder strap from her bag and set it on the ground, opening her arms to him. He stepped into them and squeezed her. Alex's eyes smarted both with joy at seeing him and with sadness knowing Megan would never get to see him as this man. "I have missed you. It has been too long!"

"It has. I've missed you, too," he said after he stepped back from hugging her and offering a *honi* on her cheek. "Since Mom's funeral, I think." His voice drifted away with the thought. Grief passed over his features but then flickered away. It was a testament that losing Megan was always there with him. The loss of Megan was with them all.

She nodded. "Yes. How are you doing?"

"Good days and bad. You know?"

"I do."

"Sometimes I forget." He looked down at his feet. "I call home, like this morning, and think she'll answer. Then Dad answers, and I remember. It's like losing her all over again."

Alex wrapped an arm around him and remembered when he wasn't taller than her waist. She recalled chasing him around the yard, him carting that football as though it were an extension of himself, of laughing at his quick wit and antics. She remembered the day he was born, and when he lost his two front teeth and couldn't pronounce the 's' sound. "I'm sorry I haven't been there, Trey."

"It's okay, Aunty Al. I think all of us have been walking around in a haze."

"How's football?" she asked, changing the subject to something less grim. "I haven't been to any of the games this year."

A smile lit his eyes, the dimples in his cheeks endearing. She thought of Adam. "I get to share playing time at tomorrow's game. First time." He leaned back and straightened his shoulders.

"Congratulations. That's wonderful!" she said. "I'll be sure I'm there tomorrow!"

"I'd love that, Aunty. I've missed you." He hugged her again. "We all have."

She closed her eyes and lost herself in the moment as comfortable as slipping into a sweater on a cool December night. But now it felt almost stolen. The truth of Adam's words came back to haunt her with a vengeance: *You've always wanted what we had, Alex. Megan and me.* Their treaty last night fused with the common ground they'd discovered had left her shaken. It was far easier to be angry with him than to explore an amiable friendship that could exist. That would tear her apart more than his anger had. Outrage made it so much easier to maintain her walls.

She pulled away from Trey. "I've missed you all as well. We should get together one of these days for lunch. Catch up," she stated.

"I'd like that," Trey said. "Maybe after football season."

"Yes. Sounds good. I wish I didn't have to go, but I have office hours. I'm up there." She pointed to the building behind him. "*Ke Ānuenue Hale.* Third floor. Come and see me, and we'll go get a bite to eat."

He followed her gaze and then turned to look at her once again. "Okay. I will."

They hugged once more.

"Good luck tomorrow, Trey. I'll be yelling extra loud for you," she said before walking away.

Alex entered her office thankful there weren't any students waiting with questions but disappointed because she'd cut short reconnecting with Trey. Seeing Trey dredged up all the loneliness and missed time with him, with Emma and Bekah, even with Adam. She felt the loss of Megan doubly, her best friend, and her family. It was easy to be angry with Adam, to feel justified because he'd been so antagonistic. But she couldn't stay in it. Last night proved that. She'd been entirely too comfortable sitting there with him. A piece of her heart was stripped knowing he had to force himself to find peaceful ground with her, and though she was used to it, she could find a way to survive. She was good at it. She was moving on. She was strong. She could go it alone.

The knock at the door drew Alex's attention away from the research article she was reading. 'Come in.'

The office door opened, and a familiar, collegial face emerged from the other side. "Alex?"

"Hey Jack." She motioned toward the chair across from her.

Jack Reynolds flashed a toothy grin and walked into the office. He flopped into the chair as though he hadn't a care in the world and brushed his longer blond hair out of his face. He reminded her a little of Geoff, her ex-husband. A tall man and still handsome though his frame seemed soft because he spent more time at work than on self-care, Alex imagined that as a young man he must have been the apple of every adolescent girl's eye. He probably still did for many women, even if it wasn't her.

"Thought you might have already left."

"And yet you still stopped in?"

"I hoped." He was still smiling his perpetual smile no matter the circumstances.

"Lucky you caught me, then. I was planning to finish up with this journal and head out to my club's practice." She tapped the article in front of her with a pencil.

Jack ran his fingers through his hair again. It was long on the top—the quintessential surfer-boy image—and he had a habit of reshaping the lock to hang to one side of his face, nearly covering his left eye. "I don't know how you do that canoe stuff."

"Paddling?" She laughed still tapping.

"Oh right. The idea of running up and down the beach barefoot, hopping in a canoe and paddling out into the ocean doesn't entice me at all."

Alex began collecting the papers she wanted to get to that weekend and piling them in front of her. "Maybe it's because you love the land, mainlander."

In the early days of their friendship, Jack had made it clear he wasn't a big fan of the ocean. She'd teased him for moving to Oʻahu, an island surrounded by the sea.

"It keeps me in shape," she said. She didn't mention how being in the water was like therapy; he wasn't on that kind of level. "What can I help you with?"

Alex didn't want to linger in the office with him. She liked Jack. He was a comfortable companion, but that was all, so she wasn't in favor of sending any mixed signals. They'd attempted to date a while back, and it just hadn't been right for her. The fact he reminded her of Geoff without the chemistry made Alex hit the brakes on anything other than a platonic relationship. She hoped he wasn't still seeking anything other than friendship. Yet, she couldn't be sure. Sometimes he'd do or say things that alerted her sixth sense. Other times it was silent.

"Are you going to the game?" Jack asked.

"Actually, I am." She pulled her satchel from under her and set it on the desk.

"Would you like to carpool?"

"Sure."

"I can drive," he offered.

She didn't like that option, feeling like it gave him too much control over her whereabouts. "No. I will. You drove last time." She placed her pile of weekend materials into the black bag.

Jack stood. "Great. Would you pick me up from my office? I've got some research to do tomorrow. No students, so I'll get more done."

"Sure thing." Alex said, and they settled on a time before Jack left.

She waited five minutes before locking her office to be sure Jack was gone. She enjoyed his company, but the truth was she found something wrong with every man she dated, not just Jack. She could admit she was rather independent. She liked her freedom. The last man she'd truly connected with had been Geoff.

When she reached her light blue car, she packed her things into the back seat and climbed inside. She started it and turned on the air conditioning. A faint smile teased her mouth when she thought about Geoff. He'd needle her for opening the windows when she turned on the air conditioning. "Why do you do that?" he'd asked, his Australian lilt an alluring factor of her faded attraction to him. She'd come up with some excuse about the rush of the air conditioner pushing out the hot air. And he'd come back with, "Don't you think the breeze outside could do that?"

The failure of her marriage to Geoff was her fault. Sure, she understood that marriages took two people, but she'd emotionally retreated long before he had. She knew that now having spent time removed from the divorce. He'd tried so hard to be the husband she needed. She never gave him credit for his strengths. She'd compared him to the false hope of an expectation she'd conjured in her head. Geoff had always accused her of being in love with another man. Thirteen years later, she understood he hadn't been wrong.

CHAPTER FIVE

Stanton Thom paced the beautiful green Persian rug of his office while his thoughts raced away with themselves. Given his analytical nature, he was sure the operation was in a precarious position and discovery was inevitable. It had been too easy.

Now, because of his panic, their mystery partner was telling him to calm down.

Stanton stopped pacing and wiped his brow with a white handkerchief. The perspiration seeped past his thick black eyebrows into his eyes. He walked over to the thermostat and tapped on the small bronze box with the clear window. Surely, that wasn't the correct temperature? Stanton removed the charcoal colored suit jacket and tossed it over the back of arms of the leather chair to his left and tapped the thermostat again.

Why didn't things ever work properly at this school?

And why had he agreed to this plan six years ago?

He blamed it on the others. He'd been lulled him into a feeling of false security thinking this would be easy, there would be no collateral damage. How wrong they'd been. At the time, he'd seen the endgame so clear in his mind and tempted into inaction. Then the dying started.

"Stanton," Dr. Black, the anonymous moniker of the voice on the other end of the line, said.

Stanton turned from the thermostat and eyed the intercom on his desk through narrowed eyes closed nearly to slits.

They didn't talk often, though Stanton was notorious for wanting to speak to Dr. Black and frequently initiated these phone conversations. Stanton couldn't escape the feeling he needed to be looking over his shoulder at all times. He'd even suggested he and the doctor meet. Of course, Stanton hadn't considered that there was a certain amount of safety in not being able to identify the face or real name of who he was dealing with. All he needed to be certain of, according to Stanton's connection to Dr. Black, was the person wasn't to be underestimated.

"I can't be calm." Stanton went to the bottom drawer of his desk and opened it. He pulled out the stashed bottle of whiskey and the tumbler then poured himself a healthy drop.

"There's no need to worry. Everything has been contained. There is nothing more to worry about."

"But we didn't do anything." Stanton's hand shook as he drew the glass to his lips. "And you are forgetting someone must have tipped her off. That is a loose end we haven't fixed."

"Nature took care of the problem for us. She left nothing behind. Eyes have watched her husband and kids for over a year." The voice paused. "As for the other issue, I believe that our threats were effective. There is nothing to worry about. Stanton, you are well on your way to a beautiful career in more ways than one."

Stanton straightened his shoulders and took a deep breath. He smoothed the white shirt and blue tie and carried his drink over to a mirror on the wall. Dr. Black was right; he was being rash. And he couldn't be rash considering his goals.

He studied his reflection: His neatly slanted eyes with their confident gaze exuded honesty and trustworthiness. They were perfect eyes. His nose was small yet straight like his mother, but the rest of him exuded his proud Chinese heritage. He smiled at his image and imagined the heartwarming look his face expressed. His brow creased as he ran a hand over his chin where he'd had a mole removed a year ago. The mole wouldn't have projected the right image for a governor of Hawai'i. It wouldn't have looked good in his governor's portrait.

The governor's seat was all that he wanted for so long.

Stanton ran a hand over his jet-black hair every strand in place and turned back to the phone call. "How much longer?"

He returned to the high-backed mahogany tinted leather chair and set his drink on the desktop in front of him. Despite his desire for the governor's seat, he knew that there was still a lot of time and risk to see this plan through, but he also knew better than to be openly combative with Dr. Black. If he was anything, Stanton was diplomatic, another very good quality for a governor.

"We are in the fourth year, but an accident-free year will solidify the research for fast-track submission."

"That's like starting over! There was an accident just a few months ago!"

The voice became quiet, only the white noise of the intercom buzzed.

Stanton's nerves sizzled. He fidgeted in his seat like a kindergarten student being reprimanded by his teacher.

"Thom," the voice finally stated, "the windfall will be worth the wait. We're close," which was followed by a dial tone.

Stanton stared at the blaring intercom and pushed the button to end the call. He swiveled in his chair to look out over the HSU campus. The mall of trees, the most photographed feature of the campus with its vibrant green canopy that sheltered the walkways underneath was visible from his office. Beyond that, and the buildings, he could glimpse where a sliver of ocean met the azure sky. Stanton tipped the glass and finished the remainder of his drink.

Dr. Black was right. Megan Kāne was a non-issue at this point in the game, and it seemed as though the problem had died with her. They didn't have anything to worry about other than her informant, figuring out who that was. He was making more of his anxiety than usual. Of course, one could never be too careful. It was always important to be prepared for any contingency—like any governor would be. Yes, he would continue to keep an eye on Megan Kāne's family.

The intercom on his desk buzzed and his secretary's voice interrupted the silence. "Your five o'clock is here, Dr. Thom."

"Refresh my memory Judy," he said, returning to his desk to stash the bottle of whiskey and the glass.

"Dr. Jeffreys, the Dean of Students."

"Send her in," Stanton said as he grabbed his jacket from the back of his desk chair and walked around to the other side of the desk to sit down. He popped a mint figuring appearance was everything.

The large, paneled door opened from the wall and in stepped a tall stately woman with short, silver-blonde hair. She smiled and shifted her briefcase to her left hand holding out her right.

"Dorothy," he said as he stood and walked around his desk to shake her hand. His award-winning smile was present on his face.

"President Thom," she said. "Thank you for taking this meeting."

"For you," he said, "this university president is never too busy."

CHAPTER SIX

Adam didn't reenter the universe without Megan until his cell phone interrupted him later that evening. When he looked up from the contract he was reading to check the cell's display window, he realized the sun was on the verge of setting on the western horizon of O'ahu. He noticed it was his youngest, Bekah, and answered the phone. "Hey sweetie. What's up?"

"Dad?" Bekah's asked. He could hear the concern in her voice. "Why aren't you here?"

"Where?"

"Em's birthday dinner? Come on, Dad. I reminded you last week."

Adam closed his eyes. He'd forgotten. "You're right, hon. I'm sorry. I forgot. Where again?"

She sighed. "Dad! Benton's."

"I'll be right there. Thanks for reminding me," he added.

"Be safe."

Adam ended the call thankful he had a set of nice clothes reserved for unexpected meetings in his car and a daughter who was willing to save his ass. He grabbed a set of contracts he had every intention of getting to that evening, but knew he wouldn't, and placed them in his satchel before heading out of the building to the car.

He parked his silver SUV in a stall at the restaurant looking forward to being with his kids and went inside to find them. Their children were sitting in an inconspicuous corner of the dim restaurant where he'd spent an anniversary or two with Megan.

Emma waved when she saw him. "Dad. Here." She looked so much like her mother with her dark blonde hair, hazel eyes, and winsome smile. He hugged and kissed her then shook her husband Grant's hand.

"Happy Birthday. I have a card for you at the house," he said with a grin.

"You forgot didn't you."

"No."

Emma dipped her chin down and looked at him. "Yeah. Right."

He chuckled and turned to Bekah. His youngest looked like him with her brown complexion and black hair; except for her hazel eyes which pierced him at the moment with frustration. She pursed her lips before whispering, "I'm glad you made it."

He kissed her cheek. "Thank you for saving me."

Finally, Trey, his middle child, stood and smiled at him, a dimple in his left cheek. He also had the hazel eyes taken from his mother along with her mischievous nature. Adam reached for his son's outstretched hand and pulled him in for a hug as well. He was struck with the realization of how tall Trey was.

"If I'd known you would forget, I would have reminded you this morning." Trey laughed.

"Ha. Ha. What is this now, Emma? Forty?" Adam teased.

"What would that make you, Dad? Sixty-two?"

"Touché," he laughed and sat down at the table. "You don't look a day over twenty-five."

"Ha. Ha." Her voice mocked him. "Since that's how old I am."

The family settled around the table laughing and talking as the waiter filled their glasses and sought Adam for the wine choice. They placed their order, and Adam sat back in his seat to soak in the energy of his children.

Emma was working on an article for the *Hawaiian Sun Times.* "I really want to prove myself with this one."

"Your mother used to say that with each piece she'd write." Adam stalled a moment, afraid he might hurt the kids bringing up Megan, but they were smiling as though basking in the sunshine of his memories of her. "She always proved her talent with each article, just like you will, Em."

"You're a great writer," Grant said and kissed her cheek.

"You're too serious, Emi," Trey jibed using the nick name he'd given her when he'd been two years old. "Instead of making names for ourselves in normal ways, I think that we should all become professional surfers like the Von Trapp Family were singers. They would call us the surfing Kāne Ohana, and we'd spend all day at the North Shore catching waves until we went on tour." By the time he finished his thought everyone was laughing.

"You do enough of surfing for all of us, Trey," Bekah retorted in good humor. "And since I'm the only one who actually attends classes—" she looked at her older brother— "I'm having a tough time with my American Government class."

"Hey. No fair. I go to classes. There's too many good looking *wahine* not to." He wiggled his eyebrows and Bekah rolled her eyes. "Who's the prof?" Trey took a sip of his water.

"Paulson."

"He's notorious but can't see through the coke bottles he wears for glasses though, so–"

"Please! Do NOT go any further than that thought, Trey. I wouldn't want to scandalize the HSU athletic program with an exposè about one of their quarterbacks, specifically my brother," Emma joked.

"Who will get to share time this Saturday at the quarterback position." Trey smiled.

His sisters groaned.

Bekah said, "You've only reminded us of that fact like fifty times."

"Fifty-two," he countered.

"I'm looking forward to the game." Adam took a sip of his wine and realized he hadn't felt this good in a while.

"A chip off the old block," Grant added.

Their dinner was delivered to the table, and Adam glowed with pride as he basked in the radiance of his children. He looked around the table at each of them and saw Megan was there, in their faces: her spirit, her wisdom, her humor. She would have been so proud. "I was thinking–" Adam set down his wine glass. "We don't get together enough like this." He hesitated a little unsure; this kind of thing had been more of Megan's expertise. "Maybe dinner once a week, or every other, to keep us more connected?"

"Sounds like something Mom would have said." Trey took another bite of his steak.

"Maybe I shouldn't have brought it up? I know you are all busy. Mom would have known what to say."

Emma smiled at him. "I think it's a great idea, Dad. And," she set down her napkin and glanced at Grant who was smiling at her, "it makes sense. Especially now that you are going to be a grandfather."

Adam's gaze darted between his eldest daughter and Grant. "A grandfather?"

Emma nodded.

Grant lifted his wine glass. "Yep."

Bekah and Trey broke the short silence with their own congratulations.

Adam sat back, his face frozen in a smile that felt as though it might look forced. He didn't want it to. He was elated. He was going to have a grandchild, but there was an accompanying heaviness realizing Megan wasn't going to be there to share the joy with him.

He reached over and placed a hand over Emma's and met her

64

gaze. Tears brimmed in her eyes that told him she knew.

After dinner and after he was home, Adam skipped pouring himself a drink, and made a cup of tea instead, then settled in to continue in Megan's journals.

> *Dear Adam... I'm not sure I ever told you this, but did you know I used to write stories about us? I'm not sure where I put them, probably in a box somewhere, but the stories all ended the same. We were married and had 2.5 children. Imagine what kind of grades I would have achieved if I had spent the same kind of energy on my schoolwork. . .*

> *Dear Adam... Do you remember the first time we went out without Michael, or Alex or some other person to hide behind? That is one of my fondest memories. I remember you asking me. You'd seemed so nervous, and I never saw you as anything other than confident.*

Adam smiled reading her memories and noted the underlined word: *hide*. He thought of Alex. He wondered if she was making any progress in deciphering Megan's words though something seemed to catch just right in his gut about her theory last night. Could Megan have been concerned for their kids? Why not just tell him if that were the case? Megan had always been straight forward.

Looking back at her journal, Adam recalled how terrifying it had been to ask Megan out on that date. While they'd gone out a few more times in a group setting, Adam hadn't been confident Mike was right. Megan showed everyone the same warmth she treated him to. She laughed with everyone. She looked each person in the eye when she spoke to them as though they were the only one in the world. She touched his forearm whenever she spoke to him. That was the only difference, only indication that she might be attuned to him. It hadn't been a heavy suggestive touch—hers was more of a light touch that brushed him like a feather and sent heat radiating to his toes. He'd watched her on those two occasions and saw the silent messages she sent to Alex when she thought no one was watching her. Adam had wondered what those messages had meant. When he'd finally garnered enough courage to ask Megan out, he followed through on an impulse instead of a plan.

He waited outside of Anderson Hall, glancing at his watch every few seconds to verify this was around the same time he and Mike had walked her to class only weeks ago. It seemed like hours passed with each glance. But he'd only been pacing the pavement just outside the main entrance for a few minutes. When a trickle of people began to emerge from the building, panic welled up in his gut. He decided to ditch the impulse and turned to leave but stopped when he heard someone call his name.

"Adam?"

He turned around and looked at a puzzled pair of green eyes. "Hi, Alex."

"First time I have ever seen you waiting outside of this building on campus. You find a new spot?" She smiled at him, her eyes brightening, and it jolted him. The warmth of her smile made his stomach flip.

He attributed it to nerves and smiled at her quip. "I was hoping to find Megan."

The brightness in her eyes dimmed, the edges relaxing, but not her smile. "She's at the dormitory. She wasn't feeling well this morning."

"Is she alright?"

"I would bet it was just a case of the I-don't-want-to-go-to-class fever. Why don't you walk with me to the dorm, and I'll get her for you? I'm sure she'd love to talk."

She turned up the mall toward her dormitory, leaving him to catch up.

He fell into step with her. "Lucky Megan has you in that class to get the notes. How long have you and Megan been friends?"

"Since Kindergarten."

"What?" Adam was surprised, thinking her answer would be like since school started. "And you're still friends?"

"Sisters. Everyone used to call us the 'twins' because we did everything together. I practically lived with her through high school. You seem surprised."

"I am. Guys generally get sick of one another if they spend too much time together. We need our space."

"Guess that's just another difference between men and women."

"Right, the women's studies major." Adam smiled.

"You say that as though it were a bad thing."

"No. It's not. A bad thing, I mean. I just have a hard time seeing how you can earn a living with a major like that."

"Money isn't the motivation."

"Obviously," Adam began to doubt the direction of their conversation. The last time they'd spoken about her major things had gotten tense.

"Here–" She held her hand out flat to the side. "If men don't choose the same profession as their father, who in most cases chose that profession because of his father, they direct themselves toward careers that can offer the most monetary reward. Maybe like a survival of the fittest for man who can acquire the most stuff. But women, who haven't had the opportunity to make career choices other than mother, secretary, or teacher, tend to choose jobs of service, and none of them are paid well enough for independent living." She paused, then added all while still walking. "Maybe my choice of major falls into the typical woman's role of service, but I want to serve other women while you have chosen the typical male career."

"You say that as if that is a bad thing."

"No. Not a bad thing." She smiled, and Adam had that feeling of familiarity once more. "Just falls into the natural order of things."

"Maybe men choose jobs that make money so that they can provide for a family."

"Maybe men don't have to be the only bread winners." She looked at him before entering the dormitory, her eyes aglow with electricity, a fire that hinted she enjoyed their discussions as much as he did. His stomach flopped a second time, and he attributed it to those nerves again. They had reached the dorm, and he was going to be taking a leap of faith by asking Megan out on a date.

But then, without thought, he blurted before Alex disappeared through the door, *"What did you mean the other night about me not remembering?"*

She stopped and looked at him. Her green eyes pierced his brown ones as a blush crept across her face. *"It was nothing. Forget it. Wait here and I'll get Megan."* Then she backed through the doors into the dormitory. *"Talk to you later, Adam."*

He watched as Alex was swallowed by the heavy glass doors of the building. Then unbidden, he began to ponder the depth of the green trees around the mall and a pair of eyes that matched each shade. Realizing the direction of his thoughts, he squelched them and tried to decide where he should stand so he'd appear nonchalant. He decided on a spot at the bottom of the steps when the door opened, and Megan stepped out.

Her angelic face lit up when she saw him, and he forgot everything else. She stopped on the step above the stair where he stood, grabbed his hands, squeezed them, then let them drop. His heartbeat reached his ears.

"Adam. I'm so glad to see you," she said.

"You okay? Alex mentioned that you weren't feeling well."

"Oh that." She waved her hand shooing away his concern. *"I didn't want to go to class. I'm usually pretty good about going, but I needed a vacation day. Alex is a great friend and offered to take notes for me today."*

"That's nice." He didn't want to talk about Alex.

Megan studied him. *"Are you okay?"*

Adam's heart threatened to pump right out of his chest. "I'm fine. I mean, well actually, I was waiting outside Anderson Hall, when Alex saw me, because I was looking for you."

"I'm glad."

"That I was waiting outside Anderson Hall?"

"Well that, and that you were waiting for me." A slight tint of pink touched her cheeks.

Adam's breath caught at her revelation, but he recovered and smiled. "Well that's good, because I wanted to ask you out."

"Out? Like as in a date?"

"Yeah. Like for dinner."

"With everyone else along?" Before he could answer, she continued, "You know with Michael and Alex and whoever else decides to join the group?"

"No. I was thinking I would like to take just you to dinner," he clarified.

"Well, I'm not sure we'd know how to act," she teased, although Adam didn't catch on immediately.

He was wondering if he misread her signals and was certain she was going to reject his offer.

"I mean, we've only been together in groups. Maybe we won't know how to talk, you know, just the two of us." She smiled at him.

Then he understood and chuckled. "Maybe I could get a few pointers from the guys on the team."

Megan laughed, the intonation a salve for his soul. He grinned with her, though he been sure the heartbeat in his ears threatened to give away his anxiety. Had she accepted his invitation?

"So? Are you up for a dinner date with a man who needs pointers from his friends? Maybe I could get Mike to sit at the table behind me and direct me what to say."

"And I could ask Alex to sit behind me. Of course, she'd need to be in disguise so you wouldn't know she was there."

Adam looked down at his feet. Though he maintained the smile on his face, he shifted his weight from side to side, the apprehension circulating through his body at full throttle.

Megan filled the silence by stepping closer to him, standing on the step just above his. She placed her hand on his arm and looked into his eyes with her golden, hazel ones. Her voice deepened into a serious resonance. "I've been waiting for you to ask me." The invitation was crystal clear when her gaze dropped to his lips.

Adam, still taller than Megan even when he was standing on a lower step, leaned into her and gently placed his lips against hers. The supple skin of her mouth was like a drink of water on a hot day, and his insides buzzed while he kept his hands in his pockets. Everything in him wanted to draw her closer, but he also knew that wasn't the message he wanted to send.

He stepped away and grinned. "I've wanted to do that for a long time."

A beautiful rose color crept across her skin and stained her cheeks in a healthy vibrant glow.

He longed to kiss her again but resisted the urge. "How does this Saturday sound?"

"Too far away," she replied. Her disappointment at having to wait was written on her face. Her brow creased, and her eyes pleaded with him while her soft mouth pouted.

Adam laughed. "Three days does seem like a long time."

"I don't have any morning classes on Friday. What about you?"

"Not until ten on Friday morning."

"What about tomorrow then?"

He was both surprised and excited by her eagerness to spend time with him. "I'll come to pick you up here at seven?"

"I can't wait." Megan admitted and leaned into him, placing a chaste peck on his lips. Without another word she bounded up the steps, turned to look at him when she reached the door with a smile, then disappeared into the dormitory.

Now, Adam's eyes fluttered open. He'd fallen asleep remembering and sat up his chair. After rubbing his head with his hands down his face, he took another sip of his now cool tea. He stood and carried the teacup to the sink, dumping the remains down the drain. It was time for bed, but he paused staring at his unclear reflection in the darkened window. He'd been dreaming about Megan, but her face in the dream kept changing to Alex. He set the cup in the sink and thought he should have had a glass of scotch.

CHAPTER SEVEN

A dam rose before the dawn, got ready and put his surfboard on his car. He was anxious to surf both because it had been a long time, and also because it had been a long time. Before Megan's battle with cancer, his morning surf session had been his ritual. It kept him grounded and balanced, but he'd given it up when her cancer returned. Then, after she died, he couldn't find the motivation, or maybe it was just he was in too much of a dark place to allow himself the light of the water. Wanting to get into the waves was like excavating a part of himself.

The cool morning air, a balmy seventy degrees, refreshed his soul as he drove, windows open. He could see the hint of the sunrise on the eastern horizon, a tease of yellow orange as it chased away the blue. He drove past Makapu'u Lighthouse around the island. When he parked, he retrieved his board and trekked down to the beach. He was ready.

The rumble of the powerful ocean beckoned him, but he stood and watched it for some time. The waves, the movement, looking for rip currents and sharks. He was glad the waves weren't too big, and the break wasn't too far, but he could see he'd have to be careful of the shore break. He wouldn't want to break his board. After prepping it, he carried his board into the water.

The sun peeked over the horizon just as he slipped into the water. The cool water slid over his skin as he paddled out beyond the break, duck-diving his head and board into the water as waves crested, fighting the current and the tide. His heart raced with joy and anticipation as he waited for the first wave.

Adam paddled the board into the *nalu* and stretched to stand as the crest of the wave caught the board. With his legs bent, he used his strength to maneuver the board through the water, becoming one with the swell as it moved toward the shore. When the wave reached the threshold of the break, Adam either sunk to his belly as the rush ebbed under him or he turned his board nose first to paddle back out once again. He spent the next hour with the water, following the same cycle, battling out to ease back in. It cleansed him as if the sea, the action of surfing purged his soul of the last of the heartache that had claimed him.

When he'd tired, he jogged up the beach, tied down the surfboard, and headed for home. As he drove home past the beaches of the eastern side of O'ahu, the mountains rose to his right, the cliffs dropped into the sea on his left. He passed Kaimana Beach Park a place he remembered surfing with his friends back in college and smiled. The image of the full moon against the black sky flashed against the backdrop of the road he was navigating along with expressive green eyes: Alex's eyes.

Unsettled, Adam pulled the car off into the lot facing the ocean, disoriented by the memory and parked it as the forgotten remnants of a distant time surface. He reached for it.

He was with two of his friends from high school, Nakoa and Keli'i-Boy surfing. Adam hadn't been able to spend much time with either of them since they'd all graduated. Nakoa had gone to the continent for school where he also played football but was home for Christmas break. Keliʻi had joined the carpenters union and was busy working.

Most of the afternoon had been spent catching swells in between Nakoa and Keliʻi ribbing him about his new girlfriend. He and Megan had been together all of a few weeks when he took her to the airport for her trip home for Christmas vacation.

The sun sank lower in the sky, falling behind the cliffs to the west.

"Shit. I stay so starving." Keliʻi's pidgin accent was strong.

"Eh, me too." Nakoa patted his bare belly.

"Let's go to Zippy's," Adam suggested as they climbed from the water onto the shore.

Several yards up the shore, a small group of people sat around a hibachi. The aroma from their barbeque teased their stomachs. They hurried to get their boards into Keliʻi's van so they could get to Zippy's right away.

"Adam?"

He turned to see who was calling his name. Alex stood at the edge of the group and waved.

After asking his friends to wait, Adam jogged over to her at the same time she walked toward him. "What are you doing here?" He looked past her to the group she was with. There were a dozen or so people, though he didn't recognize any of them. "I thought you'd be going home for Christmas vacation."

Alex shook her head and looked down at the sand. "No. I'm going to a conference for my Model United Nations group the day after Christmas. It was that or go home for the holidays. I couldn't afford both. What are you doing?"

"Surfing with some friends." Adam looked over his shoulder at his friends who were waiting for him.

She glanced past him. "I didn't know you surf too. You are a jock through and through aren't you," she teased.

He smiled. "Nah. I just love the ocean. I started surfing when I

74

was a keiki with my dad."

"You guys want to join us?" she offered.

"No. We couldn't intrude on your meeting."

"Meeting? Oh, no." She smiled and shook her head. "These are just friends of mine that are stuck in the dorms for the holidays. We came to hang out, drink a few beers, and eat."

"Really? We don't have anything to share." Adam didn't know why he was surprised she offered. "We were just going to get a bite to eat." With a bit more coaxing she convinced him, Nakoa, and Keli'i to join the party.

The night wore on. A few of Alex's friends had musical instruments, and a local guy brought a ukulele. Kanikapila ensued with singing and laughter, the stars twinkling in the sky that turned dark around them. As things usually went, people paired off. Keli'i met a girl and invited her for a walk on the beach. Nakoa took a girl back to the van. That left Adam to wait for his friends with Alex.

In his car staring at the ocean, Adam remembered sitting in the sand, their backs to the mountains watching the sea roll toward them, the white caps of the waves humming their song. The moon, large and full had appeared above the horizon, a deep yellow so close Adam wondered if he could touch it.

"Do you have a place to go for Christmas?" he asked. He was leaning back on his hands immersed in the soft white sand. "You are welcome to spend it with me and my family."

"I do. Thanks though." She leaned forward and wiped at the sand around her feet. "We are all going to go out for Chinese food on Christmas Eve, then exchanging gifts together in the girls' dorm lounge on Christmas morning."

"I think I'd rather be with you."

His statement hung in the air as though it were a balloon losing its helium. He laughed, hoping she hadn't noticed the suggestive nature of his comment even if that wasn't what he'd meant. Then he

thought about her question when he'd walked her back to the dorms
again and wondered about it. What had he forgotten?

"What do you do with your family?" She buried her feet in the
sand.

"Oh, you know. Open gifts on Christmas Eve so everyone can
sleep in on Christmas Day. Then we go to my kūpunas, my
grandparents, where the entire family gathers for dinner and
singing and surfing."

"That sounds wonderful. How many people are in your family?"
She looked at him from over her shoulder.

Adam found a rock in the sand and pulled it out. He sat up and
dusted it off, occupied his hands. He remembered wanting to touch
her, not like sexually. He just wanted to feel the concreteness of her;
it all seemed like a dream. "My dad has ten brothers and sisters."

"Holy crap!" She leaned back resting on her hands. "That's a
lot of people."

Adam laughed. "Like I said. I think I'd prefer the dorms."

He set the rock back down in the sand. As he leaned back again,
his hand covered hers in the sand. Adam curled his fingers around
hers and drew her hand up. His heart bumped against the inside of
his chest and raced. He held her warm hand, covered with the grit
of sand and studied it by moonlight. Her hand was slender, her
fingers long, and her nails were clipped short for practicality. So
like her.

She didn't pull away but fixed her gaze on their united hands.
Then she looked up at him, her green eyes shining black jewels in
the moonlight.

A girl in the moonlight. Mahina's light.

He noticed how beautiful she was. And he knew he'd thought it
before. And it was suddenly so familiar. He had that hazy feeling
again, that faint memory he couldn't quite grasp at it. Her words,
you don't remember, do you, *resurfaced.*

He glanced at her lips, perfectly shaped and slightly parted and
remembered the only thing he could think about was drawing her

down into the sand and kissing her.

She must have been thinking the same thing because she whispered, barely audible, "Megan."

Jolted back to reality by that one word—shaken by what he'd contemplated—he remembered squeezing her hand and releasing it, trying to maintain the appearance that he was in control. So, he stood, held a hand out to her, and said, "Want to walk?"

"Sure," she replied, accepting his offer for help.

He forced himself to let her hand go despite the desire to keep hold of it, to keep the fire of her touch in his palm. Electricity raced across his skin. They walked, because you couldn't kiss and walk at the same time. When they came across Keli'i walking back their way with his friend, they parted ways, the girls going back toward the group, and Adam and Keli'i to the van.

Now, the breeze whipped through the cabin of his car through the open windows pulling him back to the present. With a shake of his head, Adam pulled the car back onto the road and drove home with the vivid memory waltzing through his mind. He had forgotten that night, and for good reason. Nothing had happened, but the guilt of wanting it too would have plagued him. A distinctive feeling of peace had settled upon him and Alex that night as they had sat there, her hand in his—proof that there had been a time when they hadn't always been at each other's throats. He frowned. And maybe a subversive reason for his anger he hadn't been honest about?

He shook his head. No. He'd been completely faithful to Megan, mind, body, and soul.

When he returned home, Adam immersed himself in things that needed to be done around the house, things he had neglected for over a year, things that would take his mind off of his sudden insecurities about Alex.

Adam answered his ringing phone. "Bekah?"

"Just calling to remind you about dinner Sunday."

"Don't trust me, huh?" He smiled picturing her on the other end of the line.

"Your performance for Em's birthday was less than perfect. I mean, you did forget even with my reminder."

"Point taken. Will I see you at the game tonight?" Adam sat down at the barstool. "Are you going to sit with me?"

"I'll be there, but I'm planning on sitting with friends in the student's section. Will you be okay?" He could hear the hesitation in her voice.

"Of course. Besides, I have Emma and Grant with me."

"That's right." She sighed. "Good."

"Come say 'hi' though if you can. I'd love to see my baby." He rubbed the countertop with his index finger.

"Okay. Love you, Dad."

He told her he loved her as well before ending the call.

Done with getting things back in order, he filled a glass of cold water and one of Megan's journals to read.

> Dear Adam... The night of our first date equates to one of the most important moments of my life. I can still see you sitting across from me at the little diner on the corner of <u>campus</u>, Classico's. The red checked tablecloth, and the half-burned candle were perfect for what turned into a fairytale love affair. I always thought that finding Mr. Right would be more difficult, but that night, sitting across from you, I knew you were the man of my dreams—a true knight in shining armor to go with the fairytale beginning of our relationship. Who would have guessed we'd be where we are now?

Adam stopped and glanced at the date she'd written the entry. They'd been married for three years. Adam had just won his first bid as a new general contractor. Megan, while raising Emma at home full time, had begun to pursue her career as a freelance writer. Their first date had signaled the beginning of a beautiful relationship, but there had been tough times as well. He shook his head unsure if he was ready to relive those yet and closed the journal.

CHAPTER EIGHT

The stadium parking lot was packed by the time Adam arrived. He paid the parking fee, and drove around the outdoor stadium, a large metal structure at the edge of Pearl Harbor. Adam always thought it odd the city had chosen to erect an iron edifice at the edge of a body of saltwater, but he couldn't help but recall all of the joyful times he'd spent playing and watching the game he loved inside of it. By the time he reached the season ticket seats he purchased each year, he'd stopped a dozen times or more to talk story with familiar faces.

Anticipation flowed through him for Trey, for the game he loved, for something else on the edges of his emotions, something hopeful. Adam could still remember his own feelings on game day.

The butterflies fluttering at warp speed in his gut.

The ebullient sound of the crowd.

The heat of the lights.

The way everything went quiet in his mind when it was time to focus on the game.

All of that was minor compared to the anxiety thinking about his son. The fact that Trey was about to take his place in the football program said a lot about his football skills and even more about his work ethic. Adam was so proud and so sad not to share it with Megan.

"Hi dad," Emma interrupted his thoughts.

Adam stood and gave Emma a hug and Grant a handshake. "You're just in time for kickoff."

"Traffic was a monster, as usual," Grant observed as he passed through to his seat. "I'd planned on being here a half hour ago." He raised his eyebrows and cocked his head toward Emma for emphasis.

Adam chuckled. "Me too." He sat back down. "How's everything?"

"Excellent," Emma said, then raised an eyebrow at her father. It was such a Megan-look. "And for you?"

"Better. I've been reading those journals of your mom's."

"Really?" Her eyes grew with excitement. "May I read them, one day?"

"Sure. When I finish, you are welcome to them. Which reminds me—I've been thinking maybe you'd like to go through your mom's old research. I know she didn't finish everything she was working on, and she'd love for you to have it."

"Are you serious?"

He smiled at his daughter. "Of course." Emma's look of fire was so much like Megan's when she had been eager about getting into a new piece. He could see Emma's wheels turning. "You should come by the house. We'll pull up her files on the computer."

"I'll stop by after church." She clapped her hands together. "I'm so excited."

"Well, you can't work into the night. Grant would have my head, and we have dinner Sunday night."

"Right," she said. "Speaking of food. Grant, hon, would you get me a soft pretzel, please?" Emma pressed her hands together as if in prayer.

"This girl can eat!" Grant exclaimed. He stood.

Emma laughed and gave him a playful smack.

"Let me go," Adam offered. "You stay with your wife. Can I get you anything else?" he asked.

"I'd love some popcorn," she said, "and a licorice rope."

"Okay."

"And mustard for my pretzel."

"Is that it?" Adam grinned at his pregnant daughter.

"Some water. Please." She grinned, squeezing her eyes shut with her wide smile and a tilted head.

"Anything for my first baby," he said, leaned down to put a kiss on the top of her head, and walked up the stairs to the concession stand. After he made his purchases, weighed down with enough food to feed an army of pregnant women, he turned and bumped into a woman a few patrons behind him. "I'm sorry," he said and looked up into a pair of familiar green eyes.

"Adam!"

"Alex." He smiled.

The crowd inside the stadium roared.

"Hungry?" she asked, nodding to the plethora of items in his arms.

"Emma and Grant are waiting for me."

Adam was struck with how beautiful Alex looked. Her olive complexion was as supple as he remembered in college, but instead of red sun-kissed highlights in her hair, she now had rich silver interlaced with her mahogany tresses. When they were younger, she'd worn them long. Now she cut her hair to her shoulders. Her eyes were still that startling vibrant shade, but they were more drawn, sad. That wasn't something he remembered about her. He thought about his earlier memory of sitting with her at the beach. Her laugh, her humor. Then he thought of her tears the other night.

"How are you doing?"

She glanced to the person standing next to her.

Adam looked from her face to her companion. She was with someone. A date. A surge of jealousy weaved its way through his gut. He shook it off and dismissed it. What a ridiculous notion to feel jealous. He had nothing to be jealous about.

"This is my friend, Jack," Alex introduced them.

The man was around Adam's height, a little paunchy, and fair. His white skin was set off with fine freckles and sandy colored hair.

"Nice to meet you," Jack said and extended his hand.

"My apologies," Adam said. "I'd shake but my pregnant daughter wouldn't get her order."

Jack laughed.

"Did I hear you right?" Alex asked her eyes wide. "Emma?"

Adam smiled and nodded. "Yes. Isn't it wonderful?"

She looked down, her smile fading, but she nodded. Adam knew what she was thinking: *Megan isn't here.*

"Would you two care to join us?" Adam asked. "I've got two open seats with us. Fifty-yard line. Unobstructed view, although if it decides to rain, we'll get hit."

"Sounds better than our nosebleeds," Jack commented with a smile.

"Thanks Adam, but. . ." Alex hesitated.

Adam interrupted. "The seats are yours." He looked at Alex. "Come. Please."

She smiled and nodded.

After sharing with them the section and seat numbers, Adam walked way, his heart pacing his quick steps. He thought he was acting a fool, nerves on edge, and ridiculously jealous of a man who Alex had every right to be seeing. Stupid. He descended the steps and moved around several young ladies blocking the stairs.

He glanced at the field. The players were lining up for kick off.

"Dad!" Bekah said from the group. She attempted to hug him around his full arms. "Is that all for you?" she asked.

"Of course," he answered with a smile. "And Emma. And Grant. Want some?"

"None for me," she stated. "In training. First swim meet is this next week." After Adam cleared his arms of the concession food handing it off to Grant and Emma, Bekah hugged him. "I'm going back to the student section with my friends."

"Thanks for coming to say 'hi'," Adam said and added, "I love you."

"Love you too, Dad." Bekah kissed his cheek.

He watched her and her friends walk up the steps toward the concourse. Halfway up, Bekah met Alex and Jack on their way down. Adam saw Bekah's face light up when she saw the other woman. They spoke for a moment, and Bekah gave her a hug. His daughter pointed at him. He waved. His heartbeat sped up again. Taking his seat, he wondered what the hell was wrong with him?

"Alex and her date are going to join us," Adam told Emma and Grant. "I saw them at the concessions."

"I haven't talked with Aunty Alex in ages. Since, the funeral." The last word faded as she looked at her father. Adam knew she remembered the scene that day.

"Emma," Alex interrupted. "Your father spilled the beans. You look beautiful. How are you feeling?"

"Aunty Alex!" The women hugged each other, placing a *honi* on one another's cheeks. "I'm so glad to see you." They hugged again. "You remember Grant?" Emma moved so Grant could step forward to hug and kiss Alex.

"Of course."

The crowd roared as HSU prepared to kick off.

Alex introduce Jack. Adam moved into the row to the end so that Alex could sit next to Emma between them and Jack could sit by his date. He listened to Alex and Emma chatting so much like he remembered Megan and Alex doing. It hit him how much Alex had been involved in his children's lives.

Why did you have to be such a jerk at the funeral? He wished he could take it back, but what was done was done. At least she'd forgiven him for it.

He focused on the game. The Hurricane kicker shot the first firing round with a sixty-yard kick. Sure enough, during the second offensive series for HSU, Trey ran onto the field. Adam immersed himself in it, delighting in the performance of his son. His spine straightened with pride after each completed throw, after each well-fought first down, and the worry after a sack. Adam was so proud of the man his son was becoming, his character to persevere apparent in his play. Trey's offensive line was working hard to keep his pocket open from defenders, but Adam, having played the game, noticed the athletic talent Trey possessed with every necessary scramble.

Jack leaned over all of them. "You must be proud of that son of yours. He's amazing."

Trey optioned to the halfback for a gain of seven yards. Adam smiled and nodded never taking his eyes from the game. He didn't want to like Jack, but he seemed so damn affable. "I am."

"Reminds me of someone else I know," Alex said.

Adam swung his head around to look at her. When their eyes collided, lightning worked its way across his skin. He answered her smile with one of his own, then refocused his attention on game, wondering again what on earth was wrong with him? He was acting like an insecure schoolboy.

Grant and Emma stood for the third time that first half. "Anyone want anything from the concession? My wife needs to make yet another restroom run."

"I'll go with you. I'd like another beer. Anyone else want one?" Jack asked.

Adam shook his head. "No, thank you."

He watched Jack follow Grant and Emma up the stairway and then redirected his attention to the field. But though his eyes were on the game, his thoughts were on Alex sitting a couple seats away. He wanted to say something, but his tongue felt two feet thick. *This is stupid*, he thought. They'd known each other so long, it didn't need to be awkward. He wondered how serious she and Jack were.

Had they been dating long? And in the next instant why was he interested in knowing?

Alex is a friend, he reasoned.

You didn't treat her like one at Megan's funeral, his subconscious argued.

Adam shook away his thoughts.

"Thanks for inviting us to sit with you." Alex filled the space between them with her words. "It's so wonderful seeing Emma and Grant." She picked at something on the leg of her shorts.

Adam glanced at her tan legs, noticed how fit they were. His lower abdomen clenched, and he glanced back at the playing field. "You are welcome. In fact, consider them yours the rest of the season."

What! You don't want to sit next to Jack all season long!

"That's very generous of you."

"Well you know me, all generosity and kindness," he joked knowing his behavior had often indicated otherwise when it came to her. He glanced at her again.

The crowd booed their displeasure at a referee call.

"That I can't dispute," she said without looking away.

She was serious, he realized with some surprise. He didn't deserve her approval. He'd been an ass.

Silence pervaded.

Adam longed to fill it, longed to make a connection with her. The memory of them sitting on the beach flashed through his mind, again. They'd made a connection that night, had been at peace, before their war began.

"How are classes?" He leaned toward her to speak over the noise in the stadium.

"Good. Really good this semester, in fact." She leaned toward him glancing between the him and the field. She was relaxed, easy to be with like he remembered from so long ago. There weren't many instances of it between them in the last twenty-ish years. Adam blamed himself—his defensiveness and bitterness where she was concerned.

The clock ran down to halftime, and the band came on the field while he and Alex talked.

He listened as she spoke about her work, enjoying the light sound of her voice, the way her eyes glowed with excitement, how her hands moved to accentuate her words. For once in as far back as Adam could recall, Alex let her guard down. He liked it—a little too much perhaps.

"Your research sounds very interesting," Adam told her and realized they were connecting, carrying on an adult conversation that didn't include accusation and anger. It felt really good. Normal.

She smiled. "It is."

Then Jack returned, all too soon, his footsteps heavy on the metal stairs. Adam looked at him then back at the field, annoyed by his presence.

Alex stood and moved seats to sit next to Adam.

She took the water bottle Jack handed her. As she turned back to the field, she glanced at Adam meeting his gaze with a smile before looking away. Adam's heart softened further toward her.

The teams were lining back up for third quarter kick off.

His stomach listed in response to her. Damn, he hadn't expected that reaction; one that indicated an unfulfilled need. That realization might have upset him a month ago, but now it seemed exciting. Adam glanced at Jack and noticed a dark scowl pass over the features of the once jolly giant as he studied Alex. It perplexed Adam and made him feel protective. He wondered again how serious they were.

Grant and Emma returned to their seats just as Trey started the first offensive series for the Hurricanes, who failed to capitalize on the fifty-yard gain. The downs turned over to the opposing team and for the entire quarter, the momentum vacillated between the two teams.

The crowd roared with the action.

Starting quarterback for the Hurricanes, Jonesy Miles, executed a play action pass, but stumbled. He regained his footing only to be sacked. He got up and tapped the top of his helmet, signaling his need to come out of the action. Trey ran onto the field to replace Miles and led the team to another first down two plays later. Miles returned to the game, lining up under center.

Adam could feel the palpable energy radiating through the stands. He watched Miles drop back into the pocket to find the best pass route, but he stumbled a second time and Adam sat forward. His brow creased with concern. The movement was different, not a trip. It looked wrong. Miles pitched forward and crumpled into a ball in the same instant he was sacked by a locomotive defensive end.

The defender stood, cocky with his arms outstretched, a conquering warrior, and strutted around the field. A hush fell over the stands. Jonesy Miles lay unmoving on the forty-yard line, a still heap.

Alex's hand grabbed his and threaded their fingers as they concentrated on the flurry of movement on the field. Trainers and coaches made their way to the fallen player, and after what seemed an eternity, Adam watched a trainer radio in the ambulance. The emergency vehicle drove onto the field while the trainers loaded Miles onto a stability mat and into the transport.

Adrenaline made Adam scan the players on the sideline for Trey. He was getting to his feet from his knees as the ambulance drove away. It could just as easily have been his son being loaded into that ambulance. He squeezed Alex's hand, finding solace in their connection. She answered with a hand on his forearm, leaning closer. The siren wailed as it left the stadium. Its lights cast an ethereal glow as the vehicle passed through the tunnel.

Trey and his teammates moved out of the huddle ready to finish the battle, though it was clear they seemed subdued. Trey dropped back into the pocket on the first play and completed a thirty-yard pass for a gain of forty yards. The crowd cheered. It was several minutes into the fourth quarter before Alex loosened her grip on

Adam's hand. He was loath to let her go for the comfort of her touch but released her. He wondered if he'd sensed hesitancy in her as she released him but dismissed it.

When the clock read zero, Trey and the Hurricanes were victorious with a twenty-four to seventeen win. Adam celebrated the win with high fives all around, but the concern for a fallen player hovered around the stadium.

"Thank you for sharing the seats." Jack shook Adam's hand once again. "We really appreciated the view and the companionship." He placed his hand on Alex's lower back.

Adam noticed.

Jack smiled. He'd wanted him to notice.

Alex turned to look at the touch, then at Jack, then to Adam and said, "Yes. Thank you."

"The offer stands, the seats are yours for the season, Alex." He searched her face curious about her relationship with the Jolly Giant. Adam didn't want to sit next to the other man all season, but he would endure it if it meant developing this peace treaty further.

She looked away and hugged her jacket in front of her. "I have to take Jack home."

"I'll see you later then." Adam leaned in, hugged her and placed a *honi* on her cheek. Her hand on his back left an imprint of fire before she moved away. He watched her climb the stairs with Jack irritated with himself and the direction of his thoughts over the course of the day. He was being ridiculous.

Emma and Grant made their goodbyes, reminding him she would be over to look at Megan's unfinished work that Sunday. After they left, and the chaos in the stadium waned, Adam walked down to the sideline to meet Trey. Another of their traditions.

"Well done, son," Adam said when Trey reached the sideline where he waited.

"Thanks, Dad. Glad you were here." Trey's tone was controlled.

Adam could see that his son was shaken. Worried. "Is Jonesy alright?"

"Coach said he'd tell us more when we hit the locker room, but he did mention just after the ambulance took Miles out that he probably had a concussion."

"What did you see?"

"Everyone kept saying he'd been sacked, but I thought I saw him go down before the hit."

Adam nodded, confirming what he'd seen. "He's a strong competitor. I'm sure he'll be okay. I'm just glad that you're alright." He hugged his son over the wall, breathing in the aroma of a man covered with the sweat of a battle hard fought. "I'll see you Sunday night."

Adam watched Trey jog toward the locker room, carrying his helmet by the facemask, his pace slow and steady, steps heavy with concern. When Trey disappeared into the tunnel, he finally turned to leave himself.

He drove home zoning out on red taillights ahead of him guiding the way and replaying the strange evening in his mind. While the sports radio personalities discussed the game with fans, he thought about his evening with Emma and Grant, with Alex and whatever Jack was to her. He thought about his own irrational reactions.

"Trey Kāne, a local boy and graduate of Kapālama High, blew the Owl defensive away. He's the son of former Hurricane standout, Adam Kāne, who led the HSU team to the Rose Bowl in 1980. Trey Kāne looked very much like the quarterback of the future, and–" the announcer stopped short.

Adam pulled into the driveway of his house and into the garage.

"Ladies and gentlemen, this breaking news just in–"

He waited to hear what the announcer was going to say, the tone conveying something of import.

"Quarterback Jonesy Miles has died on route to King's Memorial Medical Center."

CHAPTER NINE

Alex waited in front of the coffee pot her elbows resting on the counter, her head in her hands. She willed it to complete its drip cycle. She usually loved the morning, but after her paddling practice the morning before and the emotional rollercoaster of being around Adam at the game, she'd been unable to get up. The thick black liquid dripped into the carafe.

Alex straightened and pulled a clean cup from the whitewashed cupboard above the coffee machine. She set it on the counter and wondered if Adam was waiting for coffee that morning. She shook her head and decided he was too disciplined to skip a workout routine. He was probably surfing.

Running into him at the game the night before hadn't been what she expected, not with a crowd of thirty thousand or more. It bothered her she'd been so pleased to see him. She had no right to feel that way. They'd reached a peace agreement and nothing more. There was no promise of friendship beyond the partnership of finding out what Megan wanted them to know. There was no security in the newfound cordial relationship they'd established for the sake of Megan, and no guarantee of leaving the hostility they were both accustomed to behind them. But there had been no hostility last night, not even the remnants of it. She could get used to the warmth and ease that had existed between them. She just knew she shouldn't.

The coffee machine hissed with a puff of steam and beeped signaling its cycle was complete. After pouring a cup of the steaming java, she crossed to the front door to retrieve the paper and stooped to pick it up from the front porch of her house. Straightening, she looked at the view. The blue shades of the sky and the ocean were so clear beyond the Honolulu skyline, so vibrant that it was difficult to determine where sky ended, and the sea began. She took another a deep breath, the floral aroma of gardenia blossoms encircled her with their comforting and familiar fragrance. She turned and reentered the house closing the door behind her.

Alex walked through the living room decorated in hues of gray and white unfolding the paper as she walked across the quaint room. When she sat at the dining table with her steaming coffee, she laid the paper flat and looked at the front-page photo. It was a picture of Jonsey Miles. The headline:

HSU Starter Miles Dies After Sack.

She drew in a sharp breath, and set her coffee on the table concentrating on the article:

> Jonsey Miles, senior quarterback for the Hawai'i State University Hurricanes, was pronounced dead on route to King's Memorial Medical Center last night around 10pm. He suffered a hit late in the third quarter in last night's game against the Oregon Owls. Witnesses to the football standout's collapse stated he was sacked by the Owls defensive end, Bill Thurston. A trainer for the Hurricanes said Jonsey Miles was unconscious when they reached

him on the field.

Medical examiner, Dwight Connolly, indicated preliminary examination pointed to possible heart failure, but he could not be certain of the cause of death until an autopsy is performed. When asked if steroids could be a possible cause, Hurricane Head Coach said that the NCAA has strict rules and testing methods, which make it very unlikely.

Jonesy Miles, a scholarship athlete from Missouri, is survived by his mother and two sisters. They could not be reached for comment.

Heartsick for a family she didn't know, she was thankful Megan hadn't experienced last night's tragedy. It hit too close to home with Trey playing in the game, sharing the same position. She rubbed her palm remembering holding Adam's hand the night before. It had been an impulse. She hadn't given it a second thought. Her adrenalin took over when Jonesy Miles went down. Her imagination putting Trey in the same vulnerable position. Her only thought was to give comfort and find comfort in the one person closest to Trey. And Adam had held her. He hadn't rebuffed the physical connection. In fact, she had been surprised that he had held her hand for as long as he did.

It made her think about the notations in Megan's journal too: *our kids.* Had she been worried for their safety? She needed to look at those again, she decided. But for the moment, she clung to the caffeine and continued through the newspaper, though her thoughts were otherwise engaged. She thought about Trey playing at quarterback and how much he resembled Adam on that field. It seemed strange to be sitting beside Adam watching his son play. Something she'd never believed possible after what happened at the funeral.

He'd been so raw. They both had been. After months of

watching Megan deteriorate, and then succumbing to the cancer, grief and the volatility of pain was ruling everyone. Alex understood that now, with time and distance. Adam had just lost his wife of twenty-five years. And though Alex and Adam had often gone nose-to-nose about something or other, his behavior that day had been so out of character. So final. She'd known him for over half of her life. They'd argued for most of it, but she'd never seen him like that—not even at her. He was always controlled and calm. His eyes bore the look of a man in control of his power even in the midst of his ire. His annoyance with her had never filtered into his expression, just the droll way he bit at her with his words. The funeral had changed it.

Though she'd forgiven him, understood it even, now, the wounds had scarred. First with bitterness. Now, with remembrance.

She approached Megan's office knowing Adam had escaped into the room to be alone in his grief. She didn't want to disturb him, but the funeral director had called with a question she couldn't answer, and Emma had been busy She knocked on the closed door and then opened it after hearing Adam say, "Come in."

She peeked into the room. "Adam?"

He stood at the windows across the room near Megan's desk, and when he'd turn to see who it was, his eyes were cold. Lifeless. Two things Adam had never been in all the time she'd known him. A chill worked its way across her skin as she walked into the room, rubbing her arms with her hands.

He turned away, hands were shoved into his pockets, the sleeves of the white shirt rolled up his forearms. The back of his shirt stretched across his strong back, the planes of his shoulders visible. His head was bent forward as if in prayer.

"I'm sorry to bother you. The director called—" She stalled when he didn't move.

Then he sighed with weighty weariness and said, "Get out, Alex."

She reached for the door. "I'll see if it's something that can be taken care of next week."

"No. I want you to get out of my house."

"Adam?" she asked confused. "I'm—" but she didn't know what to say she was so stunned.

He continued to face the window. She felt shut out even though he was speaking to her. "What don't you understand?" he scoffed.

Alex held her temper, giving Adam the benefit of the doubt. "I'll come back later."

That was when he turned back to face her and the look on his face had made him unrecognizable—that cold, unfeeling rage which didn't seem could coexist but had. It made her shiver while at the same time press against her with shame. "That's just it, Alex. You're always coming back. You're always fucking things up. Just like you did to Megan's and my marriage." He shook his head, incredulous as though she were the one saying these things to him.

"Adam. Stop," she said, hoping he'd snap out of wherever this was. This wasn't the Adam she knew. "Don't say something you can't take back."

"I won't, Alex. No, I've been holding this back for years." He shook his head and turned to face her with his whole body. His hands still in his pockets, his shoulders slightly slumped with his pain, but his resolve firm. "I've held this back for Megan's sake, not yours." He was an angry calm amid a raging storm. "You've always wanted what we had, Alex. Megan and me," he continued. "And you've never found it. Not with Geoff, not with any number of the men you've dated. So instead, you made it your mission to break up our marriage. You wanted Megan all to yourself—just like old times—no one to compete with for her attention."

Alex stepped back, colliding with the door. She shook her head partly out of denial and partly from fear that he had it right. But it had never been Megan's attention she wanted. Afraid he'd seen through her all those years. Recognized her want and the way she coveted Megan and her family.

"Deny it all you want. I know the truth. You're a bitch, Alex. A cold-hearted bitch, and you're so fucking miserable you want to make everyone around you miserable. You didn't want Megan to be happy because you refuse to find happiness. It's pathetic."

The door to the office pushed open, Alex stepped away from it which put her closer to Adam. Emma poked her head in. "Dad. The funeral director–" she stopped her eyes darting between them. "What's going on?"

Alex couldn't tear her gaze away from Adam's dark look still fixed on her. She tried to open her mouth, to speak and reassure him that he had it wrong. She would never have done anything to hurt Megan, to hurt him or the kids. But she couldn't. For once in her life, Alex couldn't speak up. And in what must have been the weakest moment of her life, tears welled up in her eyes, a weakness she was ashamed to show anyone, especially him. She'd not only lost Megan, but now she was losing the one family she'd known as her own. Rather than face Adam and his hatred, Alex turned and left the room, leaving a dumbfounded Emma in her wake.

It was the third time in her life she'd ever walked away from him.

Alex took another sip of her now lukewarm coffee, the paper opened to a page of the Island Life section. She couldn't remember turning to. She stood and grabbed the coffee pot to refresh the warm coffee with hot.

Last night, Adam had been a different man than he had been that awful day. He'd even seemed different from just days ago when he'd asked for help, when she'd visited the house. Last night, he'd seemed to see her—Alex—not Megan's friend. There'd been a difference in his gaze, in the warm expression of his is dark eyes. He seemed more like the Adam she had first known. She'd noticed something new too, something she remembered seeing in the depths of his eyes many years ago, before the beginning. Certainly, she was making more out of it than she should.

Alex shoved her thoughts away and reread the article on the page in front of her. The picture showed the smiling face of a pregnant woman holding up maternity clothes. It reminded her of Emma and her pregnancy, three months along. Alex felt a small tug on her heart at having never experienced motherhood but dismissed it. This was the life she had chosen, and she was content with her choice.

Emma had invited her to the family dinner. Now, Alex was wondering at her wisdom in agreeing to go, but Emma's plea and insistence on needing her there meant Alex hadn't been able resist. Spending time with Emma at the game, talking and laughing, seeing and hugging Bekah, speaking with Trey, the peace with Adam, all of those moments had reminded her of the ache of not being a part of their lives. So, she'd accepted.

She took another sip of coffee.

What she would learn when she arrived at dinner was whether her and Adam's peace treaty was real or not.

"Did you see the front page of the Hawaiian Sun?" Emma asked as she walked into the kitchen.

Adam had heard the front door open and got up to pour her a glass of orange juice. "Yes. Terrible news," he answered. "You're early. I didn't expect you for another few hours." He handed her the glass and leaned down as Emma pressed a kiss to his cheek.

"We skipped church today. God knows I still love him," Emma said with a smile. "And," she began, "I'm really excited about looking at mom's work. It was Grant who suggested I come over first thing this morning."

"I'm glad you did."

"I can't stop thinking about Jonesy Miles, though. His poor *ohana*."

"Me either." Adam shook his head as he took a sip of coffee and sat down next to Emma at the kitchen island bar. "I know it makes me selfish, but I'm so thankful it wasn't Trey."

Emma's silence and her head leaned against his shoulder confirmed her same sentiment. "It makes you human. The paper reported he may have died of heart failure." She sat back up. "This was a person predicted to go in the first round of the NFL draft. He had to be in peak condition. How does that happen?" Emma asked.

Adam—who would have smiled under normal circumstances as he watched Megan seep from their daughter—figured it was more a rhetorical question than one that had an answer. "It's always a shock when healthy people die unexpectedly." He thought about Megan. "People we know. Death sucks." It felt like an understatement.

Emma sipped her orange juice. "You think steroids had something to do with it?"

"Athletes, world class athletes especially, are always prone to that assumption, but like the coach said, the NCAA has very rigid rules and testing procedures."

"His poor family," Emma reiterated and took another sip of her orange juice. "This juice tastes good. I haven't been able to keep much of anything in my system in the morning because of the baby, but I hadn't tried orange juice. Can I have another glass, Dad?"

"Do you need to ask?" He smiled and watched as Emma poured herself more. "Well, my budding reporter. Let's go to your mother's office."

They entered the room. Adam and Emma shared a silent reverence for the space. He pulled out the chair for Emma and motioned for her to sit, then reached over and turned on the computer. "Here's your mom's password," he said pointing at a post it. "Look at whatever you want, hon," he said. "I think her unfinished pieces were marked 'in progress' or something like that. I'll be downstairs if you need me."

"Thanks Dad."

Adam left to the click of the mouse and slipped out of the office and down into the kitchen. There was lots of work he could do around the house, but he decided to read some of Megan's journal instead. He knew Emma was excited to get her hands on them.

Dear Adam... There was a time in our relationship, at the very beginning when I never noticed that we were different. I thought of us as two people, two humans that were learning to share our hearts. It wasn't until I took you home to meet my parents, and I met yours, that I realized that sometimes the color of our skin was relevant. Maybe not to you and me, but to the world around us.

Do you remember going to meet your family? Wasn't I a fish out of water? I laugh, now, thinking about the <u>assumptions</u> I made of the world, how everything looked beautiful through my <u>rose-colored lenses</u>. If only they hadn't cracked. Sometimes, it seems that it would be better to be ignorant of society and the defined boxes it's labeled for people. Oh, how age and experience change our ignorance.

When I'd chosen to go to <u>school in Hawaiʻi</u>, I'd never realized that it was a place with rules unlike any I'd ever known. As a new freshman, farther away from any familiar thing I'd ever known, Hawaiʻi was paradise, and I, saw nothing beyond the tip of my nose. So, my expectations about meeting your parents were vastly different from what I experienced. I'd figured that meeting your mother and father would be the same as meeting any mother and father of a boy I had dated back home. And I thought my parents were perfect. I hadn't realized they were flawed. I'm shaking my head at my <u>ignorance</u> as I write this. Oh, how you have *broadened my world, Adam, and I'm a better person for having learned from you.*

When we went home to California for the first time during that one Christmas, I saw flaws in my own family that I'd <u>been blind</u> to until then. You never want to think of your own parents in that light. My only comfort, in light of their behavior, was that they'd just been ignorant not <u>malicious.</u> I don't know why I thought that my family would be any different. I'd idealized them all my life, so I was blinded to their humanity. What a fool—okay—maybe just discovering independence and life without them. I wonder if our children will see our stains. Well, they will when they read this I suppose.

I remember that first meeting with my parents as though it were a movie in my head; the front door opening and walking into the house where I'd been raised, feeling the warmth—remembering home. Feeling wholly connected to the familiar. I see it in my mind's eye in slow motion, wondering what it must have looked like to from your shoes. You have always been gracious; it must have been torture.

Adam smiled. Megan's home—how different it had been from his own, how much he'd felt like a surfer without waves. Though he'd been to the mainland before, he'd never truly experienced life outside of the Hawai'i "local" mindset where everything remained the same and the pace and expectations were constant. Megan and her family were his first experience beyond his comfort zone.

I think that the beauty of it all is how it turned out. Look at us. We are married. We have a beautiful daughter (with more children to follow I am sure). Our lives could have been so painful with the <u>anger of</u> your <u>family</u> and the <u>ignorance of</u> mine, but our <u>families</u> love and accept the choice we made to be together, and despite the racial differences (although I still fail to see their significance), we are blessed.

I love you Adam.

Dear Adam... I was looking through our wedding album today (working on that wedding piece for the Family Life section at the newspaper) and as I looked through the album, I was accosted by one thing—regret. Not about marrying you—I will never regret that—for not being stronger about what I wanted for the wedding. Why couldn't I have been stronger? Why did I agree that we shouldn't get married at the beach because the marriage needed to be in a church? God's more evident at the beach next to the beautiful ocean as the sun dips below the horizon than in a building with stained glass that reminds us it's a place of God. And why didn't I <u>go with my instincts</u> about the wedding party, or the reception? Of course, your family didn't really want the wedding to happen at all, so I can't feel very sorry for them in the whole situation. What a comedy! Please <u>don't let</u> me <u>do that to our kids</u>, Adam.

Please remind me that their wedding is a special day for them to remember with joy and to look back on as a moment that forever changed their course. It should be a beautiful moment. Of course, don't think that our wedding wasn't a beautiful moment. The moment I walked down that isle and saw you standing at the altar, nothing else mattered. Not the location. Not the menu. Not the photographer. Not who I chose to be in my wedding party. Just you.

Adam leaned his head back against the chair and closed his eyes. He remembered Megan walking down the aisle. She had taken his breath away. He'd conjured a version of life full of possibilities, someone to share the joys and aches of life with. Megan had been that person—but not as he had envisioned. She was an artist, a writer, a lot of what Megan thought and did revolved around her life, not others. Adam sighed. He realized he'd imagined a picture of perfection when she'd died having forgotten the tough times.

He'd been contemplating their wedding and marriage himself the last few days. He looked at his hand and drew the band from his ring finger. Looking at it, the engraving inside with their initials, the metal worn with age, Adam knew he needed to let that part of his life rest. He was still here, still alive, left behind, and still had a road stretched out before him. A month ago, he wouldn't have been able to even think it. Now, it almost made him breathe easier.

He kissed the band and got up to do some chores.

A while later, Emma walked into the kitchen. "I got through a lot of it, but there's a lot more to see."

He looked up from the chair he was fixing with a new screw and stood, wiping his hands on his shorts. "Did you find anything you might be able to follow up on?"

"A few things." Emma filled her glass with another helping of orange juice. "Do you remember Mom working on something about HSU?" she asked.

He walked into the kitchen and leaned against the counter. "Your mom was always working on more than one thing at a time. She would move where the leads would take her and when something went cold, she would pursue another idea. She talked a mile a minute about all of them."

"Well, I found something in her files that confused me."

Adam crossed his arms over his chest to hold back his heart

which had slammed against his ribcage. "What was it?"

"All of her files were titled. Within each folder were either documents or subfolders all pertaining to that subject. Everything was labeled clearly."

"Sounds like your mother." His heartbeat had restarted but it was quite a bit faster.

"There was a folder labeled 'HSU,'" Emma started.

Adam remembered HSU had been one of the underlined words. "What was strange about that one?"

"Mom did the same thing—numbered all of these subfolders. But when I opened the folders, there was nothing in them. It was like everything she'd found or written had been wiped out."

"Maybe she was planning something new, and didn't have time to use the folders?" Adam reasoned, but even as he said it, he could feel that wasn't the case. Megan was deliberate and efficient. She wouldn't have wasted her energy.

"Maybe, but why go to all the trouble to make something so detailed and not have anything to put in them?" Emma set her empty glass in the dishwasher. "Will you take a look at them and let me know what you think?" she asked.

"Sure," he said.

Nervous about what he was ready to do, but knowing that didn't mean his children were, he reached into his pocket and retrieved the rings. "Hey, I wondered something?" Adam's pulsed kicked up slamming against his nerves.

Emma leaned against the sink. "Yeah? What is it?"

Adam saw her when she was three. Nine. Thirteen. Nineteen. Now twenty-five. He swallowed. "Would you like my wedding ring? I was going to give Bekah mom's, if that's okay?"

Her eyes welled up.

"I'm sorry. Too soon?"

She shook her head. "No," but she'd started crying.

Adam crossed the kitchen and drew her into his arms. Tears filled his eyes with her. "I didn't mean to hurt you."

"It doesn't," she said through her tears.

"Then why are you crying?" he asked through a chuckle, his own tears trickling down his face. He leaned back to look at her.

She wiped her eyes. "It's the right thing, I know. Sometimes I just get hit by things—normal things—and then cry. I think it's a good thing, Dad. Yes, I want your ring!" She sniffed.

Adam released his hold on her so she could get a tissue. She handed him one too. He wiped his face with it. "It's been a tough couple of years."

Emma nodded.

"For all of us in some way or another."

"I think Bekah will be really happy with Mom's ring," she said.

Adam held his band out to her, and she took it. "You okay with Bekah getting it? I'd be willing to give them both to you," he said.

She shook her head. "No. Dad. That's perfect." She leaned against him, looking at the golden band now in her fingertips. "Bekah needs mom's ring." Her phone buzzed. Emma straightened and retrieved it from the counter. "I've got to go, Dad. Grant and I are going to go and comparison shop for stuff for the nursery today. Before dinner." She smiled.

Adam walked her to the door. "Sounds like something I'm glad you are doing and I'm not."

"Dad!"

He laughed and dodged her playful swat. "See you at dinner."

He kissed her cheek and watched her get into her car. She waved as she pulled out of the drive.

Adam shut the door and leaned against it. He looked at his hand, now bare of his ring. It was strange. It had been on his finger for twenty-six years. He knew it had been the right thing to do, but the weight of the moment had taken him by surprise. The rightness of it mixed with the pain.

He took a deep breath, and then climbed the stairs two at a time to Megan's office.

CHAPTER TEN

Adam pulled into the parking garage located next to the restaurant still pondering the discovery. He'd gone up the Megan's office to take a look and just as Emma had described, Megan had created a file in her "in progress" work folder on her computer hard drive. A folder labeled "M@HSU". Within that file were other numbered files. One file was marked 051782, another 111789, in all around ten of them. When Adam clicked those numbered files, they'd opened to nothing. No new files, no documents, just empty folders. He thought of Alex's letter and the number he'd asked about.

Adam knew Megan. He knew her scent—rose with a hint of mint. He knew her laugh—a sound like a sparkling stream running off a mountain. He knew her ticks—the way Megan would twist her hair when she was thinking, or the way she tapped a pen against her desk when a moment of writer's block hit. Megan couldn't work in a disorganized space, and he knew there was no way she'd have created a file on her hard drive just to leave them blank. He checked when the files were created and saw it was prior to her re-diagnosis. He was certain she'd used the file. The question then became what had she used it for?

Adam got out of the car and locked it, walked across the lot, and pressed the button for the elevator.

M@HSU was perplexing.

While the obvious seemed Hawai'i State University, it could have stood for something else. Hawaiian Stevedores Union, except that there wasn't a number to go with the local union. Maybe Health Systems Unified, a local HMO, but the M and the @ symbol? Was it a contact, a partial email address? Adam wished he could remember the last article she'd been working on. She'd been in the research phase. She usually talked more to him in the writing phase of her work, her excuse being that talking about her ideas in the research phase was bad luck to her process.

Once in the restaurant, he checked in with the hostess. She smiled and led him toward a secluded alcove where his children were seated behind a curved frosted glass partition.

"Hey dad," Trey said and stood up from the table to shake Adam's hand.

Adam gave him a hug instead, drawing his grown son into his arms. "Sorry about Miles, Trey."

Trey clung to him a little longer than he would have normally, then stepped back. "Hell of a shitty way to gain the starting position," Trey said with a shake of his head. Adam could see his son's sadness, his eyes drooping and the frown on his face.

"Don't think of it like that—it wasn't your fault. Jonesy respected you for your play. He wouldn't want you thinking like that," Adam said and patted Trey's solid back with his hand.

He greeted everyone else, hugged Bekah, and noticed Alex was there too. "Alex." The surprise was clear in his tone, but he didn't want her to misinterpret it. He smiled, meaning it, though his insides had somersaulted and were still spinning, making him feel off balance.

"I invited Aunty Alex when I saw her last night," Emma said.

"So glad you did." Bekah leaned into Alex, who wrapped an arm around Bekah's shoulders and drew her in closer.

Adam was struck by how maternal it looked. How right. "Glad you were able to join us." He was relieved he meant it. This awareness was new territory, a continuation of a fresh perspective.

She arched an eyebrow at him with the hint of a smile on her lips and reached across the table to pat the top of his hand.

Dinner was fantastic. Conversation flowed as the wine was poured though, Emma lamented each time she had to toast with her cranberry club soda. Adam watched his children soaking in the sound of their voices and their lives. It made his heart expand and satisfaction covered him from head to toe like a warm blanket. When he glanced at Alex, he was reminded of her ease in their lives. The way the kids loved her, and how she just fit—like always.

As he pondered her, her gaze locked with his. Instead of looking away, Adam held her eyes and sought her story. What he saw reminded him of moments he'd experienced. The way his skin lit up when he'd accidentally bumped against her while taking off his jacket. The times they'd talked, and he'd felt content in those moments with her. The way his breath had caught in his lungs holding her hand at the beach. The excitement of seeing her at the game. The way he'd lost himself in her arms—wait.

He shook his head and looked down at his glass of wine. That wasn't right. Perplexed by the faint flicker of a memory that didn't seem to fit, he looked back up, but her gaze had escaped his, and the moment was gone. She was laughing at something Trey had said. Her head was tilted back, her mouth open and eyes closed as her laughter mingled with everyone else's in a harmonic chorus.

Adam looked at her exposed neck, and he imagined how soft her skin might feel against his lips. Something happened in the pit of his stomach, a lingering burn which spread toward his groin. It frightened him, so he looked away when Alex's green eyes sought his again.

He turned to Emma. "I've been thinking about your mother's work." Adam decided he needed to focus on something else.

"I was telling, Grant about that." Emma set her napkin on the table.

Grant put his arm over the back of Emma's chair. "Sounds strange to me."

"I haven't been able to think of much else." Adam picked up his glass of wine. He swirled the red contents and then finished the last sip.

"What's that?" Bekah asked, pulling herself away from the conversation Trey was having with Alex. Adam saw that they too stopped their discussion and focused on what was happening at the opposite end of the table.

"I found something off in Mom's work today," Emma said.

Adam glanced at Alex wondering if she'd hear his questions as Emma explained. *The letter? The number?* He willed her to.

"Maybe she just didn't get a chance to finish erasing her files before, well, you know–" Trey stopped talking.

Everyone knew.

"Perhaps," Adam started, and decided not to say anymore. He had a peculiar feeling in his gut, a sensation that made him realize he didn't want his children to worry. Adam looked at Emma who started to say something, but he shook his head, a minute shake meant for only her. She closed her mouth and offered a slight nodded of understanding. "That's probably it." He wanted to change the subject and was saved when the waiter came to take their dessert orders.

By the time dessert had arrived and been consumed, the discussion of Megan's strange files was forgotten, and before Adam was ready, his family peeled away. School and work tomorrow. He understood.

Emma and Grant were the first to leave. "I'm tired," she'd said as her hand rested at her abdomen.

Around ten minutes later, Bekah excused herself, announcing that she had a class at eight the next morning. "This was good, Dad," she said as she hugged him.

Trey went with her since they'd carpooled.

And just like that, Adam found himself alone with Alex. Alex who he'd learned to ignore over the years but couldn't bring himself to anymore.

She stood to go. "Thank you for dinner, Adam."

"Will you stay for another drink?" he asked.

She hesitated a moment as though questioning the wisdom of it. He didn't blame her. "Alright." She sat.

He stood up and joined her at the other end of the table, so they weren't sitting so far apart and laid an arm across the back of the chair next to him. Nervous, he smoothed the yellow tie he wore against the slate-colored shirt, then motioned for the waiter who returned to take their order.

"Okay. What did Emma really discover today?"

"You heard most of it. Remember the number I asked you about on your letter?" Adam watched her swirl the remaining wine around in her glass again.

She set it back down without taking a sip and nodded.

"The file folders on Megan's computer hard drive were labeled with similar notations."

"Know what they are?"

Adam shook his head and watched waiter set down their fresh drinks and bill. He handed the waiter a credit card. "I hoped whatever was in them would give me a clue, but they are all empty."

"That doesn't sound like Megan at all," she said. Her brow creased in contemplation of the discovery.

Adam resisted the urge to reach out and touch her. He focused on the topic at hand. "That's what I thought, too." He saw her hand curve around the new glass and twirl it. He thought about that night on the beach. Did she remember that night?

"Can I see them?" Alex asked.

"Yes. Of course. Maybe we could get together this week. I can show you then?"

"Thursday is my early day. Can you meet then?"

Adam nodded and they agreed on a time. He didn't want the evening to end just yet, but he didn't have any reason to extend it either. "I'm glad you joined us tonight, Alex." He signed the receipt.

They left the restaurant together, and he walked Alex to her car, parked only a few stalls away from his own.

She turned as though she wanted to say something, then turned back toward her car. "I wasn't sure if I should, truth be told, but I'm glad that I accepted Emma's invitation."

"I remembered something, surfing." *What are you doing?* he thought.

Alex's smile faded, but just enough that she looked as though she were trapped in the spotlight, the semblance of a smile still showing.

"What?"

She shook her head and tilted her head down so he couldn't see her face. "It's nothing, I just remember thinking that this morning—that you probably still surfed. Just the coincidence of it." She looked up again, the smile casting an ethereal glow about her features.

He grinned and felt warm to his toes at her confession that she'd been thinking about him. He had definitely been thinking about her, more than usual.

"Sorry to interrupt." Her smile faded and Adam felt the heat abandon them. "You were saying?"

"Remember that first year we met, way back in college?"

She nodded. Now her eyes looked wide, almost frightened.

But that couldn't be, Adam thought. What could she be worried about?

"It isn't bad. I promise," he said to offer comfort. "I remembered that first Christmas vacation—the one you stayed in Hawai'i for your Model United Nations conference—and we sat on the beach." He studied her face which seemed to have lost some vibrancy.

She turned away from him to search through her purse. "I think you should leave it alone, Adam."

"What? What did I say now?" he asked, dumb struck by her response. But why had he brought it up? Did he want her to remember the moment they'd shared? It was obvious she did, her indirect admission by asking him to leave it alone. Why would it bother her?

"Just let it go. We shouldn't go back there—not when we're finally getting along. The present is preferable. We've established a space where we can coexist in peace." She found the key, opened the door, and threw her handbag into the passenger's side. "I'm not sure I could bare losing..." she paused, and then said, "the kids again."

Adam was confounded by her sudden ire. This was usually his role. "Look. What happened at the funeral is on me. I'm sorry."

"You don't have to apologize again. I've forgiven you."

He took a step closer to her. "If I remember correctly, that night was pretty peaceful. We didn't argue once." He leaned to one side, attempting to reel in her eye contact.

She turned on him. Adam stepped back surprised by the look on her face. It wasn't angry like he expected. It was frightened. Her brow was creased, her eyes wide.

What would frighten her about that memory, Adam wondered?

"Please, Adam. Just let it go." She raised her hands, drew her hair up into a ponytail, then let it drop with a sigh. Her hands shook. "It's been a very lonely year for me." Her voice trembled.

Adam wanted to hug her, but he knew she wouldn't take it. "I'm sorry. I didn't–"

She held up a hand and shook her head. "It's okay. I'll see you on Thursday." She turned and got into her car. The tires squeaked against the concrete as she drove from the parking garage.

Adam waited as she drove away and knew there was no way he was letting it go now, despite her request. He had too much to make up for.

CHAPTER ELEVEN

A lex sat at a table next to the window pane. She looked up from student work she was reading at the street which ran parallel to the Java Stop. The coffee shop was walking distance to campus, and Alex enjoyed the retreat from her office on most Thursdays. The thick aroma of espresso beans, brewing coffee, and a hint of chocolate and cinnamon provided a homey warmth for her senses that made her think of holiday's with Megan's family. It provided a brief respite, even if it was a destination now lost.

She glanced again at the clock above the cash register. Then she glanced at her silver watch. Both timepieces read ten after eleven. She and Adam had planned to meet at the coffee house at eleven that day. *He isn't coming*, she thought. After her cold treatment of him the other night, of running from the past, he probably thought the peace treaty had been broken.

As a women's studies professor, she'd spent a lifetime studying women, examining their lives, their values, and the mistreatment of her gender by various societies. Yet here she sat, hopes high for the arrival of a man who'd already disappointed her on more occasions than she chose to recall. It was shameful. Alex blushed and looked around. No one knew or cared if she was being stood up.

He definitely isn't coming.

She sighed, annoyed with herself for even caring. It was stupid really and would amount to nothing regardless. She rolled her eyes and muttered, "Stupid woman." She stood and began placing papers she'd been correcting in her satchel. As she slipped the last of the papers into the bag, she heard a soft knock at the window.

Alex looked up at the sound, and her gaze connected with Adam's face on the opposite side of the glass. Her breath caught at the sight of his dimpled smile. He waved, then continued down the walkway toward the Java Stop entrance. She sat and followed his arrival, the bell on the door chiming as he entered. He walked straight to her.

"I'm so sorry I'm late," he said. "I had a negotiation this morning that ran over. I should never have made you wait."

You are so forgiven, she thought. "I was just getting ready to go back to my office."

"Would your office be better?" he asked.

She shook her head. *Public places only.* She didn't trust the giddy butterflies dancing within her. "No. This is better. More space." She let the strap slip from her shoulder and set the bag back on the floor.

"May I get you a cup of coffee or tea," Adam offered.

She tested her cup, now empty. "I'd take another cup of coffee." She handed him her cup and watching him walk to the counter.

Pull yourself together, she chided herself and took a deep, cleansing breath.

He was so handsome, the epitome of a man so ruggedly attractive with features softened by his even temperament. *In most cases*, she reminded herself. She rubbed her temples, attempting to gather her wits. She didn't need to think about how striking he looked in his white linen shirt that hung perfectly on his perfect frame, or the way the short sleeves drew taut around his biceps. She didn't need to think about how his tan skin stood out against the light fabric. She had an errant thought and wondered if he'd taste like a café mocha if she were to run her tongue along his skin.

Stop! She shook her head.

She watched him at the counter. Tall and lean, he drew his wallet from his khaki chinos which perfectly fit his frame and made her insides melt.

She looked outside and watched students file past the window. Had Megan written about Alex's secret? She didn't think Megan had told him, otherwise his behavior wouldn't have changed. He would feel justified about his comments at the funeral. Alex's stomach tied itself into a knot.

Adam returned to the table with coffee and a couple of sandwiches in hand. "I thought you might be hungry." He sat down.

"That turkey sandwich does look good," she admitted. Adam pushed one of the plates in front of her. "Thank you."

"Were you waiting long?" he asked. "I realized I didn't have your number to let you know."

"No. I usually come here on Thursdays to work, anyway."

He set his phone on the table and slid it toward her. "May I have your number?"

She stared at the device as if it had sprouted a head.

"I won't bug you. I promise." He smiled. "But if we're working on Megan's stuff, together, I might need it."

"Right." She picked up the phone and added her contact information. "Did you come up with any ideas since Sunday?" She handed his phone back to him. Their hands brushed and left a heat signature burning her skin.

"No." Adam thumbed something onto his phone. Her phone pinged. "I sent you a text, so you have mine." He put the phone away and looked up devoting his gaze to her. "I've been wondering if

Megan really thought the kids were in danger. And I keep thinking that I don't know for certain if she really felt that way. It *is* a wild assumption."

Alex nodded. She'd been wondering the same thing. She had poured over the journals that Adam had given her but had come up with nothing more to support her conclusion. It was one thing to know for sure, but another entirely to assume Megan's meaning.

Adam pulled out the envelope that Alex had given him a week ago and picked up his phone again to show her a picture he'd taken. "These numbers are the titles of the empty files on her computer." He pointed at one of them. "Look—this one matches the number on your letter. Oh-eight-oh-six-oh-four."

Alex looked at the random numbers and picked up her letter to glance at the notations made there. Sure enough, one of the file numbers matched.

"Know what to make of it?" Adam asked.

Alex shook her head and conjured Megan's image in her mind as she studied the page. *What were you thinking?* Megan smiled in Alex's imagination, then disappeared. *Think, Alex.* Megan was notoriously organized.

Adam took a bite of his sandwich and licked a remnant of mayonnaise from the corner of his mouth. Alex couldn't tear her gaze away, a vision of Adam's tongue on her body flashed in her mind. Her skin tingled. She gave her head a shake to clear her thoughts. "Let's start with what we think we know."

"Okay."

"We think Megan was worried about the kids."

Adam nodded. "And we think we know it has something to do with HSU. Could the numbers be classroom numbers?"

"I don't think so. The numbers are too large and there is no reference building."

"Extension numbers?"

Alex shook her head and finished the bite she'd taken from her sandwich. She took a sip of the latte Adam had bought her. "HSU has a double-eight prefix. Doesn't fit."

"Employee numbers?"

"Or student ID numbers? That's a distinct possibility. Can you send me this? I'll see if I can finagle some info to check on ID numbers."

He smiled picking up his phone. "Sure."

Her phone pinged again as his text came through.

It was quiet for a moment, except for the local music filtering through the shop's sound system, the huge coffee machine steaming milk for a customer's beverage, and the hushed conversations of patrons around them. Yet, Alex heard nothing but the sound of her heartbeat. She needed to fill the noisy silence. "How is Trey doing?"

Adam nodded. "He's holding up." He set the napkin on the banana leaf shaped glass plate, then slid it aside. "I'm afraid he'll think he won the QB position by default."

"And forget he was the next in line anyway? Why do teams usually have two quarterbacks share time?" Alex asked.

"Typically to solidify a starter. Sometimes to groom the heir apparent."

"And Trey hasn't thought about that has he?"

Adam shook his head and looked from the white cup in his hands to her face. He smiled and Alex felt her breath catch in her throat, the dimple in his left cheek endearing, sexy. Her stomach dipped.

She knew the pace of her heart was due to the realization she was sharing lunch and having a pleasant conversation with Adam. She hadn't thought it possible. "Did you see the article in the Sun about Miles?" she asked.

Adam nodded.

"I noticed that the coroner isn't ruling out possible steroid use. What do you think about that?" She took another bite of her sandwich.

He was shaking his head. "Trey says he doesn't believe it, and if you ask me, I don't think he could have gotten away with it. The NCAA is too strict."

"A deeper conspiracy then?" She smiled at the joke. "Someone paid off an NCAA official to look the other way."

Adam grinned at her. "Dear God, I hope not!" He shook his head again and took a sip of his beverage. "Could you imagine the repercussions of that on collegiate athletics?"

"I'd see a lot more of my student athletes in the classroom."

He laughed.

Alex took another sip of her latte and stared at the cup. She turned it around in a circle.

"Alex, do *you* think Megan underlined the words in her journal to send a message?" Adam asked.

Alex looked at his face. He looked worried, his lips thinned out and his brows drawn together. He was skeptical, but it was Megan. She understood.

"I don't know, Adam. But we both knew her. Megan was the sort of person who didn't do things *just because*. I mean, she was fun and enigmatic, but she wasn't irrational." She picked at the sandwich and felt his track her.

He leaned forward, his arms on the table. "Everything had a purpose and if it didn't, she got rid of it. Megan hated clutter. But later—toward the end?"

Her eyes slid up from the sandwich to his. "You think she did this toward the end?"

He looked out the window. The light illuminated his face and his dark eyes into a more complex color, just like him. Then he looked at her and shook his head.

"How come?"

"I thought about that," he said and looked down at his hands. He'd removed his wedding ring. Alex's breath hitched in her chest. "She was pretty clear all the way up to the end, in retrospect. It was just those last days. The journals were done already."

Alex leaned toward Adam and rested her arms on the table. "So, it seems a safe assumption she underlined those words knowing you would read them, knowing you would notice. You've always noticed Megan." She stopped the last words catching in her throat. "The question is what might she have been trying to tell you?"

"About the kids possibly being in danger?"

Alex sat back. "It does seem far-fetched." She sighed, "but, I can say this: nothing would have motivated Megan more. Have you come across any entries that connect?" She wondered about her secret, again.

"Nothing out of the ordinary. Just memories."

Alex took another sip of her coffee and set the cup back on the table. "Do you feel uncomfortable assuming Megan was worried about the kids?"

Adam looked out the window a moment and then back at her. "I would rather feel uncomfortable with that assumption than not have a theory at all and leave the kids vulnerable."

She nodded, then couldn't help but say, "You took off your wedding ring."

He looked at his hand again and flexed his fingers. "Yeah. It's strange. Gave them to the girls. Emma has mine and Bekah, her mom's."

Alex swallowed and didn't want the tears that pressed against the back of her eyes. When he looked up at her, he offered a subdued smile. "Are you–" she stopped needing to control the emotion rising. For most of their adult lives it had been Adam and Megan. Megan and Adam. When she knew she could ask the question without crying, she asked, "Were you ready?"

His eyes caressed her face, and he tilted his head to the side. It was a small movement, slight, but she noticed it. "Yes. I was ready." There was a beat of something unsaid, a moment that felt pregnant with meaning, but it wasn't born. He smiled and look at his watch. "Oh. Shoot. I have to go."

She glanced at her own watch. Almost two hours had slipped past them. "Wow. Me too." She knew they couldn't sit in that coffee shop forever while time passed. They had to go back to the real world at some point.

"What are you doing right now?" Adam asked.

"Nothing planned. Just time in my office in case a student wanders in for help. More grading."

"Can they wait?" Adam asked.

Alex's heartbeat skipped ahead of itself. "Most anything can wait, Adam. Why?"

"Come with me."

"Where?" she asked.

He smiled that dimpled smile, the one that made her knees feel like jelly and highlighted his handsome face. She remembered it from that night before she'd known his name. He'd looked at her and said, *dance with me* along with that dimpled smile. She'd melted then too.

"A surprise." He stood and held out a hand to her. "A good one."

CHAPTER TWELVE

Alex took his offered hand with one of hers and grabbed her satchel with the other. As they walked from the Java Stop out into the warm Hawai'i day, Adam kept her hand in his. It wasn't until they were on the sidewalk that he released her. She missed his hand around hers.

"Would you like me to drive?" she asked.

"Nope."

Giving up control was difficult for her, but to Adam, it wasn't as much of a struggle. She followed him to his car a few blocks from the coffee house while they talked about his earlier meeting. He unlocked the passenger's side door of the SUV and held open the door while she climbed inside. She'd never been offended by gentlemanly behavior, but she'd never been excited by it either. She'd always considered it a simple kindness, but having Adam open a door for her, waiting for her to be safely seated inside the car did something to the preserved emotions she'd stashed away.

"Not a hint?" she asked as he slid into his seat next to her.

He started the car and turned down the volume when acoustic guitar music blared through the speakers. "Nope."

"Acoustic guitar?" she asked. "I took you more for the classics like Lynard Skynard or Cream."

"I do like Eric Clapton."

"Doesn't count. Everyone likes Clapton."

He laughed and flicked on the turn signal. "Trey and Bekah got me into listening to the new alternative stuff and Jack Johnson."

"Oh, the local artist. I like him too," she said. The awareness they had something in common besides the kids and Megan hit her. "So, what about that hint?"

Adam pulled the car out into traffic. "Somewhere on campus."

"That doesn't help."

"The athletic complex."

"You want to go relive your glory days?" she asked with a laugh.

"Thanks a lot." He gave her a wry look. "I would never do that by the way."

"I know." She meant it.

Adam had never been showy. He wasn't one to take credit for his accomplishments. His achievements he always attributed to his team, workers, or someone else. His humility was often cumbersome. Who could really be that humble? He was, she knew. She'd learned that about him early into knowing him.

She'd also heard it from Megan: *I wish he had more fire*, she'd said.

Shocked Alex had told her Adam had enough fire to start a multi-million-dollar company from the ground up.

Megan hadn't been able to respond to that.

Alex gazed out the car window. The plumeria trees drifted as they drove by. The white and yellow blossoms so perfect they looked manufactured. They passed students and teachers alike walking along the sidewalk. It seemed a lifetime ago that she had walked the same sidewalk as a student, but also just like yesterday.

"Where'd you go?" he asked.

She looked at him, his eyes on the road. "Nowhere," she said not willing to share that memory of Megan. She glanced out the window again. "Just admiring the plumeria. I love it when they are in bloom. They are so beautiful."

"They are. And they smell nice, too."

When she turned her head, she noticed he was watching her. He looked away, back at the road and pleasurable chills raced along the skin of her shoulders and back.

"What? No more guesses?" he asked with a smile.

"I can't think of anything else," she said as they passed through the gate of the HSU athletic complex and into the parking structure.

"Another hint: water."

"Water?" she asked and took a moment to think about his hint. Then it dawned on her and she smiled. "Bekah's swim meet."

"I knew you could do it." He flashed her a bright smile and parked the car. "She will be so happy you've come. The kids adore you."

She looked at him. "I adore them." *I adored Megan. I adore you.*

"They've missed you." With his hands in his lap fingering the keys, he turned toward her, but he didn't meet her gaze. "There isn't a day that goes by I don't regret what I said to you that day. I know you said you forgive me, but I really hurt you. I hurt them—not having you after Megan died. They needed you."

Alex reached out and put a hand on his arm. "Adam, don't. It's done. You have to let it go. I'm here now."

He was looking at her hand.

"For them," she added, because it seemed like she needed to for the hitch in her breath suddenly coming in short bursts.

His eyes flashed to hers. He swallowed and his eyes dropped to her lips before falling away. He cleared his throat. "I'm glad I didn't fuck it up completely then." He got out of the car.

Alex took a deep breath trying to slow her heartbeat and followed.

"What events is Bekah in?" Alex asked as she passed Adam, her shoulder brushing his chest as he held the stairwell door for her. The clean scent of his cologne caressed her senses. She remembered she'd always been this aware of him, even when she'd turned it off, she'd been aware.

"The 100 fly, the 200 breast, and a freestyle/backstroke medley. I think she's the second leg in the freestyle relay, too," he said from behind her his voice echoing in the concrete cavern of the stairwell.

"Is she enjoying HSU this first year?"

"You know Bekah. She loves a challenge."

"That she does." Alex looked down at her feet to navigate the next narrow flight of stairs. She smiled, recalling Bekah as a toddler and any staircase in her path. She had attempted to tackle everyone despite the many bumps and bruises along the way. Most children would fall and bump their head and know to steer clear of the stairs. Not Bekah. She'd try climbing them again before the tears had even dried.

"She likes her coach," Adam said.

Alex looked back over her shoulder at him to listen to his comment and collided with someone coming up the stairs. The contact sent her reeling backwards into Adam who caught her, breaking her fall.

"Sorry," the person who'd bumped her said and continued up the steps, the white tennis shoes disappearing.

"Slow down, brah!" Adam called out. "You okay?"

Alex leaned against Adam who sat on the steps and lifted her gaze. She was more distracted by her current position against Adam's lap than the rude man, who had knocked her over, but she nodded. His arms were around her. His hands rested on her lower back. Her body came alive, pulsing with energy. Their eyes locked and she knew he would kiss her. Lord help her, she wanted him to. His arms tightened their hold and pulled her closer to him.

"Alex," he said, but it was quiet. His brown eyes dropped to her mouth again and despite her logical brain, her instincts took over. Her lips parted in response. She wanted so much to kiss him, to take control, and discover for herself his taste, to refill her memory with new details.

One of his hands came up and brushed errant locks of hair from her face. He pressed the skin of his palm against the skin of her cheek and God help her, she leaned into it. The pad of his thumb caressed her cheek so close to her lips. She struggled to breathe.

"Alex?" This time his voice was a touch louder, as his eyes grazed her face. A question this time. The first time her name had sounded like a wish.

She shifted in his arms to get up, afraid of crossing a line that would ruin this peace. She couldn't lose him again. She couldn't lose the kids again. Alex put her hands on either side of him to push herself away, but she miscalculated. Her body pressed closer to his, their chests in full contact with one another and her mouth even closer to his.

"Alex," he whispered, and this time a devilish grin with that endearing dimple appeared on his face. This time her name a warning.

Her heart, once racing, now melted in her chest. All reason fled as she considered just doing it. Just closing the distance. But she couldn't. She remembered how much she had to lose. But Adam didn't know the war going on within her, and he did press his mouth to hers.

She sighed. Relaxed against him and lost herself in a kiss twenty-some odd years after their first one. He was firm and strong, pliable and hot beneath her hands. She was sure stars had exploded in her body, a rush of effervescence bursting through every inch of her. She shivered and Adam's hold tightened around her, his head tilting to one side, drawing the kiss deeper, and welcoming her fully into his embrace. She burrowed in, wanting to crawl into his skin with him. One of his hands moved from her lower back to the back of her head, holding her there. The pleasure of the kiss consumed her.

Stupid woman! She heard that inner voice from somewhere in the recesses of her mind.

Shut up! She fought back. *Give me this one moment! I've waited a lifetime.*

But that inner voice was persistent, and Alex withdrew. When she opened her eyes and met Adam's, she saw the desire she felt mirrored in his gaze.

She shivered again, remembering that night so clear. He'd wanted her then too. She'd wanted him. "Adam. I—" The breathlessness in her voice was a strange sound to her ears.

"Alex." This time her name an admission. His hands framed her face, his thumbs stroking her skin. "I've wanted to do that since the game."

"What?" she asked. What was he saying? He'd been thinking about kissing her. She could hardly concentrate on his words. The gentle and persuasive touch on her face was coaxing her to turn her head and draw his thumb into her mouth. The stairwell wasn't the place, so she willed herself to remain still.

"At the football game." He grinned. Then it faded. "Oh, shit." His eyes widened with worry. "I'm sorry. I forgot about Jack. I'm so sorry." He sat up, helping Alex to stand, then got to his feet.

"Jack?" she asked confused and missed the loss of the heat between their bodies. "What about him?" What was he talking about? He'd been thinking about kissing her! He was worried about Jack. What did the two have to do with each other?

She heard Adam take a deep breath. "Come on." He held out his hand. Alex took it. "We don't want to miss Bekah's debut events." Adam led her down the remaining flights of stairs and across the courtyard to the Nui Ikaika Water Complex which housed the HSU Olympic size pool.

It was an open-air structure the beauty and serenity of the Hawai'i scenery surrounding the pool on all sides. On each length of the pool were wide concrete bleachers. At the Diamond Head end of the pool there were starting blocks, and, at the Ewa end, a dive platform. The bright blue and green logo of the Hurricanes was emblazoned on the bottom of the pool. Competitors milled about at the opposite end of the pool from Alex and Adam and where they entered.

Alex, her hand still in his, followed Adam up the concrete steps to a space where they could sit and watch the meet.

"There she is," Adam said and pointed toward the swimmers.

His voice pulled her from a daze. It was as though her world had tilted on its axis, and she hadn't regained the proper spin. She looked to where he was pointing and found Bekah who was kicking her legs one at a time, moving her arms in circles to stretch the muscles as she warmed up for her event. When it was Bekah's turn, she climbed up on the starting block. Alex, finally letting go of Adam's hand, cheered as Bekah eased through the water in her freestyle relay, her team winning first place.

Adam's shoulder pressed against hers when he leaned toward her and said, "I love watching her swim."

Alex decided she must be dreaming. Kissing Adam in a stairwell at HSU seemed more like a dream than reality. Holding his hand while watching Bekah at her swim meet. Dream. Alex nodded at his words but kept her eyes on his shoulder.

"Are you okay?" Adam asked.

She didn't know how he could be so nonchalant.

Dream. It was the only explanation. How was it possible to go from constant adversaries to kissing in a stairwell? She couldn't speak, and nodded, saved by the starting gun which signaled Bekah's next event.

Bekah sailed out over the water and entered the pool. She came up nearly three-quarters of a length later with her first burst through the water. Her head appeared above the water, her powerful arms and shoulders swung from behind her to the front in a split-second propelling her through the water as if she had wings and was flying over it.

Adam stood, cheering on his daughter. She flip-turned and headed the opposite direction submerged under water. When she emerged from underneath, she was winning her heat by a stroke. Bekah hit the wall, and though it looked like she was first, it was too close to call. They waited for the call and cheered because she won!

Adam turned to her, beaming. "Did you see that?"

She stood. "I did. Right here with you." She smiled at him. "She was wonderful!" She clapped and was suddenly in Adam's arms as he hugged her.

He leaned back to search her face but didn't let her go.

Alex blushed, the heat creeping across her skin and stepped away.

Adam released her and clapped, whistling for Bekah.

Alex wondered if he was as conflicted as she was, only he was just better at hiding it? Then she wondered if she supposed to feel guilty about kissing Adam. She didn't. She didn't feel like she'd hurt Megan at all. But that made her feel even more guilty.

She pushed her thoughts of Adam, of Megan, of her own dishonor of Megan's memory away and concentrated on Bekah's swim meet. That was a far more important endeavor for the moment instead of her self-centered meanderings. By the time the meet was over, Alex had talked herself into forgetting that the kiss had ever happened, despite the jump start of her heart every time she thought of it, or the electricity that passed through her spine every time they touched.

Alex caught sight of Bekah walking toward them, her black hair wet and combed, her muscular frame wrapped in a green and blue towel.

"Aunty Alex! You're here!" Bekah was smiling ear-to-ear.

"Congratulations on your medals," Alex said and hugged her, not particularly concerned about getting wet.

Adam exchanged a few words with his daughter before saying goodbye. Then Alex followed Adam back across the athletic complex and up through the parking garage stairwell. Her face heated as they passed the steps, her desire to do it again overwhelming her.

The silence between them was uncomfortable but not antagonistic. Alex just didn't know how to rebuild the bridge. This is what she'd been afraid of. So, she asked something that made sense: "What did you mean about Jack?" Silence broken, she decided that being childish wasn't the best way for her to deal with the situation.

"I'm sorry. I shouldn't have kissed you," Adam answered. His voice sounded contrite as though resigned to something she didn't understand.

He unlocked the door of the car and opened it for her.

That wasn't exactly what she had wanted to hear, even if she'd berated herself for it only an hour earlier. She stopped and looked at him.

"How does that have anything to do with Jack?" she asked still needing to understand the shift.

His gaze shifted to her lips. Then he moved around to her side of the door and gently pressed her into her seat. He still wanted to kiss her, she realized, and happiness flowed through her like sunshine on a spring day.

"I just stopped thinking and well. . ." his voice faded, and he shut her door.

She watched him walk around the front of the car, then as he climbed in. "And Jack?" She really wanted clarification.

He paused for a moment his hands on the steering wheel. He looked controlled and tense, a different Adam than the one she had spent the afternoon with. "Look, if I were in Jack's shoes, I would want to throttle me for kissing you. I took advantage of the situation." He started the car and proceeded to drive from the parking garage.

"Who says I didn't take advantage of the situation?" she teased. Alex didn't like the way this was going, though the kiss lingered in her mind, laughter was obviously the best medicine to get beyond whatever was bothering him. She was sure Adam must be grappling with the consequences of their kiss as well. With Megan's memory.

Levity would make it easier to face Alex decided, for both of them.

Adam laughed. "Did you?"

Alex smiled at him and refrained from answering. "Why would you want to throttle Jack? How does he have anything to do with it?"

"Alex, if a man made a pass at you, and you were my significant other, I'd be really pissed off." He looked at her. His jaw tensed and his eyes blazed.

Alex shivered. She wasn't one to desire a man's protection, but the thought of Adam protecting her was exhilarating. "Jack wouldn't care. He's just a friend."

"Wait. He's not your boyfriend?" Adam asked.

She arched her eyebrows. "The dangers of assuming things." She smiled. "Just friends. Jack isn't my type."

Adam parked the car a block from her office building and climbed out. She also got out of the car before he could get to her door and met him on the sidewalk. They walked together far enough apart that they didn't touch. She was glad. She was certain that he only needed to graze her arm, and she would throw herself at him.

"Not your type." He chuckled his usual levity returning now that Jack seemed to be out of the way.

"No. No." She shook her head. "Just a friend." She was so happy she could tell him that, but she knew that it wouldn't have made a bit of difference considering the circumstances.

"And just what is your type?" he asked. He stopped at the stairs that led to the front doors of the building where Alex spent most of her time while on campus.

She stood facing him and smiled. "I'm not sure. It's been a long time since I've dated anyone. I was thinking about joining one of those online dating things."

He laughed.

"Look," Alex said. She didn't want to talk about it, but she knew they needed to. "About the kiss."

His smile faded.

"It was really, really nice, and I enjoyed it, but I know we're both…healing," she finished. "I just want you to know I understand, and I don't want to ruin our peace treaty." She'd decided that he'd lost his mind kissing her even if they'd both wanted it. She wanted him, but she was sure he had different reasons, namely physical ones. "I don't want to risk losing you and the kids again."

"Oh, it didn't ruin our peace treaty," he said and roved over her face with his eyes. "And you won't ever lose us again, Alex. Ever." He looked over her shoulder a moment, then reconnected with her eyes, his face somber. "Thank you for allowing me to read Megan's letter she wrote to you." He stared at his car fob he was holding in his hands.

"You're welcome." She couldn't stop watching his hands but forced her gaze back to his face.

"I wondered what she meant that she didn't hold what you'd told her against you?" Adam asked. He continued to search her expression, his head tilting slightly to the side.

Alex's heart dropped off into a chasm. She shouldn't have been surprised he'd ask the question. She would have in his shoes, but it would reveal her secret. She didn't want to ruin what was happening—and that wasn't about the kiss—but about being back in their life. The kids, the companionship was too important. "You know." She stalled. She kept eye contact with him but couldn't help her wayward gaze when it wandered to his mouth.

"No. I don't."

She continued hedging out of nervousness. "It's a girl thing."

"I can respect your privacy, Alex. That's all you need to say."

"You're right. I'm sorry. I'd rather not share." She looked at him.

His head was bent, but he nodded in acceptance. "Thank you."

She had the distinct impression that he was grappling with something because he looked down again, then back at her.

"You're sure I can't wait and take you to your car?"

"It's just behind the building. I'm going to grab something from the office and go home. You don't need to worry." She smiled.

He turned away and then swiveled back her way. "You'll let me know if you come up with anything on those numbers?" He took a step backward.

"And vice versa, right?"

"Yes." He turned to go.

"Adam?" Alex called after him.

Adam stopped and turned back to her. Alex's breath caught her memories slamming up against the inside of her mind, his hands on her, his smile, his laugh. She had to force the air though her throat to formulate the words. "Thank you," she started, "for trusting me with Megan's journals."

Adam nodded. "Who else could I trust with Megan's thoughts, Alex?" He nodded again as though punctuating the thought, turned, and walked away.

Alex took another deep breath and released it. Yes. She had to be dreaming.

CHAPTER THIRTEEN

The ping of a text message drew Adam from Megan's journal back to the present. He stood and retrieved the phone across the room. It was Alex.

Alex: *You home?*

Adam pressed the information button and called her.

She answered on the first ring. "Adam? Oh my—are you home right now?" Alex's voice sounded winded.

Adam heart quickened at the sound of her voice. He'd just spent the last few moments reliving Megan's thoughts about Alex's divorce. *How do you fall out of love, Adam?* Megan had written. He wasn't sure there was an answer to it. He still loved Megan—would always love her even though she was gone. Maybe Alex stilled loved Geoff?

"I'm here," he answered. "Is everything okay?"

"Good. I'm fine, just excited. I think I figured it out!"

Adam straightened up. "Really?"

"May I come over? It would be better to show you rather than tell you," she said. "We need Megan's journals."

"I'm home. Come now."

She disconnected the call. Adam looked at the screen, then set it back down on the counter. While he waited, he went up to his room to get the journals retrieving them from a chair next to his bed and carried them down to the living room. He set the box on the coffee table.

He went into the kitchen and got a glass of water. Drank it. Paced because his nerves wouldn't let him sit.

The afternoon he'd spent with Alex a few days prior had been wonderful. Easy. He pictured kissing her. He'd acted on impulse. Maybe if he'd thought about it, he wouldn't have done it, but he had. And then her "about the kiss," speech with the "we're healing" reminder. He'd cringed inwardly at his behavior, but he hadn't regretted that kiss. No. In fact, he wanted to do it again.

He was thinking about her a lot. Ever since he'd approached her for help that day, she was always walking into his mind and memories. Remembering the beach had blown him away, the weight of his want. Then the day of the football game, realizing he wanted her on a physical level hit him like lightning. That wasn't something that he'd thought about when he'd walked back into her life. He'd assumed the feelings weren't mutual. But that kiss! It had proved him wrong, her reaction earthy, exciting, and enticing.

Was he supposed to feel guilty? He'd often wondered how someone could cheat on their spouse, but it had been nearly a year since Megan had succumbed to the cancer. It had been almost two years since they'd started fighting that battle again. Was there a societal rule that one didn't feel attracted to a woman just because she was your late wife's best friend? He wondered what Megan would think. Would she be angry with him for feeling this way?

Megan is gone, his inner voice rationalized. *Until death do you part.*

Yes. And I still love her, he answered the internal voice.

Moving on doesn't mean you stop loving her.

Adam walked into the entryway and stood at the white plantation shutter to watch for Alex. Then he paced again, the sound of his bare footfalls seemed loud on the hardwood floor. While he knew he was ready to walk his journey without Megan, now, he didn't know what that meant about his attraction to Alex. That had never seemed like a possibility, and with her "about the kiss" speech, probably wasn't still. Their memories of one another were mixed up with so much hurt. They'd spent a lifetime angry at one another.

Where did it come from?

Adam stopped. The internal question slammed against him like a baseball bat. *From my thinking Alex was trying to break up my marriage.*

Had she been?

He hadn't considered it. That had always been the only option, but in the last few weeks, he knew what he'd said at the funeral was wrong. If he knew that was wrong, then was he wrong about everything else?

Adam's heart pounded in his chest, echoing in his ears as if he were standing in an empty cavern. If he was wrong about that—and it was pretty clear he was—why had he been angry all those years? Without that excuse, the walls crumbled around him, but he wasn't sure what to think so exposed to a new paradigm.

He heard Alex's car outside the house. Her car door slammed as he opened the heavy door, and she was running up the drive toward him. She looked excited, her green eyes alive and vibrant, a smile on her face. Her face was glowing. God, she was sexy.

"I can't believe it! It was so damn obvious, Adam!" she said as she walked into the house passed him.

"What do you mean obvious?"

Alex turned to face him her. "It was just that I didn't have all of the information, but then I started thinking about the numbers and the journals–" she rambled the words coming out in a breathy rush.

"Slow down, Alex," Adam said, getting lost.

"Sorry." She took a deep breath and reached into her back pocket. "I've been thinking about those numbers with the empty file folders. Like you said, I assumed that Megan was trying to leave a message, but now I am sure of it." She pulled out a piece of paper and held it out to him. "It dawned on me to check the journals and sure enough, each of the journals that you gave me matches one of the empty file folders' numbers."

He moved to look at the paper she was holding out to him. He recognized it as the photo he'd shared with her at the coffee house.

Alex leaned closer to him. "The date, Adam." She pointed at one of the numbers. "Some of the numbers you gave me and the numbers on my letter correspond with the journals that you shared, the ones that had underlined words and phrases."

"They're dates? How simple." He was disgusted with himself for missing the simplicity. "Diligent, Organize, but simple. Should have known."

"Each of the numbers corresponds with one of the journals you gave me except one."

"Which one?"

"Oh-eight-oh-six-oh-four," Alex read. "That number is both on my letter and the files." Alex reached across him and pointed to the number on the page.

"So, if it is a date, it would be August sixth of two thousand and four," Adam said looking at the number on the paper. That was around the time Megan's cancer had returned. He moved to the box of journals and sat down knowing exactly which journal to look in because of the date, realizing that unless Megan had hidden the entry, it had to have been in the last journal in which she'd written— one he hadn't gotten to yet. He pulled it from the stack, opened it, and flipped through the journal, glancing at the dates as he went until he found the matching date, the doubled number from both his files, Alex's letter, and Megan's computer. Sure enough, there was an entry.

Adam glanced at Alex as she sat down beside him on the couch.

Their shoulders touching, Adam began to read the entry aloud:

"Dear Adam, I don't know where to begin. My heart is racing, and my hands are shaking. I don't know how to say this, although by the time you read this you will already know, but you don't know now. You are at work today securing an insurance bond for the new high rise bid you won last week. Oh, dear God, I thought we'd defeated this—that we'd already won this battle. It's back Adam, the cancer is back, and Dr. Togoshi has in as much said I need to put my affairs in order. She didn't say how long, can't say, but I could read it in her eyes—not long enough."

Adam stopped for a moment and glanced at Alex. She met his gaze, and then looked back at the journal. He continued, "So now, I'm frightened, though not of what you might assume. I'm not frightened of death, Adam, but I am frightened of not having you by my side. I'm frightened to know that the cancer will take me away from you and our babies, but Adam, I'm more frightened of the idea that a different sort of cancer has worked its way into our lives. I know you must be confused by that. Trust that I've had my reason's Adam, as you will soon learn. I have my suspicions, well, I know that the cancer is aware of me, and might retaliate. I don't mean to be cryptic, though I fear I may have to lead you on what may feel like a goose chase in an effort to protect what I have learned and you in the process. Let me start at the beginning."

Adam stopped reading the entry. "What the hell does that mean?" He looked at Alex.

"Just keep reading. She's going to explain it," Alex said. "You want me to read it instead?"

Adam ignored her question and continued with Megan's entry as Alex stood and began pacing. "In January of this year, I received an anonymous email. I'm still unsure why I have been singled out as the recipient of this information and have come to the conclusion that the informant either noticed my by-line in the paper, or knows me (and possibly, you). But truthfully, I paid little attention to the email at first. My journalistic curiosity got the best of me, however, so I did a small amount of digging. The email gave me a name—Donna Delco. The name sounded familiar, so a quick search turned up several hits. Most hits were about her involvement in a local high school swim team and more recently her standout performance as a Hawai'i State University swimmer. The hit that stood out however was the one about her death, an apparent suicide. Do you remember when that was in the news?

"Delco was a nineteen-year-old athletic standout that was supposed to compete in the 2004 Olympic Games. She was an academic all-star on her team. Does this sound like a kid who commits suicide? Sure—you could say pressure—I thought it too, but as you well know, I was compelled to dig a bit deeper. I met with Donna's parents. Saw pictures of her smiling face, the trophies and awards that she won as a swimmer and heard stories about her life. I met with her teammates, her coach, and some of her instructors all had the same thing to say, "Donna didn't commit suicide." That it didn't fit, but they couldn't prove it. I walked away from each interview with the same impression. Donna Delco seemed like a young woman with the world at her feet and knew exactly how she'd walk on it. But the evidence suggested otherwise, and there was nothing that the police or the family could do.

"Then something strange occurred. I found a postcard left on the windshield of my car. On it were the words "Back Off" in block letters (I've left it in my file cabinet marked in the file mentions and awards). I laughed it off, thinking it a fraternity prank.

"Then, in April of this year, my informant sends me another email about the death of John Bayer. The story hits the papers that night, though I'd put in a call to Tony at the news desk. It turns out that Bayer died of accidental alcohol poisoning after a huge party at an HSU frat house. I didn't think much of it until my informant sent me another tip. With the follow up, I discovered John Bayer was an HSU wrestler. I wondered, two athletes at HSU in a four-month period. It sounded strange to me, so I followed up on another tip that my anonymous informant sent me—a file left for me in the stacks at the Alexander library on HSU campus.

"Guess what I found out, Adam? Since 2001, there have been at least seven deaths at the HSU campus. I know that doesn't sound strange considering the size of the campus. HSU is a small city. What I found strange was that five of the deaths involved HSU athletes. Five of those kids that died were in peak physical condition. Why is that? When I left the library, I found another postcard on my windshield, with another block letter message: Second Warning: Back off! This time I didn't laugh. This time I didn't think that it was a fraternity prank. This time I knew that I had stumbled into a hornet's nest and the hornet was watching. But I couldn't stop there. You know me well enough that my instincts were on red alert, and I couldn't get out of my mind that Trey is starting his first year at HSU next fall and is himself an athlete."

Adam stopped. "Alex, do you even understand what this means?"

"Do you think this has something to do with Jonesy Miles?"

"What if it does? How can you explain away five, now six, student athlete deaths? Why haven't the police gotten involved?"

"Unless it goes deeper than just the university?" Alex returned to her seat next to him.

Adam stared at her and shuddered at her thought. A conspiracy wasn't something that Adam wanted to get involved in. He didn't want Alex involved in it or Emma. But Trey's and Bekah's lives could be in danger. Megan had certainly thought so.

Adam stood then and began to pace as he continued to read. "So, I went to Milton Yamane. I was thankful we had that connection with your involvement in the football booster club. He always seemed amenable, and I figured he would be the best person to approach, especially being the athletic director. As usual, Milton was kind and amiable, and when I brought up what I had found, a high percentage of HSU deaths being athletes, he didn't seem surprised. He admitted he was aware of the situation, though they weren't overly concerned considering the sheer size of the athletic program, and that of the university, the statistics fall within the norm concerning death rates on college campuses. It seemed ludicrous to me, Adam, that Milton seemed so blasé about his athletes dying. I left his office determined to find out more.

"I looked into every death since 2001 that involved an HSU athlete. Every death, except for one murder involving a boyfriend, was ruled accidental or of natural causes. Again, I couldn't help but feel that something wasn't adding up. Something isn't right about all these deaths, and I'm very afraid for Trey. I planned to investigate the lives of each of these kids, Adam, every one of them, but—well, you know that I can't, and you know why I didn't say anything, especially if you've read the note.

"And now, today, I find out that I will be facing a battle of a different kind, a battle that I may not win this time, Adam. I can't die knowing that Trey or even Bekah, if she attends HSU, could be in danger. So, I'm sorry that I couldn't come out and tell you about it. I had to make it appear that the issue was dead for your safety and the kids' safety. I know there's something wrong. Innocence wouldn't require anonymous informants or threatening notes. I have done what I can do; I hope that you can do the rest. Ask Alex for help, she has an inside connection to the school, but be discreet. I fear that the warnings weren't idle threats. Everything I've gathered is in a safety deposit box. You'll find all of the information on my desk in my planner including the key."

He stopped and looked to see if there was more, then turned back to the beginning of the entry to reread it silently. When he looked up, Alex was holding a small piece of paper toward him.

"This fell out of the book," she said her voice strangely quiet. Her eyes were wide and her complexion pale.

Adam set the journal on the table and took the post card-sized paper from Alex. It took Adam all of five seconds to read the note before he crumpled it in his hand with rage. It read:

Final warning, Bitch. We know who your kids are.

139

CHAPTER FOURTEEN

Adam walked through the double doors of the athletic administration building. It was a place on the HSU campus with which he was very familiar. They'd debated whether or not to make a meeting with the athletic director. Megan had done the same thing, and she'd described it as a dead end. What if the meeting alerted whoever was behind the threats? But they had very little else to go on other than the fact that now six of the students that had died, including Jonesy, were athletes. That statistic seemed too coincidental to ignore, and because it hit too close to home with both Trey and Bekah. He couldn't ignore it.

It had been a good thing Alex had been with him when he read the journal, or he would have stormed into Yamane's office demanding blood whether he was involved or not. She'd been able to talk him down with some common sense.

"Adam, you have to live business as usual. You don't have any proof of anything yet," she'd said. She'd placed a hand on his arm.

Her touch alone drew him back into the room with her.

He'd nodded. "You're right."

"We've only got Megan's preliminary work to go on and no legitimate proof of anything. The only thing we have on our side, right now, is if there is someone who might be behind the deaths—or these threats—they believe you don't know about it."

He'd nodded and took deep breaths to regain his composure.

After a discussion with Alex, they concluded if Milton was involved in something that was risking students' lives or behind the threats against Megan, it didn't fit. Milton had too much to lose, didn't he? But Adam wasn't going to be foolish either. His visit to Milton couldn't raise any red flags, at least he hoped it wouldn't. He couldn't put his kids or Alex at risk.

The main entrance to the athletic offices had updated since his college days and looked modern and urban. The school colors, green and blue, were painted on the concrete floor in waves from wall to wall. Retro black furniture provided seating and study space for students. Larger than life Andy Warhol style prints hung on all available wall space, depicting cartoon athletes in various sports poses. The wall near the elevators and stairs adjacent to the reception desk housed a huge trophy case. There would be trophies and pictures from yester-year providing historical insight to Hawai'i State's athletic program; his Rose Bowl team would be in the case if he went over and looked.

His footsteps echoed across the space as he approached the reception desk. A young woman had glanced up at him as he'd walked through the doors. When he stopped at the desk, and she didn't look up from her book, Adam cleared his throat. "Hello?"

The girl looked up at him, her expression bored. "Can I help you?" She didn't smile and snapped her gum.

"I have an appointment with Director Yamane."

She looked back at her textbook as she said, "Take the elevator to the third floor, turn left, and walk to the end of the hall."

"Thanks." Adam walked away. Once in Milton Yamane's office

reception area he checked in with his assistant and waited.

The green and blue carpet was decorated with the school crest. The wood paneled walls adorned with portraits of former athletic directors, Milton's, the most recent and last portrait in the ascending line. His small face smiled, one side of his smile higher than the other as if he knew something that you didn't. His small dark eyes were slanted and turned up with his smile. Despite his age, his black hair was still dark and combed to the side, a traditional style. Adam had always respected Milton, though never been able to feel as though he really knew the reserved man.

"Adam Kāne!" Milton's slightly nasal voice exclaimed. "What a pleasant surprise. It's been too long."

Adam smiled as he took Milton's extended hand. The small man had to look up, and Adam reached to shake his hand. Just as he remembered, Milton's handshake was soft. "Glad you had the time to see me."

"Come in," Milton said and stepped back to allow him to enter his office. "Garrett, please hold my calls," Adam heard Milton direct his assistant before he closed the door.

Adam noticed Milton's private office looked very similar to the outer office where his secretary greeted his guests. Aside from the large wood desk and bookcases that lined the wall and the large picture window which afforded a view of the athletic complex, the rest was wood paneled with a school crest on the green and blue carpet.

"Have a seat," Milton pointed at the brown leather wingback chairs in front of his desk. He walked around his desk and sat down. Then his smile faded, and a look of regret passed his features. "How are you doing, Adam?"

"Fine, Milton. Thanks for asking," Adam sat, drawing up his pant legs as he did. "Making it day-to-day." He didn't feel like expounding about his grief process with other man. While they had a connection due to Adam's involvement in the program, the boosters and his donations, it wasn't like he spent a lot of time in

Milton's company.

"Sandy and I were crushed about Megan. We're so sorry for your loss."

Adam nodded. "I appreciate that, though, if you don't mind, I came in to talk with you about the football program."

"Right. Right," Milton answered. "Are you ready to come back to the president seat for the football boosters? It hasn't been the same without you. We'd love to have you back."

Adam smiled and shook his head at the mention of the post he resigned when he learned of Megan's re-diagnosis. "No. No. I like the fact that I can come to the games and enjoy them, not have to work at them. Especially now that Trey is playing."

Milton laughed. "And your boy has been doing so well. You must be proud!"

"Of course." Adam leaned forward. "That is what brought me in, actually. Jonesy's passing is an awful tragedy, and as a parent, I am more than a little concerned. With Trey taking over as QB1, I just wanted to check in with you."

Milton nodded and sat back in his chair. "What are you worried about?"

"Jonesy. I would like to know if his death was in any way related to the program."

Milton smiled, one of those condescending smiles where his brows drew up on his forehead and a slight shake of his head. "Now, Adam, you know that's an outlandish question."

"Is it?" He leaned back in the chair.

"How can you say that? Coach Ferris is excellent. He runs a clean program and follows the rules."

"So we're told."

Milton's eyes narrowed.

Adam knew he wasn't engendering any good will with the athletic director, but he had to play up the concerned parent and the concerned donor. Highly attuned to Milton's nonverbal cues, Adam found it was essential tool in negotiations. Milton was annoyed with him, but not panicked. He pressed. "Look Milton, I have given a lot of money to this program. A lot."

"And we are extremely grateful."

"I want to know that one," Adam held up a finger with each point, "my son is safe, and two, my name is safe."

"Why would you think otherwise?" Milton asked, his arms folded on the desktop.

"Come now, Milton." It was Adam's turn to be patronizing. "We are not children. You and I understand the inner working of the machine. Money brings in more money. Scandal dries that well up quickly."

"Is this a threat, Adam? Are you threatening to remove your money?"

"Not a threat, Milton. Just a fact. If there is so much a whisper of scandal attached to this program, I will remove both of my children—I know both are good enough and smart enough to transfer to top-rated institutions—and all of the money I earmarked to donate will be off the table for HSU and HSU athletics." Adam put an ankle on his knee. "And I don't have to remind you, my influence has a very big reach. People ask me my plans consistently."

Milton swallowed. It was subtle, but Adam recognized the tell. The other man was nervous. "If you don't mind my asking, why would you think there's anything to be worried about?"

The hair on the back of Adam's neck rose. Milton was fishing. Adam wasn't sure if he should throw some bait. "No reason specifically, but certainly a concern when a young man in the prime of his life collapses on an athletic field. What did the coroner report?"

"Heart."

"A football player—like Trey. I also remember the untimely death of a young swimmer a year or so ago."

"Donna Delco. Suicide," Milton said and leaned back again.

"My daughter is a swimmer."

Milton nodded. "You know, Megan came to see me about Donna's death."

Adam's nerves flared with awareness. Unsure, he thought it might be strange if it seemed she hadn't shared. "I think I remember her mentioning it in passing. She'd been working on a human-interest piece for the Hawaiian Sun."

"That's right. I remember that." Milton stopped a moment and then said, "I remember I told her that this campus is a small city, with over thirty-thousand students alone, not to mention faculty, staff, and administration. In a population of that size, death, unfortunately isn't uncommon. And suicide on college campuses where alcohol is used to the extreme, isn't an anomaly."

Adam nodded, remembering a night many years ago when he drank too much after being victorious on the football field. In his mind's eye he recalled a moonlit room and a woman. That experience certainly hadn't been about suicide, but alcohol had been the fuel for reckless decision making. He shook his head to focus.

Milton leaned forward again, the creaking chair cacophonous. "I see my explanation doesn't assuage your concerns."

"My concerns are for my kids."

"And mine," Milton stated. "When Megan brought me her statistics–"

"What statistics?" Adam asked, hoping he appeared to be unaware. "Megan rarely talked about articles when she was in the research phase. I only got to read them when she was done."

Milton waved his hand as if dismissing the information, he shared, "I don't remember it off hand, but it was enough for me to work with our department. We instituted a Healthy Athletes course that all HSU athletes must take as part of their scholarship requirements. It covers healthy living in general, alcohol and drug abuse, as well as safer sex. As a sophomore, Trey has already taken it. Bekah is probably set to take it this later this year if she's not in it this semester."

"I will have to ask them about it."

"Please do. I'm pretty proud of it, and the NCAA took notice. There is talk of instituting a similar program nationwide even though several other schools have followed our trend," he paused. "I don't know if that alleviates your fears, Adam, but know that from one parent to another, we are trying to address the issues."

"That is comforting." Adam stood, hopeful he had done what he needed. "Thank you for speaking with me today, Milton."

The athletic director mirrored him and offered his hand.

Adam shook it and they walked to the door.

"Did you ever get to read Megan's article about Donna? I'd love to see it."

"I didn't," Adam said. "She found out about the cancer while she'd been working on it. Her research—her writing—everything stopped to fight that battle."

Milton looked sorrowful and nodded. "I'm sorry to hear it."

"Yes. Me too."

Adam entered the back stairwell of the social sciences building. He remembered it well having taken a few political science courses there. But he hadn't been in a rush as he was today. He took the concrete steps several at a time.

Slow down, he told himself.

His blood rushed with excitement to see Alex, to tell her what he thought about the meeting. He found her office door in a narrow hallway surrounded by other doors of professors in the Women's Studies department and knocked. It went without an answer. There was a schedule on the door, surrounded by other clippings that pertained to her discipline. Adam read the schedule and realized she was teaching. A quick look at his watch, he decided he could catch her after class and walked up another flight of steps.

Most of the doors were closed, but a few were left open, and the monotone drawl of lecturers escaped into the corridor. Adam located the classroom where Alex was teaching and, deciding that he wouldn't disrupt the class should he enter, walked into the room quietly. He sat down. Students glanced at him, but then returned to their small group discussions.

Alex's back was to him as she walked the room and spoke with undergraduates. When she turned and caught sight of him, the surprise put a stunning smile on her face that brightened her green eyes. The air was knocked out of his lungs. At forty-seven, a widower, Adam didn't think he would ever again experience the excitement he had felt as a young man regarding the opposite sex. Hell, he hadn't thought he would ever be without Megan. The thought of getting back out there, dating, finding himself attracted to another woman had seemed impossible. And now he was looking at a woman he'd known for years, feeling like a schoolboy. He needed to pull himself together. He didn't know what his feelings meant, and he didn't want to ruin anything between them. He'd made a promise that nothing would tear them apart again.

"Be sure to check in with me by next week on your topic if you're having difficulty narrowing it down. That's it for today," Adam heard her say. "Have a great weekend."

Students moved erupting sound in the room, but then Alex was surrounded by several students with questions. Adam got to observe her. She actively listened to each student, her focus on the speaker clear. Adam noticed again how beautiful she was. It surprised him how he'd been blind to it. Or maybe he hadn't. The thought startled him.

Alex disengaged from the group as they left. "Thanks for waiting. What a nice surprise."

"I was on campus."

"Did you see him already?" Her voice was low.

Adam thought is sounded erotic, and his pulse quickened. "Maybe we could talk somewhere else?"

"My office?"

"An early dinner?" he asked.

She looked at her watch. "Sure," she answered. "Come with me to my office to double check that I don't have any students waiting, and I'll get my things."

Adam liked the ease with which they moved around one another now. He called Emma while he waited for Alex to finished up with a student who'd been waiting. An hour later, they were nestled in a booth at Tino's Pizzeria. The jukebox was playing *Nightbird* by Kalapana, and a patron at the bar was attempting to outdo Mackey Feary with his rendition. Adam had just finished relaying the conversation he'd had with Milton Yamane when the waitress appeared.

"Amber ales for each of you, and Tino said to let you know that your pizza would be out in about twenty," the large Polynesian woman with Hawaiian features said.

"Mahalo, Nani," Alex said. "Tell Tino that he needs to pay you more."

Nani laughed. "Eh, I tell him that every night, but you know husbands." She was still laughing as she walked away.

"So, you weren't convinced?" Alex returned to the conversation about the athletic director.

"I don't know. My gut tells me that Megan was on to something. Milton got nervous, but it wasn't about Megan—it was about the money. When he brought up Megan, I don't know if it was me filling in blanks, or something else. The threats to Megan alone tell us she was onto something, but I'm not sure Milton was a part of it. I don't know what to think." Adam lowered his head and ran a hand over the back of his neck. He looked up. "That was all we had to go on. What if I inadvertently hurt my kids?"

Alex reached out and covered one of his hands with both of hers. "You can't think that way. You were careful. What did Emma say?"

"She's going to see what she can find out about each of the

students who died. Retrace Megan's steps."

"That makes me nervous," Alex said.

Adam raised an eyebrow.

"Megan got threats just for doing the research, Adam."

"We could give her what's in the safety deposit box."

"Think it's being watched?"

He shrugged. "So, we do nothing? Nothing is possibly getting athletes killed. Trey and Bekah."

Alex nodded. "Are you going to tell them?" She took a sip of her beer, a foam mustache left behind on her lip.

Adam suppressed the urge to kiss it away at the same time Alex licked it away with her tongue. Something familiar tugged at him. That hazy memory. He pictured the moonlit room, the party, but it was like it had been cut from his consciousness. What was it? He reached for it conjured a pair of green eyes so much like Alex's. Probably what he wanted to see.

He shook his head, almost absently as he pondered the direction of his thoughts. He forced himself to remember her question. "I don't think it would serve any purpose at this point other than to selfishly make *me* feel better."

"I guess we can always keep an eye on them." Her brow furrowed between her eyes.

He realized that she was far more worried about the situation than she was letting on. As he took a sip of his beer and studied Alex again over his glass. He didn't want her to worry, so he reached across the lacquered tabletop to lay his hand on hers.

Her green eyes jumped to his.

A jolt of electricity buzzed his insides.

She turned her hand over, their palms connected.

The buzzing electricity became and electric shock at the base of his spine. "We'll figure this out, Alex. Together. I don't want you to worry," he said.

Nani reappeared with the pizza; a thin crust covered with everything under the sun.

Alex removed her hand from his to make way for the pie.

Adam moved back as Nani placed their dinner in front of them.

Alex pulled a steaming slice from the pan and set it on her plate. "I guess all we can do now is wait. And eat." She took a bite of the slice.

Adam gulped, suddenly very hungry. He took a sip of his beer. *Platonic, Adam. Don't fuck this up.*

CHAPTER FIFTEEN

Diane threw her head back and screamed with her release. She straightened, her chest heaving after her climax as her blonde hair settled around her face, and she collapsed against her lover's chest, still straddling him. The linoleum floor of the classroom was cold against her knees. She moaned, a sound like the purr of a contented cat. "God, that was incredible."

He grunted in response. "I like being called god."

She giggled. "Maybe you'd like to come back to my place? It would be more comfortable." She leaned up on her hands to look at the man with whom she'd just had sex. He was beautiful, older, accomplished, intelligent. The kind of man with whom she'd always imagined for herself. His eyes, which reminded her of the color of the lake on a rainy day outside her family's home in Vermont, were a dark now, almost black. "I can call you 'god' all night long."

"That sounds good," he answered. "You leave first, and I will follow you in, say, twenty minutes?"

"It's got to be—what—around nine pm? Who's going to see us? We could go together."

"Too risky."

"We won't get caught. We've been very careful." Diane leaned in and kissed him full on the mouth hoping to be persuasive. When she came up for air, she was hot all over, wet, and ready again.

"Go. I will be there in an hour."

"You said twenty minutes." She pouted, hoping she'd convince him to do it her way. She rocked her hips back and forth against him wanting so much for him to move inside her once again.

"I need to go get some more condoms," he whispered in her ear, "besides, I'm not eighteen anymore. I need some time to recover." He grasped her hips and eased her off of him so he could get up off the floor.

Diane watched him pull up his black pants and buckle his belt. He left the room to walk across the hall to the bathroom, she assumed to dispose of the condom they'd used. A few seconds later, he returned and put on his black long-sleeved shirt. She admired the light hair on his chest and the trail that disappeared beneath his pants. She stood and pulled down her dress and adjusted her panties sticky from her arousal.

"One hour. That's all you get." She stepped close to him and kissed him. "It will be hard enough to wait that long."

"Don't worry. I'll be right behind you. And then I'll make you call me 'god' all night long." He leaned down, bit her lower lip and nuzzled her on the cheek. "Go." He patted her ass as he pushed her toward the door.

Diane left the room and walked down the sterile white hall to what she used as her office. She placed a few things to read through and some papers she needed to correct in her backpack, slung one strap over her shoulder and locked the door as she left.

When she stepped from the building, the darkness was

pervasive. She was glad that she didn't live very far from campus, only a mile or so, an easy walking distance. She set off toward home, a small studio apartment that she rented. It was the basement of a couple's house though she had her own entrance.

She loved Hawai'i and was glad she'd chosen HSU to complete her PhD. It was the premier biology research university in the nation, at the cutting edge of scientific discovery, and she was working with Dr. David Bennett. How lucky could one girl get? Though she missed her family, the experience of working at HSU was going to prove invaluable in more ways than one. She'd be able to work any place she wanted when she was finished.

Diane could hear the foot falls of her feet as she walked a steady rhythm that seemed to match her heartbeat. Everything was going perfectly. Her research was almost complete, her dissertation started. She couldn't wait to invite her lover back to Vermont for Christmas to meet her family. She would do it tonight, she decided.

She noticed the lack of lights on the upcoming stretch of the road and had never realized it before. Diane felt the hairs along her arms stand and a chill scraped its way along her back. "Stop it," she told herself aloud. "There's nothing to worry about." But something didn't feel right. She looked over her shoulder and saw nothing but the night and a deserted road. She quickened her pace, her senses warning her she needed to get to her apartment.

"Half a mile," she continued aloud as though the sound of her voice might frighten the unknown, the unpredictable in the dark. Diane glanced over her shoulder again, but she should have concentrated on what was in front of her because she collided with something, knocking her backward off her feet.

Dazed, she looked up to see a looming shadow, and as it stepped forward, she smiled. "You scared me." She laughed and clutched a hand against her chest. She held her hand out for help up, but confusion followed as she looked into the familiar face who didn't offer any assistance. Suddenly, Diane felt overwhelming fear take her. "What's wrong?"

A scream built from her center, but before she could release her primal fear, her attacker was on her. He covered her mouth with his gloved hand, banged her head into the unforgiving concrete, and began stabbing with the knife he held. Diane kicked and tried to push against him with her hands. He adjusted so that his knees pinned her arms. She felt as though she were being crushed. She looked up, at the face of someone she knew, her assailant, whose hand was clamped over her mouth and asked beneath his hand, "Why?"

He answered with a slice across her neck.

Diane's last thought was that of the lake behind her home in Vermont, and it was raining.

Stanton Thom sat up in bed, the night around him stifling. The humidity closed in around him and he clutched at his chest, gulping for air. Was he having a heart attack? His heartbeat echoed in his ears. The rustle of the palm trees outside his bedroom swaying in the trade winds grazed the screen. The late-night phone conversation replaying over and over in his mind, in his dreams: *Someone is poking around.*

"What are you talking about?" he'd asked Dr. Black. It was out of the ordinary to have the voice call him instead of the other way around.

"Emma West has accessed student records at Alexander library. I'll allow you six guesses who the students are."

"Who is Emma West?" Stanton had asked sinking down into his office chair. His gaze shifted around the office as though eyes were watching his every move. He'd swiveled in his chair and looked at his reflection in the now dark window.

"Emma West is a reporter for the *Hawaiian Sun*. West is her married name."

"And her maiden name?" Stanton had asked. He was afraid he already knew.

"Kāne."

"Dear God. She's Megan Kāne's daughter."

"And our friend Adam Kāne made a visit to HSU's athletic director today."

"You said there was nothing to worry about!" Stanton had said. His voice had risen an octave, his reflection stiff with tension. It was a strange sight-seeing the panic in the window's image, as though he were two separate entities.

"You have nothing to worry about regarding the Kānes. I have that all under control. However, I do need you to make sure your administrative staff is reigned in, Stanton. I've come too far to have to turn around now."

"Is that a threat?" Stanton had asked.

"I'll leave that to your interpretation," Dr. Black had said, and then hung up.

Now, the pressure on his chest seemed to ease. Stanton swung his feet over his side of his bed and leaned his elbows on his knees, his head in his hands. He took deep breaths and tried to gain control of his rapid heart rate. He had a foreboding feeling that the tenuous project he'd hoped to propel him into the governor's seat was about to unravel. Someone, like Adam Kāne or Emma West, was going to pull at the loose string and destroy everything that he had worked so hard to control, to gain.

If he were a man of vision, Stanton would mobilize for the possibility of a threat, but he wasn't. He was a pawn, a participant in a scheme concocted by someone much smarter and far more motivated than him. Besides, if he decided to react defensively, it might draw unwanted attention, and then goodbye governorship anyway.

Yes, that's it. You're overreacting, he thought to himself straightening his shoulders. *Trust Dr. Black.*

Stanton would visit Yamane like directed. That was it. He had to make sure everything was contained from his end. *Keep it together, Thom. A governor keeps a cool head in the face of adversity*, he thought.

"Stanton?" His wife's voice interrupted his internal pep-talk. "Are you alright? Did you have a nightmare?"

"A nightmare," he paused. "Yes, a nightmare."

Stanton laid back down on his side of the mattress and closed his eyes to welcome sleep. He dreamed about millions of butterflies demolishing the HSU campus.

CHAPTER SIXTEEN

Adam stepped from the glass-block shower and wrapped an ivory towel around his waist. He turned down the radio and wiped steam on the mirror away with a hand towel before slathering his face with billowy shaving cream. Thinking about what Megan had stumbled upon, Adam could feel it was something as sharp the razor he was using to shave.

The problem was that he didn't have any clue as to what he was looking for, and he knew he was in way over his head. Why were an inordinate number of student athletes dying from seemingly natural causes? Seventy-five percent of the deaths on that campus were student athletes; it wasn't a wonder Megan's investigative radar had been spinning. The question was why them? Was someone killing them to cover up a larger conspiracy? Which made him wonder if it was a conspiracy, what was its origin and how far did it reach?

With two kids in HSU's athletic program, panic tightened around his chest. The only option he had to protect them was pulling them out of school which was impossible. Trey was in the perfect position as the starting quarterback—something he'd been working hard to achieve. Bekah could transfer, but not in the middle of her season. It wasn't fair to ask them to transfer without any proof. Adam's fears were operating on a hunch and a tentatively provable one at best. He'd wait to make decisions about the kids after Emma did some digging.

The bumper music to the news played on the radio drawing Adam out of his thoughts followed by the robust voice of the radio personality. "Good morning, Honolulu. It's six thirty and your traffic report is in three minutes and counting. But first, in local news, the body of a Hawai'i State University doctoral candidate was discovered early this Monday morning a few hundred feet from the apartment where she lived."

Adam stopped shaving, his head tipped to the left, the razor pressed to his jaw. He looked at the radio through the mirror as though it were alive and speaking to him.

"Police suspect based on time of death that she was walking home from campus late last night when she was attacked, but they have no information to report at this time as to possible suspects. No further details have been released, but police promise to be forthcoming as new information is available. This is the second death of an HSU student this fall, the first being the late quarterback for the Hurricanes, Jonsey Miles.

"In other news," the female voice continued, but Adam had stopped listening.

He looked at his reflection. He'd cut himself. The bright red blood from the nick on his cheek dribbled down his neck. He unraveled some toilet paper to wipe at the cut. *Another death at HSU? A murder?* A tingle of dread moved through him like a wave across the sea. He finished his bathroom routine and got dressed for work. After grabbing his car keys from the dish in the kitchen, he headed out the door. As he turned the ignition to start the car, his cell phone rang. It was Alex.

"Hi." He switched it to hands free and backed out of the driveway.

"Adam? Did you hear?" Alex asked through the phone.

His heart reeled at the sound of her voice. "I'm assuming you are talking about the murder headline this morning. Yes." He checked both directions and drove the car out into the street.

"Have you heard from Emma yet?" she asked.

"Nothing specific. She said she's just doing some digging on the deaths."

"Do you think this murder is related to the others?" Alex asked.

"Based on the report, it doesn't appear to be. But it sure seems strange." He turned the car toward town and drove down the quiet road lined with trees and green vegetation. Bright yellow, red, and pink blossoms splashed the trees with color. The tranquility of the scenery seemed incongruous with the tumultuous murder of a young woman.

"I spoke with Jack this morning. She was a student in his department at the school."

"Jack?" He hated the surge of jealousy filling his lungs, and he had a horrible feeling he knew where her line of thinking was headed. He didn't want to spend time in the company of Jolly Giant Jack, not when the other man was making passes at Alex.

"We could talk to him."

Adam rolled his eyes.

"He might be able to point us in the right direction. We might be able to find out if she's connected to the others in anyway?"

"Do you trust him?" Adam asked.

"Of course. Why wouldn't I?"

"If you think it's a good idea." He wasn't but was willing to trust her. He drove onto the freeway and slowed for traffic. "When? I have some free time for lunch, but I'm booked for most the rest of the day with meetings."

"I'll see if I can set something up and let you know."

Adam's chest constricted with worry. "Alex?"

"Yes?"

"Please be careful."

She was silent a moment, and then replied. "I will."

Later, that evening, ensconced at home with some take out from a Korean BBQ place, Adam still hadn't quieted the thoughts that had plagued him for most of the day. While focus was imperative during his meetings, his mind was free to wander as he drove from job sites, to meetings, to the office, to home. Aside from work there were three things on his mind: Megan's research, the kids, and Alex. All of which made him feel powerless.

The anniversary of Megan's death was less than a week away, November fourth. Three months ago, he could barely pull himself out of bed because he'd been mucking about in the mire of his depression. Now, he had another woman on his mind, and what confused him was that it was Alex. Alex who he'd spent so much time dogging, purposefully trying to ensnare in arguments. Alex who he'd tried to chase out of his life because she had been such a big part of Megan's. Alex, the one he blamed for the betrayal. But there was a nagging feeling sitting at the base of his brain pressing buttons to catch his attention: *what if he'd blamed Alex because he'd been trying to push her away?*

Recalling his memory about that night on the beach—he'd wanted to kiss her. Him. He'd been attracted to her enough to forget he was dating Megan. Maybe it had scared him? Maybe he'd been the asshole to keep her at arm's length? But the betrayal—Megan's betrayal? It had been easy to blame Alex rather than assign Megan responsibility.

Deciding that he was wasting time mulling it over, Adam retrieved Megan's journal to put his thoughts to productive use. Maybe she'd left him another clue, something he could use to protect his kids.

> *Dear Adam... I sure miss you. You haven't been home before seven every night this week. The kids miss you, too.*

Dear Adam... Congratulations on your contract for the Honolulu High Rise. You worked hard on it! I have been trying to deal with things on the home front, I know how busy you are and that you are working hard for us. Thank God for Alex, she's been such a life saver.

His company had remained small up until the birth of Bekah. He'd been content to work on private residences and remodels, but his aspirations had been grander. Adam had wanted to be a big contractor, a major player in the state. Megan supported that dream, but neither of them had calculated the familial risks.

After Bekah was born, Adam's goals for success meant longer hours, which meant more time away. He and Megan had both decided it was the right choice for their family. It allowed her to stay home with the kids. It provided for her freelance work. Adam wouldn't have changed the course of his professional life, but in hindsight, he would have done more to nurture his wife and kids.

Dear Adam... I'm so sorry about last night. I jumped the gun and have been on edge, so you took the brunt of my stress. I don't mean to make excuses, but the stress of moving, and I think having three little ones makes a mother a tiny bit insane. Emma's a big help, but nothing compares to the support of you.

Adam remembered that night.

He walked into the house well after nine one evening. He'd spent most of his day in meetings between negotiations and hiring a new project manager, he hadn't had time to complete a bid proposal for a new shopping complex that bid the following afternoon. Calling home to Megan had slipped his mind. Adam had a feeling he was walking into a firestorm because she hadn't checked in with him either.

All the lights except the kitchen and hall were extinguished. Adam maneuvered his way through a maze of boxes that Megan was in the process of unpacking and set his bag on the kitchen counter, then opened the fridge in search of a bite to eat since he'd skipped dinner and worked straight through. Surprised Megan hadn't volleyed her first shots at him, Adam pulled out some cold ham for a sandwich. He closed the refrigerator door to find Megan on the other side, leaning against the wall.

She looked a mess, not her usually impeccable self. Her blonde hair pulled back in a lopsided bun and strands of hair wisping about her face. She wore a pair of tattered chino shorts, so worn that strings hung from the hem, and Adam recognized the green HSU tee shirt that had been his in college which Megan swam inside. Her cheeks were flush, her lips dawn in a taut line, and arms crossed over her chest. Even though Adam knew she was pissed, he couldn't help but smile.

"What?"

"You look sexy. Good enough to eat. Maybe I should skip the sandwich." Adam motioned to the food on the counter. He leaned toward her, still holding onto the fridge door handles.

"Don't think you can charm your way out of this one."

He straightened, defenses up, and moved to the counter, then leaned against it subtly mimicking her body language with his own. It was a negotiation ploy to make the opponent think you're just like them. He was ready for the skirmish and raised an eyebrow in challenge.

"Oh," she breathed. "You can't act like you don't know why I'm angry."

"I know. I didn't call."

She moved into the kitchen and leaned against the refrigerator opposite him. "Adam, you haven't been home before seven at all this week! I've been dealing with these kids all by myself. Alex has come over to help me out a few times, but I don't want to rely on Alex. I want to rely on you. And I never have time to write anymore."

162

"There it is," he said. "It really always comes down to you doesn't it."

"What the hell is that supposed to mean?"

"Megan, you wanted to be a stay-at-home mom."

"Yes, I did. But I also chose to work from home too. What do you think my writing is?"

"It isn't bringing in a steady income."

"It's all about the money then? Who brings in the most?"

"No. But the fact of the matter remains that I'm bringing in the steady income so that our family can survive, and if I have to work until the wee hours of the morning to do that so you and the kids are taken care of, then we'll have to suck it up won't we."

"I need time for myself too, Adam. I need time to step away from the kids and this house."

"Alex has obviously allowed you time to do that," he countered.

He had the impression that she was going to explode when she turned in a circle not sure of which direction to walk. She topped at the sink her back to him. "That's not what I'm talking about, and you know it."

"No? I hear you tell me that you are pissed that I'm not home when you want me to be home, doing what you want me to do, so that you can have quiet time for yourself. Sounds a bit self-centered, doesn't it?" he said.

"You're being a jerk. You know I didn't mean it like that."

"You didn't? Truly? Because it sure sounded that way to me." Adam watched her turn, lean against the sink with her arms crossed over her chest and level an angry stare at him. He continued adding fuel to the flames. "Maybe I should have called to let you know I would be late, but I'm doing what I have to do to make the business successful so that you and the kids don't have to worry about where the groceries come from or how to pay the electric bill." He turned to the counter and began to make himself a sandwich. "And if I remember correctly, you weren't complaining when we bought this house or the car in the garage."

"You're really going to make this about money?" Her tone was incredulous.

"That's what it comes down to, isn't it?"

She stalked from kitchen without a word. He wasn't sure if he won the argument, but he slept on the couch. He hadn't wanted to see her pout, and he was sure that because she'd walked away from the fight, she wasn't ready to make up. Besides, he ended up working into the early hours of the morning anyway.

When Megan, still angry with him, had woken him up the next morning for work, he'd promised to make sure he called when he would be late, but life went on and work never stopped. He'd fallen back into the same routine, even if he'd made more of an effort.

Dear Adam... Emma asked me today why Daddy never seems to hear her. It broke my heart, and I couldn't help but think of you and your own father. I'd always realized that marriage and parenting would be difficult, but when you hear a question like that from your child, I wasn't prepared for the sadness.

Dear Adam... There are so many times, more that I care to count or admit to, when I lose my cool with the kids. I'm like a rubber band. They pull and pull so I give and give until I have no give left, so I snap. I'm so thankful that I have Alex right now to turn to. Wonderful Aunt Alex who has saved my butt on a number of occasions.

Adam closed the journal and cleaned the kitchen before going upstairs to sleep. Reading about this phase of their marriage made him tired. It weighed on his heart, all the ways he could have— should have—done things better and hadn't. Maybe he hadn't had the tools he needed to be better, his focus on providing for his family. Alex's words surfaced in his mind: *If men don't choose the same profession as their father, who in most cases chose that profession because of his father, they direct themselves toward careers that can offer the most monetary reward...* Maybe he could have changed the outcome, but now he couldn't. Now, he didn't need to.

Adam had a pit lodged in his gut as if he'd swallowed a stone. Megan's words, the same she'd used to try and reason with him carried such a different meaning now. If she'd stood in front of him now, arguing that she needed more of him at home, he would have listened and acted. It was as though his pride and arrogance as a younger man made him untouchable, making him deaf to her words.

Adam pondered the necessity of the difference between him then and now. Then he'd needed to be risky, a little arrogant, and prideful to survive in his business, to provide for his family—the endgame being *what* he could provide them. Now, as an older man, almost having lived half of a century, over ten years removed from that man of his youth, he recognized the importance of *how* a man provides for his *ohana*, the support that he *gives*, the love with which he *devotes* to his wife and children.

Adam was thankful he'd had a chance to love Megan as he was supposed to love her beyond the pride of his youth. He was thankful that despite all that, Megan had been able to turn to Alex for support. And yet, that support by Alex had led to a betrayal so deep Adam said some of the worse things he'd ever said to anyone.

Adam sighed. He knew he'd apologized for it. He knew Alex had forgiven him. It just was impossible to forgive himself.

CHAPTER SEVENTEEN

D etective Mana Lopes donned a green surgical gown and matching green hat before he entered the morgue. As he pushed through the heavy metal doors with his back and pulled on latex gloves, the only thing on his mind was the Diane Gomes case and solving her murder. He was hopeful the coroner would be able to give him some details to open flood gates on the case before the autopsy—something to start on while waiting for the coroner's final report.

The fetid stench of chemicals mixed with cleanser and death was enough to send rookies out to spew the contents of their stomachs, but Mana was no rookie. He'd been through the drill so many times it was as natural to him as eating breakfast. Except that homicide was never palatable to him. He had the need to see justice for each John and Jane that lay cold on the coroner's stainless-steel table.

Mana had a reputation to uphold as a homicide detective. He was hard-nosed, hard-headed, and hard to read. His no-nonsense way frightened the newbies which didn't bother him. It was his job to make the bastard's trial in court a cakewalk for the prosecuting attorney. Therefore, he did his job right the first time—the only time. On his watch, Mana's team had solved every case assigned to them. He planned to keep it that way.

The harsh light that bathed the blue and white tiled room was blinding, though Mana didn't particularly notice. His focus was on the body of a female victim that had been discovered the previous morning. The coroner was usually backlogged for weeks with autopsies, but with a case such as this one, the body was priority.

"Morning Lopes," Dwight Connolly, the chief county coroner greeted him. Mana wasn't surprised to see the short, balding man there that morning, his thick horn-rimmed glasses covering his twitchy blue eyes. The fact that the Gomes case was a high-profile case made it imperative for Connolly to be involved. In other cases, and on routine autopsies it was common for other members of the coroner's team to do the work.

Mana skipped the usual salutations and got right to the point. "Tell me about this Jane," he said. He made it a point to never refer to the victims by their names when he knew them, as a rule. He didn't want to get too personally involved. He didn't want to lose his objectivity. He'd seen too many detectives allow a case to get in too deep and subsequently they lost their edge.

"Twenty-five-year-old female," Dr. Connolly began telling Mana everything he already knew. The glare of the lamp on the naked body made her form appear yellow gray under the harsh light, and the grisly stab wounds, fifteen of them to her torso were enough to cause a shudder in a less experienced cop or maybe a cop with a heart. She had yet to receive the tell-tale incision of the autopsy, but the gory slice across her neck was brutal.

"Initial evidence collected from the vic is trace under her nails, several foreign pubic hairs mixed with her own, and some fibers in her hair."

"So, she had sex before she was murdered?" Mana asked.

"No semen collected from her pelvic exam though the hairs

might indicate a sexual partner. In that case, a condom was probably used. I did however find vaginal tearing and the inside of her vagina looks like hamburger. My initial guess is that the perp raped her with the knife postmortem. No pooling blood."

Mana didn't wince. However as he did with each of his cases, he could feel the imaginary thermometer he attached to each case dip below freezing. No emotion, his motto, was crucial. It was essential for a clearer thought process. He was used to the distorted and unnatural in his line of work, but the disgust never went away. It made sense why many cops were alcoholics. The spirits had to chase away the demons of the work.

"I suspect when I open her up, I'm going to find a lot of internal damage I didn't see with the pelvic," Dr. Connolly added.

"Multiple stab wounds." Mana leaned toward the body for a closer look, but he kept his arms crossed. "Can you tell me more about those?"

"Fifteen to the upper torso, none are defensive. She might have been tied except that there aren't any contusions or burns typically seen with rope. There was some bruising on her forearms," he pointed to deep reddish-purple marks along the tops of her arm, "but without pattern or distinction of, say, a hand.

"The stab wounds are variable at an inch to an inch and a half in width depending on the degree of incision. My guess is that the perp was sitting on top of her and stabbing hence the different angles and sizes of some of the wounds. The cut across her neck was what killed her. Time of death approximately between nine and midnight. The perp hit the jugular on her left side and sliced toward the right. The depth lessens in degree in that direction."

"So, hypothetically, if the perp was sitting on her, that would make him left-handed?"

"Hypothetically."

"So multiple stab wounds, the slice across the neck caused the death, and she was raped with a foreign object postmortem." Mana checked his notes.

"Crime of passion, perhaps? Someone was very angry. Maybe a stalker who saw her get busy with a boyfriend?" Dr. Connelly theorized.

"Or maybe someone wanted it to look that way," Mana countered. "You sent all of the evidence to trace?"

"Sent a runner this morning."

"Thanks Doc. You know how to reach me," Mana stated, turned and left the room.

Connolly watched the large man leave, the shiny metal double door hydraulics hissing shut behind him. Mana Lopes never failed to intimidate him. Not only was his physical stature impressive, but his brain never stopped working. Connolly was struck with how detached Lopes was and shivered as a chill raced along his spine.

"Dr. Connolly," the nasal voice of his secretary sounded over the intercom, "You have a call on line one."

Dwight walked over to the phone connected to wall by the door exited by Officer Lopes and pushed the talk button on the intercom after stripping off his gloves. "I'll take it in here," he told his secretary. He picked up the white headset and rested it between his ear and shoulder then pushed the button to connect the call. "Dr. Connolly speaking."

"Dwight," a familiar voice said.

Dwight felt his gut spin and nausea settle in his throat. He grasped the headset to his ear with his hand.

"I need another favor."

"I've done enough for you," Dwight answered. This was no favor for a friend. It was blackmail.

"Diane Gomes," the voice simply stated.

Dwight Connolly's eyes darted to the female victim lying on the metal table. "This was murder. Totally different than the others. There is nothing that I can do." Dwight hung up the phone and waited for the voice to call back.

CHAPTER EIGHTEEN

A dam was worried for his kids and Alex. They were all connected in some way to HSU. Emma was chasing information safely from her computer, looking for anything that might signify a connection, but so far, she'd turned up nothing to bring closure. He hadn't collected the information from the safety deposit box for fear it was being was watched. That was a last resort. The last thing he wanted was for something to happen to any of them. He knew the one thing he could do was return to Megan's journals—read them for any information she might have hidden, but it took Adam several nights before he could bring himself to open them, knowing what was coming in their marriage. Though he had already lived the drama and knew the outcome, facing the tarnish of a marriage after a year of polishing the image was difficult.

Adam lit a lamp on an end table in the living room and settled into the L-shaped couch, his feet up on the square coffee table. He opened Megan's journal to where he had left off comforted by her familiar scrawl.

> *Dear Adam... something has changed. I don't know when it happened. We went from talking about our day to talking about the kids' day and forgetting each other. I don't like this empty space I feel in my chest. It's like a puzzle piece is missing, and I'm wandering around looking for it.*

He remembered the drifting too. The pain of looking at her and feeling as though there was a canyon between them without a bridge. After the fight about coming home late, he remembered putting a limit on himself and doing everything in his power to be home for dinner, but it hadn't seemed to change the rift. Megan must have used the journal to get out her feelings when he wouldn't listen while he buried himself in work. That realization was a heavy burden.

> *Dear Adam... I wonder when you stopped seeing me. I still see you, but I feel—detached. There was a time when I knew that you looked at me and I was the world. When I looked at you and felt that warm glow. But now, I ache to know that I'm not your world anymore, that instead of really looking at me you see through me. I would like to blame it on work, at least then I could justify it, but I don't know. You don't talk about it.*

> *I feel so lonely. There are times when I tell you what's happening in my life and you are emotionally vacant, like an apartment open for renters to move in. I thought we moved into that apartment together. Like tonight, after Trey finished telling us about his math test at school, I mentioned the invitation to the writer's group luncheon and the award to celebrate my*

article that I received this afternoon. You smiled vacuously, then asked Bekah about something, dismissing me. Am I invisible? That is how I felt.

Dear Adam... Things seem to be spiraling out of control. The other night, when you came home and snapped because Alex was here, seems like a nail in the coffin.

He remembered that night. He'd returned from work one evening with Alex ensconced at the counter in the kitchen talking quietly with Megan. Adam had entered the house and stopped short when he'd seen her. She'd just gotten divorced, and he remembered the way the knowledge had bothered him. She looked happier, clearer, so pretty. In hindsight, he remembered the bitterness he tasted—as though perhaps, now that she was available, for someone else because he was a married man, he'd missed his chance and would watch another swoop in to take it. Again. Had he been happy in his own marriage at the time, maybe he wouldn't have even noticed, but because of he and Megan's struggles, he suppressed his failing in anger. His feelings had been so mixed up and convoluted.

"Don't you have your own place?" he asked, announcing he was home. He'd been able to taste his sarcasm.

"Adam." Megan held a warning in her voice.

"Hello, Adam." Alex smiled. "I'm just visiting with my friend, Megan, who invited me for dinner."

"Lovely."

Alex put both of her hands in her lap. "Maybe I should go, Megan."

"Don't on my account, Alex." Adam poured himself a drink. "You won't even notice I'm here. That won't be anything new." He walked out of the room, leaving them. Megan muttered something as he left the kitchen and followed him.

173

"What the fuck, Adam?" Her voice was a hiss. *"It kills you to be polite?"* Her hands were on her hips, then she pointed at him. *"What is your problem?"*

"I don't know why she's always here." He used his head to point at Alex in the other room. *Even then he knew it was irrational, but he wasn't facing what was really bothering him.*

"She's my friend, Adam, and she's going through a rough patch. I'm going to be there for her."

"This is the third time this week I've come home to her. Ever thought I would like to spend some time with my wife?"

"Really? Like we've spent much time together lately?" Megan turned away but stopped. She added, *"Ever consider Alex has been there for me? She's the only one who gives me time and listens to what I have to say."*

He was so angry partly because what she said held a version of the truth, but also because he knew he was failing. They were failing. "Why didn't you fucking marry her then?" He took a sip of his drink unable to catch the boulder rolling downhill.

"Fuck you." Megan turned away from him and walked out of the room. He stood in the living room, drink in hand, and listened to the keys rattle as she pulled them from her purse. The door to the garage opened and closed. Still, Adam stood rooted to his spot in the living room listening to her leave.

He hadn't gone after her. How different things might have been if he had.

Trey came in through the front door a few minutes later. "Is Mom mad at you?"

Adam—drawn back to reality by his ten-year-old son—nodded. "Yes, she is, but don't worry, Trey. That happens when two people love each other as much as your mom and I love each other." He meant it, believed it, knew deep in his soul that even in their struggles, this was the woman he'd chosen, and they would figure it *out.*

Trey accepted his explanation, then asked about dinner. Adam, amused by the mind of a ten-year-old boy, took care of the kids, then waited for Megan, thinking that once she'd blown off some steam she'd come home. And he waited. When she still hadn't returned after midnight, Adam vacillated between panic that something had happened to her and regret for being an asshole. By the time Megan pushed open the door to their bedroom, the clock read two in the morning and Adam was furious. His bitterness toward Alex mounted.

"Where the hell have you been?" He growled from where he sat on the end of their bed. He'd been waiting in the dark, tossing and turning with hopes to sleep, but unable to when Bekah had woken up with a nightmare. After getting his daughter back to sleep, he'd heard Megan come into the house.

"Out. What do you care Adam? Go back to sleep," she said, her words slurred.

Adam reached over and turned on the lamp. "You've been drinking?"

"You do it, every night after work."

"At home. With you. I don't go out with my friends drinking."

"So sanctimonious. I didn't feel like being around you. I was, let me amend that, I am angry with you. Alex is there for me."

"Some friend, coaxing a married woman with three children out to a bar. She may be single, but you aren't, Megan."

She stared at him as she shrugged out of her shirt, and when he expected to see a look of conciliatory understanding, one that communicated compromise, he saw something worse. It flickered from anger and hurt then died like she'd been pushed over the edge of emotion into the oblivion of nothing. Without saying anything, she walked into the bathroom and shut the door.

Adam heard the shower start. He tried the knob to finish the fight, to fix it, but she'd locked the door, something Megan had never done. She'd locked him out.

Adam went to bed, the tug at his heart held fear of something he didn't understand and anger at himself for not having the answers to solve the problem. She wouldn't talk to him, and he didn't know how to make it better.

After that, things went from bad to worse. Megan refused to speak to him about that night, though she would carry on polite, if detached, conversation about the kids or dinner. Otherwise, she was vacant. Instead of seeking answers to the trouble that had inserted itself into their marriage, Adam did what he was best at. He went to work. He blamed Alex for seducing Megan into the desire for not wanting him or her family anymore, to drawing Megan out when he got home. His hatred festered until that was all Alex represented for him.

> The other night has changed everything. It signified a cliff in the plateau that our marriage has become. I don't know that I want to do this anymore, Adam. I don't know that I want to be your wife, because I don't feel good about myself as your wife. I don't feel like you see me and all that I do. I don't think you see the love I have for you, and now I feel like that love is changing into something closer to resentment and hatred.
>
> The other night, the night we fought about Alex being over and I left, something happened. Something that I'm ashamed of, but not so ashamed of that I haven't allowed it to reoccur. I met someone at the bar I went to that night. And I was so angry at you, had let the anger build up over the months that I wanted to get back at you. He invited me to his place. I went.
>
> Alex begged me not to go. She told me to think about

what I had before I threw it away. But I didn't listen to her. I don't know right now if I should have or not. I don't know who I am anymore. I don't know who I am with you.

Adam stopped reading. Emotion well up in his chest. He remembered. After that night, he'd tried. He'd been there wanting to make things right. He hadn't wanted to be a liar to Trey. He loved Megan, had always loved Megan, but it hadn't seemed to matter what he tried to do anymore. It was as though it was too little too late. He'd stop in for lunch to attempt and reconnect with her, and she'd be gone. She went through a dry spell with her writing, something she loved, and the kids began asking questions. "Why did you pick us up from school late, Mom?" And Megan had sputtered excuses. Adam should have known, suspected, but he'd been so selfishly caught up in his own hurt, indignation, and fear that he hadn't. He hadn't found out until they went to marriage counseling.

That day was so clear in his mind, even still.

Megan sat across from him, her arms crossed over her chest blocking him from her heart, her legs crossed, and her head turned away from him as she gazed out the window of the marriage counselor's office. She was crossing him out of her life.

"Megan?" The marriage counselor asked. "It's your turn. Adam just said that he was tired of being shut out of your life. Would you like to comment on how that makes you feel?"

Adam watched his wife, a woman he'd worshipped at one time, remain detached. At that moment, he loved her so much, there wasn't much distinction between it and the hate he felt looking at her. She continued to study the picturesque view out the high-rise office. Then something shifted in her countenance. Her shoulders relaxed, her brow softened, and she returned to the session, her eyes filled with tears.

"I've been having an affair."

Adam's jaw dropped, and he felt as though a large fist slammed into his side, breaking several ribs. "What?" He heard himself ask as though separated from his body. That can't be, he thought. One look into her eyes pooled with tears spoke volumes of her regret. He closed his mouth, pressed his teeth together with anger and anguish. She didn't shed a tear.

"An affair, Adam. I've been having an affair for the last six months."

Dumbfounded, it was his turn to look away and gaze out the window of the office. One of his hands covered his mouth as he absently rubbed it back and forth across his chin. I need to shave, he thought, as he disconnected from the moment.

"Adam? It's your turn," the counselor urged.

"I don't know what to say," he admitted, then fury stronger than he'd realized he could carry detonated within him. Six months. "Who?" Though it didn't really matter. It was a rage capable of things that frightened him seeping into every part of him. Then he exploded. "The kids? Six months? It's because you've been going out with Alex," he accused, needing an excuse, needing to assign blame to someone other than Megan. Other than himself.

Megan stared at him and simply shook her head.

Some moments I want out of this relationship, Adam. Some moments I remember the man that I married, the loving caring man that adored me and was sure to tell me that every day. I look at our children and know that I don't want to hurt them, but I'm locked away in a cell that our marriage represents. It feels like I'm serving a prison sentence right now, I wish it didn't, but it does. I don't know where my love for you has gone. I know it must still be there. We can't share fifteen years of marriage and not have something, there can we? I feel so confused.

Adam looked away from her words. Going through these times was heart wrenching. How things—looking back—could have been avoided if they'd just gotten out of themselves. If he'd gotten out of his own story to be a part of hers. But he hadn't. He'd been so preoccupied with his own experience; he couldn't see beyond the tip of his nose. He'd assigned the blame to Alex because it was easier than to admit his own faults for whatever stupid reason—self-preservation, repressed attraction, bitter jealousy—he spent so many years angry at her for a choice Megan made.

He reread Megan's words: *Alex begged me not to go; she told me to think about what I had before I threw it away.* That was something he'd never known.

He sighed, closed the journal and leaned his head back. They had made it through it. Lots of counseling, reinventing who they were in their own skin and standing next to one another. They'd figured it out and pressed reset. It had worked. A team through the first bout with cancer. A team with the kids. A team.

Reading Megan's thoughts, now however, forced him to examine his terrible behavior toward Alex. He was going to see her tomorrow. They were supposed to meet the Jolly Giant. Faced with his misguided treatment and mistaken blame of Alex all these years, Adam was beginning to think he deserved the burden of their friendship, and the pain of an unrequited attraction.

CHAPTER NINETEEN

A lex stepped out into the sunlight from the Foreman building where she'd just taught a class. The sun overhead seemed a heating element as its light touched the earth. It was so bright, Alex squinted as her eyes adjusted to its brightness. She was going to meet Adam outside of her building across campus before walking to Jack's building at the Abner Scott Science Complex. The walk, had it been a nice brisk December day, would have been refreshing, but the late October heat exhausted her. Air conditioning beckoned. How spoiled she'd become since her Peace Corps stint.

The mall was shady, the trade winds blowing through the tunnel of trees. Alex took a deep breath thankful for the refreshment against her perspiring skin and the fact her building was at the end of the passageway. She caught site of Adam sitting on the bench where she'd first seen him so many years ago and felt her heart skip the same as it did then. *You shouldn't be feeling this way,* she informed her heart. *Things are good.*

Adam stood when he caught sight of her and began walking her direction.

She realized the advice to herself was futile. The truth was, she did feel that way. She'd always feel this way. Always had.

There were defining moments in Alex's life, moments that shaped the path she'd traveled. Moments like not telling Adam how she felt outside the dorm all those years ago. Moments when she shut down her truth for the sake of someone else. Moments when she looked at Geoff and realized she'd hurt him. These moments couldn't be changed, she knew, but she should know how to recognize them and own them.

She wouldn't have suspected, however, that despite all these moments, the path would return her to what seemed the beginning. Her first choice. Adam was meandering toward her seemingly as untouchable as he was the day they had officially met. Had she failed to learn something the first time she approached this juncture and now life was offering her a do-over? Or had she accomplished everything she was supposed to and was being rewarded with a second chance? Maybe life was just throwing something she'd always questioned back in her face for a good laugh. She'd never regretted her decision, and there were three reasons for that— Emma, Trey, and Bekah.

"Alex." He greeted her with a hug and *honi* on the cheek. His hand lingered at the small of her back.

Her skin burned under his touch. She didn't step away but leaned back to look up at him. "You haven't been waiting long? My class went a little long this afternoon." She missed his touch when he stepped away.

"No. Not long." Adam glanced back at the bench. She recognized the haunted look in his eyes. "It all started here, didn't it."

For you it did, Alex thought and recalled his hands on her just weeks before that day they met at this bench.

He turned back to her. "Done with classes for the day, right?" he asked.

"I am. Jack will be waiting for us, but we've got to hurry. He's got an evening lab."

Adam fell into step with her.

"Do you need to get your things from your office?" Adam asked.

"No. I got everything already."

"Good. I'd like to take you to dinner then, if that's okay. After."

A moment. "Dinner? As in a date?"

"We can call it something else if you prefer." Adam's hands were in the pockets of his navy chinos.

She turned her face to look at him, his handsome chiseled profile. But he didn't return her glance. His jaw was set, the muscle working. She wanted to reach out and lay her hand against his jaw. She didn't. "I would love to."

"Really?" His brown eyes were open wide, and his grin was tentative. No dimple. "I thought you might say 'no.'"

Her brows drew together. "Why?"

They walked several more steps, Adam deep in thought, until he said, "You have to let me make the past up to you." His voice sounded resolute but insecure, as though he left something unsaid.

The words—the meaning of them, the weight of them, the salve of them—hit her straight through the heart.

"Adam?" She stopped walking.

Adam kept going but turned to look at her when she said his name. The light blue linen shirt contrasted so beautifully with his brown skin. His head tilted. Waiting. Her heart stopped beating, and then fell into the chasm of her body where all her want existed. She wanted him. She'd always known it, but she'd never allowed the hope of it. Never. Tears pressed against the back of her eyes, and she swallowed.

He must have noticed because he closed the distance between them and stopped in front of her. He tilted her face up to meet his. "Please don't cry, Al."

A tear slipped from an eye, and she tried to drop her head to swipe it away, but Adam held her head with his hand and wiped it with his thumb.

"I'm not," she said with words cracked with emotion.

He searched her face and smiled again. No dimple. "Don't lie."

A simple phrase. *Don't lie.* It's what she'd been doing her whole adult life. Lying to herself, to Megan, to him, to Geoff.

She stepped back and composed herself. *Don't lie.* So, she changed the subject. "Let me do the talking okay? It might seem weird that you're with me, you know. As Megan's widower."

"Alex?" he asked.

She knew he was referring to her quick change. She said: "One thing at a time? I can't walk into Jack's office–"

He understood and nodded, then fell into step with her as they continued to their destination. Alex concentrated on the faces of people passing in the opposite direction—anything to take her mind off the man next to her, though it was impossible. *You have to let me make the past up to you.* She sidestepped a professor walking head down toward them, and her arm grazed Adam's. She glanced at him. He was looking down at her, his whiskey eyes thoughtful. Goose flesh rippled upon her skin. She turned her attention away from the enigmatic man next to her.

The Abner Scott Science Complex consisted of five buildings. HSU was known for its scientific research and its medical school, the Moorehouse Medical School, which neighbored the ASSC. The architectural design stood out, each building a dome shape and made of glass, like five large atriums. Each atrium was connected to the other by elevated passageways and in the middle of the domed pentagon was a verdant tropical garden. So everywhere one looked there was a view of lush shades of green and the blue of the sky. The design embodied the essence of Hawai'i.

Alex led Adam into the second building, up a staircase to the second floor and through a hallway. Despite the glass domes, the interior of the building still consisted of normal construction with walls and ceilings; the first-floor main lobby however was illuminated by the natural light from the dome. Three quarters of the way down the hall, Alex stopped and knocked on a door.

They entered to find Jack in his cubby hole of an office, staring at a computer screen. The office was encased with bookshelves, each of which was stuffed beyond capacity. There were stacks upon stacks of books and papers in every other available space. A cup on Jack's desk was stuffed with sharpened pencils. She was grateful for the distraction from her current thoughts and amused by the reminder of what a character Jack was. He was the only professor she knew whose pencils, with their sharp lead tips, pointed out of the cup like two dozen tiny spikes.

"Alex! You made it," Jack said. He noticed Adam with her, and his 100-watt smile dimmed a bit. "Just getting ready for my next class." He held out his hand to Adam. "Good to see you again, Adam."

"Stab anyone lately?" Adam asked. Alex watched him nod toward Jack's desk.

Jack's face paled, "Excuse me?"

"I'm sorry." Adam raised his hands. "I didn't mean it like that. Bad joke." His gaze shifted to the cup on the desk. "I was talking about your pencil holder."

Alex let out a rush of air and laughed nervously.

"Oh, shit." Jack picked up the cup with a chuckle. He studied it a moment, then replaced it. "You wouldn't believe the number of students who filch pencils. You hide the erasers though and the pencils stop disappearing." He set the pencils back on the desk. "Walk me to my next class. We can talk on the way. Besides, I think you want to talk to Dr. Bennett since he was Diane's doctoral advisor." Jack grabbed a stack of papers and books near the door as they left. He shut, locked the door, and began down the hall.

"Did you know Diane?" Adam asked.

Alex stopped and watched Jack who'd turned to go back to his office. He re-checked his door to make sure it was locked a second time.

"Can't be too careful," he explained. "Research is very

competitive," he whispered, then continued in a normal voice, "I had the opportunity to speak with her on a few occasions, but I didn't know her all that well. She always seemed a very intelligent sort, though a bit preoccupied. I like my doctoral candidates focused on their dissertation and their academic study. Why are you interested anyway?" Jack asked, wiggling his eyebrows, "Curiosity seekers? I've sent several police officers and reporters his way in the last few days."

"Preoccupied?" Alex asked. She sidestepped his last question.

Jack chuckled again, his characteristic good-natured sound. "She was young for a doctoral student. Aren't most young women preoccupied?" He laughed again and chucked Adam with his elbow, as though they were good buddies. "I just think it's strange that you are so interested."

"Adam is a big donor for the University," Alex said.

Jack's eyes moved from her back to Adam. "You don't say? Must be nice."

Adam didn't respond.

"It's nice to have insider information?"

Adam offered him a patronizing smile with a lift of eyebrows.

"Thank you for the help, Jack," Alex said.

"Anything for you, Alex." Jack's intent was clear. He'd reached out to put an arm around her.

Alex offered him a half smile and extricated herself from his hand.

They walked down the hallway in silence, the awkwardness drawing them toward a destination she couldn't see. She prided herself of thinking ahead, of being aware, but in that moment, she knew she was in over her head. Tension stretched around them.

Jack breathed, sucking a breath, and she knew he was going to say something. He did. "I just can't wrap my mind around you needing to come all this way to ask about a grad student's death."

She was confused by Jack's tone, patronizing and full of challenge, as though he wanted to draw Adam into a confrontation—not a normal personality trait for Jack. Alex pushed the quietly nagging feeling of incongruity away attributing Jack's behavior to the stress everyone was under at the university. The reporters, the police, the new administrative protocols. It wasn't about her. She'd been clear with him.

"I suppose it might seem strange. I've got a company and a reputation to be worried about." Adam's jaw was set, but his voice was passive.

Alex noticed the quiet force which emanated from Adam, *mana*—as Hawaiians would say—that flowed around him, through him, from him.

"And if I know my girl, she suggested you come to see me and put your mind at ease." Jack's grin was award-winning.

"Excuse me?" she snapped, pissed off by Jack's claim.

Adam looked at her. "You know Alex," Adam said his eyes never leaving hers. "She is the epitome of kindness."

Alex forced her hands into fists and crossed her arms as Jack knocked on a door where he'd stopped.

"David is a great guy. You'll really like him." Jack pushed open the door. "Dastardly Dave?" he called.

"Dastardly?" Alex asked and sent a glance toward Adam who was staring at Jack's back. He didn't look gentle anymore.

"Jovial Jack!" A rich baritone voice replied. "Come in! Come in!"

Alex followed.

CHAPTER TWENTY

Adam and Alex followed Jack into the office.

"Dave, I wanted to introduce you to a friend of mine, Dr. Alex James, and her friend, Adam Kāne." Jack stepped back to make way for them.

Dr. David Bennett wasn't what Alex had expected. The handsome scientist was young, no more than forty with a face that could have graced a Calvin Klein advertisement. She'd expected an elderly gentleman either skinny and nerdy or portly and loveable and was ashamed to admit it given her own area of study. David was neither of those images. He stood behind his desk, thin, maybe, but lithe and fit.

"Hello. Nice to meet you." The man shook Adam's extended hand.

Bennett glanced at her and shook her hand. She didn't like his gaze and drew her hand away.

"Adam here has a curiosity about your grad student," Jack stated.

Alex was irritated with Jack's lack of tact. "Actually," she clarified, "it's my curiosity." She shot Jack a look. "I dragged Adam along, though he does have a vested interest in the university."

"How's that?" Bennett's eyes remained neutral.

"Just a donor. My company built this science center and funds a good portion of what's happening inside," Adam said.

If Alex would allow herself to cheer for male posturing—that would have done it.

"And his son is the starting quarterback," Jack added.

Alex closed her eyes and took a deep breath for patience.

"Really?" Bennett asked.

Alex opened her eyes again and inserted herself. "That's not why I'm here, however."

"Because of Diane?" Bennett sank back to his chair and indicated with the nod of his head that they could sit.

"I'd stay and chat with you all," Jack interrupted, "but I have a class to teach. I can guarantee that the natives are restless watching the clock for that magical fifteen-minute mark when they can leave."

"Thank you, Jack," Alex said.

He leaned forward and looked into her eyes. "Anything for my girl," he said loud enough for Adam to hear and planted a kiss on cheek. Then he walked out of the office.

Alex's eyes darted to Adam who redirected his attention to David Bennett.

"I didn't realize Jack was seeing someone," Bennett said.

"He's not," Alex stated.

Bennett smiled, then chuckled with a shake of his head. "Poor fellow. So why are you here?" When he looked at her again, she saw the interest in his eyes.

Alex knew it was time to do her best damsel in distress. Everything about her abhorred it, but she needed to play the part for Trey and Bekah. She needed to find out whatever she could. "I've just been fretting all week about this situation. As a woman on campus—you know." Alex played it up as best as she could. "I just wondered if there was anything you could tell me about—well—I don't know if all of us should be worried for our safety."

"And this major donor is your bodyguard?" Bennett's eyes slid to Adam.

Adam shrugged neither confirming nor denying his reason for being with her.

Bennett looked at Alex again. "I've been talking about Diane nearly all week. Reporters, police, you name them, and they have been here."

"Are you surprised?" she asked. "It's not every day that there's a death, let alone a murder of an HSU student."

Bennett nodded and seemed to contemplate Alex's statement. "A shame," he muttered more to himself and drifted for a moment in his own thoughts. He looked back at them and shifted back into gear. "Though it's also not very common for another HSU professor and her friend to come asking about a grad student who was murdered either."

"Nothing about murder is common, wouldn't you agree?" Alex asked.

"You're right, of course," he said. "She was a wonderful assistant, very intelligent and conscientious. I never had to worry about being late for a class. She made sure that every class was covered if I got stuck in the lab or at a meeting. She was a fabulous researcher, really made my job easier. I'm going to miss her," he stated.

"Sounds like you lost your work horse," Adam said.

Bennett looked away from Alex to Adam. "I'm not sure I'm comfortable answering any more questions, Ms. James."

"Doctor," she said, reaching over to put a hand on Adam's arm. "My friend meant that you've lost a very valuable member of your team. He doesn't understand the working relationship at the University." When Bennett's gaze was on her again, she said, "I can only imagine how much you will miss her. Fellows are so invaluable."

Bennett's look shifted, warming. "Yes, she was." He paused and leaned forward on his desk. "I'm not sure how I can help you, Dr. James." His gaze slid across her torso, rested at her breasts, then returned to her face.

Alex frowned at his invitation. "Did Ms. Gomes have friends?"

"She kept to herself mostly. Though the last few weeks I think she might have started seeing someone. Never met the person, however, so I can't help there."

"Why do you think that?" Alex asked.

"She seemed a bit distracted from her research. She was very secretive about the relationship though, wouldn't talk to me about it." Bennett leaned back in his chair again.

"Was it normal for your grad student to talk about her love life with you?" Adam asked.

The satisfied look in Bennett's eyes was gone the instant he looked at Adam, replaced by annoyance, possibly anger. "Grad students and their advisors work very closely together. It isn't uncommon for them to build a close relationship."

"A close relationship?" Adam's dark eyebrows arched over his eyes.

"What you are insinuating, Mr. Kāne, is highly unethical, not to mention against policy at the university." Bennett's voice was controlled, but the anger was distinct in the tight clip of his words.

Tension marred the electric atmosphere.

Alex jumped in to change the subject. "What was she researching for her dissertation?" She'd been around enough professors to know she only needed to feed their ego, and David Bennett was clearly all ego. Her research would have been directly linked to his expertise.

"It centered on the effects of human growth hormone, but this tragedy cut short her research which was to target HGH and its effect on Alzheimer's cells. She'd only finished her first round of testing on rats and mice."

"HGH—like the athletic supplement?" Alex asked. She glanced at Adam who was also connecting a dot.

Bennett continued. "In certain quantities and in varied forms. I've seen some of those ads heralding it as 'the modern fountain of youth.'"

"Does that mean there are illegal forms?" Alex asked. "You seem to know so much about it."

"I've done a lot of work on it myself. A few of those have created patents." He was proud. Alex refrained from gloating and waited for him to continue. "And its legality depends on several factors. Mainly the dosage, and it's pairing with other chemicals. Many patents have been tied up awaiting human testing and approval by the FDA."

"That's fascinating," Alex said.

Bennett continued. "Diane already knew that high amounts of HGH can affect skeletal structure as well as the reproductive system. With my help, she'd hoped to discover a possible link to a cure for the degenerative effects to the human brain due to Alzheimer's disease. Her initial research indicated there is cardiovascular and nervous system implications." When Alex looked confused, Bennett explained. "In some instances, the level of HGH in conjunction with certain other chemicals could cause short circuits in both systems." He leaned back in his chair and looked again at Alex. "I don't think this is helping you to feel safer on campus."

"Oh, but it is. Knowing there are so many knowledgeable people doing good for the world." She offered a smile even as she gritted her teeth for appearing so vapid. "Oh dear," Alex exclaimed, looking at her watch. "I'm afraid I have a meeting tonight that I can't miss." She stood and stretched out her hand. "Thank you so much for your time, Dr. Bennett. I feel better."

"David," he smiled and extended his hand. "And I would have more time for you if you need it, Dr. James."

She just smiled.

"You know where to find me."

Alex knew that would only happen when hell froze over, but she smiled anyway.

Once they were outside in the waning sunshine of the day, Alex asked, "Are you thinking what I'm thinking?"

"Let's talk about it at dinner. Unless you need to ask Jack if I can take you to dinner? Or maybe you'd rather go with Dr. David

Bennett?" Adam jogged down the steps in front of her.

She stopped walking and narrowed her eyes. "Hold up. You're mad at me?"

He turned and crossed his arms over his chest.

Narrowing her eyes, she held up a finger. "First of all—I'm my own person and can do whatever the fuck I want, Adam Kāne, even if it's going out with an egomaniac like David Bennett. Second, Jack blindsided me with his ridiculous behavior. And three, I saved your ass in there. If it weren't for me, you would have gotten jack shit information. Fourth," She started, but then stalled when Adam—who'd started walking the moment she got to number two—stopped so close to her, the lack of air in her lungs wouldn't have allowed for any more words anyway.

Adam smoothed a stray lock of her hair back into place, his fingers grazing her cheek. "I'm sorry," he said. "That was rude of me. I don't want to go back to war with you. You're right."

Her insides swirled with desire, and she refrained from closing her eyes at his touch.

"I think Jack feels quite a bit differently though, Alex."

She watched his hand as he drew away from her face. "Jack is a friend. He knows where I draw the line."

He nodded, though Alex had the impression he had more on his mind, but didn't voice it.

Adam sat across the table from Alex in the dimly lit pizza joint, Tino's, where she'd brough him before. It bothered him he felt insecure about it, as if he were seventeen again and worried about the kind of impression he would make.

He'd considered a nicer, more expensive place like Benton's, but Alex knew him at his worst. She'd seen the before and the after of him. She'd been in a fancy restaurant. She'd witnessed his tears and his rage. He didn't think she'd appreciate a showy place. Alex wasn't showy. She was real, so he wanted to keep it real.

He thought about her standing outside the science building holding up her hands and fought a smile. She was studying the menu now, her attention elsewhere. Her dark lashes fanned out over the ridge of her cheeks, and she was moving the pendant of her necklace back and forth across a chain. His heart tripped at being able to be with her this way. A date.

He loved that she'd snapped at him. He'd deserved it, and she'd been right. Without her, they wouldn't have learned any of it. Sufficiently scolded, he'd felt stupid for his foolish, jealous outburst. It had just been so difficult to watch two men flirt with her when that was what he wanted to do.

His brain reminded him he needed to keep the peace treaty.

His desire argued he was wanting something more than a friendly peace treaty, though how much more wasn't clear yet. He liked her. He liked being with her. He desired her.

Alex looked up and caught him staring at her. She smiled which made his stomach do a roller coaster loop. "Do you think we should go to the police?" She picked up her glass of ale and took a sip.

"About what?" he asked. "Excuse me officer, Diane Gomes' murder is related to all those other deaths on campus that you ruled natural or accidental."

"You're right."

Nani showed up to take their order. She and Alex bantered about Tino, then they were alone again.

"An even scarier thought is that if Diane Gomes' death is related to what she was studying, then all of the other deaths that are also related somehow to her theory means there has to be someone on the inside falsifying information."

"Someone inside law enforcement, you mean." She said more to herself.

"Possibly."

He was worried about all of stress associated with the information, mixed up with the confusing direction his life had turned. The perplexing way his heart didn't seem to align with his head. Both took a swig of their beers contemplating the implications of that statement.

"We also don't have a motive." Adam ran a finger through the condensation on his glass.

They were silent again, both weighted with their own thoughts.

Adam was thinking about Jack and Bennett. He was thinking about Alex and the way his body seemed to pulse with want when she was around. He was thinking about Megan's journal and her admission that Alex had tried to stop her. He was thinking about admitting earlier that he didn't know why she'd forgiven him. He was thinking about her crying. Adam looked at her and wondered what she was thinking as he took another sip of his beer to extinguish the fire in his belly.

"Alex–" he started but Nani arrived with the pizza.

"Here you go." Nani set the glistening pizza in front of them. "Enjoy," she stated and walked away.

"You were saying?" Alex asked. She hadn't reached for a slice yet.

"It does. I'd contemplated taking you somewhere else, maybe somewhere to impress you, but then I remembered how much you loved the pizza here." He smiled as he dished out a large slice, several olives and some sausage slipping off into the pizza board and set the slice on her plate.

Her eyes slid from the pizza to his hand, to his face.

"I'm sorry. My hands are clean." He put a slice on his own plate.

She smiled. "No." She shook her head. "Not that. I'm just not used to someone anticipating my wants." She picked up a piece of sausage and slipped it in her mouth. "I like this place. Far more impressive that you remembered."

Adam noticed she refrained from looking at him. When she finally did, he could feel the heat arcing between them.

"That's what you were going to say? Before the pizza got here?" she asked.

He cleared his throat. "I was just going to ask about earlier."

She looked down at her pizza.

"I hadn't meant to make you cry," he said.

"It surprised me—your words. I didn't realize how much I would appreciate hearing them." She picked up her ale. "Are they related to Megan's journals?"

"Yes. And no."

She offered a question with her eyebrows as they shifted over her eyes.

"Yes, because I'm facing the truth of who she and I were. Through the cancer and after she died, I painted our marriage with a glossy sheen. And now, because I'm clearer, I'm reading and remembering it for what it was—a human relationship with all of its good and bad parts." He rushed ahead afraid that if he stopped, he might lose his nerve. "So yes, I'm seeing the truth. And no, because I'm realizing that it was my behavior toward you that needs forgiveness. I'm seeing who I really am—without her. I was so wrong. I took my failings—Megan's and my failings—out on you. I made you the scapegoat. So, I can't imagine how you could ever forgive me. I don't know how this peace treaty is even in effect."

Alex plucked at her pizza toppings.

He tracked her movement and said, "I need to thank you."

Her head snapped up. "For what?" Her eyes wide with…she looked worried.

Adam continued though he filed his question about it away for the moment. "For being such a good friend to Megan. I know I was an asshole most of the time. I didn't understand. But as I've read her journals, her thoughts, you were a lighthouse for her. You picked up a lot of my slack, and I thank you for that." He rubbed his hands together, nervous.

"Please don't thank me," she said quietly, and returned to picking at the toppings. "Megan was my best friend, and your family has always felt like mine. I didn't do any more than what she did for me."

"I'm not sure that's true."

Her gaze slid up to meet his.

"That night—the one she and I got in that fight. The one she—" he struggled to say it, but then didn't shy away from the words— "the one she started the affair. She wrote you begged her not to do it."

Alex swallowed.

"I hadn't known. It makes my behavior toward you all the worse."

Alex paled and brought a napkin to her lips.

"Are you okay?"

She nodded. "Yes. Yes. I didn't know she'd mentioned that." Her color returned.

He picked up his pizza and took a bite wanting to busy his hands even if his thoughts were on the beautiful woman across the table from him.

She took a sip of her beer. Some foam remained on her upper lip. He had the urge to lean over … and … kiss … it off … She wiped it with her napkin. A memory—like a déjà vu—of a young woman at a party with beer foam on her upper lip flashed in his mind. He'd had that same image the last time he'd been here with Alex. He'd ignored it then. The image was more insistent, however. His need to follow its call which was loud, but it would have to wait. His attention on the moment.

When they were finished, they walked out into the darkness of the parking lot. The trade winds danced softly around them; the breeze raised gooseflesh along his arms. The vision continued to flash in his mind. Was it real? Or his imagination?

"Thank you so much for dinner and the company, Adam."

He held the door open for her. "Peace treaties have benefits."

Alex laughed. It curled around him and entered at his heart.

When he drove his vehicle into the deserted parking lot where

196

Alex had said she left her car, everything was dark except for the glowing light posts. The sky was blue black, no stars for the light pollution in the city. He spotted her lone car and parked next to it.

"I forgot to mention that Emma said she was going to look into Milton Yamane," Adam said.

"I wonder if she'll find something." Her hand was on the door.

He turned off the car and got out. Once around the other side, he planned to open the door, but she was already climbing out. "Let me help," he said.

"You don't have to help me, Adam."

Adam grabbed hold of her elbow to support her down to the ground. When she straightened, he could feel the heat of her body brushing his. "I want to help you," he said.

Alex looked up at him, her eyes more black than green and a lock of her hair waving in the breeze, brushing her cheek. Adam lifted his hand and gently removed a strand caught on her lip. His gaze caressed her mouth and her lips parted in invitation. With his heart pounding inside his chest, he leaned forward, unwilling to take anything from her she wasn't willing to offer. "I really want to kiss you, Alex. May I?"

"Yes," she breathed and closed the distance between them.

The kiss was a soft tentative touch. A million butterflies fluttering their wings inside him—so different than the day of the swim meet. That had been hungry. This was new. This was better. She tasted so sweet, so refreshing. She stepped into him. Their bodies finally touching, and the kiss intensified.

Adam fell over a precipice into a vat of want, and he drowned in it. His hands roved over her back, then he submerged his fingers in her mahogany tresses, one palm on each side of her face. He kissed her long, hard, and deep.

She gasped, then matched his rhythm.

A sense of déjà vu careened through him. He'd kissed her before, and this was a recreation of a beautiful dance they'd once shared. Their tongues met and the kiss deepened into something that Adam wasn't sure he wanted to control. Together, they created a rhythm, a dance that became a wish for something more.

Adam released her hair and ran his hands down her back pressing her tighter against him. He walked her backward, pressed her back up against the closed car. She was between his legs, his body leaning heavily against hers. He reveled in how they fit. She moaned into the kiss.

"Alex," he said against her jaw, as he trailed kisses to her neck. "You taste so good."

She grabbed his face and brought his mouth back to hers. She kissed him hard, seemed to lose herself in it, her hands drawing him closer, her tongue searching, her ardor equal to his. "Adam," she panted his name into his mouth, the sound filled with longing, dripping from her tongue like honey.

He ran his hands lower over the curve of her hips around to the contour of her ass and lifted her. She wrapped her legs around him, the skirt she wore riding high on her thighs. Conscious of only her, of his senses pitching wildly toward something beautiful, he carried her to the front of her car and set her down on the hood. Their tongues still intertwined, their hands still roving over the peaks and valleys of each other. He ran his hands along her bare thighs, her skin silk against his palms and slid them beneath her skirt. He grabbed her hips and drew her closer to him. She was pressed against his erection, sweet torture. "Alex. Alex." Her name was a prayer.

The desire to bury himself in her became overwhelming. Adam pulled his mouth from hers and trailed kisses along her neck. She arched her back and held the back of his head as he ventured to the top of her breast, exposed by the neckline of her shirt. "I've been dreaming about this," he breathed against her skin, and then made a return trip with his mouth from the top of her breast to her neck to her mouth. "With you."

Their lips and tongues met again in that suggestive dance.

Adam knew he had to stop. He couldn't do this now. He couldn't do this here. Alex deserved more than sex on the hood of her car in a parking lot. But he was drowning and needed air. She was the oxygen.

"Alex. Come home with me," he said between kisses.

He sensed her hesitation a moment before she pulled away.

She lurched back, blinked, and seemed to become aware of what had just transpired between them. "Oh shit." She unwrapped her legs from around his waist and slid off the car, then down the length of him.

He groaned as she passed over the length of his arousal.

"What were we thinking?" She seemed panicked.

"I don't think we were thinking about much." He smiled watching her fix her skirt. "It was nice not to be thinking. I liked it."

"This wasn't supposed to happen!" Adam could see her face by the glow of a light post. She was blushing and stepped around him to her car door. But she stopped. "I'm so sorry, Adam. I shouldn't have let it go this far."

"You weren't alone." He drew her back against him and wrapped an arm around her shoulders. His lips against her hair at the back of her head. She leaned against him, relaxed, and Adam knew she didn't regret it despite her words. "I could have stopped us. I didn't. I didn't want to. Alex. This…"

"Changes everything!" She yanked her car door open but didn't get inside, hanging her head instead. "Don't you see?" she asked. It was quiet.

"See what?" He adjusted his trousers and tried to put his hands in his pockets to keep from touching her. It was too difficult, so he crossed them over his chest. Under different circumstances, he would have laughed, but her tone was so broken, despondent. "Alex?"

"You were right."

"About what?" He wanted to reach for her, to draw her back against him.

"Everything you said. At the funeral." She lifted her chin though he could only tell because he saw her shift.

"No. Alex."

"You said not to lie, earlier, Adam." She turned to face him. "I can't lie. Not anymore. I did want your marriage. I did want what you had with Megan. I was bitter and broken it wasn't mine, and I couldn't make it work with Geoff. You were right."

He shook his head.

"I can forgive you, Adam, because you aren't the only one who deserves forgiveness." A sob caught in her chest. "I don't want to risk losing you and the kids again. This will change everything," she said between sobs.

He drew her to him then. Held her tightly while she cried. When her crying subsided, he drew back and wiped her hair away from her face. He leaned down and kissed the tears from her cheeks. "Alex James."

She hummed a response, her eyes closed.

"I understand." He kissed just under her left eye. "I won't push you." He kissed just under her right eye. "I want to take you on another date." He kissed the tip of her nose.

She smiled.

He kissed her mouth—a chaste kiss. "Is that a yes?"

Her eyes fluttered open, and she searched his face. "What about the kids?"

Adam wanted to say he didn't care. That it was their happiness that mattered, but he knew he did care, and she was right; it did matter.

"Let me think about it," she said.

He nodded.

She got into her car. "Good night, Adam. Be sure to call if Emma finds anything."

"I will. Drive safely," he said and stepped away.

She backed her car out and he watched the red taillights disappear around the corner before walking to his own car. He climbed into the front seat, the burn of Alex's body still on him—

body, mind, and soul. He sighed—there was no way he was letting her get away from him again.

Again?

CHAPTER TWENTY-ONE

Adam's heart raced as he drove home. Again? *Where had that come from*, he wondered. He took a cleansing breath to clear his mind of the everything rolling around in him. The desire, the strange déjà vu, Alex's fears, his own. None of it left him, however. Instead, he returned to kissing Alex. His want. Her response. He smiled alone in the car, flipping on the turn signal, thinking about his foolishness. He'd behaved like an adolescent boy, going at it with Alex in a parking lot. He chuckled and his skin heated. He was an adult for goodness sakes. It wasn't like he'd never kissed a woman—hell, he'd been married for twenty-six years! But he couldn't remember feeling like that. Unmoored. It unnerved him and even brought up guilt that he failed to remember that kind of excitement with Megan.

But there is that faint image of beer foam and pretty lips, his memory reminded him.

When Adam walked into his house, he knew he wouldn't be able to sleep. At least not for a while. His mind and body were amplified

with sensations and thoughts of Alex. He poured himself a drink—
needing one.

His eyes rested on one of Megan's journals on the counter.
Maybe he would find what he was looking for there, draw him
through to their final act. He carried his drink and the journal into
the living room then settled in to read. He dove into the words with
every intention of pushing Alex from his thoughts.

> Dear Adam... When we were first together, I found
> myself jealous of the other women you dated, but I
> remind myself that you chose me and love me, and
> we have three very beautiful children that exemplify
> our love.
>
> In fact (and I'm embarrassed to admit this) I was
> frequently insecure about the relationship you had
> with Alex. You had some of the best arguments with
> her—neither of you would back down. You'd be nose-
> to-nose and then Michael or, later, Geoff and I would
> laugh because you two looked ready to engage in
> fisticuffs, and I was insecure because it seemed like a
> sort of foreplay.

Adam stopped reading and looked at the dark fireplace.
Foreplay? He blushed thinking about it, about how true, maybe, it
had been. He took a sip of his drink and pictured Alex sitting across
the table from him at Tino's with foam on her lip.

He took another sip of his drink.

The familiar visual moved through his memory clawing for the
surface.

A secret.

One so buried he'd forced himself to forget it.

It rushed back in bursts, now, like snapshots.

A fraternity party.

He was drunk, full of himself, proud of a victory on the field. Adrenalin and hunting instincts were the only thing keeping him on his feet.

He wanted sex. Too young not to be careless with his body, but old enough to know better.

Then he found her. Across the room. Laughing. Gorgeous.

He hadn't known her then, but he would, later.

He'd kissed the beer foam from her mouth.

Alex. AJ.

He'd been so drunk he'd forgotten her. And when he did remember the first time—because who could really forget her—he'd buried it. He'd already been with Megan.

The second time the memory surfaced, it had been several years into his marriage, after the birth of Trey when it hit him. Emma had been three or four, and Trey just born. Megan had been sleeping, hard hit by postpartum, so Alex had been staying with them to help.

It had been another late night. Adam had just gotten Emma to sleep, and when he walked into the kitchen of the home where they'd lived at the time, the lights had been dimmed. But he'd heard singing.

He stopped in the doorway and across the room, settled into a chair with a notoriously colicky Trey in her arms, Alex was singing to him.

He watched them.

He smiled listening. He enjoyed the sound of Alex's soft voice and the cooing of Trey. That beautiful baby boy swaddled in her arms. The pride for his new son and Emma upstairs asleep filling him with contentment. His children.

Alex touched Trey's little face and smiled at the baby.

Then something happened in Adam's heart: a pressure, a burning that started like a pinpoint of intense light and spread like a fire across his chest. He tried to swallow the sensation.

Alex looked up at him the partial smile still on her face.

Her green eyes connected with his.

She smiled. Brighter.

And he remembered.

His heart collapsed and his lungs constricted.

The beautiful, mystery girl from the party had been her. Alex. The one he'd tried to find but had been too drunk to remember. Except he had once before. Before he'd been married and he'd walked away.

He swallowed down his emotions.

If he'd found, her... everything would have been different. And every moment passed through him like a movie:

The hazy memory of their coupling.

The night outside the dorm, "you don't remember, do you?"

The night at the beach when he'd thought about kissing her.

The banter and laughter.

All of it muscle memory.

That little baby in her arms, no longer there.

Emma. Gone.

Then he smiled back at her, and with a calmness he didn't feel, he walked into the room. He'd made his choice. It was Megan, and it would always be Megan.

Adam took Trey from Alex's arms and extinguished the memories that would break him if he allowed them out. He looked at his son's face, then at Alex. She'd never said anything either, but he knew she remembered. Her words: You don't remember do you.

He tore his gaze away from her and looked back at Trey now asleep. "Thank you, Alex."

"Of course," she said. "He's so precious."

"A gift," he replied, the weight of the meaning lost to her, but the burden a ton for him, difficult to hold up on his own.

Now, Adam stood, unable to sit and walked over to the window. It was dark and he could see his reflection staring back at him against the black of the night. That was the night he'd chosen to forget. And without meaning to, a seed of bitterness toward Alex was planted in his heart, one that grew and festered into something ugly and unwieldy. It had grown into resentment, anger, and finally rejection.

"You're an asshole," he whispered aloud to his reflection.

He'd been faithful to Megan in all their time together. All of it. Never strayed or considered it. Except that night when he remembered, it reminded his heart of what he'd never had. So, he built walls around his heart fortified with animosity and melancholy. They'd been erected to keep Alex out, but they'd hurt Megan just as much. He'd felt so self-righteous about her affair. It hadn't been him after all. He'd been faithful through and through, but that was a lie. He just hid his temptation in masks of distemper and indignation until he believed them to be the truth.

And Alex. Poor Alex.

He'd used her that night so long ago, and she'd thought herself forgotten when she hadn't deserved that. She deserved to be a first choice—she had been. Geoff's. What had she said earlier? *I can't lie. I did want your marriage. I did want what you had with Megan. I was bitter and broken it wasn't mine, and I couldn't make it work with Geoff. You were right.*

Adam hung his head no longer able to look at his reflection. He didn't want to be right. He wanted her. How did he deserve to hope that Alex's words had been about him? But God forgive him, he did.

Alex lay in bed staring up at the ceiling. She couldn't sleep. She couldn't close her eyes either because every time she did all she saw was Adam. All she could feel was Adam. His mouth and hands on her. The sound of his voice telling her that he wanted her.

She pressed one hand between her legs to ease the ache of want in her body, and the other hand to her heart to ease the ache of want there too.

She should be happy.

Adam had told her he wanted her.

She wanted that more than anything. That was also a lie. She wanted his love. She wanted what he'd given to Megan.

In all its complicated glory, she wanted him to look at her and see her—Alexandra James—and love her because he loved her. Alex. Not because she was available for him to ease his physical needs. And she was. That was the truth. She would give herself to him because, then, for a moment, she could feel the beauty of being connected to the only man who had ever made her feel complete. Again.

But physical wants were fleeting.

Alex wanted Adam's heart.

He didn't know what she'd done, what she'd told Megan. He didn't know how she really felt about him. Tonight, she'd equivocated—offered a partial truth to appease his need to understand. She hadn't been able to tell him, still couldn't say the true words on her heart. *I love you. I have always loved you.*

He would think she'd coveted the relationship, their marriage. She had, but it hadn't been about those external constructs. No, she had coveted Adam. She'd wanted his marriage because it was with him.

Tears slipped from her eyes and she rolled over onto her side. She stared at the window, the white curtains fluttering as the trade winds filtered through the louvers.

Alex knew she was standing at another moment in the journey of her life. Adam wanted to date her. She knew could say 'yes.' She could damn the consequences and face her heart being torn apart again when his infatuation waned. The risk might offer the reward of his love. Maybe. Or maybe he would never be over Megan and she'd remain the shadow of love lost. Alex could say 'no,' and walk away again from him, again. She could save herself the heartache of losing him. She could keep him in her life and the kids in her life and find contentment. The status quo.

She could.

She squeezed her eyes shut and pictured Adam's smiling face, felt the rush in her belly of his touch and kiss.

Damn her. She knew she would risk everything for him.

CHAPTER TWENTY-TWO

Mana entered the stark lab. The light bathed the room in fluorescence. As he strode through the space with a purpose, his shoes made soft footfalls on the tile floor. He was in a mood since he hadn't been able to dig up much on the Gomes murder, specifically a motive for her death. And Dwight Connolly's hypothesis that she was killed by a stalker was the only logical idea on which to follow up. But it was leading nowhere.

So far, he'd met with Stanton Thom, the university president whose personality wore quite thin, and Dr. David Bennett who seemed more in love with himself and his loss of an assistant than the fact that a young woman had lost her life. Neither man had provided any information that seemed of use to the investigation, though Bennett had mentioned she might have had been involved with someone. Mana had also spoken with students who had attended lab that night, janitors of the Abner Scott building, professors who worked with her and around her. He'd followed up on leads that all led to dead ends. No one saw anything. Mana was worried.

Tilda waved when he entered. The attractive Chinese woman was in a cubicle of sorts behind her lab equipment. Her eyes, a stark contrast to her spiky short black hair, were soft and feminine with long black lashes that matched her black eyes. Mana looked from her to her equipment and couldn't make heads or tails of the science of her job. But she was an ace.

"Lopes, glad you got here so quick."

"You call. I run," he stated, hoping that she had something that could lead him to the murderer.

"I sound like a booty call," She laughed. "Keani wouldn't approve."

"Sure, it's not the other way around?" Mana asked and grinned at her.

"Uh, nope. One-woman girl here."

Mana laughed. "What you got for me?"

"I wanted to show you what I picked up with trace evidence," she said getting right to business.

"Give me something I can work with Tee," he said.

"Good news or bad first?" she asked.

"Always the bad. You know this."

She nodded and continued. "Nothing. Trace found nothing. Her fingernails were clean. Her clothes were clean of fibers and foreign epithelia. It is almost as though she were wiped clean, sterilized."

"Interesting."

"I thought that was bad news."

"It's bad because it doesn't give me a lead, Tee. But it takes the case in a different direction," Mana said.

"How's that?"

"Doesn't sound like a crime of passion which was the initial hypothesis. A clean body and murder scene sound more like premeditation," he explained. "Give me the good."

"The pubic hairs we found weren't hers. And one still had its tag, though we'll still looking into the signature taxa component."

Mana smiled. "Do you have a name yet?"

"I just started running tests and the DNA through the system. It may take a while. But there's no guarantee that the donor is in the database."

"We can hope," Mana said and turned away from Tilda. "Call me."

"You know I will."

"And tell Keani I appreciate being your booty call." Mana backed out of the room.

Tilda scoffed as he walked away. "Fuck off, Lopes. Keani would kick your ass after I did."

Mana laughed—loudly—and left in a much better mood than when he'd arrived.

Stanton Thom paced his office like a caged cheetah. He moved back and forth across the room, wringing his hands. He had only to pant with anxiety to complete the picture. He moved to his desk and sat in the opulent leather chair. Then he leaned forward placing his elbows on his oversized desk and chewed his thumb nail. Then he stood, beginning the cycle anew. He had been wearing this trail in his office for close to a half an hour when his secretary buzzed over the intercom. He returned to his desk and sat once again pressing the button on the intercom.

"Yes Judith?" He forced himself to sound collected.

"You have a call from Dr. Black on line one."

"Thank you," he said, then dove for the phone. The leather chair rolled him past the desk. He realized his anxiousness and stilled before picking up the receiver. He didn't want to sound out of control, so he smoothed his suit adjusted himself in the leather chair, pulling himself back to the center of the desk.

This was it. There weren't any other options. The moment the body of Diane Gomes had been discovered the police had become involved. Stanton knew he might as well kiss his political career goodbye, if not his life entirely.

Stanton fought the urge to vomit. His overactive gut turned due to his nervousness. Ignoring the nausea, he pressed the headset to his ear. "Dr. Black."

"Stanton. You really need to stop contacting me." Dr. Black stated. Stanton could hear the impatience in the other voice and felt his eye twitch. He swallowed again. The doctor's voice was frightening and often haunted him in his dreams.

"That girl's death changes everything," Stanton whispered.

"What girl?"

"You know the one. The cops are involved now, and they never have been before. This screws everything. Did you have something to do with her?"

"Calm down." Dr. Black was clipped. "Again—what girl?"

Stanton fidgeted in his chair and smoothed his tie. He didn't want to make the person on the other end of the line angry, but they were resting in a tenuous position. "I don't know, but you told me that Adam Kāne and his daughter are poking around asking questions. That means they must know."

"About that bitch's research?"

"Yes."

"It doesn't matter who looks into it, Thom. Kāne, his cunt daughter, or that whore Dr. James."

"Who?"

"One of your professors in the Social Sciences. Did you know she was a close friend of the family?"

"No idea." Stanton deflated, sinking against his leather chair. It creaked under him. Three people—a donor, a reporter, and a professor—poking around with the police. This was going to be the ruination of everything he'd held dear. He had the governorship within reach. And now this. "If Kāne suspects anything, we might as well kiss the payoff goodbye. He is a very powerful voice in this state. You said yourself we need at least another year. At this rate we need to pull the plug." Stanton's voice had raised an octave. He lowered it again after a pause. "I do not want to go to prison. Do you understand? I can't go there."

"Stanton. Stanton. Stanton," Dr. Black chanted like a clicking tongue. "You have no faith. The governor chair awaits you if you stick with the plan. Our roadblocks are temporary, but the windfall will be worth the struggle. You aren't looking beyond the moment."

Stanton rocked his head back and forth on his neck to crack it and alleviate the discomfort of a headache starting. He pinched the bridge of his nose. "That's difficult to do. I've had to speak with homicide detectives. Do you understand the stress that I am under? Diane Gomes' death has changed everything. The school and her department are now under a law enforcement microscope. I don't think *you* get it."

"Are you questioning my judgment?" Dr. Black asked quietly, too quiet.

Stanton grimaced and opened a desk drawer. He reached in for the Rolaids package and popped three in his mouth. "No. I'm not questioning you. I just don't think you understand the stress of my position."

"I understand perfectly."

"Do you, Dr. Black? When I agreed to this plan, I did it for one reason—the governor's seat. Murder on my campus does not reflect well on that plan." He shoved another antacid in his mouth.

"There you go again, Stanton. That sounds very much like you are working up to a threat." Dr. Black paused. "Let's be clear, Dr. Thom. Nothing stands in my way. Anything that attempts to disrupt my endgame is eliminated. Now, I'll ask again. Are you questioning my rules?"

Stanton swallowed the dry, chalky chewable, then wiped the sweat on his upper lip with a kerchief. "As much as I would like to, I don't have the stomach for it, Dr. Black."

"Hence the reason I'm the brains behind this operation. You just do your part. I'm doing mine."

Stanton took two cleansing breaths. "And in the meantime?"

"The less you know, the better."

Stanton couldn't argue with that. He needed a way out of this mess if the time came. "Okay."

"In the meantime, call me only in case of emergency. You don't want to have to worry about a phone tap, yes?"

Stanton looked at the phone. The idea that there could be a tap there now drained the color from his face. "What?"

"Focus, Stanton. Just follow my directions, and you will be fine."

"I understand," he stammered.

"Good."

The click on the other end of the line signaled Dr. Black had hung up.

Stanton sat down in his chair again and put his face in his hands. He wished with every fiber of his being that Dr. Black was right. Stanton didn't feel so confident.

CHAPTER TWENTY-THREE

I t had been a year.

A year without Megan.

A year since she took her last breath, though the leaving started long before that.

Adam looked up at the November sky. It was a clear, star-filled night. He felt clearer too, the cosmos of his body filled with burning stars as well. He wondered if Megan was watching. If she understood his journey without her? He wondered if she would approve.

After walking across the lot and taking the elevator to the correct floor, Adam entered the restaurant where he was to meet his children to celebrate Megan's life. And Alex. She would be there too. His body was buzzing, excited to see her again. Since his revelation, it was all he could think about. He wanted to talk to her. He wanted absolution.

The hostess smiled at him when he approached the podium. He gave her his name. "Right this way, Mr. Kāne." He followed her through the dimmed restaurant. She turned and looked back at him, smiled, her blonde hair falling over a shoulder. Adam thought of Megan as if an apparition of her turned to look at him, flashed a dazzling smile, and then dissipated as the hostess presented his table.

Standing at the opposite end was Alex.

He blinked, the sensation that Megan had led him to Alex sent chills along his skin.

"Adam?"

He approached her. Her pretty dress accentuated every curve she possessed. "You look beautiful," he said and leaned closer to offer a *honi* on her presented cheek. He laid a hand on the small of her back, needing to feel she was real, and pressed his lips to her cheek, breathing in her gardenia scent. There was so much on his heart to say, but it wasn't the time. He recalled the kisses they'd shared, setting him aflame. He drew back, but not enough to look into her face, just enough so his lips could still graze her skin. "I'm so glad you're here." As soon as the sentiment left his lips, he recognized the truth. She belonged there. She was as natural to the ebb and flow of his life as the sea. The idea of her not in it made his chest tighten.

She turned her face toward him, her mouth close enough to kiss, then looked up. "Me too."

They should probably have taken their seats but didn't. Lingering. Adam's hand heavy on the curve of her back. He wasn't ready to move away, but he did, drew out her chair, before sitting in his own. An overflowing silence spilled around them. There was so much to be said and nowhere to begin.

Alex finally said, "I can't believe it has been a year." Her eyes filled, and her throat worked to keep her tears in check. "I'm barely holding it together." She offered a teary smile.

Adam reached over and covered her hand with his.

"If you try to be strong for me, I will most certainly break down." Alex's giggled a teary laugh. "I really miss her."

"Words can't express how much," Adam added, but as he said them, he had the strange sensation Megan was there, between them, but not in a way he might have expected. There wasn't any guilt in the presence. Megan had been his youth. She had been his gift, provided life to his children, shared in the struggles of his youthful arrogance and pride, taught him to be a better man. She had been his first true love. Nothing and no one could ever take that away. His eyes slid to Alex—and perhaps—just like Alex had stepped away to make way for his youth with Megan and their children—Megan was offering him this gift of a second chance now.

"Oh my god! Alex? Is that you? What a surprise! Adam." A voice split the intimate moment down the center.

Alex's gaze slipped away from his toward the voice.

Adam's eyes followed and rested on a familiar face. "Jack." Adam stood and extended his hand to shake the other man's.

"Did you find what you were looking for the other day?" he asked Adam as he put a hand on Alex's back.

She tensed.

Adam returned to his seat and rested an ankle on his knee. "As much as can be expected."

Jack's eyes darted between them. "Anytime. You two on a date?"

Adam suppressed a smile. Clearly, Jack was trying to stake his claim. Adam wondered if Jack knew Alex at all. That wasn't the tact to take with her, and he sensed Alex wasn't happy about Jack's overtures.

"Of sorts," Adam said.

"Yes," Alex said. She turned her head up and looked at Jack. He removed the hand from her back. "We are."

Adam smiled now. No need to suppress it. He loved that Jack's plastered smile faded for a split-second.

"Which is it? Sort of? Yes?"

"Yes," Adam replied and looked at Alex. Her gaze met his, the edges of her eyes curled up with a smile. "Do you have a date tonight?" Adam asked Jack, turning the tables.

"No. No," he said. "Meeting some colleagues for drinks. There's a conference in town. Networking and all of that. You know how research is."

"No." Adam shook his head. "I don't. But don't let us keep you from your evening."

Jack paused, the dismissal clear. He turned to look at Alex as if he wanted to say something, but when Alex wouldn't return his gaze, he seemed to wilt into acceptance. "Yes. Right. Have a nice evening." Jack finished with a nod and walked away.

Adam watched the Jolly Giant move into the bar and greet a group of people standing there. He didn't seem particularly phased—still jolly. Then he recognized one of the faces: Dr. David Bennett. Their loud laughter kept his attention for the moment. Bennett handed Jack a drink, who then said something and laughed bawdily with the others. They drank.

If Adam was a distrustful man, he would have thought it strange that Jack and David Bennett happened to be at the same restaurant as he and his family, but he wasn't usually suspicious by nature. He supposed Megan's research and the threats against her made him distrustful of anything that moved lately, but he dismissed the suspicion. Jack hadn't lied. Bennett was a colleague in the same department. It would be normal to get a drink together.

He filed it away for later. For now, he had another more important matter on which to focus.

A waiter came over to take their drink order.

"How are you?" Alex asked him after the waiter left.

Adam wanted to make his confession to her vacillating between the impetuous desire to just blurt it out and the wisdom of finding the right time. He was saved by Emma and Grant's arrival.

Hugs and kisses were exchanged, and as they were about to take their seats Trey and Bekah arrived, and the flourish of greetings were exchanged again. Joy overwhelmed him. His family. Their noise. The love. Adam contained the tears forming from that well spring. Warmth spread through his chest: contentment.

Alex reached under the table and took his hand in hers.

Chills raced up his arm, and he looked at her.

She smiled and looked away, her gaze soaking in the action of the kids around the table.

A little later, Trey closed his menu and leaned forward. "Can you believe there was a murder on campus?"

Adam's contentment waned with the topic.

"It wasn't exactly *on campus*." Emma leaned toward the table as she said it.

"Same difference. Someone from campus, then." Trey offered her a sarcastic look.

"You're such an adult," Emma replied.

Trey offered another look this time accompanied by the middle finger.

Emma shook her head and Bekah interrupted. "It's pretty much all that anyone can talk about." She looked up from her menu. "What are you getting, Trey?"

"The lamb. Always."

"Can't you branch out at all? You always get the lamb. Besides, it's cruel."

"I like lamb. When I don't like it, I'll get something different."

Bekah rolled her eyes. "I heard it was a crime of passion."

"They say that if you're attacked, you usually know your attacker," Grant offered. His hand was on Emma's neck, massaging her with affectionate kneading.

Bekah shuddered. "That's terrifying. I know that I've been looking over my shoulder more often."

Adam turned cold. "Why? Have you been followed?" His eyes darted from Emma to Alex who both understood his concern.

"Chill out, Dad! I didn't mean I've been followed, just that it's creepy knowing someone was murdered—like it could happen to anyone."

"Truthfully, Bekah, I've thought about killing you—multiple times," Trey stated, picking up his water.

"Trey!" The entire table erupted with censure.

He held up his hands. "Sorry! Sorry. Bad joke. But for real, Bekah, if you don't hook me up with your roommate." He laughed and ducked when she tossed some bread at him.

"You're so morbid, Trey. And if you want to hook up with anyone, you're on your own," Bekah replied.

The waiter came to take their order. The party laughed at the banter, enjoyed their food when it arrived, talked about Megan and memories, shed poignant tears. Adam sat back and basked in the glow of being with his family.

A bit later, he raised a glass. "I'd like to propose a toast." The party around the table hushed their conversation and followed his lead. "To a wonderful woman who we miss tremendously, without whom we wouldn't be here together today. Our common thread." He felt a lump rise in his throat but refused to allow it release. Tonight, was a celebration. They drank.

"Here. Here," came the answer followed by tipped glasses in unison.

"Wow, Dad. That was deep," Trey said. "Didn't know you had those kinds of lyrics."

Adam laughed.

As the night wore on, Adam had a distinct feeling of peace settle over him. It was like walking into the surf on a rainy day, the warmth of the ocean wrapping its arms around him. The feeling bespoke of the absolute clarity and truth of the moment. Adam knew he was ready to finish reliving the memories of his life with Megan. He was ready to look ahead to a future infused with her presence as an enchantment which made him better and whole. Adam was ready to say goodbye and to let go.

"Ready, Bekah?" Trey asked, pulling Adam from his thoughts.

"Has this carpooling always been a thing?" Emma asked her siblings.

"Four letters," Bekah said and spelled, "K-A-R-A."

"Kara?" Adam asked with an arched brow.

Trey smiled.

Adam chuckled.

"My roommate," Bekah informed them.

"You are my hook up," Trey said.

Bekah shook her head.

"I doubt you need the hook up," Grant said. "I'm sure being quarterback for the HSU Hurricanes doesn't hurt."

"She doesn't watch sports," Trey said, his expression incredulous. "But she's hot."

"Won't last," Emma said.

"Who said I want it too," Trey wiggled his eyebrows.

"Oh dear."

"See!" Bekah pointed an accusing finger at him. "That's my point. You'll get what you want, then leave me to clean up the mess. I'll be stuck in the middle," Bekah said and stood.

Trey pressed his hands to his heart. "I'm touched, Beck. You think I have that kind of play."

Both were still arguing as they rounded the table giving *honi* and handshakes before leaving. Adam watched them depart the restaurant, Trey laughing at something Bekah had told him.

"Any news?" Emma asked. She lifted the glass of water to her lips, the yellow rind of the lemon a bright contrast in the clear liquid.

Adam and Alex shared what they had learned from Dr. Bennett. "That's him over there, next to Jack—the one you met at the game." Alex told her.

Emma glanced over. "The handsome blond one?"

"Handsome?" Grant scowled. "He looks rather effeminate to me."

Emma laughed and poked her husband with her elbow. "He does not. You really need to go get your eyes checked." She wrote down the researcher's name. "I'll do an internet search for him and see if I find anything of interest. There might be something to follow up on."

"Okay." Adam signed the bill.

The foursome stood and walked from the restaurant. Adam

guided Alex through the restaurant, his hand at the small of her back. He felt a keen awareness that they were being watched as they left, chills standing on the back of his neck. As they walked through the doors, out into the night, Adam turned to identify whose eyes were on them but didn't notice anyone's attention. Even the Jolly Giant was nowhere to be seen.

They said their goodbyes to Emma and Grant, then took the elevator to the parking garage.

"I feel better than I did this morning," she said, watching the numbers on the elevator. The elevator stopped and the doors slid opened. "This is me."

"I'll walk you to your car," he said and held up his hand when she opened her mouth to argue. "I feel better too. There's always something about being around the ones you love."

"Yes," Alex answered quietly.

Adam was aware of what he'd said. He'd put her in that group. Did he love her? He knew he cared for her.

"Here I am." She stopped and turned to face him. "Thank you for inviting me." Her wrap fell from her shoulder to the ground.

Adam bent and picked it up. "Let me help you." He wrapped his arm around her, swinging the fabric over her head remembering it had been the same phrase the other night which led to the kissing. He resisted the urge and instead arranged the fabric so that it rested around her shoulders.

Alex lifted her hands to help him set it in place. Her fingers grazed his.

"Thank you for being here. It was important, I think." He took the key she'd retrieved from her clutch and ventured between the cars to unlock the door for her.

Alex stood in the void of the open car door and looked up at him. "Important?" she asked.

Adam handed her the key, then put his hands in his pockets. "Yes. You are as much a part of this family as me or any of the kids. It was important you were here. I stole that from you at the funeral, over this year. I know I can't fix what I did, but I'd like to give what I can back."

She'd pressed her lips together and dropped her gaze. When she looked back up, her eyes were full of unshed tears. "Thank you for that."

"It doesn't deserve a thank you, but I'm glad–" he stopped trying to find the right words. They seemed to dart around his mind. He couldn't catch them. "Well. I'm just glad you're putting up with me."

She wiped at her eyes with her fingertips, then smiled. "Adam Kāne," she laid a hand against his cheek. "I will always put up with you."

He leaned into her touch and smiled.

Her eyes expressed there was more as he searched them, but he didn't ask. He needed to finish the journals. He needed to close that chapter.

And he needed to deserve Alex. He had so much to make up for to earn her trust.

She removed her hand. "Let me know if Emma learns anything, alright?"

"I will," he said.

She hesitated a moment, then turned, getting into her car.

Adam pushed the door closed and watched her drive away. He turned and walked back to the elevator to take it to the parking level where his car was waiting. He had some journals to read.

CHAPTER TWENTY-FOUR

"**D**r. James! Dr. James!"

Alex stopped on the mall and turned to look at who was calling her name. There were dozens of students walking in different directions to their destinations. Other students sat on benches, leaned against trees, or lounged on the grassy knolls of the mall. About a hundred yards from her and closing, Alex watched a young woman jog across the walkway toward her. As she approached, Alex recognized her as a student she was supposed to have seen in her last class.

By the time the young woman caught up to her, she was out of breath, though not so much so that she couldn't carry on a conversation. "Dr. James." She took several deep breaths. "I tried to reach you before the end of class," the cute girl said. She looked the all-American, girl-next-door with her blonde hair, a sprinkle of freckles and a button nose.

"*Aloha e* Claire. Good to see you." Alex raised her eyebrows.

"Missed you in class." Alex turned and continued walking toward Ke Anuenue Hale and her office. Claire fell into step next to her.

"I know. I know. I'm sorry."

If it had been any other day, Alex was doubtful Claire would be chasing her through the mall, but the fact that the midterm essay had been due that morning made it far more plausible. It wasn't the first time an undergraduate had chased her down with an assignment they'd procrastinated doing and chose to finish it instead of attending her class.

Claire continued, "I had cheerleading practice last night and again early this morning—we're pulling double practices for competition—and so I overslept. But my paper was done, I swear. I have it here." She waved the white sheets she was holding. "I wanted to turn it in."

Alex shifted the satchel on her shoulder to a more comfortable position and cast a glance at Claire as they continued walking. She glanced at the stapled, white sheets of paper. The young woman was a good student and unlike many of her other undergraduates usually attended classes. Alex didn't have a reason to doubt her excuse.

Alex stopped walking and turned to face the student. "I have to say this, Claire. Being a student athlete is tough and, though it isn't always fair, you are held to a higher standard. You have double the work because you have academics and sports as responsibilities. But you chose it."

Claire nodded.

"So," Alex continued and held out her hand for the paper. "I have to treat your paper as I would any other student's. It's late, so as agreed upon in our syllabus, I must dock 15 percent."

Claire's face fell, but then met Alex's eyes and handed her the paper. "Okay."

"But," Alex offered a carrot. "I'll be offering some extra credit not mentioned in the syllabus later this semester, so listen for it to make up the points."

Claire nodded and smiled. "Thanks, Dr. James. I really

appreciate it."

"Good luck with the competition," Alex said. Claire turned on the ball of her foot and bounded away.

Alex tucked the paper under her arm and opened the door to the social science building. She hustled up the two flights of stairs and walked down the narrow hall until she reached the door to her office. Once inside, she dumped the satchel on her desk and set Claire's paper next to the black bag.

She unloaded materials she'd used for her last class from her pack and replaced them on the shelves in her office. As she did, she passed the shelf dedicated to her family. One photo of her real father, who had since passed, and a stepmom with whom she didn't really get along. A half-brother who emailed to keep up and sent images with his wife and kids she'd met a handful of times. Most were snapshots of Megan and the kids, school and athletic portraits of Emma, Trey, and Bekah. There were family photos that included Adam.

Having determined she was willing to take the risk to be with Adam, it had given her a sense of freedom. Alex knew engaging in a romantic relationship—even if it was just physical—ran the risk of losing him and the kids. Even though he'd promised that wouldn't happen, Alex also knew, based on her own life's journey, one couldn't make promises like that. She'd married Geoff thinking he was forever.

Adam hadn't tried to kiss her, though the tension had certainly been present. A chill raced down her spine and spread through her lower back thinking about it. She knew Adam wouldn't have—not last night. They'd been there to celebrate Megan's life. There was something sacrilegious somehow about desecrating her memory in that way. Though, Alex wasn't exactly sure how one day mattered over another. The thing was, Megan had known Alex loved Adam. She'd told her. She didn't think Megan would have asked her to watch over Adam. She wouldn't have asked Adam to find her for help. It was almost as if Megan had set a final plan into motion and hoped they'd figure it out. Though, Alex wasn't sure she was figuring anything out at all.

Alex picked up a bronze-colored frame and looked at the man she had spent a lifetime loving. It had been so easy to be with him last evening. They'd shared each other's space as though it were the most natural thing ever. The kids accepted her presence, though she hadn't expected anything less from them; she was Aunt Alex after all. Adam had been different, however, though she couldn't exactly put her finger on how. Settled and peaceful, somehow. Contrite. That idea struck her and reminded her of his words: *I stole that from you at the funeral, over this year. I know it can't fix what I did, but I'd like to give what I can back...Thank you for putting up with me.*

Alex leaned in and looked at his face. He and Megan had been in their thirties when the picture had been taken. Emma around ten or eleven, Trey seven or eight, Bekah a year younger. She focused on Adam. The confidence of his smile, the curl of his eyes as if amused by something Trey said, the swagger of his stance, his strong hand resting on Emma shoulder and one behind Megan. Last night, this man was there, but different, somehow.

It made Alex wonder, why? Had Megan written about Alex's admission and now he knew? It was a possibility, but she didn't think Adam would stay silent about it if that were the case.

She set the picture frame back in its place and began getting materials she would need for her last class of the day, but as she did so, thought about Adam. She thought about kissing him the other night and imagined doing that again—hoped to do that again—soon. She remembered the impulsive one night stand they'd shared so many years ago—the one he'd never remembered he'd been so drunk. She'd been so ashamed about it for so many years, the one secret she still carried with her. She'd never told because she'd been embarrassed for being so impulsive, for sleeping with a stranger. Then she and Megan had met Adam, and he hadn't remembered, her shame increased. When Megan liked him—staked her claim—and Adam was into her, it just wasn't the right thing to do. At least, not until it mattered.

After pulling the same book twice and replacing it on the shelf twice as the wrong one, Alex shook her head to clear her mind and tried to focus. She took a deep breath, turned back to her desk, and sat down in the chair. She pulled the essays from the satchel and glanced at her watch, deciding to start on the papers to help her focus. She picked up Claire's paper.

The title was interesting enough: *Media and its Effect on Body Image* by Claire Thomas. Intrigued by the topic, Alex opened to the first page and began to read. Halfway through, Alex stood up with the paper in hand, her heart beating rapidly. Excited, she said, "Oh shit."

> Human growth hormone, a legal substance in many formulas has found its way onto the college campus where it is provided to athletes for athletic performance enhancement. For example, at HSU, the cheerleading squad takes an HGH formula that the athletes believe helps them maintain their weight and keeps them athletically viable. But many athletes are persuaded to take HGH supplements simply because of the effect they have on musculature and body definition providing a more toned physique that is deemed desirable by media.

Alex stopped reading and glanced around her office as though someone was sitting there to tell. She refocused on the essay and finished it. The pounding of her heart continued even after she'd completed reading the paper. She reached for her phone and dialed Adam's cell number and paced her office. She listened to the ring until Adam's message picked up. Then she tried his home phone and left a message. Alex dialed his cell again. "Come on Adam," she muttered holding the phone to her ear still pacing. "I think I just found our answer."

Adam turned off his vibrating cell phone after looking to see who was calling. Alex. While he was ecstatic to be getting a phone call from her, he couldn't answer it and promised himself that he would call her as soon as he could. Now, however, he was with Emma, pretending to be her cameraman. He had a camera looped around his neck and was snapping photos. He was a contractor for goodness sake, not a private investigator. Yet there he was, sitting in the office of a stranger, playing a part.

Just that morning, right before Adam had left the house for work, Emma called. "I said I'd investigate Milton Yamane, and I still am, but I diverted a bit and started researching what you and Alex uncovered regarding Diane Gomes. I found someone willing to talk to me, Dr. Sarah Billings at Milner Pharmaceuticals. She's the lead researcher on an HGH supplement Milner is creating."

"She's willing to talk about Diane Gomes?"

"No."

"Then what's the point?"

"Figured I might be able to work in some questions about Gomes once my foot was in the door."

"Very enterprising of you."

"Can you come?" Emma asked.

Adam agreed, not that he could have said no to his daughter.

Emma picked him up at the jobsite and once she had him in her clutches said, "Here's your camera."

"Camera?"

"Yes. Just hold it and maybe pretend to take a few pictures."

"Why?" he asked.

Emma looked away from the road and directed her gaze at him.

"Because," she started and returned her attention to the road, "Dr. Billings thinks I'm there to interview her about the approval process for new drugs."

"What?"

"I knew she wouldn't see me if I flipped the Diane Gomes name at the onset, so we're there to ask her about her research."

Adam was silent. He understood, and he could appreciate not approaching the table with your hand showing, but this undercover guise was out of his comfort zone. He dealt with businesspeople, money, and negotiations.

"You are just a cameraman, Dad. You won't have to say a word accept to take a few photos, okay?"

"Fine," he said. Getting to the bottom of Megan's mystery for the safety of his kids was more important than a few minutes out of his comfort zone.

Now, he sat there, watching Emma work her investigative magic and couldn't help but feel proud of her. She drew Dr. Billings into the conversation. Emma's questions smart, pointed and well researched. Her hands moved when she talked though never distracted from the discussion.

Adam looked at Dr. Sarah Billings and lifted the camera. One thing he could do was look for tells, so he did what he could to read the other person. The doctor sat forward in her seat, her arms on her desk, and she looked attentively at Emma. Once in a while, she'd cast a glance in his direction, attempting to include him in their conversation.

Adam couldn't shake the feeling that he had seen the doctor before. She was a lanky woman, her silver hair cut short to her head and vibrant contrasted with her beautiful, dark, russet skin. She was attractive and had a regal, self-assured quality about her. But Adam couldn't place her.

"So, you see," Dr. Billings continued with her answer to Emma's question regarding the FDA approval of new drugs, "new drugs must go through rigorous testing before they even get to human trials. The last stage is human trials, but if there's ever a question or an error in data in the first two phases, the drug gets bumped back to the previous phase for additional testing. That doesn't even cover the committees it has to get through. All in all, from start to finish without any roadblocks, it takes a new drug at least eight years to get approval."

"I feel safer knowing that." Emma took down her notes. Adam could see she was formulating her next question in her mind. "What if a drug produced fatal results in animals?"

"It wouldn't make it to the next phase and would go back to lab."

"What about this new athletic enhancement technology you are working with–" Emma paused with an 'um' sound. Adam recognized the technique as he had also used it in negotiations. She was hoping that Dr. Billings would supply the information herself and therefore come across as leading the conversation.

"The HGH conversion hybrid? Yes. We've been in animal testing now for—let's see, we're in our second year. It looks as though we've created a successful supplement and human trials are less than a year away provided the committee approves our findings."

"Congratulations. HGH you said?"

"Why yes, fascinating hormone."

"I read that Diane Gomes, the HSU student that recently died was researching HGH."

Dr. Billings smile faded a notch, and she looked from Emma to Adam. "I wasn't aware of that."

Emma feigned innocence. "You were mentioned as the leading source of information about HGH on O'ahu by–" Emma looked at her notes– "Dr. David Bennett?"

Adam noticed Dr. Billing's body language shifted. "No. Well, I've met him, but I don't know him well. This interview has nothing to do with the FDA approval process does it?"

It was a rhetorical question, but Emma went with it. "Absolutely,

Dr. Billings. I was wondering though; would you care to comment on Diane Gomes research regarding HGH?"

"I haven't read it, and no, I don't care to." She stood indicating the interview was over. She held out her hand to Emma. "Thank you, Ms. West. Mr. Kāne."

Both Emma and Adam stood, shook Dr. Billings hand, and left the office. They walked into the elevator. Once the doors slid shut, Emma turned to look at Adam. "Did it seem to you like she knew something?"

"She certainly clammed up when you mentioned Diane Gomes research," Adam said. "She seemed really familiar to me." His mind was preoccupied trying to place her.

"We didn't learn much though. I'd hoped she would give us something to follow up on."

"She did give us something, Emma," Adam answered as the elevator doors opened to the lobby. "And I just figured out where I know her from."

"Really? Where?"

"Our dinner for Mom. Remember Alex's friend, Jack?" Adam paused while Emma nodded. "We saw him at the restaurant. He was meeting fellow researchers for a networking type dinner."

"Right. The handsome blond guy—David Bennett."

"He's not *that* handsome."

Emma rolled her eyes.

"She was there. I saw her at the bar."

"Okay. We've established that she's a researcher and has dinner with other researchers. That isn't out of the ordinary, Dad." Emma walked through the door that Adam held open for her to the outside.

He squinted in the sunlight and looked at Emma as she opened her purse to look for her car keys. "Think Emma. She's the lead researcher in a new drug being developed."

"Right. The HGH conversion hybrid."

"Diane Gomes research doesn't cast a positive glow on HGH now does it?"

"Motive," Emma breathed.

Emma and Adam stared at each other a moment in the sunlight, wondering if their assumptions were farfetched. They weren't extraordinary people with amazing detective abilities, but the solid ground on which they usually walked had somehow turned to quicksand.

Adam waited on the passenger's side of the vehicle. "What do we do next?"

Emma had found her keyless entry remote and opened the doors. "Maybe it's time to go to the police." She got into the car.

Adam got into the car just as Emma was turning down the radio. "What if the police are in on it?" Adam asked.

Emma turned in the seat and looked at him. "You think so?"

"Come on, Emma. You are a journalist. Are civil servants any less immune to corruption?" He turned and looked out the windshield watching the cars drive passed on the busy thoroughfare.

"You think all of them are dirty?"

"That's unlikely, but how do you tell one from the other?" Adam paused, then added, "It's all conjecture anyway, but let's play pretend."

Emma put the automatic in reverse and backed the car up. "Okay."

Adam watched the road as Emma pulled the car from the parking lot into the traffic. "Let's say that Diane Gomes was murdered because she found something out about HGH. And then let's assume, hypothetically speaking, that Dr. Billings' research is on the line because of Gomes impending discovery."

"How is it connected to Mom's research?" Emma asked. She drove the car onto the H3 Highway. Adam watched the tall buildings thin out and the lush tropical vegetation thicken as she continued to drive.

"I don't know, but what if they are connected somehow? What if the athletes are somehow connected to Diane Gomes findings?"

They drove up the mountain in silence. The dark green peaks

rose sharply and contrasted like a brilliant emerald against the azure sky. Adam thought of Alex, reminded of her beautiful green eyes, and then rubbed his forehead with two fingers. He felt a headache starting.

Emma broke the silence. "I still don't see how that means the police are involved."

"I can't know that for sure. The amount of student athlete deaths in four years is astounding. Even more so at one school. Why is it that no one is asking questions? Add the fact that all the athletes seemed to…" Adam lost his train of thought. He rubbed his forehead again and yawned.

"Seemed to what?" Emma asked as she yawned too. "Funny how yawns are contagious."

Adam's eyelids were heavy. He blinked trying to chase away the sudden exhaustion. "The athletes all died from natural circumstances—natural circumstances that none of them should have had considering their peak physical condition." He looked over at Emma who blinked, as if in slow motion, then shook her head trying to refocus on the road.

"With that logic though, Dad, you could just as easily imply that the media is involved."

Adam saw Emma yawn again. Then he closed his eyes. His head was throbbing. He had a distinct feeling that something wasn't right. "Emma?" he asked and opened his eyes to look at her. She was asleep at the wheel. "Emma!"

The car drifted toward oncoming traffic. Adam reached for the steering wheel though his arms felt so heavy. He yanked the wheel toward him. The car veered a sharp right. The sound of a blaring car horn was the last thing Adam remembered as he succumbed to darkness.

CHAPTER TWENTY-FIVE

Alex stepped onto the maternity ward. She'd already been to the ER but was informed Emma had been transferred for observation by a text from Bekah. What about Adam? It was a mantra feeding her rushed steps through the hallway. What about Adam?

Alex had been finishing up her last class when she'd gotten a call. She hadn't answered the phone—she never did in class—and it was haunting her now. She'd waited to check the messages, and when she'd seen it had been from Trey, her heart and sputtered with trepidation.

Aunty Alex, there's been an accident.

Now, with her adrenaline and anxiety fueling her, she was trying to find her family. Her heart hadn't ceased its anxious rhythm that dropped acid into her gut and made her feel nauseous. What about Adam?

The maternity ward of King's Memorial Hospital was a maze as Alex navigated its peach-colored hallways. She remembered working her way through the same hallway years ago with the birth of each of Adam's children. When she finally discovered the inner sanctum of the nurses' station to ask for directions to Emma's room, a pretty, Filipina face pointed her in the right direction.

Alex knocked and pushed the heavy door open. Grant, the first face she saw, looked drawn and pale with worry. "Hey," he told her and met her at the partially drawn curtain.

"How is she? The baby?"

"They're doing fine." He crossed his arms in front of him and looked back at the other side of the curtain. "Thank God."

Alex put her arm around him in a half hug and moved around the curtain. Her heart expanded, then floated away. Adam was there, a dressing on the right side of his forehead above his right eye but relatively injury free. Her throat closed, and her face fell into her hands with a sob. Relief. Fear. Regret. What if she'd lost him?

Strong arms encircled her. "It's okay. It's okay," Adam murmured.

She wrapped her arms around him and clung to him. "I couldn't. If. Without you." She couldn't string together anything coherent, but his arms tightened around her.

He held her. It didn't matter that Grant was witness to it, or that Bekah and Trey walked into to find them that way. Alex couldn't bring herself to release her hold. Adam didn't move either. "I'm so glad you are here," he said.

When she did finally find a place of emotional balance, Alex moved, but not away from Adam. Just enough to look at Emma who was asleep. Her face was battered, a big black and blue mark on her cheek. Then she looked at Adam, leaning back to search his face. "And you?"

"Shaken up," he replied. "A terrible headache. Hit my head against the window when the car veered from the road onto the shoulder. We were lucky we were where we were."

He stepped back and ran a hand over the bandage and returned to Emma's side. "They gave her something to rest. She was pretty upset about the baby."

"What happened?" she asked.

"She was taking me back to the jobsite—in Kailua—where I'd left my car. It was just after the Likelike exit. She just fell asleep. I was feeling off too—a terrible headache—and so damn tired. I grabbed the wheel, I think, to keep us in our lane."

"The H3?" Trey asked.

Adam nodded.

Silence descended like a storm cloud, full of all the awful possibilities had the car been anywhere else along that highway. They wouldn't be in the maternity ward with minor cuts, bruises, and monitoring; they'd be in a morgue.

Alex took a deep breath and shuddered. She felt sick to her stomach.

"Grant?" Emma's groggy voice cut the silence in half. "Dad?"

"Here, Emma." Grant bent over his wife.

"I'm here, baby," Adam said on her other side.

"Dad? Are you okay?" she asked, but her eyes stayed closed. "They want to watch me and the baby overnight, but they said the baby is fine." Emma's voice was thick with sleep. Her hands went to her belly.

Bekah started crying, a quiet, broken sound. Alex raised her hand inviting Adam's youngest into her arms. The younger girl walked into Alex's hug. She held Bekah, offered comfort she needed, and somehow received herself by holding onto Bekah. She glanced at Trey who was standing against the wall with his arms crossed in front of him, his expression static, and lacking his usual spirit.

"I'm alright, sweetie. Grant is keeping us informed. You rest." Adam squeezed her hand. Alex watched him rub his thumb over the bandage on Emma's right hand lost in thought while all of them observed the rise and fall of Emma's chest.

Alex offered a prayer of thanks.

"I'm so sorry, Grant," Adam said.

"You have nothing to apologize for, Dad." Grant reached across Emma and placed a reassuring hand on Adam's.

A knock sounded at the door. The same Filipina nurse entered, "There's a Detective Lopes outside looking for a Ms. West or Mr. Kāne?"

Adam glanced at Alex as he straightened.

"I'll be here," Alex told him.

Adam stopped in front of Alex who was holding Bekah. He put a hand on Bekah's head but met Alex's eyes. With a nod to her, a quick check on Trey, he left the room.

"Mr. Kāne?" a big man asked. He was taller than Adam and broader. A giant local man with russet skin and burly arms. His face was as wide as he was with strong brows and large dark eyes. He was dressed in plain clothes, a pair of khakis and a blue aloha shirt. He held out his hand. "Detective Lopes."

"Detective." Adam shook his outstretched hand.

"I'd like to ask you a few questions, Mr. Kāne?" He pronounced Adam's Hawaiian last name correctly unlike most people who assumed the Western pronunciation. "I'm sorry to hear about the accident this afternoon, and the timing of my visit. Is your companion alright?"

"My daughter. May I buy you a cup of coffee at the cafeteria?" Adam walked toward the elevators. "I'm feeling like I need some."

Detective Lopes fell in step with him, and they left the maternity ward. "And your daughter is okay? And her baby?"

"How did you know?" Adam asked.

"The maternity ward."

"Right. Sorry. My mind feels thin right now and slow. Baby

seems to be fine."

"Let me get to the point. I'm investigating a specific case and you and Ms. West were brought up in conjunction with it. What can you tell me about the murder of Diane Gomes?"

Adam leaned against the wall of the elevator, crossed his arms, and studied the younger man. "Diane Gomes? This isn't about the accident?"

"Let me be frank," Detective Lopes said as they stepped from the elevator out into the hallway. "When they pulled you from the car and brought you in, you were rambling about Diane Gomes. That's my case. I got a call, so I came down."

They walked into a large room in shades of burgundy and tan. It was surrounded on two perpendicular walls of windows. Outside, the view of the jagged mountains and a lush green tropical canopy provided a calming backdrop

With coffee in hand, Adam found a table next to a window and sat down across from the detective. "Do I need a lawyer?" Adam asked.

The detective's eyes widened with surprise. "Do you?"

"I don't know. I spoke with an officer earlier about the accident, but now you're telling me you want to talk about a murdered woman that's all over the news."

"Do you know something about it?"

Adam leaned back in his chair and sipped his coffee. "Do you know anything about my accident today?"

"Other than what's been reported—no." His eyebrows drew together with irritation. "Mr. Kāne, what do you know about Diane Gomes murder?"

Adam knew he was in over his head. And now with the accident, he knew he needed to trust someone, but was it this cop? "I'm trying to figure out if I can trust you."

Detective Lopes tilted his head as if confused. "What do you have to lose?"

"Oh, perhaps my life."

Detective Lopes leaned back and crossed his arms. Adam was sure he'd probably offended the cop, who waited for Adam to explain.

"My daughter and I were driving from speaking to a researcher named Dr. Sarah Billings with Milner Pharmaceuticals. My daughter is a journalist. But you already knew that, didn't you? Did you check up on our accident after we were brought in?"

"That isn't my case," Detective Lopes said.

"I have the impression you go the extra mile, since you're here, speaking to me for mumblings. That if some guy came in rambling about your case, you'd try and find a connection." Adam took another sip of his coffee, then set it on the table. That same fact might mean the detective was clean. When the officer didn't reply, Adam leaned forward and placed his arms on the tabletop. "Because I don't think our accident was an accident, and it scares me to consider the ramifications. I don't know who would do it."

Detective Lopes studied Adam, his jaw working, then seemed to come to a decision about something. He leaned forward. "A homemade device was found on your car that rerouted the exhaust into the main cabin. Who would do that Mr. Kāne?"

"I don't know." Adam said and looked out at the mountains hoping to find something peaceful in which to escape for the moment. His heart pounded with impotent rage. Someone had tried to kill Emma. Someone had almost succeeded. He looked back at Lopes and ran a hand over his face before he said, "Like I said, I don't know who to trust."

Lopes held Adam's gaze with what appeared to be an earnest one of his own. "You can trust me."

Adam realized he was at a crossroads.

The detective's watched him. "Look. I'm here to solve my case and get the bad guy."

Adam maintained his silence, worried and vacillating on speaking to the detective. Everything about the detective seemed on the level, but Adam wasn't trusting himself. His *na'au* seemed off.

"My daughter was interviewing Dr. Billings about HGH."

"Diane Gomes research?" A brow arched over other man's eye.

"Not specifically, no. She knew she wouldn't get Dr. Billings to agree to speak to her, so she went in under the guise about finding out about the drug approval process."

"Why? What led you there?"

Adam sighed. "It's going to sound—crazy."

"I've seen crazy, Mr. Kāne. You'd be surprised at the crazy I've seen. Try me."

Adam leaned his elbows on the table, his hands around the paper coffee cup. He measured his words hoping the risk he was taking was with an ally, but picturing Emma lying in the bed a few floors above where he now sat, seeing the fear on Grant's face, Trey, and Bekah's emotional struggle, and Alex's fears, he couldn't do this anymore. His who-to-trust options were limited. "I can't prove anything I'm about to share with you. My late wife was a writer who wrote human interest stories for the Hawaiian Sun and contributed regularly to a few national magazines. I discovered–"

"Megan Kāne," the detective interrupted.

Adam nodded. "I discovered," he continued, "only recently that she received a tip about something happening at HSU. She investigated a lead about the Donna Delco death." Adam continued relaying the story. Midway through the tale, when he revealed that all the deaths were HSU athletes, Detective Lopes leaned forward in his chair. "I assume you are aware what Diane Gomes was researching for her dissertation?" Adam paused.

"HGH," Lopes stated.

"And, I can see that the connection to HGH to athletics isn't lost on you," Adam added as Detective Lopes nodded.

"Why Dr. Sarah Billings?"

"My daughter, discovered she's the lead researcher on a new anti-aging drug containing–"

"HGH," Lopes finished. He was quiet a moment. "You don't know if you can trust me because you think someone inside—

possibly the police department—is in on a cover up."

Adam took a sip of coffee neither admitting nor denying it.

"That's an interesting story."

Adam didn't respond to the statement, but did say, "If what Dr. Billings shared today about Milner Pharmaceuticals wonder drug is true, and it was about to be refuted by Diane Gomes research. It seems like a very strong motive."

"One I find I have the desire to follow up on," Lopes stated.

"My wife left all of her research in a safety deposit box."

"Do you have it?"

Adam shook his head. "We knew she was being watched. She was threatened at least three times, so we didn't want to alert anyone by collecting it from the bank. You are welcome to it." Adam knew he could be handing over everything to a possible enemy, but he was tired. He couldn't do this anymore. He needed his family safe.

Detective Lopes stood and held out a hand to Adam. As they shook hands Lopes said, "I'll be in touch."

Mana Lopes returned to the station, his first order of business to validate the claims made by Adam Kāne and thus rule out his possible involvement. He weaved his way through the desks in the room and went directly to his cubicle. He sat down. The center of the desktop was clear though on each side were stacks of files that either needed completing or refiling, a chore he never got to.

Despite the outlandishness of Kāne's story, there was a certain credibility to the man's assumptions, which put Mana's senses on high alert. With Tee's discovery nagging at the back of his mind. The clean crime scene with very little evidence meant someone knew what they were doing which hinted at possible premeditation, Mana needed to find the link. How did Gomes fit with the other deaths? Did she?

Mana decided to verify the validity of Kāne's claims by pulling the death records of each of the names given to him. Thankfully, all were loaded into a linked database between the health department and the police department. With the ease of touching a few buttons, Mana was able to call up each case.

Once each report had been pulled up on the computer, the first thing that he looked for was a cause of death, the second was the investigating officer, and the third was the coroner who attended to the autopsy. As an investigator, his job was to read between the lines. More often the not, Mana was impressed with the fact that the key to most investigations was the least obvious. That meant going through all of the details with a fine-tooth comb, looking for things that struck a nerve or sent the hairs standing on end. And then sometimes, it was those things that you didn't want to see, a fact slamming you in your face that you failed to connect.

As he looked through the case files, the first thing that he noticed was that in each case, the athlete's death appeared from either what appeared to be natural causes or self-inflicted wounds. The second thing that he noticed was that each case had different investigating officers. That gave him hope that the police department wasn't involved in some way but could also mean that the web spread further than he'd like to imagine. The final point set off an alarm in Mana's investigative instincts. With any death, the county coroner that examined the body had to sign off on the death certificate. In the Oʻahu Police Department, there was one senior coroner, but three other coroners that had the authority to sign. With each of the athletes' cases only one name was signed on each certificate: Dwight Connolly.

Mana sat back in his chair. The old metal creaked under his weight. His mind began working. Dwight Connolly. What did he know about the coroner? Better yet, what didn't he know? Mana sat forward in his chair, metal groaning again and signed onto the internet. He typed the name into the search engine.

CHAPTER TWENTY-SIX

Adam drove home. He was familiar with driving in the dark, but after the experiences of the day, it seemed sinister. After speaking with detective Lopes, he'd returned to Emma's room only to be interviewed by yet another police officer investigating the accident. *A device was found on the car.* When he'd finished, he could think of little else than being comforted by the sight of. But to his disappointment, she hadn't been there.

"Where is Alex?" he'd asked Grant.

"She went to feed Barney for me," Grant had said referring to their dog, "so I wouldn't have to leave Emma."

Adam had nodded. "Bekah and Trey?"

"Back to school. Alex wanted me to tell you she'd come by your place after feeding the dog. She said something about needing to show you something."

Adam had nodded though grateful he'd get to talk to her.

When Adam walked into his house, it felt like a refuge. The house was dark, but it was familiar, safe. It seemed surreal all that had occurred since he'd left that morning. He went to the counter that separated the family room and dining room listening to the messages on his phone. "Adam!" Alex's voice. "I've been trying your cell. I can't get through. I need to talk to you." The line clicked indicating she'd hung up. He was looking forward to seeing her.

The doorbell chimed.

He went through the entryway hall and opened the front door. Alex was there, her face weighted with worry in the artificial light of the porch. He was so glad to see her, as though returning home had been incomplete until she arrived.

She stepped into the house. "How is Emma?"

"She and the baby are doing fine. The doctor visited right before I left and said that barring any unforeseen circumstances, she should be able to go home tomorrow." He let Alex pass him though he wanted to draw her into his arms. She walked into the dark living room, and he followed her down the steps.

"I asked her to stop investigating. She gave me a look that reminded me of Megan then said she'd do her best to leave the police work to the police."

Alex turned, her eyes shining with unshed tears. "Megan wouldn't have wanted this." Adam couldn't see her clearly but could hear the emotion in her voice. "Not for you. Not for Emma."

"Alex–" Adam started and stopped.

"I think it's gone too far. I couldn't handle it if anything happened to you," she stopped and then added, "or the kids."

Adam studied her. Her hands were shaking. He reached out to take them but folded her into his embrace instead. She felt so right there. The realization sent an elixir of contentment pulsing through his blood mixed with the adrenaline and cognizance of what could have happened today. He tightened his hold on her. "I know. The thought of something happening to Emma, Trey or Bekah, well, I can't bring myself to contemplate it."

"Or you."

Adam kissed her temple.

"Did you tell the police?" she asked into his shoulder.

"I did. I couldn't hold off now that this happened," he said.

"Because of the accident? It was an accident, right?"

He leaned back to look at her face, to draw strength from the new emotion that had infused the shell of a man he had once been. "It doesn't appear so. No."

Alex looked up at him and in the next instant stepped away, removing herself from his embrace. Her hand at her mouth. She turned away to look out into the blackness of the windows. All the things still unsaid were heavy weights. "Adam," she said, "if something happened to you."

"I heard your message on the machine. Is that why you called?" Adam asked.

She faced him. "No."

He held out his hand to her. "Let me fix you a drink. I could really use one." He smiled.

Alex took his hand and allowed herself to be led into the bright kitchen.

"What happened today?" Alex asked.

Adam led her to a barstool and sat her at the counter. It was an affectionate gesture that both confused Alex and sent her heart racing. She listened as he explained about the interview and then its aftermath. Dread built within in her realizing how close she'd come to losing him and Emma. She shuddered.

"Are you cold?" Adam asked and set a scotch in front of her.

"I just can't fathom what could have happened."

Adam stared into his own drink and Alex watched him get lost among the glaciers in the glass. Her heart expanded having always loved that reserved, quiet quality about him. His humility had always been endearing. His overt confidence that night so long ago had obviously lit Alex's fire. She smiled at the thought.

"A smile—a good sign," Adam said, interrupting her momentary lapse into the past. He sipped his drink.

Alex blushed having been caught strolling down memory lane. "Just thinking back to the time, we met," she said. His abrupt cough caught Alex off guard. Confused she added, "That day outside Ke Anuenue." She took a sip of her scotch. It burned all the way into her gut at the lie.

Adam's brown eyes searched hers, a thorough perusal as though looking for something, a hint, a clue to a lost treasure. "Yes," Adam's answer was measured as his tone drew out the word. He set down his drink on the counter. "I remember."

Alex got up from the bar with sudden listless energy she needed to burn. Her nerves were exposed. She turned away from Adam's gaze and walked into the family room. "With Megan. At the bench," she said. She didn't trust herself to look at him and be nonchalant about it.

She heard him walk toward her, then felt his powerful presence behind her.

"I remember that was the first time I met you, Alex, and Megan," he answered.

She was aware that if she took a step back, she would be able to lean against his strength, but she didn't.

"I also remember meeting AJ, Alex James. Do you remember AJ?"

Her heart stopped as she whirled around. "You remember?"

He had a slight smile on his face, just big enough to offer a glimpse of the dimple in his cheek.

"You remember." She was suddenly angry, and tears smarted her eyes. To think she'd been carrying that memory around, afraid that he would hate her if he did remember. "How long?" Her voice sounded frozen in her ears.

Adam hesitated. He ran a hand through his black hair. "Alex..."

"Don't patronize me, Adam. How long have you remembered?"

"I'm not sure," he answered. "I didn't at first, Alex. I didn't. And then it was a few nights ago, that I remembered with clarity. Once I remembered, it was like all of it rushed back."

"And you never told me? You let me believe that I was just a random girl you sacked? A notch in your belt so unmemorable you couldn't remember me sober?"

He looked at her. "I tried. I did, twice." His gaze was back to challenging her in the next instant. "You didn't say anything."

She made a disgusted sound. "Like I could? You were dating, and then married to my best friend. I would never do that."

"Neither would I," he said and hoped she understood.

It silenced her and a myriad of emotions moved across her features. "You tried?"

Adam could see she was hurt. He sat on the family room sofa. He certainly owed her the explanation. "I remembered I'd been with a beautiful woman, but I'd been too drunk to be smart. I hadn't gotten her number. All I had to go on was the impression and the name she gave me: 'AJ.' I tried asking around, but no one knew or remembered the pretty brunette I was asking about. It was what? A week? Two after that party that we met by the bench?"

Alex sat down in a chair. She looked so small, her arms wrapped around her middle.

Adam continued. "By the time I was able to piece together the connection between AJ and your name, Alex, I was already involved with Megan, but I promise you Alex, I was in agony knowing it. I remember the day I figured it out, I'd gone to the library to find you. I'd known you would be with Megan there, but I remembered that you had class and she'd stay. So I'd waited outside for you. It had been raining." He stopped and looked at Alex.

Her gaze slid up to meet his. "I remember," she said. "You'd been waiting at the end of the walkway—drenched. You'd looked upset. And I remember I told you Megan was in the library. You'd said—"

"—I know," Adam finished. "And you asked me what was wrong. In my head, I was swirling around what I'd remembered, the small hints you'd given before Megan and I got together, and that night on the beach, the night I'd wanted to kiss you so badly, but didn't."

"Because of Megan."

He nodded. "I'd told you I'd been looking for you."

"And I'd been surprised."

"And I knew that if I said anything, it meant things would change. It meant, that it would end what was happening with Megan, and even if I admitted it, I couldn't be with you either. I didn't want to come between your friendship. It was an unsolvable problem. So, I chickened out and made up an excuse about something."

"A gift for Megan. You wanted help with planning some date for her. So, you just forgot?"

"No." He shook his head. "I just compartmentalized it, put it into a box and stashed it on the shelf."

"And the second time?"

"The second time, I didn't try to tell you, I just allowed it out." He took a sip of his drink.

"When was that?"

"After Trey was born."

She leaned forward in the chair.

"Alex–"

She shook her head. "All this time."

"Yes."

She stood up and walked back into the kitchen, lifted the snifter of scotch and drained it.

Adam stood but didn't walk toward her. "Alex?"

"I just–" she kept her hands on the counter and her back to him. "I just thought I was carrying the memory alone. That I'd never been good enough to be remembered."

Her words stabbed him in the heart, but he knew she wasn't trying to be manipulative. She was hurting. "I can't—I mean, I don't have an excuse for it. It was just easier to put up a wall, act like an asshole to try to forget."

"Don't say that," she said.

"Why not? If the shoe fits," he answered his smile wry. "When

I allowed it out after Trey was born, I was so ashamed of how I'd treated you, I shut down. It makes no sense, but I got so angry."

She turned, tilted her head. "Why?"

He didn't answer for a moment suddenly afraid. He was looking at himself in a mirror and didn't like the reflection, but he owed her the truth. "I was bitter. I realized the possibility I'd sacrificed to acquire what I'd gained: my family. And—" he looked down at his feet.

"And?"

His throat closed with the emotion of what he was going to admit, but he had to. He had to lay himself bare. "I hated myself. It was like I was given these incredible gifts: the kids and Megan, and all I could think about was what I hadn't gotten. How selfish is that?" He looked up at her. "Gifts you had given to me, Alex. Everything. And I repaid you with anger."

She sank onto a barstool, tears filling her eyes. "It took two of us, Adam, that night and everything else over the last twenty-seven years. There wasn't a day that went by I didn't wish maybe I'd made a better decision." Tears spilled down her cheeks, and she swiped at them with her hands.

Adam wanted to go to her, lift her up, draw her into his arms and plead with her to forgive him, but he knew he didn't really deserve it. He stayed rooted to his spot, hands in his pockets. Her words, now, sent pangs of grief through him that she'd regretted things. "Better? Meaning you'd take it back?" The thought she lamented that night twisted his heart. Being with her wasn't what he had misgivings about. He regretted everything else but not that.

Alex was silent for what seemed a lifetime. "No, Adam, I wouldn't take it back," she said eyes downcast as she studied her hands. "Would *you* have done things differently?" Her eyes lifted to his and begged him for the truth.

"I don't know, Alex, I don't think so. I wouldn't trade Emma, Trey, or Bekah for anything. I loved Megan. But I also would never have chosen to let you think that I'd forgotten you because you were insignificant. Never that. I would change the way I've treated you—all that animosity—all these years."

She offered him the hint of a smile. "Thank you for that."

Adam wasn't sure what was next. Now that it was out there—the admission, the hurt, the shame. Where did one go forward from there? So, he spoke unfiltered truths sitting on his heart, even if he wasn't exactly clear what it was all about. "When I was in the ER, the only one I wanted to talk to was you. And when we celebrated Megan's life, the one I wanted to be with was you. And when I go to sleep at night, the one I want to tell about my day is you."

She stood and turned away from him. He wasn't sure how to interpret her. Maybe he'd gone too far. Maybe he didn't deserve to tell her what was on his heart. So, he cleared his throat and asked, "What were you trying to call me about today?"

She sniffed. "I'm not sure I want to share it now, considering what happened today."

Adam walked across the room and stood next to her. He glanced at her and noticed the tear stains on her cheeks. He noticed how her mahogany curls framed her feminine face. Adam suppressed the igniting spark he felt in his center, the itch he felt to run his fingers through Alex's hair. To turn her face to his and draw her lips to his, to remind them of how good that night had been to stay with them for nearly three decades.

He turned away from studying her and frowned shaking away the want. "The police are involved from this point on." He walked out of the kitchen and went into the living room, turned on the gas in the fireplace to ignite a light against the darkness and the cool air. "Whoever it was would be foolish to think of trying anything again now that the police are involved."

Adam heard Alex follow him into the room. "Do you trust them?"

"Have to now. So, what did you want to tell me?"

Adam watched her turn away from him and gaze into the fire. The light flickered against her features reposing them in a strange light that reminded Adam of the reflection of water. He almost smiled, realizing his thoughts, thinking of Alex like fire and water, opposing forces equally powerful and equally necessary to life; she was exactly that. And just like that he realized it: he loved her. He loved Alex James, and the realization sucked him down under the waves and held him there.

That night twenty-seven years ago, he'd wanted her, but despite the strange and bumpy journey they'd both traversed, he'd fallen in love with her along the way. Maybe he'd known it was love that day she'd held baby Trey, when it was impossible, and he's insulated it in his bitterness and anger. He didn't know—hadn't allowed himself to analyze it. But now, with the insulation peeled away, he could see it. He loved her.

His heart was bursting with it, but he couldn't say it now. And if he did, there was every possibility she would tell him to *go to hell*.

Her voice interrupted his thoughts. "I got an essay today from one of my students. The topic was about body image in the media, but interestingly enough, guess what a portion of the paper is dedicated to?"

"HGH?" Adam guessed, getting his mind back on the same track as hers.

"Right."

"Would this author happen to be a student athlete?"

Alex nodded and looked back at the flame. "HSU cheerleader."

"Can we talk to this student?" he asked.

"I thought the police were investigating from now on."

Adam nodded. "Right."

"But she is my student. And, to appease my curiosity, I wouldn't mind hearing her story."

Adam smiled. "Right."

"She won't be back until after Thanksgiving Break. She's left for the mainland for a cheer competition."

Adam nodded. What could happen in another week?

CHAPTER TWENTY-SEVEN

lex stood. "I should go."

Adam mirrored her. "You don't have to."

She looked into the depth of his gaze and knew she did. It was a contrasting juxtaposition of her heart and her head. Her heart alighted with the knowledge he'd remembered, but her head was filled with the weight of the knowledge. She didn't have to carry that burden any longer, but now there was what she'd told Megan. It was one thing to have their one-night affair out in the open, but her letter to Megan—what she'd said—that was something different.

"I do." She collected her purse and put some distance between them. "I have things I need to do tomorrow, paddling practice, grading. Regatta season is approaching."

"Will I see you at Trey's game?" he asked.

Alex walked toward the front door with slow steps. Adam trailed her. "I don't know." She wanted to be there more than anything, but she wasn't sure she could do it. Maybe she should just tell him—tell him about her letter. He'd opened up and bared everything. How come she couldn't do the same?

Because you're afraid. Afraid he'll still reject you. Afraid you'll lose him. Afraid things will change.

She stopped and turned at the door. Adam watched her, his hands in the pockets of his jeans. Her eyes caressed his bared arms and the sinew of his muscle and veins strong and beautiful. Sexy. Her heart fluttered in her chest, leaving her wanting. She wanted to feel his hands on her, his kisses, to remember with clarity what it had been like to be connected to him completely.

"I'd love to see you there." His voice was quiet and made her feel as though he might be as insecure as she felt.

She took a step backwards feeling for the door handle with her hand to keep from reaching for him. "I'm glad that you and Emma are alright," she said.

"Alex. I've tried. I can't." Adam closed the gap between them.

And then she was in his arms, her back against the door, his hands framing her face. His mouth pressed against hers. "Alex. Please."

She granted his request and kissed him with everything stored up inside her. She ran her hands over his back, found the hem of his shirt and flattened her hands against his skin underneath the fabric. It burned, so hot. It made her ignite, everywhere, the rush of want intense.

"I'm so sorry," he said between kisses. "I'm so sorry that you thought I could forget you. I'm so sorry that I hid from it and allowed it to fester between us." His tongue sought refuge with hers, and she opened to him. His hips sought hers. He tore his mouth away from hers and trailed kisses along her neck as his hands moved to her hips, drawing her against him.

She was bursting into flame. She moaned aloud and thought she might burn to ash.

Then he stopped, breathing heavily and rested his forehead against hers. He squeezed her hips and drew her close. She could feel the evidence of his need rigid against her body. "Alex, I want you," he said.

She couldn't find her voice and nodded instead. Her tongue was thick with longing and missed the entanglement with his.

He straightened, pulling her away from the door and into his embrace. "I'm sorry."

Breathless with desire she melted into his embrace. "Please. Adam. Don't."

He kissed the top of her head. "I wanted to deserve to be with you. I want you to want to be with me."

There was irony in the statement. Despite the peaks and valleys between them, she'd always wanted to deserve him. She had never *not* wanted to be with him.

Adam leaned back and caressed her face with his eyes, then leaned forward pressing a gentle chaste kiss to her lips. The depth of intimacy in that kiss added to her desire in equal measure to the passionate kisses they shared only moments earlier.

Then he smiled, that dimple deep and delicious, and reached around her to open the door.

She felt his breath hot against her ear.

"You can stay if you want to," he offered.

She willed her legs to move but as she walked away, she was beginning to wonder why she was walking away at all. Why was she fighting against the very place she wanted to be?

Adam leaned against the pillows in his bed. He'd spent the better part of the last ten minutes attempting to read Megan's journal before closing his eyes to sleep but couldn't concentrate. He was preoccupied by his evening with Alex and emotionally spent.

He loved Alex. He smiled.

The kisses they shared before she left were apparitions in his mind haunting him. He couldn't get the feel of her mouth and hands on his body from his thoughts. He wanted her so much he ached. She wanted him too. He could feel that, but she was holding back, and he wanted all of her. Realizing that he loved her changed things for him. He wanted her love too. He didn't want her holding anything back from him. It was why he'd stopped. He didn't want to be that arrogant jerk who used her again.

Adam closed the journal and tossed it on the other side of the bed. As he reached to turn off the lamp, a white corner of paper slipped from the gilded edged of Megan's journal peeking out as though screaming it wasn't supposed to be there. He leaned over and opened it. A plain white envelope was tucked into the back of the journal between the last page and the cover. Adam pulled it from the book. It made a slight cracking sound as the piece of envelop was unstuck from the cover, the adhesive from the envelope holding it in place.

Adam opened it. Folded inside were several sheets of paper—a letter. Adam removed it, but it wasn't in Megan's handwriting. He looked at the last page and was surprised to find that it was a letter to Megan from Alex. Adam due to everything that had transpired today, suddenly felt as though he might be trespassing on a private conversation. But Megan had put it in journals written for him. Her last journal. She wanted him to read it. Adam opened it and read the words:

Dear Megan:

We've known each other a long time, friend. You are so very important to me, and that is why this will be one of the most difficult things I have ever said to you. But I fear that if I don't tell you what is on my mind, I won't have been as true of a friend as you have been to me. Your confession has not only shocked but rocked me off center. You've always been a guiding star for me and watching you struggle with a choice such as this, so wholly out of your character, is frightening.

I remember when we met. That fateful day in Kindergarten at Mills Elementary. You'd approached me and said with a smile on your face, "See my new shoes? They have blue flowers on them. I like your purple shoes." It was as though I was supposed to find you that day and you were supposed to find me. Inseparable since.

In the early years of adolescence, I envied you for what you had and wanted it for my own. You had the best family though they welcomed me with open arms. I couldn't help but be jealous because my own family was so dysfunctional, and though I confess, I was envious of your family, I worked through those feelings in time and came to realize that in a different way, your family was my family; I didn't need to be jealous. As we've grown up, you've always had things come easy to you. School was easy, making friends simple. Your winning personality has always been your strength, Megs. Please don't think that I begrudge you these things.

When we attended HSU, we grew into women together. We shared our triumphs and our failures in every arena of our lives. You know things that I have never told a soul, not even my ex-husband Geoff. Megan, I have trusted you with every facet of my life, and I treasure that bond. I'm so happy for your success and your blessings. You are my sister and my friend. I love what you have achieved, and though I may have questioned my own life in comparison to yours, my envy has never crossed into your life, except for one thing, Megan. I have envied you one thing which brings me to why I'm writing you this letter.

Remember the bet we made, about that football player our

freshman year of college, the football quarterback? Yes, Adam. You bet me that you could get him to initiate talking to you within fifteen minutes, and I'd taken the bet. I remember telling you that he looked too shy. I'd won the bet, although I had thought at the time, I would lose it. You see, I had already met Adam before. He was the one, the one-night stand—remember from the weekend after school had started? Yes, I mentioned that night, never told you who he was (I never expounded on any details I'd been so embarrassed about the whole affair). I'd made that bet with you thinking I would lose because he hadn't been so shy with me that night. I figured he'd come across as the smooth player that I thought he was. I'd seen him around campus over the course of those next few weeks and practically hid when I saw him, afraid he'd recognize me, afraid he wouldn't. I was so horrified that he'd never contacted me, but I realize he had been so drunk that night that he didn't remember who I was.

As we walked across campus that day, he didn't say a word to me. I had built in my head he was a smooth operator, that he'd just wanted a one-night stand because he hadn't tried to contact me, and then, when he had the opportunity to try and hit on me like the player that I'd conjured him to be in my head, he didn't take it. That was when it started, when I began falling in love with a guy with whom you were infatuated. It was the first time since feeling envious of your family that I coveted something that you wanted.

I tried to stifle the feelings I had for him. Not only was I infatuated with a guy who had aided me in abandoning my principles, a guy who didn't even remember me, but also, I was in love with a man who could destroy a friendship I treasure. It was so difficult participating in all those group dates, watching the bond between you grow and wanting so much to be the one he wanted. But I wasn't who he wanted; _you were_. It was obvious in his eyes how he felt about you. Adoration and affection, and though it was painful, I reminded myself that you are my sister. I was happy for you. There was no way that I would jeopardize my relationship with you. But that didn't cure my attraction to him, and instead it grew as my relationship with him changed. Even as his animosity developed (an animosity I have never really understood) I couldn't fight the one-sided love that had blossomed.

I worked hard at fighting it. I dated others, joined the Peace Corps and figured getting away would kill my yearning from my best friend's by then fiancé. The Peace Corp didn't help me forget, but I met Geoff and thought that everything would be normal again. Adam was a memory, an infatuation of a college girl who'd grown up and seen the world. But when Geoff and I returned and tried to be the suburbia married couple, I couldn't help but compare him, compare us, to what you and Adam had built. Poor Geoff, he'd gotten the raw deal from the get-go, because I couldn't let go of something I would never have. Please don't think I blame anyone other than myself for my failed marriage, or that I write this because I want you to feel sorry for me. I have built a satisfying life and feel fulfilled in the choices I've made.

I witnessed you and Adam grow together, a love, a friendship that has no bounds. As the years have gone by, your relationship seemed to deepen with the addition of each of your children. But lately, I have seen you and Adam drift. I think maybe he blames me for what's happening to your marriage now. I can shoulder that burden if you can save what you have.

You see Megan, the other night, when you made that decision to begin what now has become an affair, I tried to tell you. I told you to think about what you have before you make a rash decision, but you made it anyway, and I knew it was a mistake. So, I'm willing to put our friendship on the line by sharing all of this with you, by taking Adam's side instead of yours.

I have spent a lifetime coveting your marriage and the man that you are married to. I have watched how your husband has loved, admired, cared for, built a life dedicated to the family you've created. I know he's not perfect—he's human after all—but he is an amazing husband and an amazing father. I have grown to love him even more deeply than I can fathom ever having loved someone.

I would NEVER have shared this with you. I'm content to take this secret to my grave, except that you are throwing away the best thing that has ever happened to you. I love you, Megan, so much so that I'm begging you to end this mistake that you are making. This temporary man, the one that you have decided to use to punish Adam, isn't a speck of the man he is. Please don't throw away the beautiful life that you've created with Adam for something so temporary and fleeting. It won't be worth it to lose the man I have watched you love with such depth and devotion nor to lose three beautiful children that are a testament to that love. Please don't continue down this path; you won't like the destination. Turn around. Tell Adam. Work on healing your marriage. He loves you. He will forgive you and become a better husband because that is the kind of man he is.

I love you and though I may lose you because of my blatant confession of this secret, it will be worth it, because two of the people I love most in this world are on the verge of losing something beautiful.

Your sister forever,
Alex

Adam placed the last page of the letter behind the previous pages as he sat in stunned silence. He read it a second time, then a third, trying to wrap his mind around it. Alex loved him? Had always loved him? And Megan had known. He studied the date at the top of the letter and a quick check back in her journals, he realized it was dated before marriage counseling, before Megan had told him the truth about her affair. She'd known then, and she had taken her friend's advice. A stirring in his chest moved his heart with new awareness.

Now he understood why Alex thought he'd been right. The day of the funeral he'd accused her of trying to break up his marriage. His face burned with the understanding that she'd been the one to save it, but perhaps she thought he would see this letter as proof? Alex who had loved him then. Did she still? But Adam thought he might already know the answer, and that spark in his heart ignited into a flame.

CHAPTER TWENTY-EIGHT

The early morning sun crawled through the clear sky, a bright yellow orb that promised unrelenting heat later that day. Alex slowed to a walk as she neared her starting point, her footprints in the sand distinct impressions though rather formless in the fine substance. As she reached her starting point, she sank to a seated position and willed her breathing to regulate. She had punished her body enough that morning with paddling practice and a nice run over the white sandy beach.

She pulled a yellow towel from her bag that she'd unceremoniously dumped there that morning before practice. It was filled with easily replaced items in case someone decided they might like her bag more than she—but so far, no one had ever felt the need. She wiped the sheen of perspiration from her skin and laid the towel across her lap. She pulled her legs up and rested her elbows on her knees. An onlooker might have assumed that she was contemplating the ebb and flow of the ocean as it tugged at the shore, but her thoughts were otherwise engaged.

Instead, she was thinking about the time spent in Adam's embrace the night before. She couldn't get his voice out of her mind. And his words: *you must know I want you.* They had pushed her that morning. Even her teammates had noticed her preoccupation, teasing her about her lack of concentration. She'd had to refocus her energy on her duties in the canoe.

She couldn't do this to herself anymore, she realized. She was fighting a losing battle. As she watched the flow of the waves, breaking like giants and crashing against the land as they rushed toward her she recognized that was how she felt. Only, she was swimming against the tide and so tired. In one swift moment, the ocean would drag her under, and she would drown the more she fought. The alternative was to turn into the tide and allow it to wash her where it wanted to. She could relax and take it one moment at a time, seeing where it would take her. But she knew where it was headed.

You must know I want you.

She wasn't exactly sure what she was fighting anymore. Before it was clear. Megan was Adam's wife. He was her best friend's husband. It was easy to fight because she knew why. But now, with Adam and the kids returned to her life after a terrible year missing them, was her reticence just because she feared losing them again? Would she? Maybe she wasn't giving Adam enough credit, but she'd also spent a lifetime walking around with her heart outside of her body. If she admitted her feelings for him, followed the tide toward him, acquiesced to her desires would she survive another heartbreak?

Alex shoved her hands into the sand and filtered it through her fingers. Watching the grains moved through like water, she realized that she'd been holding onto the memory, the love she felt, the secrecy of it for twenty-seven years, and now things were changing.

She looked up at the ocean again. Everything about it—the water, the tides, the sand, the shore—was moving, changing, but she wasn't. She'd been stuck and fear was keeping her stuck now. That wasn't what she wanted.

What do you want? She heard an internal voice ask her.

I want Adam, she replied, and tears surfaced in her eyes. She had always wanted Adam, and she knew she couldn't fight it anymore.

Alex tossed the towel over her bag, stood, and walked down to the surf. She waded into the water. The surf rushed up over her feet. The waves pushed and pulled at her legs and waist. The sea rushed against her skin, and she dove into the next wave. The cool salty water baptized her with acceptance and hope. She didn't want to fight anymore. She was done. She didn't need to hide, or fight against her love, or fear what could happen next. When she reemerged from the depths, it was as though she'd washed off her old paradigms and was ready to face something new. It filled her with joy.

Alex turned into the tide and allowed it to take her back to shore. She climbed from the water, the surf getting stronger as it tried to pull her back out. She stood and wiped her hair away from her face then stopped short. Jack stood next to her bag, his hand outstretched with her towel. His blue eyes were upturned with his bright smile.

"Jack," she said. Surprised gripped her. "Wow. I'm surprised to see you here. I mean, you've said you aren't a big fan of the ocean," she added and continued walking toward him.

"I finally yielded to your suggestion of getting out to the beach." He handed her the towel when she reached him. "Been coming out as often as I can."

"Really?" She wiped her face, then wrapped the towel around her body. After all of the misled attempt to persuade her to be more romantically involved with him, she felt an intense urge to cover up.

"Well, you have been singing the praises of the ocean since I met you. I figured I would give it a try. You've talked so often of how much you enjoy this beach at dawn."

Alex pulled her surf shorts on under her towel. "That is true. There's something kind of spiritual about it when the sun climbs above the horizon." She pulled a fitted white tank over her head and yanked the towel from her body at the same time.

"Yeah. I see what you are saying now. I've been trying to get out here a few times a week. I realize now how much time I have spent cooped up in my lab."

"Really? Turning a new leaf then?" she asked. She stuffed her belongings back into her bag, pulled her car key from a pocket in her shorts, and slung the bag over her shoulder.

"So, you could say, I suppose."

"Well, I'm headed out." She turned and walked up the slope of the beach toward the parking lot.

The sound of Jack jogging to catch up with her followed her up into the lot. "I just meant that, well," he hesitated a moment as though gathering his words. "I haven't seen much of you lately–"

"I've been really busy," she interrupted. "Things have been hectic."

"If doing the things you enjoy can ensure seeing more of you, then I want to make a change," he finished.

Alex stopped and turned to face him. She stood a few feet from the hood of her car. "Jack," she started.

"I know. I know. Just friends," he said. "I got it."

Alex was cautious. "I get the feeling you are hoping it might turn into more though." Her words sounded cold to her own ears, but she couldn't risk the miscommunication. "It won't."

He hesitated and looked down at his feet. Alex had a quick vision of what he must have looked like as a little boy. And she knew her question was right on. "Maybe, but I'm willing to take what you can give. If it's only friendship—okay." He lifted his hands and shoulders as though shrugging, a movement that seemed to signify his acceptance of the situation.

She smiled at him. "Well, good, then." She turned and closed the short gap between the car and herself. "Enjoy your swim."

She heard the crunch of loose gravel as Jack walked behind her. "Are you going to the football game tonight?" he asked.

She suppressed the urge to sigh but didn't turn. Instead she opened her trunk and put the bag inside. "No. I don't think so," she said and unlocked her car door.

"How come?" he asked.

That was a good question. She could see Adam. The idea had a certain appeal. Then again, she wanted to get a sense of herself, her wants before confusing what she wanted with being near him. So, she said, "I've got a lot of papers to get through before Thanksgiving break. I'm sure you're swamped too."

"Aren't we all. Come to the game though. A bunch of us are meeting up to enjoy some time away from grading. There are five of us. You remember David Bennett, right?"

"Thanks, but I didn't make a plan to go. You know how I am with spontaneity," she said, thinking it was a viable excuse if a bit over exaggerated.

"We are riding the carpool bus that leaves from campus at five this evening."

"I'll think about it," she said. David Bennett's name was an interesting prospect to contemplate. Maybe she should go, use it for research. She thought about Claire's paper. Maybe she could learn something.

"Do," he said.

Alex signaled to her car seat with her thumbs. "I have to go. It was good seeing you. Maybe I'll see you at the game."

He backed away. "That would be good. I'm going to go get my swim in," he said, smiled. "Glad I saw you." He turned and walked back down the sand.

Alex started her car. Maybe she would go to the game. She would be able to watch Trey play, and though it wouldn't be with Adam, who she really wanted to be with, she could do a bit of reconnaissance. Yes, she would go—for Trey and Bekah, for Claire, for all the kids who'd lost their lives that Megan thought was connected, for Emma and the baby. Getting to know Bennett a bit better might be just the break they needed.

Adam had lived another day without Alex in his life. He had gone another twenty-four hours without seeing her. Adam wasn't particularly sentimental, but if he was being honest, he was driving himself crazy thinking about her. And he was aware how much he missed her. He hadn't reached out because he was giving her space.

Now, Adam sat alone at the football game attempting to concentrate on Trey's last home game of the season and all he wanted to do was be sitting here with her. He was cheering for Trey. He was cognizant of the fact that Trey was having a stellar game. He could hear the fans around him. He could see the colors, hear the sounds, smell the scents, but his thoughts were with Alex.

The discovery of Alex's letter to Megan had rocked him, leaving his nerves exposed and raw. Needing to move and dispel the nervous energy rocking through him, he went to the bathroom at the end of the third quarter.

"Adam?"

He turned and looked at the familiar face of Milton Yamane. "Milton." Adam held out his hand. They moved off to the side, a bank on the side of the human river. "How are things?"

"Good. Good. Feeling any better about that issue you came in to see me about a couple of weeks ago?"

Adam kept a poker face though each of his senses took on an edge of heightened awareness. *Was he fishing? Is he responsible?* Adam felt a little nudge of guilt knowing Emma was looking into Milton's background. He'd always seemed to be the upstanding guy, a friend to him and Megan, but how could the athletic director not be aware of what was happening to his athletes? And with his kids at risk, he couldn't let the guilt stick. "Not particularly. Seems there's a lot of questionable things happening on that campus, now with the death of that Gomes girl."

The other man's face gave nothing away. "I've been thinking about it." His eyes darted away from Adam's face momentarily as he looked at passing faces. "Maybe we could get together."

"Sure."

"Let me get back to you?" he asked.

"Sounds good. You know how to reach me," Adam answered. They shook hands again. He watched Milton wade into the current and disappear within the crowd.

His thoughts a jumble after the encounter with Milton, not to mention his preoccupation with Alex, Adam dialed Emma's number on his cell phone. He needed to wrap his mind around something of substance before he lost it all together. "Em?"

"Hi Dad. How's the game?"

"Good. Trey rushed for a touchdown in the second quarter. How's my grandbaby?" Adam stepped back to let an elderly woman pass by.

"So, that's how it's going to be huh?" There was a smile in the lilt of her voice. "We're both great."

"Guess who I just saw?"

"Who?"

"Milton Yamane."

"Really?"

"Learn anything we didn't already know?" Adam turned so that he was facing a wall and held a hand over one ear to hear Emma better.

"Not much. He's a pretty typical guy. Graduated from a local high school in '69. He went to college on the mainland, played golf for Stanford. His first athletic department job was through Stanford in '80. He worked his way to Director at HSU in '90. The only blip I found was in his bank records."

"I know most of that. How on earth did you get into his bank records?"

"I have my sources," she said. "He had a very lucrative year in '99 with four sizable deposits that stand out. He was audited in 2000 but came out okay."

"1999, huh? When was the first death of an athlete that we are aware of?" Adam asked.

"2000, I think," she answered.

"And no strange financial activity after?"

"No. Everything looks legit."

"Okay." He paused and watched the passing faces. "Thanks hon."

"You know what I'm thinking?" she asked.

"I'm afraid to ask, but I think I know." Adam waded back into the crowd to return to his seat.

"Looking into where those sizable deposits came from."

"Emma—you terrify me." Adam ended the call after saying goodbye.

He blinked as his pace slowed. He was thinking about Alex too much. An apparition of her stood a few yards away. Someone in the crowd bumped him. He blinked again. With Jack. A jealous fire ignited in his gut and hurt spread through his body like a tidal wave. Alex looked up and her green eyes met his. He knew he had no right to feel jealous, and the fact he was jealous made him even angrier. Alex had every right to move on with anyone—even though he wanted it to be him. And dammit, he wasn't going to give up without a fight. But Jack?

She smiled and offered him a slight wave. In as long as he'd known her, he knew her smiles. This one didn't reach her pretty eyes. It wasn't quite fear, but something else he didn't recognize. He took a deep breath and assuaged his anger with the understanding she must have a good reason to be with Jack. He trusted her. He had no reason not to, but his hurt was rooted in the disappointment she hadn't chosen to come with him. She was with Jack, who was tripping over himself for her. Adam did not like Alex with another man.

And yet she loved you while you spent a lifetime with Megan.

The realization cooled him. "Alex. Jack," he said with what he hoped sounded even and noncommittal.

"Adam," Jack boomed. He was all smiles, most certainly because Alex was with him. In all the time he'd known the Jolly Giant they'd been engaged in his one-sided pissing contest. This was a win in his book and made Adam irritated. Maybe it wasn't so one-sided.

"Adam," she said. Her face was pale.

A moment of concern for her hit him, but when he noticed Jack's hand on the small of her back, he dismissed it. "Good to see you both. I'd love to talk story, but I can't stay," he said. "Fourth quarter is about to start." He walked away even more confused about his feelings and Alex's.

He settled back into his seat at the stadium intent on focusing on the final quarter of the game. He was making more of the letter—written eleven years ago—than he should be. She had moved on and maybe it was with the Jolly Giant. Adam had no one to blame but himself. He'd been awful to her all those years.

But she carried that torch for sixteen years before writing that letter.

He shook the thought away in time to center his attention on Trey as he dropped back and completed a sixty-yard pass bringing the crowd to its feet. He stood and cheered for his boy.

Adam knew he would have to see Alex, maybe he would know how to act his age by then.

Alex watched Adam walk away, her heart aching, and stifled the need to go after him, to explain why she was with Jack, but her own pride, her own sense of justice ignited knowing Adam had jumped to conclusions. *Let him stew*, she thought.

But she wasn't going to let Jack get away with his crap. "What the hell was that?" she asked.

"What are you talking about?" Jack asked his eyes wide with innocence.

"I'm done with this." She turned away from him and walked

down the concourse toward the exit.

"Alex!" Jack called after her. She could hear his footsteps on the concrete behind her.

She continued walking.

Jack's hand wrapped around her arm and pulled her around to face him. "What's wrong? I don't understand why you are so upset. Are you and Kāne, like, a thing?" he asked.

She shook her head. "That isn't any of your business." And she fought the tears beginning to work their way into her eyes. "And I don't appreciate this stupid game you are playing."

"What game?" he asked.

"Don't play dumb, Jack. It's an insult."

"Jack. Alex. I came to see if you needed help with the food," David Bennett said as he approached them. He was smiling and Alex noticed his gaze shift to her chest.

Alex rolled her eyes and walked away.

"Alex! Where are you going?" Jack called after her.

She turned and walked backwards toward the exit. She'd get a taxi home. "I'm out. Have a nice fucking life, Jack."

"Alex. Don't leave."

She didn't turn around but offered a half-hearted wave.

She heard Jack shout, "I'll call you later."

He was an idiot, she decided. One of those super smart people who had no clue about social relationships. To make things worse, spending time with him and Bennett and the others at the game had been a waste of time. She could have gone with Adam, or she could have been grading papers at home and had a better evening. She'd given Adam the impression she wasn't coming to the game and did the opposite. She could tell he was hurt. His jaw set in that familiar way when he was bothered. She'd seen it so many times. All the rumination earlier about how she needed to move forward and now she was right back to where she and Adam always were angry, hurt, and embittered. It felt terrible.

CHAPTER TWENTY-NINE

Milton Yamane looked up from his desk to see Stanton Thom coming in through the double-door entrance to his office. Milton stood, "Stanton. You were just here. A shock. What brings you out this way?" He motioned for Stanton to sit and then took his own seat again.

"Milt," Stanton stated using a nickname Milton hated. "We go back a long way, don't we?"

"Yes, we do Stan. Is there a class reunion coming up?" Milton was being patronizing, and he knew it, but couldn't resist. At one time the two men had been great friends. Milton had respected Stanton and jumped at the chance to work for him at HSU. At one time he would have trusted Stanton with his life. But time, and mortality, rubs a person much like water over rocks, wearing them down, eroding them.

Stanton leaned forward in his seat so quickly that Milton was knocked off guard. "Don't be stupid," he said. "You know why I'm here."

"Can't imagine," Milton stated.

Stanton stood and walked to the large window, his hands clasped behind his back. "This is a nice office. Great view."

Milton swiveled around in his chair to look at Stanton. He remained silent.

"You have a lot to be thankful for, Milt, a great job with a nice salary, a cushy office, an amazing home, fantastic kids, and a beautiful wife." Stanton stopped to look at Milton.

"Are you threatening me?" Milton asked. His heart had stopped beating, then restarted at an accelerated pace. Rage ripped through his veins.

"What? Is that what you think?" Stanton feigned surprise and innocence raising his hands in mock surrender. "I'm just checking in with a friend. Speaking of friends, how is Adam Kāne?"

So, there it was. Stanton was having him followed. He'd wondered and now he knew. "Not sure."

"Oh," Stanton said. He moved over to the bookcases and fingered objects on the shelves. "I heard that you saw him at the last home football game."

"You're having me followed, Stanton?"

"Just checking to see if I smell a rat."

Milton ignored the comment wondering if Stanton knew. "I didn't know you knew Adam Kāne," he evaded.

"Who doesn't, one of the greatest quarterbacks in HSU history with a son moving in the same direction? A major donor to the university. A possible contributor to my bid for governor. It's my job to know him. I'm curious what he had to say to you."

"Seems natural that a former athlete would be friendly with an athletic director."

Stanton swung around to face Milton. His eyes were slits and his teeth bared. Milton couldn't help but picture the rat that Stanton had just referred to. "Don't play games with me."

"I didn't start this game, Stan. You did."

"Allow me to remind you of something: You're just as culpable in this as I, so don't start forgetting the part you played. Your

272

conscience isn't going to do you any good at this stage in the game." Stanton had walked over and was now leaning on Milton's desk, an obvious tactic to try and intimidate him. "The trail that leads to me, leads to you." He stopped, letting that sink in and then stood up. "I know Kāne's been asking around. He'll be taken care of as well as anyone else who gets in the way of this project." He let the meaning of his last statement hang between them.

The last statement made him wonder about the recent murder. "Are you through, Stan?" Milton asked.

"I'd keep in mind all that you have to lose, friend." Stanton said and he walked out of the office.

Milton turned to face the windows that looked over the athletic complex. Had he known, he never would have agreed to what Stanton had described to him. Milton had just thought it was kickbacks, something that happens all the time.

Had Milton known then what he knew now, he never would have agreed, but he was long past making the right decision. Milton was in deep. He leaned his elbows on his desk and buried his face in his hands hoping for a way out of the mess he'd gotten himself into. Nothing was more important than his family, not even the truth.

Mana Lopes tipped the large glass of ice water back and gulped it down. Those around him, other detectives and police officers gathered to celebrate the retirement of a dinosaur detective, tipped mugs of beer, shot glasses of tequila or whatever other alcoholic preference that brought the numb. Mana preferred the harsh bite of reality and chose not to drink alcohol, and not in the middle of a case. The Gomes case was a case he needed to solve. He didn't need to be blurry.

"Speech, Ramirez! Speech!" The loud cheering rose above all of the other sounds within the small Irish pub at the edge of Honolulu town. The room with its green walls with their mahogany wainscot decorated with black and white photographs of everything Honolulu from police officers to sports stars like Duke Kahanamoku was packed. Mana stood toward the entrance, his mug in hand for the toast. He watched Detective Ramirez make his way to the bar, slaps on the back and handshakes propelling him forward. The tall thin man turned to address his fellow officers, his face bright from imbibing his alcoholic preference.

As Detective Ramirez began to speak, Mana heard the telltale ring of his cell phone. He set down his mug and left the bar, stepping into the humid air outside the bar. Though the temperature was still warm, it felt refreshing next to his skin from the crowded heat of the pub.

"Lopes," he said into the phone.

"I had the device we found on the car checked," a male voice answered. Mana knew it was Tony Jorges, a detective working the accident involving Adam Kāne and his daughter.

"Let me guess, no prints."

"You got it."

"What's your next step?" Mana turned up the street and started walking toward the parking garage where he'd left his car. He didn't want to tread on someone else's investigation, but he had a feeling they were connected.

"We're going to have to go to individual parts and see if we can't tag where the perp purchased the ingredients for the carbon monoxide cocktail."

"Thanks for keeping me in the loop on this."

"No problem, Lopes. You think the cases are connected?"

"Who knows," he answered and took the stairs several at a time. He had three flights to walk, and the corridor smelled like piss.

"Well, I'll keep you looped in."

"Thanks, Jorges."

Mana disconnected the call and walked through the doorway

274

into the concrete building. His footsteps echoed in the space, sounding hollow. He went to his car and climbed into the vehicle. Though it was a Sunday, time didn't work that way for him. He had a case to solve, and he worked until he solved it.

His most pressing problem now was that he seemed to be at a dead end. He was waiting for Tee's DNA results. He was waiting to see if Jorges and his detectives discovered anything on the car accident. And his search for Dwight Connolly had turned up an interesting coincidence. He had worked as a research scientist for a pharmaceutical company in Texas many years before moving to Hawai'i and becoming a county coroner. But Mana couldn't question the man. Not yet. He didn't want to alert any players if he did—not yet anyway. And there wasn't anything linking Connolly to Gomes or Dr. Billings in any way.

Mana drove the car out of the garage and turned it toward the station. He would park there and go through the case files again. He missed something. He just had to figure out what.

CHAPTER THIRTY

Adam pulled his car into the Zippy's parking lot and went into the restaurant, a staple establishment for the Kāne Ohana. He ordered some chicken, chili and rice, and waited for the food, before heading out to Kaimana Beach Park with his surfboard strapped into the jeep. Trey had suggested that the family opt for a day out at the beach for their weekly get together, the beach a favorite Sunday activity for the family. Before Megan's illness.

Traffic thinned the further he drove from Honolulu and merged into one of the two lanes on Kalaniana'ole Highway, the road dropping off into the sea. Jack Johnson crooned, *Better Together*, from the car radio, as Adam drove along the highway. His thoughts shifted to Alex as he thought about the words of the song and pondered the coincidence of how the words matched their situation—as if the artist himself had known about them when he wrote it. Adam smiled at that absurdity. He still felt raw at the sight of Alex with Jack the night before, but after having had time to ponder it, he realized he had jumped to conclusions. Besides, she was her own person, and she didn't owe him an explanation, even if he wanted one.

Even more than that, Adam wanted to know if she still loved him. He wanted to know if his love for her was a dead-end. He wanted to know if it was too late.

Adam kept circling back to the realization Megan had known. She had known for the last eleven years of her life that Alex had loved him, and she'd held that, hadn't said a thing. Or had she? Adam recalled Megan in hospice, right before the end.

He'd been sitting with her, his hand holding hers. She'd been in and out of wakefulness, the drugs keeping her comfortable. It had been during one of her salient moments, after talking about the kids, about new issues at work, and just contentment of being together, but the extended time had begun to wear on her.

"Megan, hon," he'd said, "You need to get some rest, save your strength."

She'd shaken her head. "I need to tell you–" her voice had been thin.

"You can tell me after you've rested."

"I have a lot of time to rest. Adam. It's coming," she'd said. "Alex," she'd said the name so quiet, and then her eyes drifted to the observation window as a serene smile passed over her features. She'd shut her eyes again.

Adam had turned to see Alex standing at the window, her hand pressed against the glass, a salutation. He'd turned back to Megan and waited for her to finish her thought. But she hadn't. She'd drifted back into drug-induced sleep and never mentioned it again. It hadn't been long after that she'd succumbed to the cancer.

Adam blinked away the difficult memory and continued to drive. When he reached the eastern side of the island where the cliffs rose right out of the dark blue ocean, his spirit soared along with him as he drove. It lifted from his soul and climbed beyond the car, surfing the wind as he sped along the road.

He drove the car into a gravel parking lot at the beach park where he was to meet the kids and parked. The kids had obviously been there for a while and had secured a spot in the grass on a bluff that overlooked the surf. They'd erected an open tent for added shade. Underneath were two coolers, a plastic folding table littered with goodies to eat and chairs. Two of the chairs were occupied, one by Emma, the other by Grant. Bekah and Trey weren't in the shelter.

"Oh Zippy's!" Emma stood when she saw him. "How did you know that's what I wanted Dad?" She hugged him.

Grant shook Adam's hand. "You saved me. She was just trying to talk me into going and getting Zippy's for second lunch. My wife is a hobbit." He laughed. "I was about to have to drive back to town to get some!"

"There's enough here to feed an army." Adam set the pink and white plastic tubs with their contents on the table. "What time did you folks get here?" Adam asked. He looked at his watch which read three o'clock.

"About seven this morning," Grant replied. "Set up the tent."

"Where are Trey and Bekah?" Adam asked.

"Where do you think?" Emma remarked and nodded with her head toward the ocean.

Adam turned to look out at the surf, the aqua water bending and folding as the white water rushed over the sand. The white caps rushed up onto the golden beach and left its imprint before it sunk back into the granules or slipped back into the surf. Adam found Bekah right away, clad in a bright yellow bikini top and white board shorts. She was shredding across the wave front until it folded over her and encased her in its strength. Her board with her ankle tethered popped up, and she slipped back onto its shiny surface and headed back out.

Trey paddled toward the shore to catch an oncoming wave. His board was caught by the force of the cresting water, and he stood. Adam could see that Trey moved with the board as though it was an extension of his feet. He dipped and touched the water inside the wave as it rolled over into a barrel and disappeared inside the tube. As the wave collapsed Trey shot out with the water and went belly to board.

"Let me get your board," Grant offered.

"Sure. Thanks," Adam said and told Grant where he parked. "Did you bring yours?" he asked his son-in-law.

"No. Mine broke the last time I was out, and I haven't replaced it."

"Welcome to fatherhood." He chuckled. "Take mine out, if you'd like. I'll catch it when you are done."

Adam sat in one of the chairs, turning it to face the surf so he could watch Trey and Bekah, while enjoying his oldest. Emma took his hand in hers, and they sat for a while, at peace with their surroundings. There was nothing to bother them there. No threats, no worries, no fears. There was only family, love, joy. There was the sound of the ocean and the feel of being connected to the 'aina. Adam for a split-second wished for Megan, and in the next moment realized she was there. She would always be there in the faces and spirit of their children, in the quiet meadow spaces of his heart. It was then he realized while he was missing Megan, his heart was seeking Alex.

"This is wonderful," he said breaking the silence. He squeezed Emma's hand as they watched Grant join Trey and Bekah in the ocean.

"Yeah," she answered squeezing his hand in response. They sat for a while longer, enjoying the moment.

"Dad?"

Adam hummed a noise of acknowledgement, then looked at his daughter.

"Are you okay?"

"Yeah."

She looked back at the ocean. "Are you lonely?"

"Why would I be lonely? I have you guys," he replied, but he knew what she meant. Was he lonely for companionship, for the romantic love that had been stripped from his life? The answer was, yes, but he knew who he wanted to share it with if she'd have him. He glanced at Emma unwilling to burden her with that knowledge and wondered what she and the kids would think. Would they resent Alex? Would they feel they were cheating on their mother's memory?

"Why?"

"The other day, at the hospital, Grant and I had a tough conversation about if one of us left the other behind." She glanced at him and squeezed his hand. "If something happened to me, I wouldn't want Grant stop his life." She smiled. "There should be sufficient weeping and near-death starvation for missing me so much, of course." Her face turned serious. "But I would want him to find happiness again. It just got me thinking about you and Mom."

Adam didn't say anything. He didn't need to.

"Dad?"

He made another noise and looked back at Emma.

"Mom wouldn't want you to be lonely."

A rush of emotion welled up in Adam looking at his daughter— so much like Megan. He had to look away and focused on the energy of the ocean. He nodded. "Thanks, Em."

She squeezed his hand again and got up. "Shall we wait for them before dipping into the chili?" she asked.

"My grandbaby waits for no surfer. Eat."

She opened the containers and scooped rice and chili onto a plate. "Would you like something?"

"I'll get it."

"I was looking through Mom's research again."

"Em. The police got it. I turned over all of her files."

"I know, and I'm being safe. Just thinking about it. She had an informant contact her, that's how she got the initial name. Someone known as m-y-a-l-l-y."

"My ally? As in my friend?"

"That's the partial email address."

"I wonder if there would be any possible way to look into who sent them—hypothetically, of course?" Adam stood at the end of the table with a plate in hand.

"Not without the original emails. But I did find something interesting," she said. "Guess who was a classmate of Yamane's."

"Who?" Adam added some baby carrots to his plate.

"Stanton Thom."

He stopped to look at Emma who stood at the opposite end of the table. "You're kidding. The HSU president?"

Emma nodded. "So, I decided to look into Stanton Thom. I didn't find much, except for one thing." Emma picked up an olive off of her plate and popped it in her mouth.

"The one thing being?"

"Sizable deposits in his bank records. Same time as Yamane's but more sizable and more frequent."

"He wouldn't be that stupid Emma. The man wants the governor's office so bad he can feel the leather chair on his ass." Adam dished out a helping of ahi poke with onion and shoyu, his favorite dish.

Emma laughed. "Okay. But it doesn't change the fact that they are there." She walked back to her chair and set the plate down on the empty table.

"Did you find the source of Milton's deposits?" Adam followed her.

"Bonus checks from a second income. Everything checked out with the IRS. It looked like one of those wellness companies" — Emma made the quotations with her fingers— "named Apex. I looked into the company. Their primary focus is on anti-aging, physical enhancement, and weight loss."

Adam raised an eyebrow. "Physical enhancement you say? Maybe the kind of products that contain HGH?" He picked up a carrot.

"My next step." She smiled at him.

Adam chuckled and shook his head. "You are your mother."

They were silent for a while shoulder to shoulder, watching the ocean. Grant was paddling into a wave and pulled himself up onto the board. As he floated on the board toward the shore, Grant sunk to his belly to lie on the board and rode the swell onto the beach. He picked up the board and headed toward the tent. Adam noticed that Bekah and Trey were right behind him.

"Grant must have told them I picked up Zippy's," Adam laughed. He turned and sat down. "Thanksgiving is this week." Last year they hadn't done much but stare at one another over a pre-made meal.

"We're having it at the house, right?" Emma asked.

"As if somewhere else was acceptable," he replied with a smile. "What do I need to do?"

"Get the ingredients. I can email you the shopping list. I'm going to enlist Bekah to help me with the cooking."

"What about me?" he asked. "I'm hurt."

Emma snorted. "Whatever. You are never a help on Thanksgiving during whatever football game is on that day."

Adam chuckled and clutched his heart though he knew that to be true. "I'll toss in the turkey first thing and prep something in front of the TV. Are you inviting Grant's family?"

"No. We'll stop there in the evening. Have you invited Aunty Alex?" she asked.

"No," he answered though the thought had crossed his mind.

"You better do it soon—before she makes other plans."

"Wow," Adam chuckled. "I didn't realize you felt so strongly about this."

"About what?" Trey asked a bit out of breath from jogging up the beach. "Hey, Dad." He punched Adam's shoulder before heading to the table with all the food.

"Inviting Aunty Alex to Thanksgiving," Emma stated.

"Um, yeah. She's family," Bekah picked through what was on the table, popping a chip into her mouth. "Last year was shitty, but even more so without her there."

Emma, Trey and Grant nodded in agreement.

Bekah kissed the top of Adam's head and went back to the table to pick through the food again. "Yes. Zippy's!" she exclaimed and in the next breath said, "I can ask her."

"I can do it," Adam stated. When he saw they were all looking at him like he might have sprouted a second head, he added, "I was supposed to call her anyway." Then he formulated in his head the best way to do it realizing he would need to pass her neighborhood on the way home.

CHAPTER THIRTY-ONE

Alex looked up from the essays she was grading when she heard a noise. She'd been aware of the sound of a car door shutting, but she'd dismissed it. In her neighborhood everyone parked on the street in front of their houses. It wasn't uncommon to hear that sound, though the fact that the sun had sunk below the horizon over an hour ago should have placed the sound of a car door on her radar.

She'd spent a better part of the day grading term papers, trying to finish them before the Thanksgiving holiday. But she'd also spent countless minutes reading and rereading page after page because she wasn't concentrating on her task. She couldn't get Adam out of her head. More than anything it was his look, the stubborn set of his jaw, but more than that, she'd glimpsed something else in the depths of his eyes. Had it been hurt? If there was hurt, could that mean he felt more about her than she'd thought?

She shook her head yet again from her wandering thoughts, directed her concentration to the paper, glanced at the stack and realized she had made some headway. Around thirty papers to go. She closed the paper she was reading, noting her observations in the margins with her green pen, and put it in the finished stack.

Closing her eyes, she leaned her head against the back of the sofa. She took a deep breath. *A cup of tea sounds just right*, she thought.

A light knock at her front door snapped her head up from the couch. Her brow creased in suspicion. *Who could that be*, she wondered, afraid it was Jack. An evening visitor, any visitor for that matter, wasn't a common occurrence at her place.

Alex stood and went to the front door. She peaked through the window to the right of the door and her breath caught in her throat while her heartbeat doubled its rhythm. Standing at the top step, Adam stood, his profile turned to gaze out at the Honolulu city lights. He made the most breathtaking sight standing there, hands on his hips, the blue t-shirt pooling around his hands. He'd been to the beach, new sun darkening him from a deep tan into a healthy umber brown.

She unlocked the door and opened it. "Adam?" she asked and stepped back to let him enter. "What are you doing here?"

"Did you even check who was at the door? What if it wasn't me and was someone with sinister intentions?" he asked.

"I checked." She laughed. "Besides, I don't think someone with sinister intentions would take the time to knock."

Adam slipped out of his leather slippers at the doormat and walked into the house ignoring her humor. She shut the door behind him. "I hope I'm not intruding," he said.

"No. In fact, I was just going to make some tea. Would you like to join me for a cup?" She walked past him and into the kitchen.

"I would love some," he answered.

She heard him follow her from the other room. After filling the tea pot with fresh water and setting on the stove, she turned up the heat. The movement eased the erratic dancing of her nerves inside her body. She opened the cupboard and retrieved two cups along with the tin filled with tea bags. "Any flavor in particular?" she asked.

She looked over her shoulder and her stomach flipped at the sight of him. He stood in the pocket door between the living room and kitchen. His shoulder rested against the wall, his ankles crossed, and his hands crossed under his chest. The ridges and planes of his body stretching the jersey fabric of the blue shirt in all the right places. His board shorts rode low on his hips, one side a fraction higher than the other. He was smiling at her, that damn dimple making her insides feel like butter.

She looked away. "I like orange spice."

"Whatever you like," he said.

She pulled two tea packets from the tin and placed a tea bag in each cup, then carried the cups to the table. She was so glad she had straightened up the house of clutter earlier that day. She looked up at Adam, who hadn't moved but followed her movement with his eyes. He was still smiling.

"Why are you looking at me like that?" she asked. "No wait." She held up her hand. "I'm not sure I want to know."

"I'm just admiring the view." He pushed away from the wall and walked toward her. To her chagrin, he passed her to sit down at the table.

She looked down and realized what she must look like. She was wearing an oversized pair of pajama bottoms, a chambray blue that hung on her hips, a white, cotton-knit camisole, and a well-loved gray cardigan draped over her shoulders. She lifted a hand to her hair and felt the clip that held her locks in a relaxed French twist, unruly tendrils dancing about her face. She was a mess but wasn't overly concerned about it as she sat down across from him at the oval table.

"Well, I wasn't expecting company," she said.

"I'm sorry. I should have called."

She laughed. "Don't get all conciliatory on me. I wasn't accusing you of anything."

He grew serious. "I was surprised to see you at the game last night," he said. His voice was quiet, even.

"I know. I thought you were angry."

"I was. But I didn't have any right to be. I'm sorry," he said.

"Truthfully, I hadn't intended to go. Then I saw Jack at the beach after my morning workout. He mentioned he was going with David Bennett and some other colleagues and invited me to join them." She glanced at Adam whose brows were drawn together. Her heart soared noticing his emotions on his face. "I thought it would be a good opportunity to maybe get some information."

"That doesn't sound like 'let the police deal with it.'" Adam sat back in his chair, one arm slung over the back of the seat, the other bent so that his head rested in his hand. Alex's insides twisted and she looked away. "Did you learn anything?" he asked.

"Unfortunately, no. Other than seeing Trey, it was a wasted evening."

The tea pot began to whistle. Alex got up and took it off the heating element on the stove. She turned the stove off and carried the teapot and trivet to the table. "I'm surprised to see you," she said.

"I was at the beach with the kids today."

She poured the steaming liquid into the cups. "How was it?"

"Great. There were six-to-eight-foot faces today so we got some great sets."

She placed the pot on the trivet. She pulled a leg under her as she sat down. "How is Emma?"

"Doing great. Feeling strong. Can you believe she's five months along, now?" He smiled at his teacup.

"Trey and Bekah?"

"Busy. It looks like HSU will make a bowl game."

"Really? The Aloha Bowl or another?" Alex placed her hands around the hot cup.

"The Aloha Bowl." His eyes held hers.

"So, you stopped by because you went to the beach?"

He smiled and leaned forward to look at his tea. Then he relaxed back against the seat before looking at her again. "No. I wanted to invite you to join us for Thanksgiving. The kids were adamant about it today."

"You're here at the kids' insistence?" She looked at her cup a bit disappointed it was the kids who had pushed him to come to see her. She lifted it to her lips and sipped the hot liquid.

"Maybe a catalyst in me stopping by tonight, but I had every intention of asking you." His gaze locked on hers and delved into her soul, searching.

She could almost feel his hands on her, rifling around to find her truths, and then it made her hot thinking about his hands on her. "I don't want to intrude on your family dinner." She took another sip of her tea. She set it down and moved her thumb back and forth across the cup handle.

Adam's gaze rested on her thumb. "You aren't an intrusion, Alex." He eyes came back to her face. "In the words of the kids, 'Aunty Alex is family.'" He smiled.

Alex looked at her tea, picked up the tag attached to the tea bag. She dunked it a few times, and realized she'd forgotten a plate to set it on. She stood cupping her hand under the dripping tea bag, the water already a comfortable warm as it dripped on her skin. She retrieved a plate and went back to the table.

"I want you there." Adam stared at her. His face was serious and his eyes intent.

The beating of her heart was a rhythm so fast and heavy she was sure that he could see her pulse. He wanted her there. The joy of that statement filled her.

You must know I want you; his words replayed in her mind.

She knew she shouldn't get her hopes up and shouldn't long to be with Adam and his kids. But she didn't want anything more than that. She wanted to be a part of that family, her family. "Well, then I would love to be there."

"Good." Adam smiled.

A silence ensued. Adam seemed to contemplate his tea. Then his eyes rose from the cup and locked on hers again. Alex felt a tingle work its way down her spine. It was an anticipation of what was about to happen. And dear God she wanted it. She wanted his hands on her. She wanted his mouth connected to hers. She wanted to feel his skin beneath her hands. His brown eyes seemed to promise her that and more.

And then the promise was gone. Adam stood. "I have to go," he said. "I'll see you on Thursday?" He carried his cup into the kitchen and set it in the sink.

She stood.

Adam wiped his hands on the side of his shorts, a nervous action, like he didn't know what to do with them. He looked at her again and seemed to hesitate, as though he wanted to say something else, or do something else. Alex's heartbeat hitched at his perusal. Then he walked past her out of the kitchen and into the living room.

She followed him.

Adam stopped at the door, a hand resting on the doorknob. "Make sure you lock the door. And don't open it for anyone who hasn't called first."

She laughed. "You didn't call first."

He grinned. "It was a test that you failed."

Alex laughed again. "Whatever, Adam."

He chuckled and met her gaze. His smile faded and the color of his eyes darkened. He leaned toward her, and Alex leaned to meet him. But instead of kissing her senseless like she wanted him to do, he kissed her cheek. "I will see you Thursday." His voice was quiet, speculative.

"Thursday," she answered.

She shut the door behind him, locked it, then leaned her head against it. Her breathing was quick, and her pulse rapid as though she had just been for a run along the beach. If Adam could do that to her without so much as a kiss, it was hard to fathom what more would feel like.

Alex pushed away from the door and wandered back into the kitchen to finish her tea. She was energized enough to tackle the remaining essays but knew she wouldn't be able to concentrate on them to save her life. The only thing she would be able to contemplate until that coming Thursday would be Adam, and the look of nearly abandoned control he'd given her when he'd left the house.

CHAPTER THIRTY-TWO

Nervous energy flowed through Adam's veins like molten lava. He couldn't stand, he couldn't sit, and already, Bekah had asked him twice if he was alright. He wandered into the family room where Grant and Trey were watching a football game. He sat and attempted to focus on his favorite pastime, but even that couldn't draw him into the calm. He felt ridiculous, like a giddy teenager, but it was like there was a promise in today, a promise that would tell him what would happen with the rest of his life. He was at a crossroads. One way led to Alex and the other was a wide lonely road. He didn't know what she wanted. He suspected, but he wasn't sure.

The front doorbell rang. A deep breath escaped him. *Be cool*, he told himself and stood. He walked into the hallway to open the door.

Alex was on the other side. The sun, at her back, produced a sort of halo that reflected the dark auburn highlights in her hair. She smiled, and Adam couldn't help but conjure the picture of a guardian angel. She wore a stylish skirt, an aqua color that reminded Adam of the ocean, and a fitted black shirt that detailed her beautiful curves. The image of her dressed in her loose pajama bottoms and white tank the other day when he'd dropped in to ask her for Thanksgiving dinner floated through his mind. She had looked so beautiful, so natural. He'd wanted to show her how much on the top of her kitchen table. Not reaching for her had been one of the most difficult things he had to do.

"Hi," he said and leaned forward to take the grocery bags from her hands. She smelled so good. The skin of their hands brushed imprinting him with heat. He resisted the urge to gather her in his arms and kiss her until she was as hungry as he was and instead gave her a traditional *honi*.

"Happy Thanksgiving," she said and stepped into the house. "There's wine in one of those bags."

"I'm glad you're here," he said.

She stepped cross the threshold and stopped in front of him but far enough away he felt a canyon still between them. "Me too."

When she smiled and looked up at him, her eyes locking on his, he saw the answer to his question. Did she still love him? Her eyes bespoke all of the adoration and unconditional love in her heart. Adam was hit with it, slammed with the gorgeous weight of knowing he didn't deserve it and immense gratitude of her willingness to give it. And suddenly, he realized now she had always carried that look in her green eyes, except now he understood it.

"Alex," Adam started to say something impetuous and probably foolish. He felt like an adolescent boy with so much emotion pent up inside him he needed to relieve the pressure. "I–"

"Aunty Alex." Emma saved him as she walked around the corner into the hall. She stopped short at the sight of them standing far closer than was necessary.

Alex stepped around him toward Emma in the next instant, as though no time had passed between Emma rounding the corner and seeing them together. "What can I do to help?" She took Emma's arm leading her back toward the kitchen.

Adam closed the front door and headed back through the kitchen to the family room. He set the bags on the counter and unloaded them, content to watch the movement of his girls in the kitchen. Bekah was peeling potatoes at the kitchen sink, commenting on something Trey had yelled at her from the family room. Emma and Alex stood shoulder to shoulder near the oven. Alex lifted her eyes to look at him as he put something in the refrigerator, and he saw as much longing in them as he felt. A promise. He glanced at Emma who was looking at him and failed to understand what was in her expression.

"Can I make you ladies some refreshment?" Adam asked.

"I'd love a glass of wine," Alex stated.

"Would you like one Bekah?"

"That would be great, Dad," she said.

"I'd love one too," Emma stated, "but I'll take a glass of water instead, Dad. If you don't mind."

Adam fixed the ladies their drinks before forcing himself to return to the family room. Even the football game couldn't keep his attention. He couldn't help but allow his thoughts and watchful observation meander toward what was occurring in the kitchen. What he found were three women in total harmony, laughing, smiling, and enjoying each other. Emma didn't look upset at the strange picture she'd happened across in the hallway. It seemed forgotten. But he was certain he'd hear from Emma later.

Thanksgiving dinner was a beautiful picture of family life. Adam couldn't escape the heartwarming realization of what a picture his family made, knowing that he'd been blessed beyond what he deserved. He watched the interaction of his children, adults now, and Emma with her husband, soon-to-be parents, and the awaiting grandchild growing within Emma present too. She was radiant and smiled at something Grant said. The joy and laughter flowed, and Adam was moved, containing the emotion by swallowing the lump that had formed in his throat.

He glanced at Alex who was looking at him. Though neither had said but a few inconsequential words throughout the day, her eyes spoke volumes about what was in her heart. And Adam was sure she could read his feelings in his looks and smiles. He was an open book, and he refused to shut it again.

He had mourned the loss of his wife, his treasured friend, a wonderful woman who had strengthened the blessing of his life. He had grieved so hard he didn't think that he would ever find his life again, yet she had given it back to him with her words. And he had learned that he could feel again, live again, and maybe even share love again.

"I'd like to make a toast," Emma said. She held onto the chair as she stood. Conversation around the table died and all eyes focused on her. Adam raised his glass of wine, the yellow liquid absorbing light. "First, I would like to toast Mom who we all miss wholeheartedly, without whom there is a missing piece, and who we will never stop loving." She stopped allowing that to sink in.

"Here. Here." Those around the table replied. They tipped their glasses and sipped their drinks.

"And second," Emma continued, surprising Adam. "To living again. To finding life after loss." She looked at Adam, her hazel eyes resting on his, and in that moment, he understood she approved. She offered him a slight nod, then a knowing smile before she tipped her glass of apple cider to her lips and sipped.

The remainder of the evening passed, dinner, the men cleaning up while the ladies laughed in the family room. Then they played a Spades tournament, Bekah and Trey the victorious partnership at the card game. Though Grant speculated it was because they had developed secret nonverbal cues to name the trump suit. Laughing, they enjoyed their time together. But time waits for no one and the clock expressed the aging day.

Emma yawned, obviously exhausted. "We better get to your *ohana*, hon," she told Grant. "I'm running out of gas."

Grant laughed, collected their belongings, and helped his wife to her feet.

"Stay," Adam said. "There's a room open."

"Thanks Dad," Grant answered, "But we have to stop in at my folks for a few."

Adam nodded, shaking his son-in-law's hand. "You are a good man, Grant."

Grant hugged Adam and walked through the front entrance. Emma whispered, "Good choice." She kissed his cheek, then escaped out the front door grabbing her husband's hand. They walked away. She didn't look back.

Adam returned to the family room to find Trey and Bekah hunched over a newspaper at the dining room table. Alex sat in a chair in the family room watching them, her feet curled under her. His insides melted at the site of her. She looked so right there.

"I don't want to watch any chick flicks," Trey said.

Adam walked into the kitchen and leaned against the counter. Alex glanced at him, amusement in her eyes.

"You're such a jerk, Trey. Why do you always have to be a misogynist?"

"Speak English," he countered.

Alex laughed.

"I am speaking English, you, turd."

"For the record, I do not hate women. I happen to like them *very* much," he laughed and wiggled his eyebrows.

Bekah punched his arm. "Okay then. What did you want to see?"

"What about the new *Harry Potter* one? At least it will have action to keep me awake after all that turkey."

"Great. Let's do it," Bekah agreed.

They debated on a time.

"Do you two always have to argue?" Adam asked. He was smiling, thinking of them as children engaged in the same pastime, just a more grown up activity.

"You would miss it if we didn't," Bekah said.

"Would either of you like to come?"

"To *Harry Potter*?" Adam asked. "I think I would have preferred the chick flick." He laughed.

"Aunty Alex?"

"No, thank you. I should be getting home."

"Shall I keep the porch light on for you?" Adam asked his kids.

"No. I'm going to drop Bekah at her place before I head to my apartment. Maybe get a glimpse of Kara." He smiled.

"You're not staying here tonight?" Adam asked. He wasn't sure if he was disappointed. The thought of waking up without them seemed sad, though he was sure they would call in the morning for breakfast.

"You okay with that?" Trey asked.

"Sure. Your choice."

Bekah retrieved her jacket and walked into the kitchen. "I'll call you in the morning, though," she said and kissed his cheek.

Adam smiled. "Have a good time." He walked them to the garage door and followed them out to make sure the garage was closed after they had gone through to Trey's car.

When he walked back into the house, Alex was no longer sitting in the chair, and it seemed excessively quiet except for the music that had been playing on the house sound system since dinner. "Alex?" he called.

"In by the fire," she answered.

CHAPTER THIRTY-THREE

She sat on the couch, wine glass in hand, staring into the flames, whose light and shadows danced on the walls around her.

"I was afraid you'd left," he stated standing at the top of the three steps that led to the living room where she sat. He held a bottle of wine and leaned against the corner wall to watch her.

Alex blushed, the comfortable heat of the fire scalding her cheeks. "I probably should."

"Do you want to?"

Alex stared at him, the beautiful man that he was. His tall frame clothed in comfortable denim pants that hinted of his strength. His trim waist tapered. The celery green polo that set off his complexion and showed the muscular outline of his body, the slope of his shoulders. His brown feet were bare. She knew that she would do anything that he wanted, everything she wanted. Her stomach felt light and jittery.

"No." She sounded calm to her own ears, a million miles from how she felt inside. The implications of her statement hung in the air between them.

Adam pushed away from his perch with his shoulder and walked toward her. "I've been thinking about being alone with you all day."

She smiled.

He stopped in front of her. After setting down the bottle of wine, he held out a hand. "Dance with me, Alex."

She looked up at him and remembered him saying that to her twenty-seven years ago. *Dance with me.* She took his hand, and he drew her up and into his arms. They swayed to the music, one of her hands in his, the other wrapped around his shoulder, her fingers teasing the skin at his nape. The music stretched and molded around them as they swayed together.

Alex rested her forehead against the strength of Adam's chest, the words of the song weaving magic around her, pulling her into its hypnotic beat. Her heart raced, and she noticed Adam's heartbeat matched hers.

"Alex?" His voice rumbled through his chest.

She drew her head back to look up at him.

"I read it. Your letter to Megan."

A trap door opened up under her belly, and it dropped through. She searched his face and knew Megan had left it for him to find. "She put it in her journal, didn't she?"

Adam nodded. "She wanted me to know. You saved us. You, Alex. She wanted me to know about your love. Why would she do that?"

Alex looked away at the fire and as tears escape hearing what he hadn't said, *Megan had brought them together.*

Adam stopped moving to the music and coaxed her to meet his gaze. "Please don't cry." He wiped away a tear with his thumb.

"Don't pity me," she whispered. "I couldn't take that."

"Is that what you think?" he asked.

"A woman locked in a one-sided infatuation that she can't get over. Waiting around and unable to move forward. It is pathetic."

She tried to step away, but Adam held her fast.

"Don't say that, Alex. You are the strongest, most determined, most selfless, woman I've ever known. Your loyalty to Megan, and even to me—well, it amazes me." He leaned in and kissed the tears. "When I read it," he added and kissed another tear, "all I could think, was how much I wanted to know if you still felt that way?" He pulled away and moved his head to meet her gaze.

Alex waded into the ocean, the tide tugging at her waist, and she met Adam's gaze. "I've never stopped feeling that way. It has always been you, for me. Always." Tears continued to slip from her eyes over her cheeks to her jaw. Adam's eyes follow the trail of her tears. He leaned in and kissed away another one, his tongue touched her skin.

She sucked in a breath.

He dipped to catch another tear with a kiss on her neck and spoke against her skin. "I have so much to make up for, Alex, and I don't want you to think for one second that I'm standing here today with you in my arms for any other reason than my selfish desire to have you here." Adam drew away and looked at her, his brown eyes locking with hers, and she saw the truth. "Somewhere along the way—I don't know when—but I fell in love with you, Alex James."

Adam pressed his lips to hers, and Alex responded in turn, the soft heat between them a comfortable fire, a slow burn that began to build. His hands pressed the small of her back, drawing her closer to him. Alex marveled at how they fit. Every sensation heightened. His muscle bunched at her touch and then relaxed as he pulled her closer.

He drew his mouth from hers and stopped, his eyes searching her face, diving in to see into her soul. "Alex, I love you," he said again, his breath ragged, but he smiled his dimple undoing her. "But I don't want to go any further if this isn't what you want. All it."

Alex silenced him her mouth on his and her tongue sharing her want. This time the burning between them became more frenzied. "I want this, Adam," she said.

Adam traced the curve of her body with his hands, pulling her tightly against him, and Alex rested in his embrace, content in his strength, at one with her desire for him. Their tongues met, dancing together, matching the hypnotic rhythm of a new song. Adam's hands at the small of her back slid lower, gripping her backside and drew against his length. She stood on her tiptoes wanting to crawl inside his skin. His need pressed against her intimately sent her over the edge with heated desire all her own.

"Adam," she moaned his name, emotion bubbling up from the center of her being. "I love you so much." The tears escaped again, but this time from elation, of being told by the man she'd spent a lifetime loving that he loved her too. She felt alive.

He ran his hands along her waist. "I think I might be terrible. It's been—"

"Shh," she said knowing it had been a long time in so many ways. She silenced him, kissing him with all the passion she'd held for a lifetime and lifted his shirt over his head. She tossed it away and pulled away to look at him. She ran a hand along his torso, still chiseled and beautiful, the many years kind to him. "I've dreamed of touching you, Adam," she told him.

He drew in a quick breath at her touch, his muscles responding to her.

She leaned in and kissed his chest. The skin and soft hair tickled her.

He drew her back up to meet his lips. "I don't know how much I can take of that." His hands framed her face, and he smiled as he dipped to kissed her again.

Then he moved, drawing away to divest her of her shirt. She looked at his face, his eyes smoldering with passion. He touched her neck with his hand, the skin-to-skin contact like fire and ran his hand from her neck over her collar bone and stopped at the top of her bra.

Alex shivered with want and watched him take her in. When his eyes slid back to hers, he was a fire. He replaced his touch with his lips and blazed a new trail with his tongue.

Then the black lace was off. She had laid bare her emotions and now bared her body.

"You are so beautiful," Adam said, touching her and molding her until they were kissing again.

Alex fumbled with the buttons on his jeans as he kissed her, tugging the button-fly open and working them over his hips. He helped her by pulling them off all the way, everything gone. Then he helped her with her skirt, unzipping it at her hip the aqua fabric and black lace pooled at her feet. They were left to look their fill at one another, the firelight dancing around them.

"Tell me again," she told him.

He closed the gap between them. "I love you." He kissed her. "I love you, Alex." He kissed her again, and she turned her face up to meet his, her heart and body melting into the moment with him, converging with whatever had finally brought them to this moment. Whatever it was, she was so grateful.

Adam drew her down with him onto the carpet, where she settled on top of him, straddling his body. Their most intimate skin burned by the other. Alex needed to be joined with him like she needed air and water to survive. There were no secrets left. There were no hidden memories. There were no barriers remaining. It was just them.

Him.

Her.

The love that had somehow found a way across a lifetime to draw them back together.

This moment.

In all her life she'd never felt something so moving, so powerful.

She kissed him as his hands mapped her body, then drew him so that they were both lying face-to-face on the floor. Adam leaned up on an elbow, still kissing her. Alex rolled onto her back as he moved over her and settled in between her thighs.

"Yes, Adam," she breathed delirious with want.

He lifted his chest from her, the rest of him still gorgeously pressed to her and searched her face.

She was struck how beautiful he was. Tears slipped from her eyes.

"Tell me, Alex," he said through a ragged breath. He was struggling to control himself, his body quivering against hers.

Alex looked at him with everything she felt in her heart as though it originated in the beginning of time. "I want you, Adam, I have always wanted you." She could feel him waiting for the right moment to join her vulnerability and longed for it, reached down and grabbed his backside. "Please, Adam," she whispered lifting her hips. "Don't make me wait any longer."

He entered her, and Alex gasped at their joining, the perfection of it. The rhythm they created together building a new memory that would sustain her forever, feeling the movement of them together once again. It was a coupling that healed old wounds.

Alex breathed with Adam. The fire built and spread its hot fingers through every inch of her body and Alex climbed into heaven, grasping at a feeling that she knew before but had never experienced with such fulfillment. And when she reached the pinnacle of her climb and cried out, Adam's name on her lips, Adam too reached his threshold. But he didn't yell, he whispered in her ear the most beautiful sound that Alex had ever heard, would ever hear in her lifetime. "I love you, Alex."

CHAPTER THIRTY-FOUR

Adam was warm. He stretched feeling content, happy, satiated. He noticed the soft skin of the woman beneath his hands and opened his eyes, smiling. He tightened his arms wrapped around Alex on the living room floor, covered by the throw blanket he'd pulled from the back of the couch. Their naked bodies were entwined together and sleepy from love making.

"If I'd known it would be that good," he'd told her after the first time, "I wouldn't have let you leave the other night."

She'd laughed.

Then they'd gotten up, Alex wearing his shirt and him wrapped in the throw that now covered them to pick at Thanksgiving leftovers. They'd talked about life, about the strange twists and turns that had somehow drawn them back together. They'd shared their worries. For her: the kids. For him: the kids.

"Emma knows."

"She does?" Alex had asked.

"Not about this," he'd clarified with a smile. "No, about how I feel. She approves," he'd smiled and drawn her naked body back to his. "Can we do that again?" he'd asked.

"I thought you'd never ask," she'd said and kissed him into the oblivion of want and need where both were the same. And the second time, he savored her.

Now, laying here with her in his arms, his body responded remembering and he willed himself to relax, wanting to make love to her again. He chuckled. He was forty-seven years old, yet he was behaving like an adolescent who'd just discovered what his penis could do.

"What are you laughing at?" Alex's voice broke his thoughts. She turned in his arms. Her hair pooled around her head. He looked at her gorgeous face and smoothed an errant lock of hair from her cheek. Then he ran a hand over her skin, from her cheek to her hip. Her eyes closed as if she relished his touch. Then she said with a smile, "Laughter after sex makes me nervous."

He laughed again. "I was laughing at myself."

Her eyes opened, and she offered him a puzzled look, her brows working over her pretty green eyes. He moved to touch her creased brow with his lips. "You've got me hornier than a sixteen-year-old schoolboy, Ms. James."

She stretched, smiled, and moaned. He liked the way her body moved, the heaviness of her breasts, the soft swell of her hips and belly. Her dark lashes fanned across her cheeks and Adam thought she looked like a cat who'd gotten into the milk. She giggled and looked at him, her eyes gleaming with mischief. "I've been laying here listening to you sleep." She reached up and traced the outline of his chest with her fingertip.

"Was I snoring?" he asked, but he wasn't thinking about his snoring. He was thinking about her fingertips moving across his skin and how hard he was getting. Again.

She shook her head. "No. But I was thinking about how good it felt to be lying next to you. My body fits so nicely next to yours." She pressed him onto his back, leaned up onto and elbow to trace the dark hair across his abdomen.

Adam wanted her again. And again. And once more after that, he decided. He would always want her.

She traced the trail of hair from his belly button and caressed his length. Her gaze never left his, a smile dancing about her mouth.

"Be careful," he warned her.

Her expression darkened, pulling the corners of her lips down. "I've spent a lifetime being careful. I don't want to be careful anymore."

His earlier attempt to relax was negated by her words opening a floodgate of desire. Adam leaned up, grasped her by the nape, and kissed her. His other hand stopped her gentle stroking. He didn't want to lose himself that way. It was too lonely. He grasped her hips. Alex straddled him. Adam looked up at her, her hair falling around their faces as though they were in their own cocoon.

She moved so that their tender flesh just touched.

He drew in a breath. "You're making me crazy."

"Good." Her eyes were hooded with passion. "Adam," she breathed as they joined again.

"Tell me, Alex. I'll never get tired of hearing it."

She bent down so that her full breasts rested against his chest. He grasped her hips, his hands splayed over her flesh. Her lips rested against his and she rocked her hips. "I love you," she whispered against his mouth.

They made love again. Lingering and slow, learning each other's body language. Adam made sure Alex reached her climax, rolling her onto her back to control their rhythm before falling over the precipice himself.

When they were done, Alex giggled.

"What are you laughing at? Laughter after sex makes me nervous," Adam, on his back, parroted her words. His eyes were closed. He was so happy.

"I feel so–" She stopped searching for the right word.

"Perfect?" he asked.

She leaned up. He opened his eyes to looked at her. She smiled and kissed him. "Yes. Perfect."

In the silence of the moment, Adam's brows snapped together at a noise he couldn't place. "Did you hear something?" He rolled her onto her back and held his breath to listen. Something at the door, maybe something outside the window?

"Hear what? I didn't hear anything."

Adam got up and pulled on his jeans, then stopped to listen. "Probably nothing. My imagination," he said and turned around.

Alex was propped up on her elbows, looking rather beautiful, her naked body lush, the firelight dancing against her skin. "How did I get so lucky?" he asked as he knelt, a knee between her legs. He tried not to crush her but loved the feel of her bare skin against his, her soft breasts juxtaposed with his rough exterior.

He lowered himself on her and kissed her again, but within another second his head snapped back up tearing his lips from hers. No. He had definitely heard something that time. "Wait here," he said and got up.

Adam buttoned the first two buttons of the fly.

"What are you going to do?" She drew his shirt over her head. It reached to the top of her thighs.

Without wariness he should have possessed, but didn't, Adam went to the front door and turned on the outside light. He looked out the peephole and after seeing nothing opened the door. He stepped out into the cool night. The soft sound of palms fronds swaying in the breeze mixed with the clicking of lizards was all that moved in the night.

He turned to go back into the house. Alex was just inside the door watching him. He walked back but looked down at the ground when the texture of the porch changed underneath his bare feet. He stooped to pick up a plain piece of white paper stuck to his foot and carried it into the house, shutting and locking the front door behind him.

Alex flipped on the entryway light and stood next to Adam as he opened the paper. His heart began to pound as he read the words on the page:

BECAUSE I KNOW YOU'RE INTERESTED, YOUR KIDS ENJOYED THEIR MOVIE TONIGHT. I'VE ENCLOSED A MOVIE TICKET IN CASE YOU WANT IT FOR A SOUVENIR. AND I GOT TO ENJOY MORE THAN A MOVIE TONIGHT. PLEASE TELL DR. JAMES, THANK YOU, FOR THE SHOW. I'LL ENJOY SEEING MORE OF HER ON CAMPUS IF YOU CATCH MY DRIFT. IN THE MEANTIME, IF YOU CARE ABOUT ANY OF THEM, YOU'LL BACK THE FUCK OFF, OR WHAT HAPPENED TO THE CAR WILL SEEM LIKE CHILD'S PLAY.

Inside the envelope was a movie ticket for the Harry Potter movie.

Alex lifted a hand to her mouth. "Oh dear, God," she breathed.

CHAPTER THIRTY-FIVE

Adam jogged up the stairs to Alex's office. Though he hadn't been without her the last several days because he hadn't wanted her out of his sight, especially after receiving the threat, he couldn't be with her while she was at work. He also couldn't let work slip but had scaled back delegating what he could to the competent people who worked for him. He wouldn't risk something happening to her, and couldn't shake the foreboding feeling they were waiting in the flats and a dangerous swell was about to roll in.

Adam knocked and stepped through the door of Alex's office.

"Hi." She smiled at the sight of him and stood. "I'm so glad you are here."

Adam enfolded her in his embrace. "I missed you."

"I just saw you a few hours ago." They'd been sleeping at her house. Well, sleeping some.

"I'm just worried."

"You too?" she asked into his chest.

"Just this weird feeling."

"Have you heard from Detective Lopes?"

"About the note?" Adam shook his head. "He has it." His brow also creased with worry. "What if this is another dead end. I want this to stop. I don't want you or the kids hurt."

Alex sat back down behind her desk. "Let's hope for more."

Adam leaned against the desk, then toward her so he could kiss her frowning mouth. The kiss was soft and undemanding, a joining of two souls at peace with each other amidst a storm. But Adam suddenly had even more to lose and it fueled his need for the comfort that she provided.

Alex disengaged. "My student will be here any moment." She raised her eyebrows as a look of warning but smiled.

"I can't help myself." He dove into her green eyes. "I can't get enough of you."

"Whatever." She laughed. "Later."

A knock sounded at the door. "Dr. James?"

"Come in," Alex called out and Adam moved to sit out of the way.

The door opened and in stepped a cute girl with long blonde hair pulled back in a haphazard bun at the base of her neck. Her denim skirt was short, and her tight HSU tee had been tied so it clung to her curves.

"Hi Claire. How was the competition?" Alex gestured for the student to sit on the chair opposite her desk.

"It was good. We made it through regionals but missed the top ten at nationals by two points."

"A heartbreaker then? Still good, though." Alex glanced at Adam. "This is my friend, Mr. Kāne."

"Hello." She smiled and held out her hand.

He shook it.

"Thanks so much for coming in."

"You're welcome. What did you want to see me about?"

"I was intrigued by your essay and wanted to talk to you about it a little more."

A proud look spread across the young woman's face. "Sure."

Adam listened as Alex began with questions that seemed to put Claire at ease. As Claire answered Alex's questions and talked about her paper, Adam perused Alex's office. Along the left wall were bookshelves. The shelves closest to her desk was burdened with book upon book, a typical office item for any college professor. The shelves closest to the door were decorated with photos and small knick-knacks. She'd displayed things that she had acquired while in the Peace Corp, things Adam had seen when she had returned. There were pictures of Megan and Alex as girls, as students, and as young women. There were pictures of Emma, Trey, and Bekah, even newspaper clippings of their triumphs at their selected sports or activities. Adam's heart expanded yet again learning something new about Alex, seeing how much his family met to her.

Adam listened to Claire talk freely about her essay very adamant about the media's impact on the psychology of the female. He turned his attention to Alex who was concentrating on Claire and her work. Her office was more uncontrolled than he'd envisioned. Alex was such a walking advertisement for control that he had assumed her working environment would have reflected that. Though it wasn't chaotic, the desk was littered with items. It looked a bit in disarray, though somehow organized, as though each item had a purpose, a pencil here, two stacks of papers—one graded the other not completed. There was a travel coffee mug, a pad of note paper and various other supplies she would need at hand. It looked rather efficient.

"How does HGH fit into your thesis?" Adam heard Alex get to the point of the conversation and tuned in.

"Like I said in my paper, young girls are beginning to abuse substances for that perfect body, like steroids, and HGH is another common substance found in physical enhancement supplements."

"Like athletic supplements?"

"Yes. Didn't I mention that HSU athletes are very performance conscious and most take legal supplements to gain that edge? My coach, in fact, gives the squad these." Claire reached into her purse and fished out a white plastic bottle, a label absent.

"Do they help you?" Alex asked.

Claire paused, "I'm not sure. Maybe cradle catches and basket tosses aren't as difficult." She laughed.

"Does everyone on the squad take them?" Alex asked.

Claire nodded. She glanced at Adam and then back to Alex. She seemed to register that Alex's interest had shifted. "Dr. James?"

Alex leaned toward Claire as though imparting a secret between friends. "Can I have a couple of the vitamins you have there?"

Claire's gaze shifted to Adam again. "You're not an NCAA agent or something?" She looked panic stricken. "Is this stuff illegal? Coach Swann said it was just a vitamin supplement."

Adam played off Claire's assumptions about him. "Could you give us a sample to test?" he asked. The last thing that he wanted was for Claire to get scared. "No one is in trouble. You would really be helping me out."

"Sure," she answered the dimples in her cheeks showing. "Here. Take the whole bottle." She handed him the container.

"Could I ask you one more favor?" Adam asked, smiling back at her. Claire continued to smile at him. "Can we keep this between the three of us?"

"Sure."

A few moments later Claire left. Alex shut the door behind her. "Can we keep this between us?" she mimicked lowering her voice.

He stood up and pinned Alex between him and the door by placing a hand on each side of her head. "You jealous, Dr. James?" He smiled and looked at her lips.

"Of course not," Alex replied but a contradictory flush crept across her features.

"I used to have this fantasy of getting it on with a hot professor in her office."

"Oh, did you, now?"

He laughed. "I only have eyes for you, AJ," he whispered and kissed her, his desire for her pounding in his ears. He came up for air. "How about dinner, Dr. James?"

"Dinner's good. How about at my place?" she asked.

"Even better." Adam kissed her again, then reluctantly stepped back. "I better get back to the office."

"I have a class in fifteen minutes," she said with a sigh.

"I'll drop off these to Lopes this afternoon," Adam stated rattling the bottle of supplements that Claire had left for them.

"Leave me a few of them? I'll get to Jack to test them."

"Jack?" Adam frowned. He didn't like that one bit. "That guy is handsy." He grabbed Alex and drew her against him.

She laughed. "You jealous, Mr. Kāne?"

Adam grabbed her elbow and swung her around to face him, pulling her back into his embrace. "I'm the only one who gets to be handsy with my girl."

A slow smile spread across her face.

He kissed her again, then said. "Please be careful. We don't know who we can trust."

"I know. That's exactly why I want to take them. Just in case." Her eyes faded and her expression became serious.

"Just be careful, alright?" he said.

"Of course." Alex nodded. "And I'll meet you at my place. For dinner and dessert." She kissed him leaving the implications on his mouth.

Adam left with a smile on face, but it faded as he walked back to his car. He didn't like that Alex was going to go see Jack, but he resolved that he could be a grown up.

CHAPTER THIRTY-SIX

A dam was surprised to see Detective Lopes walk into his office a while later. His tall frame took up most of the doorway, his dark scowl powerful. Adam wondered if the detective had something to share with him about the note or the car accident. Either way, Lopes's appearance saved Adam a trip to the main station downtown he'd planned to make later that afternoon.

"Mr. Kāne," Lopes stated, holding out his large hand.

"Adam," he replied, taking the offered hand. "Please sit." Adam motioned toward the mahogany leather seat opposite his desk. "Either you have news for me or a question."

"Maybe both." His tone was forthright but hinted of his good nature. "Unfortunately, like the device we found attached to your daughter's car, the note was also a dead end. We're attempting to find a lead through alternative means."

Adam grabbed the bottle of supplements and slid it across the desk. "I'm glad to see you anyway. It saves me a trip."

"What's this?" Lopes took the container and held it up to examining it.

"A professor friend and I tracked down a student athlete who wrote an essay that referenced HGH supplementation at the school. She gave us these samples of whatever her coach has been giving her. I'd planned on dropping this off to you today." Adam nodded

313

at the bottle. "Maybe a lead."

Lopes lifted his eyebrows in response, a sort of 'impressive' look. "I do like gifts. I like leads better. Thank you."

Adam laughed. "I'm surprised to see you."

"I had wanted to let you know about the note, but the lab did find something that I can't comment on that might open the Diane Gomes case, possibly provide a connection."

"There's a common link?" Adam asked.

"Could be," Lopes evaded. "I was hoping for a clearer correlation. Maybe you have just provided it." He held up the bottle, then slid it in the shirt pocket on his red and ivory Aloha shirt emblazoned with hibiscus and leaves. "I need to fill in the blanks." Lopes's cell phone beeped. "Hold on, I have to take this," he said after checking the display. "Lopes," he stated as he held the receiver to his ear. "Glad to hear it, Tee."

Adam watched the other man carry on his conversation. Curious, but trying not to intrude, he turned his attention to a bid contract he had been looking over before Lopes had arrived. Attempting to focus on the black and white of his computer screen, Adam reread the same line as he picked out the indiscriminate mechanical drawl of the voice on the other line.

"Are you sure?" Mana stated and leaned forward in his seat. "That's Texas, as in the state?" he asked, paused, and listened.

Adam noticed Lopes was looking for something with which to write, so he handed him a pad of paper and a pen. Lopes wrote down the information. "That was Jackson?" He clarified and then tore off the page pushing the notepad back to Adam with a nod of thanks. "I love you. Tee. I owe you dinner," he said and paused. "Naw. She won't care." He smiled into the phone. "Oh, and I have some goodies for you to analyze when I get back. I know. You love me too."

Lopes hung up the phone and sat back in the chair, looking at the notes he had taken. Adam studied the other man, his expression dark, deep in thought. Then clarity seemed to move across his features as though the sun had broken through a storm. He lifted the pad and pen and set them back on the desk. "Thanks Adam, I've got to go and check something out. I have a hunch that needs following up. Maybe the break I need." Lopes stood.

Adam shook the detective's hand. "Glad that you stopped by. Let me know if there's anything I can do."

Lopes cracked a smile, a slight one, and added a nod of his large head.

Adam watched him leave and sat down to get back to work. His thoughts drifted to Alex as he glanced at the clock. He calculated she'd still be in a class and in an hour or so would be taking her sample to Jack at the lab. With some more time before meeting her at the house, Adam bent over the pile of work he had to get done and barely noticed the second hand of the clock. The next time he looked up, his cell phone was ringing, and it was nearly an hour and a half later.

"Hi Emma."

"Dad. I got something interesting for you." Emma's voice sounded excited. "Remember our conversation about Stanton Thom's and Milton Yamane's extra cash flow."

Adam nodded though Emma couldn't see him. "Yes. I do." He reached for the blank notepad that he'd handed detective Lopes earlier and picked up a pencil. As was his habit while he was on the phone, he doodled and shaded the paper with a pencil.

"It turns out that Apex is not just a wellness company. In fact, I had to do quite a bit of digging, but I turned up an interesting tidbit I think fits quite conveniently with Mom's research. Apex is... well was a small pharmaceutical company based out of Texas before becoming the wellness company a few years ago. It turns out they were under investigation in Texas by the FDA because of illegal procedure in drug testing and approval protocol."

Texas, he thought. *It had to be a coincidence.*

Adam sat forward. "Okay." He continued to rub the plain white paper with the edge of his pencil. "Any specific drug that they got caught trying to push through?"

"No, not a specific name but the resource labeled it 'an experimental anti-aging drug.' The president of the company, Harvey Lingle, was a college roommate with someone we know."

"Milton Yamane?" Adam guessed as he continued to draw on the paper.

"No. Stanton Thom."

Adam stopped his pencil rub for a moment allowing the information to sink in, then resumed, noticing a void on the page as he drew. Remnants of Lopes note. "So, we can connect Stanton Thom to Apex Pharmaceuticals through Harvey Lingle, but we have nothing else Emma, nothing that proves Stanton Thom or Lingle or Apex has anything to do with the deaths on campus. It's circumstantial at best."

Claire's vitamins?

"True. But there's something else. It turns out that one of the drug developers, the lead research scientist for the drug that nailed Apex, had a record of attempting to push his 'fountain of youth' drug into human trials before he'd cleared the necessary committees. He got caught, though he didn't serve any time. Lingle and Apex simply paid their fine and changed the company."

"Okay? What happened to this researcher?" Adam stopped the pencil rub and looked at the void realizing that it was looking at a name—one very close to a name he recognized. *Maybe the break I need*, Adam recalled Lopes' words.

"Not sure. I have a name here, but nothing else. Jackson Reynolds."

Adam shot up from his seat. "Oh shit." He was staring at the matching name on his pad of paper. Jackson. Jack. Everything in his body constricted with dread.

"What is it Dad?"

He was around his desk. "Call Bekah and Trey. Tell them to go straight to your house."

"Dad what is it?"

316

"Just do it, Emma. I don't have time to talk about it now." Adam moved quickly. He grabbed his keys and left his office. "I just don't want you, Bekah, or Trey anywhere near the school. I have to call the police. Alex might be in danger." He hung up the phone to dial Alex's cell.

He emerged from the lobby of the Kāne Builders Offices and sprinted toward his car in the garage he was trying her cell for the third time. "Pick up, Alex," Adam muttered as he weaved his car through traffic, the cell phone ringing over the car speakers. He raced through a tail end of a yellow light just as it turned red earning a blaring horn from a car in the turn lane of the fresh green light. Alex's cell phone continued to ring until the voicemail answered.

"Fuck!"

He pressed the red button on the steering wheel of his car to disconnect and pulled out the card detective Lopes had given him at the hospital from his wallet. Adam dangerously drove the car and dialed Detective Lopes's number.

He drove through another yellow light and accessed the freeway viaduct. The phone began to ring. Adam nervously tapped at the gray steering wheel checking his mirrors as he merged into steady moving traffic on the H-1.

"Lopes," the distinctive baritone answered.

"Detective. Adam Kāne. I know who you are looking for."

There was a second of silence. Adam had expected the confusion. "What? Why didn't you say anything when I saw you earlier today?"

"I didn't know at the time. My daughter, Emma, called with some information she uncovered regarding some officials at HSU. It turns out that one, the University president Stanton Thom, is connected to a former pharmaceutical company called APEX."

"I'm not following, Kāne." He sounded impatient.

"Jackson Reynolds," Adam stated, skipping the connection.

"Where'd you get that name?"

Skipping the fact that he'd pulled it off the notepad Lopes had used in his office, Adam replied, "He was a researcher for APEX; he was arrested and convicted of FDA violations in drug development."

"And you know where he is?"

"He's a professor at HSU."

"In the same department as Diane Gomes," Lopes deduced. "Hence the DNA match. I know him," Lopes said more to himself.

"My friend, Alex, Dr. James was on her way to see him this afternoon. I can't reach her on her cell phone."

"We're working on the warrant as we speak, Adam." Detective Lopes spoke to someone, the conversation inaudible. "We're on our way to HSU. Stand down."

Adam hung up his phone unable to listen to the detective. Though his intentions were in line with the law, there wasn't anything that was going to keep him away from going after Alex. He'd just found her, and this time he needed to fight for her. He dialed her cell again and listened to the ring drone.

CHAPTER THIRTY-SEVEN

A lex walked across campus toward the Abner Scott Science Complex. She'd just finished her final class for the day. Students filtered past her as solitary figures in the fading day, others in pairs or small groups. Most were young and alive with the chatter and laughter.

She took a deep breath, happiness filling her lungs and seeping into her bloodstream. She'd passed her youth an independent woman allowing her the ability to develop a self-identity and self-worth. Though she'd been lonely at times, she was at peace with her past, and now was blessed with the gift of openly loving a man she'd been born to love, enjoying his children, who she couldn't love anymore had they been her own. *Oh Megan, you've granted me such wonderful gifts in your family,* Alex thought, hoping her friend could hear her prayer. Alex looked up at the sky, an azure expanse, jeweled like blue topaz that stretched about the trees and ombre range of blues headed toward sunset. Alex had the distinct feeling that if Megan were looking down from heaven, she was smiling.

"Aunty Alex!"

Alex saw Bekah smiling at her, her hand suspended in midair with a wave. She smiled and noticed the feminine embodiment of Adam in his youngest daughter. Her beautiful brown complexion paired with the rich raven colored hair was a dazzling combination. Her hazel eyes, the one feature that was distinctly Megan's, shone like jewels. Alex felt her heart skip in excitement.

"What are you doing?" she asked.

"I have a make-up lab at Abner," Bekah stated using the ASSC nickname.

"I'm headed that way myself. Let's walk together."

Bekah fell into step beside her.

"Missed a lab huh?"

"Swim meet. I don't mind, though. I really like my science courses. I'm thinking about a pre-med track."

"You'd be a wonderful doctor, Bekah. You've got the temperament for it."

"That means a lot coming from you, Aunty."

They continued to walk along the path, the trees thinning out from old campus to newly constructed campus. "I sure missed you last year, Aunty. I'm really glad that you've become part of the family again."

Alex smiled and wrapped and arm around Bekah. "Me too." It was a validation of how she felt about them.

A popular hip-hop song rang out. "That's my phone." Alex dropped her arm, and Bekah opened her gray and black backpack to fish out her cell phone. "I wonder who's calling," she said and checked the display. "It's Emma." She smiled as she answered. "Hey."

Alex glanced at her watch, checking the time and hoping that Jack hadn't gone home for the evening, but leaving before dark would be unusual for him. She heard Bekah talking into the cell phone and had the urge to check her own. She opened her purse and rummaged inside. In the next instant she pictured her phone sitting on her desk. She'd forgotten it. "Damn," she muttered.

Now, she would have to walk all the way back to her office to get it instead of going straight to her car. She was looking forward to dinner with Adam and didn't want to waste time going all the way back to get her phone. She contemplated not giving Jack the sample to look at and just let the police deal with it. She just as quickly dismissed the idea. She wasn't sure what Adam's contact in the police department would do with it. The sample could get buried under a pile of backlog or perhaps lost on purpose.

"I'm on my way to class. Aunt Alex is with me," Bekah stated. "Emma? Emma?" She pulled the phone away from her ear to check the display. "We got cut off," she said and frowned. "Horrible service by this building. I'll just call her after." Bekah stashed her phone as they walked through the front doors of Abner.

"Where is your lab?" Alex asked.

"Second floor, 207."

"I'm headed in the same direction."

"What are you doing at Abner? Your building is on the other side of campus, right?"

"Checking in with a friend. Dr. Reynolds. I have something I want him to look at."

"That's my lab teacher for this make-up session. I usually have Dr. Gray on Monday's."

They climbed the stairs and headed down the dark hallway lit only by light that escaped from solitary windows inset in doors or leaking from between the floor and a closed office door. Jack's office door was ajar, the light seeping into the hallway.

"I can wait for you," Alex told Bekah. It made her nervous knowing that Bekah was going to be alone after dark, and with the Gomes case still unsolved.

"That's okay."

"No. I'll wait. I can work on some grading." She patted her bag.

Bekah nodded and smiled. "Wish me luck."

"You don't need it." Alex watched Bekah proceed down the

hallway and disappear through a door on the left side of the hallway a few doors down the hall from Jack's office.

"Jack?" she asked and pushed open the door. Jack stood on the opposite side of his desk with the phone pressed to his ear. Alex was taken aback by the pallor of his face and the translucent quality of his usually blue-gray eyes.

"I've got to go, Connelly," he stated and hung up the phone. "Alex." The rigid tone of his voice sounded strange to her ears. In as long as she'd known him, Alex had only known a happy-go-lucky Jack.

"Are you okay? You look really pale. Bad news?" She nodded at the phone.

"You could say that, but nothing that can't be remedied. I'd rather not talk about it if you don't mind."

Alex nodded and felt her skin prickle a silent warning. Her brows drew together. Something was amiss.

"I haven't seen you since the other night at the football game." He didn't smile and Alex knew he was angry with her. "What brings you this way? Last I remembered you told me to 'fuck off'."

"You're right. I apologize for my words. I was pissed."

His demeanor shifted like a change in the wind. He smiled, happy again. "All is forgiven." The smile didn't touch his eyes. "What brings you all the way to Abner today?"

"I have a favor to ask," she stated. "Aren't you teaching a make-up lab for Dr. Gray?" She pointed with her thumbs at the hallway.

Jack glanced from the papers he was shuffling on his desk to Alex. He nodded. "The favor?"

"I'll get to that after you get Bekah started in her lab. I don't want to take up your teaching time." She nodded her head toward the lab.

"Bekah?" Jack asked. He seemed preoccupied and didn't look up with his question.

"Yes. She's making up a lab. You met at the football game several weeks ago. You're covering her make-up lab tonight."

His head snapped up and his gaze locked on her face. "Adam Kāne's daughter?" A fleeting look passed over his features that Alex didn't understand. A strange glimmer darkened his eyes further until they were unfamiliar and nearly black. Chills race up her spine and ended at the top of her head. That indistinct, foreign feeling was screaming again that something was wrong, but she couldn't put her finger on it. Alex, however, wasn't one to dismiss her instincts. Maybe his call had been dreadful news and he was trying to show a brave face? But a warning bell went off inside her head, her instincts pressuring her to listen.

"Meet me at the lab. We can talk there." Jack looked around the office. "I've got to get a few things before I go. Pack up."

Alex turned and stepped into the hall after watching Jack open a drawer of his desk. Maybe enough time to get Bekah out of the building. She didn't know why, but she trusted the feeling and rushed down the hallway hoping she was quiet enough not to draw his attention.

The lab had two entry points. Alex entered the room at the closest entrance. The opposite wall from the door was sheer glass paneled windows that afforded a view of the tropical garden in the midst of the five building pods. As the sun sank in the sky, the shadowed green looked eerie against the windowpanes. The illuminated fluorescent lights cleansed the room of strange shadows and reflected in the glass. Bekah was seated at a metal stool, her backpack and notes spread out on one of the four parallel monolithic black counters that ran perpendicular to the windows.

"Bekah."

Bekah's head snapped up. "Oh." She clutched her chest. "You scared me."

Alex hurried across the room. "Let's go." She glanced at the door, dread seeping into her bones.

"I can't. I have to make up this lab or I can't get anything higher than a B in the class."

"Bekah," Alex looked behind her. "A B is great. Let's not worry about that right now. Let's just get out of here. Leave your stuff." She exhaled nervous energy, the door and room still devoid of Jack. Her heart was racing. She didn't know how much time she had. She looked back at Adam's daughter. She would not leave Bekah. "Trust me?"

Bekah's brows came together, and she nodded. "What's wrong?"

"No time to explain." Alex held out her hand to Bekah. She was surprised at the confidence of her voice and the fact her fingers weren't trembling. Her insides were jittery as if she were over caffeinated.

Bekah took Alex's hand, stood, and then stopped short. Her complexion turned ashy. The saucer like look of fear in her hazel eyes and relaxed open mouth, dropped in awe frightened Alex. "Bekah?"

"She's fine," Jack said from the doorway behind her. "Just scared is all. As she should be."

Alex turned around, the gruff sound of his voice grating her like the sound of fingernails on a chalkboard. Jack Reynolds stood in the doorway, but it wasn't the man she'd known for six years. This was a stranger whose eyes were now glazed with an uncertain sanity. He held a gun in his hands fixed on her and Bekah. Alex could no longer contain the trembling within as it escaped her control.

CHAPTER THIRTY-EIGHT

Jack moved further into the room and shut the door behind him with his foot. Alex glanced at the opposite door—still closed—and wondered if she could dart across the room to get out, but she discarded the thought. There was no way she was leaving Bekah exposed. They were in this and would escape this together. She dropped Bekah's hand and stepped between her and Jack's gun.

"I'm faster," Jack smirked as though he'd read her thoughts waving the gun as he spoke. "And just so you know, screaming isn't a good idea either. There aren't very many people around, seeing this is make-up time. The cleaning service is on the other side of the building. Besides, I'd hate to use this thing more than necessary."

"What's going on, Jack? I don't understand." Alex stepped back until she could feel Bekah's body behind her and reached her hand back until she felt Bekah's arm. She slid her hand down to grab Bekah's hand with her own. Bekah's fingers curled around hers.

"Don't you? I mean, I knew you were dense about us. I was willing to overlook that, but after all your sleuthing, you haven't put it together yet? Your boyfriend is really something." He was sweating. Beads developed on his forehead and perspiration was beginning to stain the underarms of his red shirt.

"What are you talking about, Jack?"

"Adam Kāne, Alex. Fucking, Adam Kāne," he spat. "That stupid family. Nosey fucks!" Spittle escaped his mouth, and some landed on his lip.

Bekah tensed and gripped Alex tighter but was smart enough not to do or say anything that would draw Jack's attention to her. "I'm not following you, Jack. What does Adam have to do with this?"

Jack sighed, momentarily looking down at the weapon in his hands and then back to Alex. "Everything, Alex. If he'd have just left well enough alone. First his wife. Now him. And he had to drag you into it."

"What are you talking about, Jack?" She was wracking her brain to understand. He had something to do with Megan's research.

"You don't have me fooled for a second. I've been watching. I'm not stupid. He went to the police. That was the wrong move. Do you even realize how fucking close I am?" he yelled. The vein on the side of his forehead protruded, his face turned red. "One more year! That's all I need. I'm sure of it."

The pills. The ones in the little baggy in her bag.

She took another step away from him and maintained ignorance to keep him talking. "A year for what, Jack?" She had to figure a way out of this.

"The formula. One more year for the formula to be perfect. I told Thom to sit tight. I was sure that I could smooth things over, but that damn woman, Megan Kāne and her informant." He shook his head. "She couldn't leave well enough alone."

"Kids were dying, Jack. Of course, she couldn't."

"I had it under control!" He brought the gun up higher, but he wasn't really cognizant of it as a weapon. His thoughts were rambling like his words.

"Jonsey Miles. Donna Delco. The others. Why were they dying, Jack?"

"You know that."

"I do?" She was confused.

"The pills."

"Your formula."

"Yes. My formula.

"How did he figure it out?" Jack yelled waving the gun at Bekah. "You told him. You and your brother."

"She doesn't know anything. She has no idea what you are even rambling about, Jack." Though it dawned on her Bekah and Trey may have had the pills all along.

"But you do. You're fucking him. I'm sure he'd blab to his whore. What did he have that I don't?"

Bekah started to say something but remained silent when Alex squeezed her hand. "Jack. Why now? If everything was going as planned?"

He grimaced, bringing the tip of the gun to his head to scratch something on his temple. "I already told you. The kids were lab rats, collateral damage for one of the greatest scientific breakthroughs of our time. I'm on the cusp of it. Imagine the possibilities of never aging, of cell regeneration, the actual fountain of youth in a pill. Imagine the ability to slow the clock, to stay young. I'm there, Alex. Me!" He spoke so loudly she had the impression he was speaking to a nonexistent crowd behind her. Sweat poured from his head. "I'm on the verge of the formula that incorporates HGH into the equation, granting human beings more time to be young and vigorous, to slow the aging process, to cure things like Alzheimer's."

"Imagine what people will pay for that ability," Alex said as the portrait of greed came together. She took a few more steps back to put more distance between them.

"It's not about the money, Alex. Not for me. The others couldn't stop seeing the dollar signs, but for me–"

"–the recognition," Alex finished.

He smiled. It was maniacal, his sanity falling over the tipping point. She didn't know how much time she had.

"Do you realize how many have looked for it? The Fountain of Youth? It would be like Einstein and his Theory of Relativity." His concentration drifted a bit as thought gazing into the future, his future as a scientific god. But it was a momentary lapse Alex couldn't capitalize on. He was staring her down again, the gun leveled on her. "I wanted to take you with me on that ride," he stated, the nose of the gun dropped a fraction, "as my life's partner," and then came back up when he remembered his purpose. "But fuck Adam Kāne and is fucking family."

"You messed up though, didn't you?" Alex scrambled to keep him talking. "Diane Gomes. Her research was going to break open all those deaths."

"Very good, Sherlock."

"But the papers said it was a stalker." Bekah's voice was higher than usual.

Alex almost missed the tremble in it but didn't. She gave Bekah a reassuring squeeze to remind her she wasn't alone. She had to keep her head clear and willed herself to stay calm, to try and think one step ahead of Jack. She had to get Bekah out.

Jack smiled at her, but his smile faded just as quickly as it surfaced. "It's easy to manipulate how people think. A few choice words, a twist of the knife there. Stalker." He moved toward them, as though hunting.

"You left evidence. That's why the panic, otherwise you wouldn't be doing this. You are as good as caught."

"No!" His voice raised a notch.

"That was the phone call," she guessed. "Someone tipped you off. Who was it?" She tried to recall the conversation. He'd said a name.

His lips drew together in a thin line.

"Someone on the inside. Who would help you hide the chemistry?"

He advanced another step. Alex answered with a retreating step. "I have friends, Alex."

"I thought we were friends," she said.

"Friends. Ha! I was never your friend, Alex," he sneered the words. "I just wanted what I wanted, and you whored yourself to the enemy."

"This isn't neat and tidy," she stated continuing her cautious retreat. "How do you expect to get away with shooting two women?"

"You disappoint me, Alex. You came to confront Ms. Kāne about her resistance to you dating her father. Things got very ugly and you shot her. Consumed with the guilt of killing your lover's daughter, you turned the gun on yourself. I just happened to stumble upon you. I called 9-11 for fuck's sake—a good Samaritan."

"And your fingerprints?"

"Wiped clean. Only your prints will be on the gun Alex. And any other trace of me would be normal. I work in this building. I teach in this classroom." He waved his arms out and Alex had an image of Jack in rapturous worship, his arms raised with reverence. The image washed away. He leveled his gaze on her and advanced again. "It is such a tragedy," he added, feigning his comment to the press. "I never suspected Alex of murder. You think you know a person."

Adam's SUV climbed the curb and drove across the grassy decline, then the wide cement pathway and came to a stop just outside the front of the ASSC. He flung open the door just as his cell rang.

"Alex?" he answered with hope, but he already knew it wasn't her. He already knew where she was. She was with Jack, giving him the sample. His only hope was that Jack didn't know the police were onto him, but with an inside source, that was unlikely.

"Dad, Bekah's with Alex." It was Emma her voice threaded with static of their weak phone connection.

"What?" The ground tilted beneath him.

"I got ahold of her, she said she was walking with Alex to her class, and then the phone cut out. I tried to call her back, but I couldn't get through. Trey is on his way here. Dad, what's going on?"

"Oh, dear God." Adam's heart dropped into his gut. "Jackson. Jack. The one from the game."

"Oh. Oh shit."

She was saying his name as the call cut out. He pocketed the phone and raced up the stairway to the front doors. There was no way he was losing Bekah or Alex. Not like this. Not now. He had only just learned to live again. He couldn't do this again.

He entered the glass doors and rushed up the stairwell to get to floor where Jack's office was located. When he reached the hall, he slowed, stopped at the edge of the hallway and listened. It was quiet, too quiet.

A light at the end of the corridor illuminated shadows which reached for him. All of the doors were closed, but light crept out into the dark passageway as though apparitions. Adam stepped into the blue gray darkness and allowed it to swallow him whole. He vowed he wasn't going to emerge alone. Bekah and Alex would be with him.

He didn't know where they were but, he went to Jack's office first. His heartbeat hitched and sped up as it pounded in his ears. He took deliberately slow steps down the hall, keeping close to the wall. His left hand caressed the cool smooth surface as he walked, a guide, an anchor. Across the hall from him were classrooms, all empty. As he approached Jack's office, he hesitated a moment to listen. He checked the door and found it locked. He listened again and heard a faint murmur of a voice. It was coming from a classroom further up the corridor.

He crossed the hall and noticed light flowing from the window in the door. He crouched down and listened. Jack's voice. And then Alex's. His heart fell into his stomach and acid began to churn. He eased up to peek through the window, an inconspicuous glance. Jack's back was to the door, his arms out in front of him. He could see Alex. She was shielding Bekah; her eyes locked with Jack's while she listened to his diatribe. They were talking, but it wasn't an easy conversation based on Alex's terrified face, based on her body language. Terror dispersed through his bloodstream affecting every part of him.

He tested the doorknob which moved all the way, releasing the mechanism to open it. Elation jumped through Adam's insides. He hoped the other door was open as well and crouched low again, making his way to the opposite door. A quick check confirmed it open as well. He pushed himself against the wall, eased up and looked through the window. He couldn't see Jack from that angle, but he saw his hands, and there, sheltered in a grip that whitened the other man's knuckles, was a gun pointed at two of the women Adam loved.

Adam's breath caught as he slunk back into a crouch, and then it came rapid and shallow. *Oh Fuck.* What could he possibly do to that might be effective against a gun? Another look, and he saw Alex was moving away from Jack, pushing Bekah backward down the aisle between the tables. His eyes locked with a pair of familiar hazel eyes, and he saw the fear in Bekah's expression. He looked at her. *I love you*, he thought hoping she could see it in his eyes. *I'm here.*

He waited just on the other side of the door, the one closest to the gun. He wasn't trained to take down an armed man and wondered how close Lopes was. He could wait, but it didn't sound like he had the time. Jack was saying words like "time" and "making a move." He was going to do anything within his power to save Alex and Bekah.

Heart racing but determined to protect two people he loved at any cost, Adam opened the door and stepped inside.

"No," Alex said when she saw him. She shook her head. "No

Adam."

"Dad." Tears fell from Bekah's eyes, terror etched on her features, the wide eyes, the pallor of her brown skin.

Jack spun, the gun now pointed at Adam's chest and took a step back to keep all of them in his line of vision. A giant smile spread on his face. "Look who graced us with his presence. This is good. Very good."

"Hello Jack. Or should I say Jackson of Texas?"

"Figured it out, I see."

"Actually, the police did. They're on their way here now."

"I know."

"Who?"

"Dwight Connelly."

The coroner. With a heartbeat that settled into a calm rhythm out of necessity, he took a step into the room, leaving the door open behind him.

"Don't move Kāne." He swiveled the gun to point toward Alex and Bekah again. "You wouldn't want me to accidentally fire."

"No. I don't. I think maybe we should negotiate." Adam raised his hands. "You and me."

Jack cocked his head to the side. "You have any bargaining power. I have it all."

"But there must be something you want that I can give you. For example, me for them."

"No," Bekah cried.

"Shut up," Jack snapped. "No. The police are on their way. Why would I release two bargaining chips?"

"I think you're underestimating your position to bargain with police. They know you killed Gomes." Adam was reaching. He didn't know if that was the truth, but for the moment, it didn't matter. He needed something with which to unsettle the psycho with the gun.

It worked. Jack's eyes flicked to the door. A frown tugged at his mouth and doubt creased his brow.

Adam knew, then, Jack was capable of killing in the name of self-preservation. He'd done it before. "You won't get very far," Adam added. "It's an island. They will have the airport and harbors covered the moment it hits the radio."

Jack's shoulders dropped a moment, the realization he was trapped setting in.

"Just keep me. Use me. Let the women go."

The gunman's arms tensed, his body straightened, and he leveled his sights on the women. "I don't think I need to wait to shoot then, Kāne. You took everything from me. Now, I get to take everything from you."

Without thought to his own safety and only the desire to protect Alex and Bekah, Adam lunged at Jack. He made it to the other man. Knocked him off his feet but not before the gun fired. Adam landed on Jack, who chuffed and grunted under Adam's weight as they hit the floor. Stools skittered across the floor, and the gun clacked against the linoleum as it slid out of reach. Jack struggled for breath, fought to get out from under Adam, but Adam held fast to keep the other man from the gun.

"Freeze," Adam heard someone say.

In the next moment, Lopes poured into the room with a herd of officers through both doors dressed in tactical gear and weapons drawn.

Chaos filled the room around him, he was dragged away from Jack, his only thought about Bekah and Alex's safety.

Jack was silent.

"We've got civilian wounded," a voice said.

Adam tried to move his head, an officer subduing him. Civilian wounded? He couldn't see. "Bekah? Alex?" he called out.

"Don't move," an officer told him again."

"Are they okay?

"Dad," Bekah sobbed. "Dad. She jumped in front of me."

"Let him up," Detective Lopes told the officer.

Adam scrambled to his feet.

"I told you to stay put," Lopes said.

But Adam's gaze swung toward Bekah, who rushed into his arms. Alex was in a pool of blood collecting around her on the white linoleum.

A siren wailed in the distance.

"She just jumped in front of me." Bekah repeated her breath ragged, fast and furious, tears falling from her eyes. She buried her face in his chest.

"Alex," Adam said. He couldn't reach her, the officers administering first aid. "Talk to me, Alex. Please. Alex," he chanted over and over with Bekah in his arms. "Alex."

She moaned. "Did you get him? Is Bekah okay?" she asked.

Lopes, who'd crouched down next to her, looked at her as the EMT's hustled into the room. "Yeah. We got him."

CHAPTER THIRTY-NINE

Alex could feel her body. It was heavy, as though she were loaded down with weights and sloshing through water. Her eyelids were sealed, but she pried them open and blinked. The light of the sun cascading through the window caused her to squint. She opened and closed her eyes until they felt comfortable open. Alex hurt too much to move. She winced.

"Hey."

She tried to look to her left where she'd heard the voice but was granted reprieve from moving when she saw Adam, now leaning over her. She wanted to smile but couldn't. Her mouth felt weighted as well, so she just captured his eyes with hers and stared at him wanting to immerse herself in the depth of his look.

His hand slid over hers. She turned her palm up so that she could feel his hand better and was happy when he laced their fingers together. She opened her mouth to speak but her dry mouth startled her. "Water?" The word hurt her throat.

"Ice." Adam moved and returned with a cup and spoon. He spooned some ice chips into her mouth. Alex wanted to close her eyes at the relief she felt of the ice-cold water melting in her mouth but was afraid she'd never open them again. She parted her lips to accept more when Adam offered the ice.

"You gave me a scare," he said.

She attempted to smile.

"You need more rest, though. I'll be here when you wake up," she heard him say. She wanted to tell him she'd slept long enough, but her eyes had already drifted closed.

Adam oriented himself though his thoughts were fogged. His eyes drifted open to a stark room, a strange shade of green and a billowing curtain on runners in a putrid shade of puce with yellow and green plaid stripes. Strange electrical outlets, a monotonous beeping, and a bed. He realized that his lower back ached from the awkward position in which he'd slept. He sat up and rubbed his eyes, and face, feeling the stubble on his unshaved skin. Then he remembered with surreal clarity that he was at the hospital where he'd been the last several hours.

He looked at the hospital bed where Alex lay sleeping. She'd opened her eyes the night before, smiled, and gone back into the drug induced sleep.

"She's going to make a full recovery," her doctor had said after surgery the night of the shooting.

The relief he'd experienced at the doctor's words had been like taking a breath after being held under a series of a waves one after the other. When he thought he might drown, and then somehow, he made it to the surface. His muscles ached with the relaxation.

He loved Alex with a a depth he'd never thought he'd achieve again, only different, more nuanced and layered with experience and wisdom. He'd been gifted a second chance with Megan's own words. They'd drawn him out from the darkest time in his life and reopened his heart. Megan's journals had given him freedom.

Adam stood up and went to Alex's side, touching her cheek and forehead with the back of his hand. Her skin was cool to the touch, soft and pliant. Knowing she'd stepped in front of Bekah to the detriment of herself made him see her, the lengths she would go for her family. She'd sacrificed herself for him and Megan. She'd sacrificed herself for Bekah. And he knew, if push came to shove, Alex would do it again. It was the depth of her love. It was unfathomable he was being given a second chance with such a wonderful woman when he had done nothing to deserve it.

A few days later, the family was gathered at Adam's. Alex was set up on the couch in the family room, being nursed by three Kānes and two and a half Wests. Adam had insisted on taking care of her there despite her insistence she could take care of herself at her own place, but secretly, she loved he'd insisted.

"Read it aloud," Bekah urged Emma. She was sitting on the floor holding Alex's hand

Alex looked around the room. She was surrounded by Adam's children, Bekah, Trey, Emma, and by extension, Grant. Adam sat on the coffee table across from her. Aside from a few personal issues, he hadn't left her side since bringing her home. Constant vigil even going so far as to sleep on the floor next to her. He'd gotten up with stiff joints but insisted he was fine. She was feeling good enough now that she'd showered, her dressing clear and clean with Adam's help, though she wouldn't be paddling canoe any time soon. She would start physical therapy for her shoulder and arm in the coming weeks.

"You sure?" Emma asked. She was sitting in the chair across the room behind Adam. "It's a pretty long article."

Trey laughed. He was leaning against the back of the couch. "Go ahead and feign humility, sis. We all know you want to read it."

"Since when do you use words like 'feign,'" Emma asked, her expression wry.

"Just read it," Trey said with a smile.

"I'd like to hear it," Alex said. "I need to get caught up anyway."

"Here goes," Emma stated and began to read the newspaper she was holding. "O'ahu Police Department detective, Mana Lopes with his team, cracked the Diane Gomes case. No one could have guessed, however the deeper implications of one woman's death. Prime suspect, Dr. Jackson P. Reynolds, formerly of Texas, is awaiting arraignment for the murder of the graduate student and the attempted murder of another HSU professor, though it's clear according to Douglas Ying with the Prosecutor's office, the district attorney may be linking him to several other deaths at the university beginning from 2000 through the death of Ms. Gomes.

"Reynolds, a scientist at the university, was attempting to skip the Food and Drug Administration drug approval process, and as an unnamed source at HSU reports, may have exposed university athletes to unapproved human drug testing. The deaths of standouts like quarterback Jonsey Miles, who died during a football game early this season, and swimmer Donna Delco, who died in 2004 among others are being reinvestigated in light of this new information. Dr. Sarah Billings of Milner Pharmacuticals in Honolulu stated, 'The FDA drug approval process has been structured for checks and balances for the very purpose of safety. Forgoing protocol puts others at risk.'

"Reynolds has implicated other individuals in the conspiracy and several arrests have been made. Among those arrested are University president Stanton Thom, athletic director Milton Yamane, O'ahu County coroner Dwight Connolly, and the CEO of Apex Wellness, Harvey Lingle, also of Texas. Each of their involvement has yet to be commented upon.

"Harvey Lingle, a former classmate of Stanton Thom is also the former employer of both Dwight Connolly and Jackson Reynolds who both served as researchers for Apex Wellness. Milton Yamane, a former classmate of Stanton Thom at a local high school on Oʻahu, has also been implicated."

Emma stopped to turn the page before she continued. Alex could see the large color photo of Jack on the cover. His head was ducked as he attempted to hide his face. She expected to feel fear regarding her attacker, but she felt disgust and rage at the site of him.

Emma continued, "Detective Mana Lopes stated, 'Reynolds might not have been stopped had it not been for the help of the late Megan Kāne. Without her research, we wouldn't have had a starting place to uncover the atrocities occurring at the college.'

"Megan Kāne, a Hawaiian Sun contributor who succumbed over a year ago to ovarian cancer left detailed research which has since been turned over to detective Lopes by Kāne's family who hopes that those responsible will be brought to justice. Kāne's widower, Adam Kāne added, 'Megan had a big heart. She only wanted to do what was right.' Detective Lopes also mentioned that Ms. Kāne had an informant who they believe has been taken into custody and will be questioned accordingly."

"Wait. What?" Alex interrupted.

"Milton Yamane," Adam stated. "When I turned over copies of relevant entries to detective Lopes, it turns out Yamane claimed he'd sent emails to Megan divulging information for her to uncover the crimes. He knew the email address which Megan had written about. No one else could have known—it was only in her journals."

"Myally was Milton Yamane," Emma added, and then continued to read: "Reynolds will be charged on separate charges of terroristic threatening, kidnapping, and attempted murder of a fellow HSU faculty member and HSU student.

"The University has yet to comment on all the arrests of several key people on campus though Robbie Delagon, a secretary for the school's legal department stated that, 'the office has been fielding a lot of phone calls.' The school has also named Dr. Dorothy Jeffery's as the interim president. She will be naming some additional interims until court proceedings have concluded.

"The arraignment is set for next week Tuesday." Emma closed the paper, refolding it along the indentions.

"The school is going to be in a world of hurt if Thom and Yamane are found guilty," Adam said.

"Sue job," Grant added. "I never thought our alma mater would have such a dark spot," he sighed.

They were quiet as the ramifications settled in their minds.

Alex broke the silence. "That was a great article, Emma. I loved the part about your mom."

She smiled. "Yeah. Me too."

"Your mother would be proud." Adam turned and looked at Emma over his shoulder.

"Thanks, Dad. I think she'd be proud of all of us."

A moment of silence stretched between them, each of them in their own thoughts about Megan and her missing presence in their lives. Until they remembered they were Kānes which required loud and excessive banter. After another half an hour of it, Adam ushered everyone out, claiming Alex needed more rest. Kisses were given and promises to be over the next day. When they were gone, Adam walked back into the room.

"They seem to be okay with their Dad's affection for their mother's best friend."

He chuckled and sat down on the couch drawing her feet into his lap. "Yes."

He massaged her feet. "Have I mentioned that I love you?"

"Yes. And I never get tired of hearing it." She smiled, leaned back, and looked up at the ceiling overhead. "What are they going to say?" she asked referring to the kids.

"About what? Us?"

Alex nodded. "I can't think that they will be so accepting of me when they find out I've weaseled my way into your life."

"Is that what you did? Weaseled your way into my life?" He chuckled, squeezing a foot. "I wondered how that happened." He continued massaging her toes.

"Adam. You know what I mean."

"They seemed fine to me just now," Adam said.

"Of course, they did. They don't know."

"Alex. I already told them. Besides, it was a bit obvious with me hovering about in your hospital room and then bringing you here."

"You already told them? And they were fine with it?"

"Why wouldn't they be? You are a wonderful woman who they love, who loves them, who their father loves. What's so difficult about that?"

"I thought they'd be upset, like I was trying to take Megan's place."

"Are you?"

"Of course, not."

"All of us know you'd never try. You aren't Megan. You are Alexandra James." He smiled and squeezed her toe. "Emma wasn't surprised. Bekah said she can sacrifice me to the woman who saved her life. Trey was a bit resistant, though I don't think it has anything to do with you—just loyalty to his mom. I think maybe the girls got to him, however. He seemed fine just now." He let go of her feet and moved up the couch until he was hovering over her. "I think I'm the one who doesn't deserve you."

She drew his weight down on her. With her free hand, she ran her fingers through his hair. "You know what I think?"

"What?"

"I don't think we should look back. I think we should enjoy every moment we have in the present together, no weight of what *was* hanging between us. We don't know how much time we have, so we should make the most of it." She continued, caressing his head, running her hands through his hair. "If this last two years has taught us anything, you never know what the day or the hour will bring."

"Speaking of the past," he said and looked up at her. "I believe that you promised me a dinner last week."

Alex laughed. "And dessert."

"I mean to make you keep your promises." Adam moved up and pressed his lips to Alex's for a chaste kiss. "I love you AJ, and I'm never going to let you forget it."

Alex smiled under his lips, "I don't want you to."

He stood up. "You need anything?"

"Help me sit up. I'm tired of laying here."

Adam helped her get comfortable, then sat down across from her. He leaned forward, hands folded in front of him. "May I ask a favor?"

She nodded.

"I need to return to the past for only a while more, but I want you to go with me, if you're willing."

"How come?"

"I've got Megan's last journals to read."

"And you want me to hear it too?"

Adam nodded. "I was actually wondering, if you'd read them." He stood and walked across the room, disappearing behind her. He reappeared a few moments later holding the burgundy book and held it out to her. She ran her hand over the leather a poignant realization that the book had once been Megan's, her friend, her sister. She opened the book to the page Adam had marked with a folded bunch of papers.

Alex glanced at Adam with the paper in hand, and he nodded to her indicating she could open it. She unfolded the document and recognized her penmanship. It was the letter she'd written to Megan. She looked again at Adam who sat next to her. She set it aside and turned her attention to the entry.

"This doesn't look like her handwriting."

"It isn't." When Alex asked him the question with her eyes, he said, "It's Emma's."

"Emma wrote the last journals for her mom?"

342

Adam nodded.

"You've already read them."

He nodded. "Yes. I asked Emma about it a few nights ago."

She turned her attention to the entry.

"Dear Adam," Alex began, "I wish that I could have a magic potion to stop time. The potion would stop the clock, and if you wished hard enough, it could take you back to the exact time you wanted to go. You could choose to stay there, forever, or move forward again, making changes to the choices you'd made along the way. I wouldn't make any changes, Adam. Each choice, some right, some wrong led us to the beauty of us, but I would stop time and go back to when there wasn't any cancer. I would stay there living forever with you at that time in our lives. Too bad the potion doesn't exist.

"And since it doesn't, I have to say my goodbyes. I don't know how much longer I have—it doesn't feel like long, which is why my gorgeous, beautiful Emma is writing this for me."

Alex stopped and pressed a thumb into the water stains on the pages. Tears. She glanced at Adam who was staring at the floor. She continued. Megan's next three entries were dedicated to Emma, Trey, and Bekah. With each entry, Alex stopped to look at Adam. He hadn't moved, his face unreadable.

"This is the last one, Adam," Alex stated as she flipped the page back and forth checking to see if there were any other entries. "Dear Adam, you are a rock. Did you know that your name means, 'Man of the red earth?' It's a Hebrew name but isn't it interesting that Hawai'i is red earth. My *Akamu*. In Hawaiian your name means 'formed by God.' My Adam. You are my grounding, my earth. And your Hawaiian family name, Kāne—man. I always was such an optimist that I couldn't keep my feet on the ground. And there you are, my rock, my foundation, keeping me solid and giving me the ability to keep dreaming. I'm still dreaming, thinking about that time potion.

"Adam, I'm not afraid to die. I know where I'm going. There is only one thing about which I'm afraid. I'm afraid to leave you behind. I'm fearful because you are my man of the red earth, rugged and stubborn. You are fierce. You dig in those feet, stand strong, and then because of that beautiful loyalty, you will choose to stop living. I can see you, the rock in the earth, hardening into the black lava, still and stuck while you keep everything else out. You'll exist by breathing alone and move only because you have to. Maybe it's presumptuous of me, but after twenty-five years, I think I know you pretty well.

"If there is one thing, I can beg of you, Adam, please don't stop living. Please love me, remember me, but don't feel trapped by my memory. I want you to return to joy. Don't lose sight of the kids. Connect with them as adults the way I won't be able to. They are in your hands now.

"Adam, I want you to find love again. It's out there waiting for you and that person will open your world in a new way. I love you with every fiber of my being. I rest in the knowledge you love me the same way. I don't doubt you will continue to love me when I'm gone, and I know that I will always have a place of your heart, as you have mine. Give the rest to someone else, for you deserve to have that.

"One last thing, I have enclosed a letter here I want you to see. I don't know what it will mean to you—maybe nothing, maybe everything—but it isn't mine to hold onto anymore. It always belonged to you. Remember I love you, then, now, and forever."

Alex stopped. She'd come to the end. She stared at Megan's last written thoughts, her tears blurring those words. Alex wiped them away and looked up at Adam. She wouldn't have known that he heard except for the shimmer in his eyes, a gleam that she might have mistaken wasn't there. "That's it." She could hear the tears in her voice.

He wiped his eyes with the back of his hand. She leaned forward and put a hand on his thigh. "Thank you," she said. "For sharing it with me."

He moved, scooping her up, and sitting down with her on his lap. With his arms wrapped around her and her one good arm around him, he buried his head in the crook of her neck and shoulder. She caressed his back.

"She gave us her blessing," Adam said.

Alex swallowed her tears and when she was able replied, "She did."

EPILOGUE
(January over a year later)

Adam stood with his eight-month-old granddaughter in his arms. She was beautiful. Her black hair was thick and curly. Her hazel eyes were never without the merriment of the moment. Her chubby fist was in her mouth as she gnawed happily on the skin of her hand. Adam was thoroughly in love with Megan Kapua West.

"Did you know, my flower, that your *kupuna kāne* is a very happy man?" he said quietly. "Your new *kupuna wahine* makes him so."

She reached a chubby hand for a bright red plastic ornament.

Adam took it off the tree and gave it to her.

She gurgled with excitement, and then drew her brows together in a serious scowl as she studied it. She brought it to her mouth.

"Don't tell your Mommy," he whispered. "She'd have my hide for letting you play with that."

"You know, you need to share her."

Adam turned from the Christmas tree holding his granddaughter toward Alex as she pushed away from the wall and walked into the living room of their new home. "How long have you been eavesdropping?" he asked with a smile.

She stopped right in front of him. "Long enough." She leaned up and kissed his cheek. He smiled thinking about standing at Kaimana Beach Park a week ago on Christmas Eve. The sound of the ocean surf and soft breeze floating around them as they'd shared their vows with Emma, Grant, little Kapua, Bekah, Trey, and the minister officiating their wedding ceremony.

He made a humming noise of dissent and turned his face so he could kiss her lips. "Hello, Wife." He felt her lips curl in a smile against his.

"I love the sound of that, Husband," she said and put her arms around him and Kapua who was now wagging the ornament in the air and pressing it and all its sopping glory against Adam's shirt.

"The game is about to start," she said.

Alex looked away from Adam to the baby and used her best baby language to draw her away from him. After a few moments, a large grin spread across the baby's face, and she leaned toward Alex her arms outstretched, the ornament falling from her hand to the floor. Alex took her, nestling Kapua in the crook of her arm on her hip and sent a triumphant look to Adam.

Adam picked up the ornament and put it back on the tree.

"You coming?" she asked the question directed to Adam but never took her eyes from Kapua.

"Right behind you," he said.

Alex leaned over and kissed Adam on the mouth, then she turned and walked away talking to the baby as she went.

Adam watched them walk out of the living room and stopped a moment as he was struck with a memory. Alex holding Trey, singing to him. He looked up at his wife disappearing around the corner. His heart awash with an all-encompassing contentment, he followed them into the family room grabbing an ale as he passed through the new kitchen. He sat down in near Alex and the baby on the couch and looked at each of his family members, all but Trey.

"There he is!" Bekah exclaimed.

Adam turned his attention to the TV in time to see Trey run from the tunnel onto the field amidst his teammates, the green and blue uniform vibrant on screen. He was the junior QB who'd led his team to the Fiesta Bowl. A National Championship.

"How do you think he'll do today?" Emma asked. She was sitting on the floor in front of Grant whose hands rubbed her shoulders.

"Trey? He always does good," Grant said, though his opinion was skewed. "The team should do pretty good, too. Trey proved the team has what it takes this year—they wouldn't have made it to this game if they hadn't."

"It should be a good game. The analysts are predicting that the Hurricanes will win by a field goal." Adam sipped his beer. "They haven't made it this far since–"

"Since you were playing, Dad," Bekah stated.

"Trey's a much better player than I ever was."

"So humble," Alex said with a smile. "Your father was amazing."

They watched the captains of the team make their way to the fifty-yard line for the coin toss, among them Trey. Adam's pride surged, a feeling he couldn't help when he watched each of his kids participate in something they loved. For Trey it was football, for Bekah it was swimming, for Emma it was reading an article she'd written and seeing her with her daughter.

He glanced at Alex, who was watching him instead of the game. Kapua leaned against her playing with a plastic toy and tested it with her two new teeth. Alex held out her hand across the arms of the couch, the brand-new ring on her finger winking at him. He smiled and took her offered hand in his own. They interlaced their fingers electricity of her touch sent a surge of excitement through him.

Adam sent a thank you to *ke Akua* for the many blessings he had received even though he didn't deserve them.

"I love you," he said for only her.

"I love you, too," she replied.

He turned his attention back to the game to find the watchful eyes of Bekah, Emma and Grant on them. "What?" he asked.

They laughed.

"You two are hopeless!" Bekah laughed. "I love you," She mimicked and received a pillow to the head from Adam. "When do you leave for your honeymoon?"

"Not soon enough!" he said and turned to smile at Alex who had blushed.

They laughed together and turned their attention to the TV screen as Trey lined up under center for the first snap of the game.

ACKNOWLEDGEMENTS

A book—the idea and the writing of it—starts with the author, but the end—what makes it into a reader's hands—is the effort of a plethora of eyes. *The Letters She Left Behind* is no different. I own any and all mistakes.

I need to thank several people who supported me through this novel.

First, Cari Lynn Webb, author extraordinaire, tirelessly read this manuscript over and over and over again in its early years and helped me shape it into the novel presented here. Thank you, Cari, for listening to me whine when I just couldn't seem to get it right. Thank you for being an amazing Critique Partner and for the companionship when we were writing in isolation and going through the tough process of trying to make dreams happen.

Thank you to Janine Caroline, another indie author, who was instrumental in telling me "You can do this" when I was paralyzed with fear. Thank you for the reading, the feedback, and the fellowship in what can be a very lonely creative world.

To my family, who always gets the short end of the stick when I'm writing. My focus is pointed, my patience is thin, and my time is guarded. Thank you so much for loving me and supporting me on this journey. I know it isn't always easy for you, but you give me hugs anyway.

Finally, to my Lord and Savior, Jesus Christ without whom I wouldn't have the stories and through whom all blessings flow. I fretted sharing this book because of the love scenes I'd written. I fretted about not being *Christian* for sharing it, and I heard His quiet voice say: "Stop. Did I not create sex?" I laughed (and cried), and He added, "I want you to present humans as humans are in truth—beautifully flawed and in need of redemption—that is all I have asked you to do. It is there where the perfection of Me can be glorified. Now do it." So, in faith, I follow where He leads.

 **BOOKS**

Also by CL Walters

Available Now!

AN EXERPT from SWIMMING SIDEWAYS

1

WISHING FOR THE AWESOME POWER OF INVISIBILITY

Good Abby has the job of keeping Bad Abby in place on her first day at a new school. I'm hopeful Bad Abby will stay in her cage, though at times, keeping her caged is more work than it's worth. It's important, however, and Good Abby knows this more than anyone. This is a chance to start fresh.

When the teacher says my name, "Abby Kaiāulu?" I cringe, wishing I could throw that in the cage too. My Hawaiian name doesn't allow for anonymity and that is a rule of Good Abby: *remain anonymous.*

"Here," I say. I've chosen a tone to communicate indifference. Not too loud to express exuberance, but not too quiet to raise any flags of social concern. Instead, an even tone to express, maybe, boredom but without an edge should be neutral enough to be forgettable.

Another rule by Good Abby: *Don't draw attention.*

The teacher looks at me. She's cute with wire-rimmed glasses perched on the end of an upturned nose. Her white skin is dotted with freckles, and her auburn hair cut short and fluffy around her face. "Did I pronounce your last name correctly?" She smiles. Classic teacher move: disarm with a smile.

I nod—even though she's butchered my name—to steer the center-stage light onto whatever awaits us in US History. While being at a new school is a positive thing, Good Abby knows how important it is to make a good first impression. It is imperative to hide the truth of what I did, to keep what happened at my last school from happening here too.

Next rule established by Good Abby: *Stay under the radar.*

Freckle-nose teacher asks, "Would you say it please?"

I sigh. "Abby Kaw-ee-aaawww-oo-loo."

Teacher makes a note on her clipboard.

I return to doodling waves in the margin of my clean notebook, wishing I was in the waves at Makaha with perfect sets of four to six faces rolling in on a clear, calm, sunny day. I imagine the azure water stretching toward the horizon, the *kai* wrapping around my body like a hug. Sitting inside a school room for lessons about US History would be pointless.

But pixie-teacher isn't thinking about waves at Makaha Beach like I am when she says, "Such a pretty name, Abby. What is the ethnicity? It's so unique."

I blink and work hard not to roll my eyes, keeping Bad Abby in check. Every pair of eyes in the room, at least twenty of them, are now on me at this third, pointed question. I sink a little lower in my desk chair and answer her. "It's Hawaiian."

"Hawaiian. Wow!" Her eyes grow to nearly the same circumference as her glasses, and her smile is extra bright. "I want to travel to Hawaii," she adds.

Bad Abby thinks the following snide observation: *you and most of the rest of the world.*

Good Abby keeps Bad Abby's snarky comment internal, however, and focuses on Tinker Bell teacher's words.

"We'll study the overthrow of the Hawaiian monarchy later this year, the imprisonment of the Queen, and the annexation," she says.

Guilt bubbles up a little at Bad Abby's ill-manners, and I wonder if Perky Teacher will teach that annexation was illegal?

"Welcome to Cantos, Abby," Good Fairy Teacher finishes.

I force a slight smile to acknowledge her comments, but not too flashy. I don't want to encourage this interrogation any further.

Even though the teacher finally moves on to today's lesson about how to take notes for the lecture, I can still feel the eyes of the other students in the class boring into me, trying to mine me for secrets. Everyone else has had nearly two weeks to acclimate to the school year, and for many of them a lifetime of knowing one another. It's my first day as a junior at Cantos High School. Right now, I'm wishing that CHS stood for Camouflage High School, a place where I can blend into everything around me due to my awesome power of invisibility.

EXCERPT

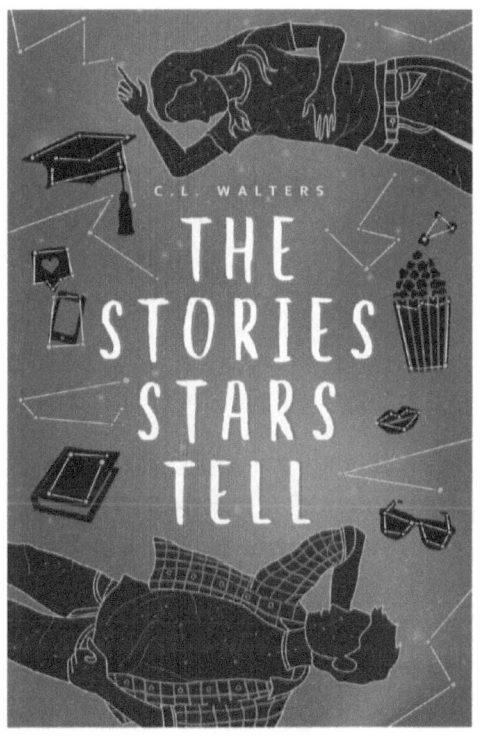

Available Now!

senior year
14 days before graduation

emma

I squeeze my eyes shut, terrified I'm about to screw this up. Three deep breaths. Slow. Steady. In. Out. The sound of my breath echoes in my head like the rush of the wind through the tree leaves in my backyard, and the fear of failure, which always sits in the front of my brain, drips down through my body into my stomach.

I could forget my part.

I could ruin everything.

I could be sick.

I picture Cameron, standing in front of his dad's red Ferrari in his khaki pants and suspenders over his dark brown shirt ranting about conquering his fear right before he kicks the shit out of his dad's car. Okay. He's a fictional character from one of my favorite movies of all time, *Ferris Bueller's Day Off*, but still. I'm going to kick the shit out of this, like, speech-Ferrari.

Breathe in. Breathe out.

"Emma?"

The sound of my name, as though it's being called through a tunnel, draws me back. I open my eyes and look into the familiar bright blue eyes of my best friend, Liam.

"Emma? It's almost time. You're doing your breathing thing?"

He's dressed in a business suit, charcoal gray and red tie with those chic pants and shoes that make him seem like he's stepped out of a male fashion magazine. Far more fashionable than most males in these competitions who look like they're wearing their father's Sunday suits. He is beautiful. Dark haired, thin and fit, handsome and not into me at all (I'm not into him either). We've been best friends since third grade in Mrs. Hale's class.

My insides shimmy, but I nod. "Cameron. Remember Cameron."

"What?" He adjusts his black-framed, hipster glasses which he pulls off to perfection.

"Just channeling Cameron." I tug on the bottom of my matching charcoal gray jacket.

Liam reaches out, fixes my collar, and then takes both of my hands in his. Leaning forward, he presses his forehead to mine. He smells like wintergreen mint, familiar and comforting. "We've got this. We've practiced this. We know it. We. Know. It."

I close my eyes. "We do," I repeat, and my heartbeat slows to the rhythm of his words. Liam. My best friend. "Our last time in duo," I whisper. Tears threaten to fall. "What am I going to do without you?"

He pulls back but keeps hold of my hands. "Do. Not. Cry." Hand squeeze. "You have to keep your make-up looking good. Game faces. Let's kick the shit out of this speech, like Cameron did the car."

I smile, because he knows me, and I nod. "Let's do it."

Our names are called. We walk from the wings out onto the stage and take our marks.

We slay it. Of course we do, because that's who we are.

Later, Liam and I are at my house for our usual Saturday night John Hughes movie of the week. It's what we always do on a Saturday night, except for that one Saturday junior year when I went off the rails. The popcorn is made, drinks are chilling, and *Pretty in Pink* is cued up. While we wait for Ginny — our other bestie — to arrive, we both scroll through Instagram.

"Look at this one," Liam says. He's on the floor with his back against the couch. His legs — fit in cotton twill — are stretched out in front of him, crossed at the ankles. He holds up his phone.

"What is that?" I ask.

"It's Baker's house."

"Baker? As in Atticus Baker?"

He nods. "Party there tonight." He continues to examine his phone, and I watch him.

Instead of scrolling through the feed, he stops and scrutinizes Atticus Baker's page. Picture after picture, even reading the comments. It strikes me, because Liam hasn't ever expressed an interest in anyone specific (he's kind of private like that). As he looks through Atticus Baker's feed, it dawns on me how much of a risk Liam took to tell his truth. How lonely it might be in our small, conservative town. Lately, with graduation impending, I've thought about what kind of risks I've taken in my life (that one time junior year notwithstanding), and the answer has been none.

"I see you, Liam. You think Atticus is hot," I say with a giggle.

"Who doesn't? He's gorgeous."

He continues to study every single picture Atticus has posted, and I recognize familiarity in his actions. I've done it. My own phone, at the moment, is open to Tanner James's IG feed, as per usual. I press on his story and watch a video of him walking into Baker's party, but I don't show Liam. He doesn't approve of my infatuation with one of the biggest f-boys at school. I don't blame him; it's suspect.

Instead, I reach out and ruffle Liam's hair, which I know he hates. "But you like him like him."

"Stop!" He lurches forward to get out from under the destructive force of my hand and adjusts his hair back into place, not that I could have done much to those product-laced locks. "And shut up. I don't." His ears turn red.

"You are so lying." I grin and search for Atticus's IG feed on my phone. "He is really handsome," I say when I find it.

I select a gorgeous picture of Atticus and turn my phone to show him. Liam glances at it but looks away, aloof and noncommittal. Even I can't detach from the beauty. Atticus is gorgeous: tall, black, stylish, fit. He's a basketball player at our high school and got a full ride to St. Mary's in California. All of his pictures have this low-key, I'm-so-casual vibe in a matching filter, so there's no way it's casual. But, damn.

"Liam. He's so hot, you have my approval," I tell him, even though I know how horrible and objectifying it sounds. Not that Liam needs my approval.

He groans. "Stop, Emma. For real. Atticus is like–" He pauses and turns his shoulders so he's facing me. "Look–"

"Mr. Liam, sir, I don't much feel like one of your lectures," I interrupt in my best patronizing student voice, because Liam is always lecturing me. Mansplaining. The jerk.

"Atticus is like — out of my league. And that's *if* he's gay." He looks down at his phone again. "I mean, I think I got some vibes, but my vibes are inexperienced. I have no idea what I'm doing. Besides, how many openly gay men do you think there are in this backwater, hick-horrible town?" He offers an old man grunt of disgust and readjusts himself with his back against the couch's seat again. "I can't wait to get out of here."

I understand his sentiment, though my prison is of a different kind: Christian family, striving for perfection where nothing real ever happens. Okay, maybe that's not fair, but it's how I feel sometimes. I can't wait to leave and distance myself from stifling expectations to experience my own version of freedom.

I try to give Liam a pep talk anyway. "None of us know what we're doing. We're all faking it. Ferris is the only one who seems to have it all figured out, and he's a fictional character. No one is like that."

"Has what figured out?" Ginny asks from behind us. Liam and I turn and watch her walk into the finished basement from the stairs. "Your dad said to come down, and he'll bring us some fresh cookies when they're out of the oven."

The third of our Bueller troop flops onto the couch next to me with her fresh-coated vanilla scent. She's been on a new kick to live as a 1970's hippie in order to explore the ideology of antidisestablishmentarianism, mostly to annoy her dad and stepmom. The outfit today: tie-dye cotton maxi-skirt she made herself and a black shirt without a bra (which is very noticeable because of her gorgeous boobs and high beams she's been very proud of since she got them).

361

The whole no bra thing has really pushed the buttons of her stepmom which Ginny loves to do more than anything. She lays her head on my shoulder and threads her arm through mine.

"Life," I say, in answer to her original question.

"Our parents don't even have life figured out. Obviously," Ginny replies. "Case in point: my dad and step-monster. How could we — mere eighteen-year-olds? I take that back. We might have it more together."

"Something new?" I ask. The last installment of *The Life and Times of Ginny Donnelly* had her stepmother forcing her to paint her bedroom since she's leaving for college soon. Her stepmom is determined to convert Ginny's room into a fitness haven and has been taking measurements for her equipment.

"Besides Operation Kick Ginny Out of Her Room? Nothing new. I don't want to talk about them, or the fact that she made me go through my closet to consolidate everything into boxes for storage."

"Sorry, Gin." I squeeze her arm with mine. "On a happier note, we were discussing something intriguing. Specifically, Liam's crush on Atticus Baker."

He turns his back to us and resumes his stylish leaning against the couch, looking like a modern James Dean. He's got it all: the hair, the glasses, the pout.

Ginny sits up. "Atticus Baker? Man, he's hot."

"That's what I said."

"Is he gay?"

"We could run a new operation: Find out if Atticus Baker is Gay," I offer. "We could all slide into his DM, and see?"

"Emma." Liam's voice is threaded with a warning, like a brother who has reached the threshold of annoyance.

I smile. "I'm sorry, Liam. Am I hurting your feelings?" I lean toward him and nuzzle his ear.

He moves to get away from me again. "No." He swats at me. "And no offense, but we know how the last operation you planned went."

I glance at Ginny, who raises her eyebrows and tilts her head. "He has a point."

I know they're referring to the junior year debacle. To be fair, if I was going to sneak out and go to a party, I was going to go all in. Especially if getting caught by my parents was a risk. I hadn't gotten caught, but I had gotten what I'd been after: a kiss — a gorgeously memorable hot kiss that I hadn't been able to forget. From Tanner James. "Everything turned out okay. We didn't get into trouble. Really, when you list out the successes against the failures, that was a win-win."

Liam looks at me like I'm delusional, and perhaps I am. "Emma, if you think you won in that situation, you're wrong. You haven't stopped infatuating about the school's biggest douchebag since. And for someone who claims to be a feminist, that's some contradictory bullshit."

I look to Ginny for backup, which I don't get. "He's right." She shrugs and flops against the couch. "It's been over a year, and you're still struggling with it."

They're both right. I sigh because I *am* infatuated with Tanner James, and I know better. "It doesn't matter. Graduation is two weeks away. We're going to kick ass, say our smarty-pants speeches, and leave for college. Which I will cry about later. Tanner James will be old news. My infatuation with him will be spent as I walk onto a college campus as a co-ed surrounded by beautiful men and women and a playground of sexual awakening."

Ginny and Liam glance at one another with saucer-shaped eyes and then collapse with laughter.

"Emma! I can't believe you just said that." Liam laughs even harder.

"Sexual Awakening. Emma." Ginny shrieks, falling away from me at her waist.

"Wow. You're giving me a complex."

When their laughter subsides, Liam climbs up onto the couch.

With me in between them, sulking, my arms crossed over my chest, I say, "You make me sound like a prude."

"That's not what we mean." Liam pats my leg. "I'm sorry if I hurt your feelings. I just–" He pauses and looks at me over the top of his glasses, reminding me of his dad. "Emma, you're pretty conservative when it comes to stuff like that. And scared about, like everything."

"What? Sex?" I say, still pouting but knowing he's right. I haven't done much in my eighteen years besides masturbate. I'm not ignorant about sex. I may have been raised with Christian parents, but they have been open and frank about sex. While the discussions have moved around the naturalness of the act, the underlying message has been an expectation to wait until marriage. Besides the junior year operation, I'd kissed a couple of other guys. Add to that my date for junior prom, Chris Keller, who tried to pressure me into sex and went so far as to grope me in the limo. I'd slapped him (so much for uncomplicated). Without a doubt, I'm curious and interested in sex, but it's clear my wiring leads to the red wire, not meaningless romps in the back of limos.

"Yeah, sex," Ginny says. "You overthink everything. Sex, like, isn't a thinking endeavor. It's all feeling."

I stand up to get away from them and their words, which I recognize as true but don't want to. "I'm not scared of sex."

Liam stands and mirrors me. "Emma — you're Claire." He points at the TV screen where *Pretty in Pink* waits for us.

I narrow my eyes at him. "I'm not Claire, who's in *The Breakfast Club*, by the way. I'm not a stuck-up, snobby, princess, tease."

"No. Not like that part. Like the sexually repressed part," Ginny says. "The one who secretly likes the bad boy but won't act on it."

"Except–" I hold up a finger for emphasis– "I went into the closet with bad boy John Bender just like she did, only it was junior year with Tanner James." I want to lash out at Liam who's checking out a guy but is too scared to find out if he's gay. And Ginny, who slept with her last boyfriend because she wanted to "get over" her virginity. With my hands on my hips, ready to deflect, I pause and bite my tongue. It's petty and mean, and I love them too much.

"Emma." Ginny's chin falls against her chest, and she stares at me under her lashes. "You had to be drunk to do it."

She's right. *Operation Kiss Tanner James* required me to be drunk, because I couldn't muster up the courage to be bold. But then when had I ever? If it wasn't about church, or school, or duo with Liam — things that I could control — when had I ever been brave?

"Fresh cookies, hot from the oven." My dad with plate in hand maneuvers down the steps into the basement. He looks up with a smile when he reaches the bottom and pauses a moment, assessing the tension in the room. "Everything alright?"

"Perfect." I cross my arms over my chest.

"Those cookies smell delicious, Mr. Matthews," Liam says, turning on the couch to face my father.

Kiss ass.

"How many times have I said it's okay to call me Mo?"

Liam snags a cookie from the plate as my dad sets it on the table between the couch and the TV. "Thanks, Mo."

Dad straightens, walks over to me, and gives me a side hug.

"Thanks, Dad."

"*Pretty in Pink* night?" His eyes bounce from me to Liam to Ginny. He lingers and clears his throat. "Not many of these left, huh?"

We all mumble affirmations at him. I'm sure none of us are truly ready to come to terms with that fact yet, even if we say we're ready to leave.

"I'll leave you to it, then." He squeezes me against his side once more and then disappears back up the stairs.

After he's gone, I look at my friends feeling hurt and vulnerable. They might as well have just said I was the most boring person on the planet — and they'd probably be right.

Ginny pats the couch cushion next to her and holds her arms out to me.

I walk into them, flop forward, and lay against her awkwardly.

"Your Emma-think isn't a bad thing. It's an Emma thing. You're awesome. When you're ready — you'll know," she says. "In fact, because you're you, you'll probably have the best first experience of us

365

all. All that thinking and analysis to make sure."

I move off of her to sit.

"And," Ginny says, "believe me. You don't want a Dean on your hands." Each of us snorts in reference to her first, the aftermath of just trying to "get over it." She shudders and takes my hand in hers. "Maybe it will be like a sexual awakening in college next year, or maybe it will be a hot someone this summer. Perhaps it will be in four years, or maybe it will be on your wedding night. It doesn't matter. What matters is YOU get to decide that for yourself, and that will make it perfect."

Liam sits down on the other side of me and takes my hand. "And I'll be there cheering you on for your first encounter with the D, or the V — whichever you prefer."

"I don't know why this suddenly became about me."

"Here. We can make it about me," Liam says. "I'm still a virgin."

"A status you'd like to change with Atticus Baker." I wiggle my eyebrows at him.

He smacks my shoulder. "Shut it, bitch." Then he chuckles.

"Let's get this John Hughes night moving already. Turn on the movie. Wait, Pretty in Pink? Maybe we should switch it to The Breakfast Club." Ginny lets me go and leans forward for popcorn. "We've got some analysis to do on that dialogue between Allison and Claire tonight, I think."

After an argument about sticking with our planned movie schedule, we watch *Pretty in Pink*. Ginny relents because Andie needs analysis of her attitudes about men: douchebags versus the best-friend. I point out one of my best friends is gay and the other one isn't; it's not an option in all circumstances. We're all in agreement that Andie should have ended up with Duckie (cue giant eye rolls), but as the movie plays, I'm distracted. I attempt to stay in it with my friends since our John Hughes movie nights are dwindling down to a handful. My mind keeps turning back to junior year. I think about how I'd played that night and the aftermath and wish I'd been braver.

366

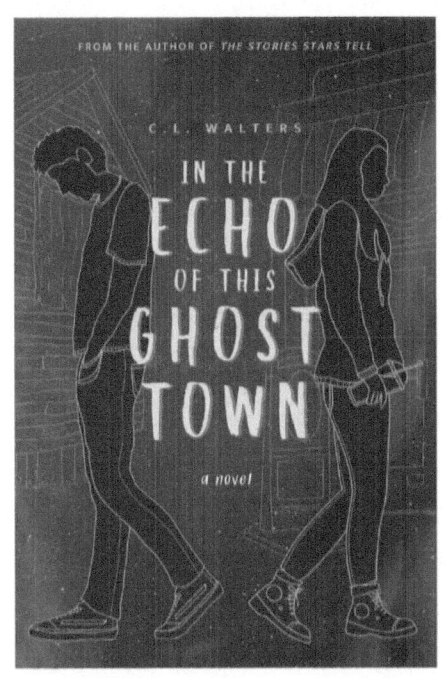

Releasing Fall 2021

Excerpt from *When the Echo Answers*
Releasing Fall 2021

"Dad." I breath the word like a prayer when the house comes into view through the pickup's window. I should be used to the condition of the houses on move-in day—I've lived in so many of them—but this one might be one of the worst I've ever seen. Besides the anemic-looking siding, the wrap around porch resembles broken bones held up with weak crutches while the ghost of its foundation sits in the middle of a field in dire need of surgery. I think, perhaps my dad has lost his mind.

"I know it looks a fright," Dad says as he turns our rusty pickup into the drive.

A fright is an understatement. The house looks like a strong wind will blow it over after the ghosts finish their century-old party in it.

"Dad," I repeat. I'm not sure why I'm surprised. Not really. Over the last eighteen years of my life, we've moved ten times, and with each move, the house has always looked like a dump, maybe with the exception of house three. "There's no way you're flipping this before

I leave for school."

We bounce along a driveway that needs repaving—or our truck needs new shocks. It's hard to decide which. Maybe both.

The sun wanes in the afternoon sky, lighting everything in beautiful hues of gold, but it doesn't seem to help the dilapidated building I'm about to call a temporary home look any better. I can't look anymore and turn away from the house, thinking about the plan he shared with me on the drive: fix this one up in a hurry—before I leave for college—flip it to help pay for school expenses not covered by my scholarship, and move onto the next one closer to school. It isn't going to happen. Eight weeks isn't enough time.

"I know it looks bad. I know." He puts the truck in park. We sit next to one another in Rust Bucket, facing a front door that's cracked up the center. Silence stretches a few extra beats, then my father adds, "But, I'm going to hire someone to help with this one."

"Dad." I shake my head this time as the air leaves my lungs. He's never hired anyone before, aside from tradesmen who help with stuff he doesn't do. Taking on a hire sounds like a lot of extra cash. "For real?" I ask.

"Sure," he says and taps the steering wheel, as if offering himself reinforcement to make it so. He looks at me and smiles. "When we sell this baby—for sure."

"Dad—" I can't seem to find another word.

"No. No." He shakes his head and looks at the house. "It's got amazing bones," he says—just like he always does—and so far, in my eighteen years on this planet, he hasn't been wrong. We've always had a roof over our head, even if sometimes there are holes in it until he fixes them. And we've always had food to eat, even if we don't always have a place for a table. He's always made sure I had clothes and shoes, even if we've had to shop at thrift stores. Truthfully, I haven't ever wanted for much, even if I'm not one of those kinds of people who wants much.

"Come on," he says. "Let me show you." He climbs out of the truck, the door squealing as he pushes it open.

I follow him but leave my bag inside the cab.

He high steps through the grass and looks over his shoulder at me. "Wait. I'll make a path for you."

I watch my dad push down the grass with his feet. That's my dad, my knight in shining armor, willing to brave the grasses with his boots so that I'll be comfortable. I'm wearing shorts, and I shouldn't have. I know better. First night in a flip is always about jeans, long sleeves, and hard-soled shoes. Sometimes I think Hazmat suits have probably been in order like house number five when we had to go get a hotel room for a couple weeks.

I hadn't thought my clothing choices through this morning, annoyed that we were doing this yet again. It might be early July, but summer months don't matter to a house that's falling apart. The rodents don't care either. Or squatters. Or whatever kinds of other items we might find inside I don't want to consider.

When it's clear the stubborn reeds aren't going to lie flat, he walks back to me and offers his wide back.

"Hop on, Max-in-a-million."

"Dad. I'm a little old for this."

"Aw. Humor your old man."

I jump up and let him piggyback me to the porch, which I can see needs to be completely redone. I'm factoring cost. The crack in the front door looks like the crack in Amy's wall in the first episode of the eleventh iteration of Doctor Who. Shit. Replacement. Cha-ching. Rodents guaranteed.

"Don't worry. We'll patch it up until we get the replacement."

As if the front door is the only thing needs replacing, I think but don't say it.

When Dad sets me down, he climbs the steps that buckle under his weight with creaks and groans but thankfully don't snap. He looks over his shoulder at me with one of those excited twinkles in his stormy-sea-colored eyes which are striking in contrast to the rich, sun-kissed hue of his face. "You ready to see this masterpiece?"

"As ready as I'll ever be."

The front door opens.

And it's a dump, just like I thought.

He has to push the door open through a pile of dirt, and, upon closer inspection, leaves, which makes me think there must be a broken window. The stairwell is intact, but a few of the stairs are cracked like chipped teeth. There's a musty odor of decomposing wood. The condition of the house is terrible, and I look at my dad with wide eyes.

"Remember, Max–" Dad turns to me, hands on his jean clad hips—he obviously knew how to dress, though in my whole life, I can't remember my dad ever wearing anything different– "you have to look at the place as it can be, not how it is. See through the damage to all the ways we'll fix it to—"

"—make it new," I finish for him. "Yes. I know, Dad. But—"

"No 'buts,'" he says, holding up a hand. "Just look."

I sigh and nod.

It's an old farmhouse, but under the grime, age, and harsh reality of time, I can see little treasures. The hardwood floor is mostly intact for some spots, though I'm wondering about that subfloor that creaks as our steps echo through the empty rooms. There are gorgeous, stained-glass windows still intact, set in the framed doorways between rooms. The kitchen needs a complete gut, and it makes me hear alarm bells of all the cash about to bleed out into the remodel. The shiplap looks shot, but the fireplace in the living room is beautiful with what looks like original river rock.

"Well?" Dad's voice is hopeful.

I follow him up the stairs. "I can see why you like it."

He flashes me a grin, which is infectious. It always is.

I share a smile with him. My reciprocation seems to relieve some of his tension when his shoulders droop to normal position.

At the top of the stairs, the walkway splits and the spindles of the banister forms a U around the stairwell. Closed doors outline the space. I follow my dad to the left. "I think this could be your room, but you can choose."

He pushes open a door.

I have to give my father credit. Even though the house is a dump—and looks like it might be haunted—the bones of this room are magical. The steeply pitched ceiling, dormered windows with places to sit though they look like they might have nests of something. The walls are bleeding old wallpaper, but I can imagine a new pattern, a beautiful room. "It's got potential," I tell him with a grin.

His eyes twinkle again. "Let me show you the rest."

After the tour, I can see the promise of the house, but I don't see how he's going to get it done in eight weeks—even with help. This will take months, which makes me look sideways at him again. My dad is a smart man. He's been doing this a long time, and while his timing isn't always perfect, he must know this is going to take the better part of a year to finish even with help. Looking around, I know he knows it, and I wonder why he's adamant about the timeline.

"I'll order us some pizza for dinner?" he asks. A tradition on the first night of each of our moves.

"Perfect," I say and wipe my hands over the back of my shorts, then realize I've probably wiped grime on my ass. I glance over my shoulder and twist to check, though I'm not sure why I'd care.

"It could be our last one." I look up at him and notice his gaze flick away. He swallows, then with a dip of his head says, "I'll start moving stuff in."

"I'll sweep up the sleeping spaces for the mattresses and lay the tarps. Don't move mattresses without me."

He nods. "Wouldn't dream of it."

I move out the front door, down the porch, and through the tall grass to the pickup to get my change of clothes. As I open the truck door, I look back at the house as Dad emerges from the doorway to grab the first boxes we'll need to settle for the night. My heart expands in my chest, already missing him, though I haven't left yet. With my leaving-for-college deadline impending—eight weeks away—Dad's strange timeline coincides. I wonder if it has more to do with me leaving rather than the actual completion of the house. Maybe it's his way of trying to make me feel better, or himself.

The thing is it doesn't make me feel better.

I change my clothes and get started on my assigned move-in day tasks. By the time the pizza arrives, I've swept the bedrooms and laid the tarps for the mattresses; Dad and I have moved our mattresses and important boxes from the trailer hitched to the back of the truck. We'll have the rest to unload in the morning. The sun has gone down, and without electricity, we're living by lantern light.

"Dad, you have definitely underestimated how long this house is going to take," I say, drawing a piece of pepperoni from the box. "I mean, Holmes Street was about this size but didn't have as much work. We were there for two years."

"True," Dad says and takes a sip of his cola he just opened. "But it also had a basement that I finished, and I had that full-time job." He takes a bite and finishes it. "Remember Misten Avenue? That one was terrible, and we were there for less than a year."

I'd forgotten about that. "Give me that." I take his soda and hand him his water bottle. "You can't drink that."

He gives me one of his looks, his mouth tensing with impatience. He shakes his head. "I didn't hire anyone to help at Holmes or Misten. And I like soda."

"Soda is diabetes juice, and you're predisposed."

He chuckles. "Look at this temple." He flexes, which makes me laugh because he always uses the same lines. "It wasn't too long ago I was a linebacker–"

"–averaging two and a half sacks, a game. Yeah. Yeah. Drink the water, Dad."

We eat in silence a moment.

"What's the rush, Dad?" I ask, plucking at a piece of pepperoni.

"You're leaving for school," he says as if he's announced the date of my birth, just matter of fact.

"What does that have to do with it?"

He looks up at me, and I see a look I don't recognize on his face, but it burns out just as quickly when he covers it with a smile. "Just seems like a natural point to shoot for. Look for a new place closer to the college so you don't have to travel so far to visit."

"It's only three or so hours from here. An easy bus ride," I point out.

He maintains the smile, but I see it's not in his eyes. Maybe that's the lack of light cast by the lantern. He nods and takes another bite of his pizza. "What am I going to do without you to keep me on track? I might go off budget."

I swallow and take a bite of my pizza, feeling guilty. It's always been us. Dad and Max-in-a-million against the world. "Aw, Dad. I won't be far," I remind him. This is why he'd relented on this place. Besides being a steal—which he loves for the eventual bottom line of the flip— the school I got accepted to was just a few hours away by car. "We have phones. Goodness. And eight weeks to flip this dump." I wonder if the reason he's adamant about his unrealistic timeline is because he's as scared to be on his own as I am to be on mine. I haven't considered the impact of my leaving on him. I haven't allowed myself to ponder it. It's complex and stitched together with a complicated history I know I can't unravel.

He gives me a chuckle. "Don't you worry your head. Your old dad's got it."

"Can we afford help?" I ask.

He sniffs and knuckle itches a spot on his nose, which makes me wonder if he's coming up with a lie. It wouldn't be the first time he's given me just enough truth mixed with a version of optimism riding the line of a lie to keep me complacent. "I'll have to dip into savings."

My eyebrows rise with a question. "Dad. I need the truth."

He raises his hands. "For real. I have a few side gigs lined up already—legit—and I'll offset it with some savings so we can get started right away."

I nod. "And while you're working the side gigs? How is this house—which is generous identification by the way—getting done?"

"The hire."

I give him a side eye.

"You and me plus one more. I think we could knock this out in no time." He smiles around his bite, and I have the sense he's telling himself this story as much as he's telling me. "Have I ever steered us wrong?"

I shake my head. He's taken us into some pretty horrible houses, but he's always made it out of them just like he's said even if his timelines haven't always been accurate. There are always unforeseen complications, and I'm one hundred percent sure this house is full of them.

"Dad?"

"Yes, daughter?"

"Aren't you tired of fixing houses for other people? Don't you ever want to find a place of your own?" This is a question I've asked him before, but his answers have been as shifty as the houses we've lived in, taking on characteristics of whatever house it was at the time. I'm expecting him to say something metaphorical about the stained-glass inserts, but he doesn't.

He clears his throat.

"Dad?"

"Home is where you are."

And I'm leaving.

I don't think he understands that this answer makes me feel like I'm carrying the world on my shoulders, like I've got to hold it up for both of us. I swallow the bite. "What about when I leave for school?"

He doesn't respond.

"Dad?"

"I messed this up, didn't I?"

"What?"

"Being your dad?"

I set my pizza on the paper plate. "What are you talking about?"

He looks at me, his gaze connecting with mine. "I just—I thought it would be an adventure after–" He stops. I know he was going to say, "after your mom left," but can't bring himself to say it. His regret is written on his face even after thirteen years. This isn't because I think he's still in love with her, but her abandonment left both of us as ghostly as the houses we inhabit.

When I was younger, I used to resent the moving, but now that I'm eighteen, I can understand it. I scoot closer to him and lay my head on his shoulder. "Our adventures have been the best," I say, and I'm being honest because they've been with him, even if there's resentment mixed in. I want him to know I love him, but I can't—won't—be a heartbreak, too. "I'm just worried about you when I go to school. You being alone."

This is the first and thickest thread wrapped around my heart. Dad has chosen me every day. He's lived for me. He's been my number one, and now I'm leaving him alone. If I thought too long and hard about it, my breath turns to steel in my lungs. I'd consider not leaving. Dad wouldn't allow it. Going to college feels a bit like abandoning him—like mom. Worse yet, I want to leave so bad, and I'm afraid it makes me just like her.

"What's this?" He wraps a strong arm around me. "Last I checked, I'm the dad. Don't you worry. If all goes well, I'll be right behind you looking for the next place."

Thing is, I can't help worrying about him.

I was five when my mom left us. Indigo Denby—in as much as I can piece together between what my dad has said and what I remember—was a free if unstable spirit unable to be saddled with a husband and a child. A hippie wrapped up the privilege of growing up wealthy, she disappeared, and after a search, was found strung out on drugs (not the first time) and incoherent. Her parents—grandparents who I've had very little interaction with—admitted her to a rehab facility. The divorce papers were delivered to Dad shortly after, and he was given complete custody, her rights as my mother signed away. We haven't heard from her—or my grandparents—since. These are fragile threads I don't understand as clearly since I was only five at the time, but threads that stitch together my experience, nonetheless.

Later, after Dad and I have cleaned up dinner and escaped into our own spaces to get some rest, I wait for the quiet to steal around the house. In the dark of the new room, my lantern glows in the horribly stark space with new shadows and new sounds. I eventually sneak from my bedroom, taking great care to keep my steps from creaking as I move to the stairs. A strange noise reverberates through the belly of the old farmhouse, and I freeze at the top of the stairs, wondering if I should have braved the window and the tree. I hold my breath.

I wait.

My dad clears his throat.

When the silence settles again, I take a step down the stairs. It squeaks. There's a moment when my heart speeds up with fear, thinking maybe I'm going to alert my dad, but I don't hear any movement from his space in the house. I keep going, moving slowly until I'm on the ground floor and out the cracked front door now covered with a plank of plywood.

As much as pizza is a first day move in tradition with my dad, sneaking out that first night is wholly mine. My ritual started at house five. Up to then, my dad and I bunked it in the same room, and his presence gave me bravery. When I turned twelve, there was a shift in me wanting to be brave and independent, to prove I could sleep in my own room by myself. My fear of the new places and my imagination, which conjured all sorts of terrifying creatures stretching in the shadows, did a number on my confidence. Instead of going to my dad, I snuck out into the dark where it felt safer. That night, I found a way to claim some power. After that, I continued to sneak out every first bedtime in a new place. Disappearing into the darkness of a strange place isn't because I want to sneak around. Rather, it feels like one of the only things in this pattern of living over which I have control. Tonight is the last time, I figure, because it's my last move with my dad and is more about the nostalgia of the routine of things rather than the compulsion to control something.

House nine, he caught me sneaking back in.

He was pissed. "Do you understand how dangerous it is?" The panic was clear in his eyes. "Why didn't you just ask? I would have taken you somewhere."

I recognized the disappointment, and I hated disappointing him.

"Why?" he'd asked.

I just shrugged. I didn't know how to put into words the why, not without hurting him. I was being dragged all over the country to fixer uppers by a loving dad, running from the ghost of a drugged-out mom who was too broken to choose us. I had this awful truth of being an outsider—always an outsider—to face the trepidation that pressed in against us every time we started over. I'd been seventeen then, and the sneaking out felt more like a sticking middle finger at the world. A loud "fuck you" to the universe, to every kid that had made fun of me, to my mom, and even my dad on some level.

I didn't think he'd get it, and I refused to hurt him because even if it was a small rebellion, I knew he didn't deserve it.

As I walk down the driveway, I consider that part of the reason I think my dad was so panicked that night he caught me wasn't just because he was scared for me. There is this part of him that probably thought about my mom. The way she walked out into the night and never returned to us, and how he couldn't fix that. My dad can fix anything. Seriously. He's made nine houses look like custom homes. Any problem I've brought home—cuts, scrapes, and bruises both physical and emotional—he's been both Dad and Mom to restore me to normal working order. He couldn't fix my mom, and I'm pretty sure, knowing my dad like I do, he gave it his best go.

As I walk out into the darkness beyond the farmhouse, I wonder if I hide my first night sneak-out from him because I don't want to hurt him like my mother did. I've thought about what it would feel like to just keep walking. The idea took root when I was fifteen—house eight—I thought about just going, finding a place to settle down for good. I was smart enough to know it didn't work like that, which brought me home. It made me wonder if Mom had found it easy to leave us. To leave me. I'd gotten caught up in how much that would hurt Dad, which I knew I couldn't ever do to him, and I wondered how it couldn't have been a part of my mom's thinking. I don't specifically remember the leaving. She was there one day and gone the next. Each time I walk out into the night, I wonder if she weighed us in her decision, and I can't think she did.

When I was younger and asked my dad why she left, he'd just say, "Indigo was a free spirit."

Back then, I imagined her like a bird needing to fly. Now, as I walk toward the streetlights ahead, I don't think of anything so romantic as a bird needing freedom. I just think she was selfish, and maybe—I worry—I'm exactly like her.

I've got eight weeks in this dump since college races toward me. I can hear the sadness and the fear in my dad's voice when he talks about it, but his fears don't change the fact that I'm leaving. It's always been us, and when I look ahead to that eight-week deadline, what I feel is the impending anticipation of freedom weighted with a heavy cost: leaving my dad behind and alone. I finally get to make choices for me. I finally get to make friends. I finally get to stay somewhere—four years—in one place and grow some roots even if my dad jumps around business as usual. As much as I love my dad, I'm looking forward to leaving this vagabond lifestyle for something that's mine, of creating a permanent home. As much as I want my dad to settle somewhere, I don't know that he ever will. The thought makes me bitter, tired, and sad all at the same time. What it boils down to is I'm leaving him and no matter how I try to dress that up, I know I'm just stepping into my mother's skin. And I'm cognizant of how selfish that makes me.

ABOUT THE AUTHOR

CL Walters writes in Hawai'i where she lives with her husband, two children and acts as a pet butler to two pampered fur-babies. She's the author of the YA Contemporary series, *The Cantos Chronicles* (*Swimming Sideways*, *The Ugly Truth* and *The Bones of Who We Are*), the YA/NA Contemporary romance *The Stories Stars Tell*, and the adult romance, *The Letters She Left Behind*. *In the Echo of this Ghost Town* and *When the Echo Answers*, her sixth and seventh New Adult Contemporary novels publish October 2021. For up-to-date news, sign up for her monthly newsletter on her website at www.clwalters.net as well as follow her writer's journey on Instagram @cl.walters.